The Dead Machine

by

Zackary Richards

ARI PUBLiSHING

ARI PUBLiSHING
P.O. Box 622
Lake George, New York 12845

Library of Congress 1-6955286901

Published in the United States by Ari Publishing Lake
George New York

The Ari Star logo is a registered trademark of Ari
Publishing

Dedication

**To Darryl DeCrescenzo. A young heart that gave out
too soon.**

Chapter One

"Virgil? Good heavens, Virgil, is that you? Is that really you!?"

Virgil's eyes immediately widened and his heart leaped at the sound of her voice. His hand trembled on the dials as he fine-tuned the transmission.

When the hissing lessened he replied with unrestrained excitement, "Yes, yes it *is* me! It's Virgil!"

There was a moment's hesitation, then she asked, "How... how is this possible?"

He stared at the speaker, imagining her face, longing to see it again. He paid no attention to the cold or to the steamy vapor escaping his mouth as he breathed. Nor the drafts that bit into his fingers and snaked up his pant leg. He even ignored the acrid smell permeating every inch of the barn.

Nothing mattered, nothing but this moment, this incredibly special moment.

Shaking with excitement, Virgil leaned into the microphone. "Do you remember, just before you were taken away, me telling you that no matter what, I would find you, and that we'd be together again?"

Through the crackling static came a reply. "Yes, but that... many years ago. And in th... situations people say things, knowing that... comforting things... lessen the hardship, to lessen... pain. I never thought that ..."

"That I'd actually find you?"

The static grew louder and panic gripped Virgil. He jumped out of his seat and scanned the computer screens, recalibrating and synchronizing the feed.

"...have found me. Oh, Virgil, somehow you've done the impossible!"

"Nothing is impossible!" Virgil shot back. "They all scoffed. They ridiculed and dismissed my work as a delusion, as fantasy. My grants dried up, my investors backed out; even the military gave up. But I never gave up! I made you a solemn promise and today, that promise has been kept."

1

"Virgil, I don't know what to say, I..."

Virgil interrupted as he scanned the computer screens. "What are your surroundings? Describe them for me. Can you see the stars?"

The static increased. The reply broke up. All four computer screens flashed Recalibrating⋯

"...The horizon in the morning... when I look out... the lights are always on... when we gather as a group..."

The hissing overwhelmed the rest of the sentence.

Virgil's hands flew over the controls.

Recalibrating⋯

"Mostly, we have a..."

Recalibrating⋯

Some background noise seeped into the transmission, then a stranger's voice. "Virgil...? Lillian, did I just hear Virgil? Where...it coming from?"

"Bert, this is...private conversation and..."

The man ignored her. "Virgil? Is that you? Where are you? It's me, Bert Langley. Remember me? I... science teacher... down... block? You used... newspaper to my... when you... kid. And I... tip you a whole..."

"Get out... here, you bastard," Lillian bellowed. "Virgil doesn't... about you! He wants... talk to me!"

Virgil heard a grunt, a huff and a shuffling of feet.

"Okay, he's gone, and yes, we... several times a week... socialize and talk about.... back home."

Virgil felt a lump in his throat. "You still miss us? Even after all this time?"

"Of course, Virgie! It's knowing that our... care for us is...keeps us together. You are... thoughts each and every day."

Tears spilled down Virgil's cheek. "You are in mine each and every day too and..."

Virgil stopped when he heard Bert Langley's voice again. It grew louder as he moved back into the transmission field. "Over there, see? I told you! Lillian is... with the outside. What? No!

2

problem. Despondent, he scoured the internet, the latest scientific journals, anything that might help. Then he came upon a blog touting the talents of Mary McGuernsey, a local self-proclaimed Psychic Detective.

Noting her decades of experience, the large number of apparently satisfied customers, and the fact that he had reached a dead end, he made an appointment.

And she led me right to her, he recalled, staring at the Blue Barn.

"Her spirit is inside," she had told him.

And tonight his machine proved it.

As he started the engine and was about to drive off, he noticed the envelope with the water and soil test permit on the passenger seat, along with permission from the state EPA to use the Blue Barn as a testing facility. He made a mental note to thank his long time buddy, Colonel Wilgren from the Army Corp of Engineers, then popped open the glove compartment, tossed in the paperwork, put the car into gear and headed home.

The glow of success was still with Virgil when he opened the side door of his opulent house and entered the kitchen. His wife Dora, a plump, 35 years old, with streaks of premature grey in her blonde hair, stood by the stove, stirring a pot of boiling liquid. She was wearing a blue jogging suit and flip-flops.

She turned. "Well, you're finally home," she said, brushing a lock of hair out of her face. "You've been gone eleven hours. For heaven's sake what are you building, a rocket ship?"

His warm glow and good feelings all but disappeared as he hung his sports jacket on the hook on the back of the door. He gave a half-hearted smile but did not reply.

"Well, whatever it is, it better bring in some money," she continued as she pulled two paper towels and wiped her hands. She ran her forearm across her brow, slipped on oven mitts, lifted the pot and poured its contents into a strainer in the sink. Steam billowed around her. "You know, if we don't get on top of things soon, we're going to be in some serious financial trouble."

Virgil nodded and continued to smile, but inside his head he was screaming,

Shut-up! Shut-up! Shut-up!

But since telepathy was not one of Virgil's gifts, Dora simply prattled on.

"Oh don't give me that look," she said, jutting her face forward. "I'm just reminding you that we're falling behind. Besides, I thought the government paid top dollar? Considering all the work you've done for them, I figured we'd be driving around in a new Cadillac by now. When is that thing going to be finished?"

Virgil waved her off as he walked into the adjoining dining room, pulled up a seat at the table and dropped his six-foot-two, one-hundred and sixty-pound frame into it. He folded his hands on the white linen tablecloth. "You know I can't discuss my work."

Dora stepped into the doorway and put her hands on her hips. "I'm not asking what you're working on. I'm just asking when you're going to get paid. You haven't brought home a paycheck in six months."

"I'll get paid as soon as it's done."

Dora huffed in frustration, turned away, then after a moment, turned back. "Well, maybe we should sell some of that equipment in the basement. I've got an account on e-bay. Maybe we can bring in a couple grand selling the stuff you don't use."

"Out of the question. I use all of it."

Dora walked back into the kitchen, grabbed the used pots and tossed them into the sink with a clatter. "Well, what choice do we have?" she called back, her voice rising in anger. "Our bank account is nearly empty. Our stocks are in the toilet and we'd have to take out a home equity loan just to get the house in a decent enough condition to sell it."

Lowering his head to his hands, and with his stringy black hair laced between his fingers, Virgil peered out from behind thick eyebrows. "Will you please stop?! We're not selling the house!"

Dora poured egg noodles from the strainer onto a plate, ladled on some sauce, stormed into the dining room and dropped it on the table. "Fine! Here's your dinner. I'm going to bed."

As the bedroom door slammed, Virgil thought about what his wife said.

Damn it, she's right. Too much going out and nothing coming in. And of course it happens just when I'm at a critical juncture. I don't need these distractions. What I really need is someone who knows how to handle money so I can focus on...

His eyebrows suddenly raised and he picked up his fork.

Mom?

A grin spread across his face. He began eating with newfound enthusiasm.

Of course, Mom!

Chapter Three

At eleven o'clock, Virgil decided it was time for bed.

"Dora?" Virgil said as he opened the door and stepped into the bedroom. "Dora," he called again. As the soft light from the hallway illuminated her side of the mattress, she reached up and, using her hand, formed a visor over her eyes.

"Virgil, I was asleep! Couldn't this have waited? You know I got a doctor's appointment in the morn ..."

"Dora!" he said. "Don't worry about the bills. I've figured out a way to take care of them."

Dora dropped her hand from her eyes, pushed down the blue comforter and sat up in the king size bed. "You did? How?"

Virgil waved his hand from side to side, "That's not important. All I'm saying is that in the next few weeks there's going to be a real turnaround."

Dora reached over and turned on the bedside lamp. She skooched back to the headboard with a smile on her face, but when it became clear he wasn't going to elaborate, she held out her hands. "Well, that's great, but where's the money coming from?"

"Well..." he began, but when he realized he couldn't explain...

Her smile quickly faded. She scowled, then folded her arms. "You wake me up from a sound sleep to tell me you're going to solve our money troubles but can't explain how?" She smirked. "You want to make a game out of this? Fine, let's play 20 questions. First question: did you win the lottery? No? Find a magic lamp? No? Sell one of your inventions? Not that either huh? A wealthy relative kicked the bucket? Did..."

She saw Virgil's stunned response when she mentioned the wealthy relative. "Is that it?" she asked excitedly as she leaned forward. "Some relative remembered you in his will?"

Virgil didn't know how to answer. He was an amazingly bad liar and Dora knew it. Still, he wasn't ready to tell her about his breakthrough, especially since Dora and his mother, although cordial, were never close.

When he saw her staring at him, with her fat face and annoyingly goofy grin, he wondered how their relationship could have deteriorated so badly. When they first starting dating she was funny and pretty and entertaining and...

Fourteen years ago Dora was in great demand as an entertainer at children's parties, especially for the offspring of the well-to-do. One afternoon, Virgil had stopped by the house of a defense contractor to drop off some blue-prints and was invited in for a drink. While making small talk, he saw her in the garden surrounded by balloons, streamers, pink crepe paper and a large group of children. They were watching her intently and hanging on every word, and no wonder, she was engaging, vivacious and obviously talented. With permission from his host, Virgil stepped outside to catch her performance.

He was amazed when the lithe, attractive, blue-eyed beauty vocally impersonated any cartoon character the children requested, Sponge Bob, Dora the Explorer, Scooby-Doo, Bart Simpson, it didn't matter; she switched from one to the other seamlessly. Even more amazingly, she could throw her voice so the kids would think there was someone behind the bushes or under the stairs. By the time she juggled filled cups of soda, (Virgil still had no idea how she pulled that off) he was smitten.

Following the show he introduced himself and asked her out. She accepted and the two began dating.

In the early days of their relationship, they got along well. His sharp, analytical and scientific mind appeared to be the perfect foil to her quick and comical wit. He took her to meet his mother and although the matriarch was clearly cool to their relationship, after a few visits Lillian reluctantly accepted her son's choice and made an effort to be personable.

If Lillian's acceptance of Dora had not already sealed the deal, what happened one night on their way to Virgil's apartment from Lillian's certainly did.

They had stopped for a light on Wheatfield's main drag when Lillian called out from the backseat, "Virgie, pull over to Kirshman's Deli, I need cigarettes."

9

"Okay," Virgil replied as he snapped on the turning signal. "As soon as that truck…"

He suddenly jerked in surprise and spun around. There was no one in the backseat.

He turned to Dora whose face was beaming with excitement. "Pretty good, huh? Had you fooled for a second, didn't I?"

He started at her wide-eyed. "That was amazing! You sounded exactly like her."

Her grin grew ever larger. "Thanks, I've been practicing for weeks but after listening to her tonight, I was really able to nail it."

In those early days, they were always trying to come up with ways to entertain each other. One afternoon while she was taking a shower, he slipped into the bathroom, sat on the beige toilet lid, slipped on a 'Cookie Monster' mask and watched her shadow as it played on the sunflower imprinted shower curtain.

After turning off the water, drying off and wrapping a bath towel around, she stepped from the shower and was surprised to find Virgil there.

"Virgil!" she said sternly as she placed her hands on her hips. "You scared me! What are you doing in here and what's with the Cookie Monster mask?"

"Me not 'Cookie Monster'," Virgil replied doing his very best to accurately imitate the famous Muppet. "Me his twin brother."

Dora smiled. "Oh, really," she said. "Cookie Monster's twin brother huh? Okay, then what's your name and what do you want?"

Virgil stood. "Me 'Pussy Monster" and me want pussy!"

With that he ripped off her towel and began chasing her.

With a squeal of delight she playfully ran from him, out the bathroom and through the house as he followed and cartoonishly yelled, "Me want pussy! Pussy yum, yum!"

She sprinted into the bedroom where she let him catch her. Within moments they were making wild and passionate love.

A grin spread over his face.

"Well?" Dora said glaring. "Are you going to answer me?"

Virgil snapped out of it. "All I can say is that it involves my mother. Give me a few days and I'll have more details."

"Oh, your mother, huh?" Dora said, rolling her eyes. "Well then I won't hold my breath." She turned her back to him, skooched down and pulled up the comforter.

"What do you mean by that?" he asked as he approached the bed with a confrontational look. "Why do you always have to be so nasty? For heaven's sake, she never said a bad word about you."

Dora let out a deep sigh, sat-up, turned to him and shook her head. "So we're going to do this again are we? All right then, let's do it. Only this time," she said pointing a stern finger at him, "we take the train to the end of the line. None of that whiney bullshit about me not understanding her, got it?"

Virgil gave a reluctant nod.

She nodded back. "Okay, it's true. I hated your mother. Why? Because the woman was, to put it bluntly, a pathological liar, AND..." she said holding up her hand when Virgil attempted to interrupt. "...And, I know you loved her but those stories are true."

"They are not!" Virgil shouted.

"Yes they are!" she shouted back. "When our engagement was announced, I received not one, but two anonymous letters, both warning me about her. They said she was a grifter, forger, and former prostitute. Both suggested she was responsible for your father's mysterious disappearance. So, just before we were married, I hired a private investigator to do a little snooping."

"What?!"

I wanted to know what sort of family I was marrying into."

This information startled him. "You...you had no right!" he said.

"Oh shut up, I had every right!" she snapped back. "Turns out your mother never told the truth a day in her life. The P.I. I hired brought me a stack of pictures and official documents three inches high. Your mother was featured in nearly all of them. She was arrested eleven times, from prostitution and drug dealing to financing a meth lab and forging Social Security checks. Somehow, she beat every charge."

11

"That's because she was innocent!" Virgil said smugly, as if his comment just won the argument.

She gave him a dismissive glance. "Really? Eleven times? Do you know anyone, other than dear old Momma, who has ever been charged with a felony? No, you don't and neither do I. Why? Because we're decent, law-abiding people, which is what Donnie Pascal said about you."

"Who?" he asked.

"He's the P.I. I hired. Said he did an extensive check into your background. Said he wanted to be extra careful because he believed the apple never fell far from the tree. But in your case, you were everything you appeared to be. Honest, bright, hardworking, and emotionally stable. So I went ahead with the wedding, but kept a healthy distance from your mother. And when she got sick and died, I did what every dedicated, loving wife is supposed to do. I comforted you, saw to it that her remains were properly attended to and kept my mouth shut. But it's been eleven years and it's time someone set the record straight. And if that money you're talking about is in any way, shape or form connected to dear old mommy, pass it up. It's probably from some meth lab or some poor old lady's social security check."

Virgil threw open the cedar chest at the foot of the bed and yanked out a pillow and blankets. "You're the most hateful person I know. I'm sleeping in the den," he said as he stormed to the door.

"Whatever," she replied and shut off the light.

Virgil went to the living room's wrap around couch and stopped. Too wound up to sleep he dropped the bedding on it and sat.

What a freakin' day.

Although he had succeeded in contacting his dead mother, the transmission was weak and unsustainable. The conversation had broken up at vital intervals and the information he received was spotty. He had to establish a clear line of communication.

And, he thought. *I've got to keep meddling idiots like Bert Langley from getting involved.*

12

He suddenly thought of the ectoplasmic chamber, one of the many devices he had invented months earlier when he was trying to locate his mother.

Well, I would have to reposition the vacuum ducts to properly circulate the gasses and increase their viscosity, but once done I could isolate her by reconfigu…

The phone rang.

He walked to the table but didn't recognize the number on the caller ID. He picked up the receiver.

"Hello?"

"It's me. I need your help," said the voice on the other end. Virgil recognized it immediately.

"What did you do now?" Virgil asked with a sigh.

"Does it matter?" the caller asked in an impatient tone. "I'm at the police station. I need someone to pick me up."

Virgil growled. "Ahhhh! All right. I'm on my way."

"Thanks, Virg," the caller said. "I knew I could count…"

Virgil slammed the phone down. "Fucking idiot."

Dora hurriedly opened the door and stepped into the hall. "Who's was that on the phone?"

Virgil pulled a jacket from the hallway hook. "Jimmy McCracken," he said, shoving his hands through the sleeves. "He got picked up by the cops."

With a look of disappointment, Dora sighed and bowed her head. Without comment she stepped back into the bedroom and closed the door.

Chapter Four

When Virgil entered the Wheatfield Police station, the harsh lights stung his eyes. With his hand over his eyebrows he searched the area, noting the communications center with its array of monitors and a staircase that led down to the holding cells. Off to his right Jimmy sat on a bench with a Styrofoam cup in his hand. A female officer stood over him like a scolding parent. As Virgil walked over, he noticed Jimmy was wearing dirty jeans, high-top sneakers and a T-shirt that read: *I'm Magically Delicious*. His long brown hair was partially tucked inside a wool cap with a marijuana leaf patch on the front.

Jimmy was only 23 years old but had a war weary look of a much older man. When he turned away from the officer, Virgil saw his eyes were red and the dark circles beneath them gave him a hauntingly sallow appearance.

Virgil shook his head in exasperation as he came up and addressed the officer, "I'm here to pick him up. What's he done this time?"

Jimmy's bleary eyes looked up. "Hey, pal," he said, reaching over and patting him on the forearm. "Thanks for coming."

The officer was around 30 years old. She had her brown hair tied up under her hat and wore a name tag that read, M. Cavanaugh. At 5 foot 4 inches tall, she seemed a little overweight until Virgil realized she was wearing a bullet-proof vest.

She glanced down at Jimmy then back to Virgil. "I was on patrol when I found him wandering the streets, obviously high and ranting about how some guy named Virgil really did it this time. So I brought him in to keep him out of trouble. When he finally started coming down, he asked to make a phone call."

"Is he being charged with anything?"

Cavanaugh shook her head. "I checked his sheet, a couple of misdemeanors over marijuana possession but nothing worth holding him for. My concern was that in his condition, he could have easily walked in front of a bus."

"Yeah, well maybe next time we'll have better luck," Virgil mumbled under his breath.

"Huh?" Cavanaugh asked.

Virgil shook his head, "Nothing. Can I take him now?"

Cavanaugh nodded. "You might want to get him into rehab. He looks like he could use it."

Virgil's expression made it clear he couldn't care less what Jimmy needed. He looked down. "Can you walk or do I have to drag your dumb ass to the car?"

"I'm fine," Jimmy grunted and he rubbed his index finger under his nostrils. "It just got away from me, that's all." He looked up at Cavanaugh. "Thanks for the coffee and well, you know, for looking out for me."

As Jimmy stood and tossed the empty coffee cup into the wastepaper basket, Cavanaugh nodded and walked away.

"Thanks again for coming, Virg," Jimmy McCracken said as he slipped into the passenger side of Virgil's Volvo.

Virgil frowned and gave Jimmy the once over as he buckled his seatbelt. He started the engine and put the car in gear.

"How long are we going to keep doing this?" Virgil asked as he pulled onto Main Street.

"For as long as it takes," Jimmy replied with a smirk.

Virgil didn't appreciate the attitude. "Ever hear the story about the kid who cried wolf?"

Jimmy held up his right hand, fingers splayed. "Ease up, buddy. I'm not crying wolf here and you know it better than anybody. I never asked for this. You're the one who put me through those tests."

Virgil shot him a look. "I put a lot of kids with your talent through those tests and you're the only one with so-called problems. Remember, none of those tests contained drugs of any kind."

"No, no drugs. Just radioactive isotopes, chemical dyes, ultrasounds…"

Virgil slapped the steering wheel. "Listen smartass, I did nothing illegal. I just rounded up kids who claimed they could talk to the dead. And out of the 26 subjects, only twelve of them,

15

including you, appeared to have any real ability. So I did some tests, and I paid your parents handsomely for the opportunity."

"Yeah, right, like any of us saw a penny of that money…"

"So take it up with your parents!"

"Virgil, you gotta listen…"

"No!" Virgil shot back. "You listen. I've read the reports. Apparently, over time some people with your talent become mentally ill. And that has nothing to do with my research. The fact is, your brain and brains like yours are genetically abnormal. You can see visual spectrums no one else can and hear sounds normal people can't. All I did was measure your abilities through MRIs and scanning devices to see what sections of your brain lit up when the dead spoke to you."

Jimmy grinned, his color was coming back and his eyes had lost that glassy look. "Is that so?" he replied. "Then how come the tests were always done at night? How come there were never any technicians around? Why did we always have to enter through the back door and how come it was always the janitor who let us in?"

The barrage of questions caught Virgil off guard. "Well…the general scientific community…"

"Oh fuck me, the scientific community and all that bullshit!" Jimmy said with disdain. "You were experimenting on teenage boys and girls and paying shitloads of cash to keep our parents quiet."

"All right, all right," Virgil said with a sneer. "You've made your point. You're a scarred, sensitive, little fuck up. Boo-hoo. So what's it going to take to get you out of my life?"

Jimmy smiled. "Nothing you've got, Mr. Scientist. Besides, this is the first time I've called you in six months, so lose the put upon attitude. Anyway, I need to talk to you about something. Despite all the drugs I've been fed; I'm still the soft shoulder the stiffs cry on. And today you're the guy they're all talking about."

That caught Virgil's attention and a wave of anxiety clutched his stomach. "Why? What are they saying?"

Jimmy smirked. "Oh, so we're buddy-buddy again?"

"Just tell me what they said!"

16

Jimmy reached into his pocket, pulled out a breath mint, examined it for lint, then popped it in his mouth. "Well, from what I've heard, it has something to do with you and your late mommy. So I'm figuring you've finally cracked the code and are yakking with the great beyond."

Virgil paled. Jimmy McCracken had, by far, the strongest abilities when it came to contacting the dead. So strong that in Jimmy's presence the spirit would often take physical shape in ectoplasmic form. It took Virgil months of analyzing and testing prototypes before he could duplicate what Jimmy did on a regular basis.

Apparently, the conversation with his mother was no secret on the other side. Still, Virgil had no intention of showing his hand.

"I don't know what you're talking about," he finally replied.

Jimmy pulled up his foot and retied the loose lace on his sneaker. "Listen, I know you're obsessed with talking with your ma, but you gotta cut it out," he said dropping his foot back to the floor." You're messing with stuff that can harm you in ways you can't even imagine. Seriously, this is Pandora's box you're fooling with."

"I still don't know what you're talking about."

Jimmy stared at him, grinned and then leaned back against the passenger door. "That's absolutely right. You don't have any idea and that's why you need to stop. You're like some drunk at a party showing off by juggling bottles of nitro-glycerin."

Virgil shot him a sideways glance as he slowed for a red light. "That's a little melodramatic, don't you think?"

"Since you're not taking me seriously, I don't think I'm being dramatic enough."

When Virgil stopped and the pedestrians entered the crosswalk, Jimmy reached over and placed his hand on his shoulder. "Listen, there is an important reason why, once a person is dead, they remain dead, for good and always. And why people like me, who can communicate with them, don't want to. And why those who claim they can conjure up a specific member of the departed are full of shit."

17

Jimmy saw the light turn green and let go of Virgil. "Pull over to the curb. I'm just in time for my shift at work."

When Virgil did, he saw they were alongside the parking lot of Lumberland, a do- it-yourself warehouse. "You work here?" Virgil asked, clearly surprised.

Jimmy opened the door. "Yeah, I got a restocking job."

Virgil studied him. "Okay, but are you in any condition to work?"

Jimmy nodded and pulled an amber colored vial from his pocket. "Yeah, the meds wore off. I shouldn't have taken them in the first place." He popped the lid, opened the door and poured them into the storm drain. "My stomach is in such bad shape that the doctors keep prescribing these damn anti-anxiety pills. I should know better. Every time I take them I wind up either cock-eyed or climbing the walls. Anyway, Virg, I'm sorry for getting you out of the house so late but I had to warn you about, well, you know."

"Yeah, well it was quite the inconvenience you know."

Jimmy slowly nodded. "No doubt, but let's face it—if I called and said we needed to get together, you would've blew me off. One last thing, you don't need to worry about me calling you anymore. I finally accepted the fact that everyone in this life gets a bag of crap to carry. Diseases, pedophile relatives, blindness, accidents etc, etc. We all get something. Me? I got stuck with the dead wanting to chat. Could be worse, I guess. But I wasn't kidding. There is a damn good reason why the dead and the living aren't supposed to communicate."

Virgil leaned over as Jimmy climbed out of the car. "Yeah? And why is that?"

Jimmy smiled as he buttoned his blue jean jacket. "Ask Mary McGuernsey," he replied, then closed the door, waved good-bye and walked away.

Virgil's eyes widened. *Mary McGuernsey?*

He slapped the steering wheel, leaned back and put the car in PARK.

How could Jimmy know about Mary McGuernsey? I never mentioned her. And come to think of it, McCracken's right. I

18

*haven't spoken to him in six months. That was long before I even **heard** of her.*

Damn it!

And now he knows about the machine, maybe even where it is. What if he blabs to the cops or the newspapers?

And just when I'm so close.

Virgil spent the next several minutes in silent debate.

I can't take the chance. I have to go back to the house, haul the equipment out of the basement and bring it to the barn. If I can just get the ectoplasmic chamber running, that should strengthen the feed enough for me to talk to Mom without breakups or interruption. Then once I explain my problem, I'm sure she'll come up with a solution.

Virgil put the car into gear, pulled back into traffic and raced home.

Chapter Five

At sunup the following morning, as Jimmy returned home from his shift, he unlocked the door and entered. The apartment was dimly lit and empty and had the lingering smell of last night's Chinese food. After making a mental note to take out the garbage the next time he left the house, he locked the door behind him, turned and discovered...

He wasn't alone.

It grinned at Jimmy through yellow, rotted teeth that looked like a broken picket fence. It rubbed its sparse beard that was as thin as prairie grass.

"Only a matter of time now, boy!" it said with a drawl as he paced before him. Wearing dusty jeans, a red shirt with suspenders and a grey floppy hat, the specter placed one hand behind his back, held up the other and shook it like an old time, fire and brimstone preacher. "Your buddy ain't payin' no mind to your warnin'. Don't reckon he's gonna. Better get ready." He grinned, placed his fists on his hips and gave a quick nod. "Like I said, only a matter of time."

Jimmy shrugged, kicked off his shoes, opened the bottle of rum on the kitchen counter and took a swig. Most people in that situation would be overwhelmed with terror, panic stricken.

Not Jimmy.

He wasn't afraid of the dead. The only way they could hurt you was for them to solidify the ectoplasmic gasses that pooled in certain natural locations and use it to push or shove material objects. Yeah, it could be dangerous if you lingered at the top of a staircase or under heavy objects, but he never put himself in those situations.

Jimmy made a popping sound with his mouth after swallowing the rum. "Ahhh, just what the doctor ordered." He capped the bottle, leaned his elbow on the counter and said, "Hey old timer, did you ever notice how turds turn white when they get old and dry? Well, that what your face looks like but with little kernels of corn jammed in all haphazard to look like teeth."

"Don't smart mouth me, boy!" the specter snapped.

20

With bottle in hand, Jimmy waved him off, walked into the bedroom, opened the end table drawer and pulled out a half-smoked joint. The specter followed. "Doin' more sinnin' I see," he said.

Jimmy sighed, dropped his hands and stared at the ceiling. "I would tell you to fuck off and die, Ike, but you've already done the die part, so how about just fucking off?"

The specter pulled back, angry but unable to do anything about it. "You know and I know there's going to be a reckoning. Inevitable, I say," the specter said smugly as he drew near. "When it comes, everybody is gonna get their due! Startin' with you and when it does..."

Jimmy rolled his eyes, put the bottle on the end table and plopped down on his bed, "Will you just shut up! I get it all right? A reckonin' is a'comin'. I'm going to get my just desserts! Message received loud and clear, but in the meantime, why don't you let me smoke this joint in peace?"

Angry and frustrated, the ghost faded and Jimmy lit up but he knew it would take a lot more than a half-smoked bone to bring him any solace.

As he exhaled and picked up the ashtray from the end table, he considered calling Virgil, but soon realized it wouldn't do any good. The man had worked every spare moment for eleven years to contact his dead mom. A guy that obsessed doesn't stop just because someone told him it was dangerous.

That momma's boy is going to screw up the whole world and apparently there isn't a damn thing I can do about it.

Jimmy took another hit and wondered. *Really, how do you stop someone like that?*

He pondered the question for a few moments then realized that short of killing him, you couldn't.

He slowly exhaled. "Yep, looks like the old coot was right. Apparently there *is* going to be a reckonin'. Oh well, fine by me," he said with a smile as he put the joint in the ashtray, uncapped the bottle and took another swig of rum.

Chapter Six

That same morning, Mary McGuernsey got up from the kitchen table, walked to the coffeemaker on the counter and poured herself and her friend Jess a cup. Mary was 67 years old with long, silvery hair. She stood about 5' 6" and was relatively thin. Today she was wearing a pink blouse, blue jeans and cowboy boots.

Her house was decorated country style. Objects from craft fairs, quilting bees and local artisans were on the walls, tables and fireplace mantle.

"You've been acting a little strange lately," Jess commented as Mary handed her the coffee.

As Mary sat down, she replied, "Feel strange," then gazed out the window.

"How so?"

Mary slumped, let out a sigh and eyed Jess. Stared actually. Five or six different sentences ran through her head but none seemed to convey what she truly wanted to say. Finally the seventh was close enough for her to blurt it out. "I think I may have met the most dangerous man on Earth."

Jess tipped down her John Lennon type glasses and stared over the top of the frames. "That's one heck of a comment. You want to throw in a little detail?"

Mary chuckled. "You'll think I'm out of my mind."

"Always have," Jess said smirking as she pushed up the sleeves of her red sweater. "So what happened? Satan stop by?"

Mary scrunched up her face. "I wish I could joke about it. Wish I could just pass it off as a weird feeling on a weird day in the company of a weird man. But I can't."

Mary ran her hands down her upper arms as if she felt a sudden chill. "This is going to be the strangest thing I've ever said to you, but here goes. About six weeks ago I met a man who I believe might bring about the end of the world."

Jess nearly spit out her coffee.

Mary waited until Jess resumed her composure then continued. "When he showed up for his session, he handed me his mother's key ring purse. Well, that thing nearly vibrated out of my

22

hand, which told me that whoever owned it had a very strong and powerful personality. The man...his name is Virgil, said he was having dreams about her. This is common when the two people have a very strong bond, so I wasn't surprised.

"The vibrations led me to this blue barn I had never seen before, smack dab in the toxic end of Dohesley Township. We were both wearing boots so I wasn't concerned about the mercury in the soil, but when we stepped inside that barn, I gotta tell you, Jess, every hair on my body stood straight up." She paused for a moment then added. "That woman's presence was so strong I almost expected her to yank that change purse right out of my hand! And there was something else there too, something, I don't know, abnormal maybe? But whatever it was it, it rattled me, made me want to run out and never look back."

"Evil?" Jessica asked leaning in.

Mary pressed her teeth together and slowly shook her head. "I'm not sure what it was, which is why I didn't mention it before, but the more I think about it, the more I'm convinced that leading that man to that blue barn was a terrible mistake." She stirred her coffee. "So I decided to google him and get a little background."

"What did you find out?" Jess asked. She was concerned. She'd known Mary for over three decades; had witnessed hundreds of psychic readings and had never seen her this unsettled, this troubled.

"I discovered this Virgil Vanderhill has a number of high-tech patents, mostly for electronic military communication gear. So I've been stopping at Lavender Hill, you know, the part that overlooks Dohesley Township, during my daily routine just to see what he's up to. As far as I can tell, he's there from sunup to sundown and he's bringing in electronic equipment, lots of it, including a number of satellite dishes. After I finish this coffee, I'm going to run over and do another check. See if I can figure out what he's up to."

Jess took a breath, let it out and placed her coffee cup a little forcibly on the saucer. Mary looked up.

"I saw this comedian on TV the other night," Jess began. "Funny guy. He said one of the differences between blacks and

23

whites is that you white people do things that get your dumb asses in trouble. You never see black people being abducted by aliens or possessed by ghosts or wiped out by some weird religious cult. Why? Because when black people see UFOs and aliens with huge heads, or haunted houses with ghosts with bloody meat cleavers, we say, 'This looks dangerous. Let's contact the appropriate government agency.' White people, say, 'Let's go inside and look around.'"

Mary put her hand to her chin. "Am I to assume you don't want me to go?"

Jess placed her teaspoon on her saucer. "That depends. Am I in your will?"

*

"I think he was here all night, but it looks like he's getting ready to leave," Mary said to Jess as she quickly checked her watch. It was shortly past noon. They were sitting in Mary's Ford F-350 truck atop Lavender Hill. Mary had a pair of binoculars in her hands and was studying the Blue Barn.

Jess leaned over for a closer look. "How do you know?"

"It rained last night but the spot under his car and carry trailer is still dry."

"Nice detective work, Mare," Jess said, sitting back.

Both women were dressed in flannel shirts, jeans and hiking boots and had clipped thick waterproof gloves to their belt loops just in case it became necessary to touch the soil. Since Mary and Jess were the same size it hadn't been necessary for Jess to return home to change. She simply borrowed some of Mary's clothes.

"I was right, he's pulling away. Ready to go down and have a look?" Mary asked.

"I don't know why I let you talk me into this craziness but yeah, I guess I'm ready," Jess replied, buckling her seatbelt. "But I don't know what good it'll do. Nobody stores expensive equipment in a building without locking the door."

Mary put the binoculars in the case and nodded. "You're probably right. But remember this is an *old* barn, there's got to be a loose knot or a warp in the boards somewhere. If we can just peek inside…"

"What do you mean 'we' kemosabe?"

Mary put her hands on her hips. "Oh c'mon, you old bat. How much longer do you expect to live anyway?"

Jess tilted her head, stared momentarily then tossed up her hands. "Well, since you put it like that, we might as well get right to it. Maybe if we get killed quick we can be poolside at Jesus' house in time for cocktails."

After Virgil left the Blue Barn and disappeared down Route 727, Mary eased her truck down Lavender Hill, carefully avoiding the thorny bushes and partially uprooted trees. She was especially careful as she made her way over the scattered railroad ties and rails near the former Dohesley Township Railroad Station.

After a particularly jarring bump, Jess said, "Yep, nothing like spending a beautiful spring day ass deep in a toxic and highly poisonous waste dump. Perhaps next week we can picnic inside Chernobyl. Seriously, this is not a good idea."

"Stop yammering, you almost made me hit that two-headed rat."

"What?!" Jess said as she jerked back in her seat.

Mary turned with a devilish grin.

"Not funny, Mare," Jess said.

When they reached the Blue Barn, they saw the padlock on its white door.

Mary shut off the engine and, as they stepped down from the truck and studied the area, Jess began coughing. Mary pulled a tissue from her pocketbook, handed it over, then laid her pocketbook on the ground and walked to the two barn doors.

"Locked tight," she called out after trying to yank them open.

Mary suddenly shivered. "The vibes are ten time stronger than when I was last here."

Jess continued to cough.

25

"You gonna live?" Mary asked as she walked alongside the barn and ran her hands along its walls.

"Unfortunately, yes," Jess called out, tucking the tissue into the cuff of her shirt. "Just my allergies acting up. See anything?"

"No, not yet. There's got to be a hole or a crack in this thing somewhere." The wind picked up and Mary saw the malformed trees move up and down like hands with admonishing index fingers.

Moments later, she called out, "I got something!"

Jess came over and saw the knot on the wooden wall. "Think it goes all the way through?"

Mary scanned the ground for something to pry it loose.

"Only one way to fi... Hey! Here we go!" she said, bending down and grabbing a partially rusted L bracket. She and Jess gave it the once over.

"Well," Jess said, stepping back, "give it a rip!"

Mary slid the L bracket between the slats and against the half-dollar knot. She twisted it so the vertical end would have the most leverage. After several yanks the knot popped like a cork.

Jess gestured to the hole. "Well, we came this far, might as well take a gander."

Mary rubbed her hands and drew a breath. As she was about to look in...

"Wait! What did I do with the camera?" Mary asked scouring the ground.

"It's in your pocketbook, remember?" Jess replied. "You left it at the front, near the truck."

As Mary started toward the front of the barn, Jess held out her hand. "I'll get it. You go see what's inside"

After Jess left, Mary peered into the hole. She was surprised at the amount of equipment, far more than she expected.

That's why it was dry under his car. He must have been unloading equipment all night.

She saw several computer screens and a number of odd mechanical devices but what genuinely startled her was something she only recently saw on the Biography Channel. It was a Tesla coil standing center stage in the barn, larger than any other piece of equipment. It was humming with the occasional electrical discharges lighting the inside in several-second bursts.

After one burst she thought she saw…

It couldn't be.

Mary stayed glued to the hole. During one small burst she saw a glass cylinder filled with swirling gasses of various densities and colors.

What was…? Was that a…

There was another large burst and for a moment light filled the room. This time she saw it. Definitely.

"Jess! Jess!" she called out, keeping her eye focused on the cylinder. "Come quick! You will never believe what that nut's got locked in here! I can see a woman…"

As the words left her lips, the womanly figure inside the cylinder turned, and from the swirling gases a face took shape.

"And I can see you too, dearie!" a voice whispered into Mary's ear.

Mary jumped back. "Jess! What in blazes are you…"

But Jess was 30 feet away walking toward her, rummaging through Mary's purse for the camera. Suddenly a strong wind buffeted Jess and sent several of Mary's business cards and ATM receipts into the air.

Jess finally pulled out the camera and smiled with satisfaction. But when she saw Mary's staring wide-eyed and panicky at the knothole, her smile disappeared.

Chapter Seven

Brother Martaine placed his hand on his companion's arm. "You look troubled my friend. What is wrong?"

Father Hector Santiago shifted his weight to get comfortable in the small commuter plane. He and Brother Silvio Martaine were on route to Albany, New York, to give a lecture at SUNY University on the dangers of dabbling in mystic writings and the conjuring of spirits. Using a quote from Nietzsche the lecture was titled, *As You Gaze Into The Abyss, The Abyss Also Gazes Into You.* They were already an hour from Montreal and expected to arrive soon.

Father Santiago, a tall, rugged looking man with black close-cropped hair and dark eyes, turned to his companion, made a dismissive gesture and said. "No, my friend, no trouble. Just an unsettling dream."

"Just now, on the plane?" Brother Martaine asked as he ran his hand over his bald pate. He was a very large, portly and jovial man, 6 feet 4 with a bull-like neck and big sturdy hands. "I need to pay more attention. I hadn't noticed you were sleeping."

Father Santiago nodded. "It was only a few minutes but the experience was chilling."

"How so?"

Santiago held up his hands. "Silvio, we both know few things are as tedious as listening one tell, in excruciating detail, the events of their dreams."

"True," Brother Martaine replied as he shifted toward his companion and placed his elbow on the arm of his seat, "but we still have some time before landing and I'm starved for entertainment."

"You are quite the compassionate clergyman."

"Out with it!" Brother Martaine said with a smile and an expressive wave of his hands.

Seeing he wasn't going to dissuade him, Santiago began his tale. "I was riding in a car with my mother, may God rest her soul, and on our way to a train station. When we arrived, I took her hand and we climbed the stairs to the platform. It was a mild, sunny day

28

with a warm breeze. The station was well maintained and located in a rural area with trees and bushes in all directions.

"Minutes later, the train pulled in and we said our good-byes. She boarded and as I watched, she made her way down the aisle and took a seat by the window. As I raised my hand to wave good-bye again, I noticed that the train windows were darkening. My mother noticed this too and became frightened. She jumped out of her seat, pressed her hands against the glass and called to me. 'Hector! Hector!'

"She started pounding on the panes as they grew darker. Seconds later I could no longer make out her form. I stepped back, startled, confused..."

With a troubled expression, Father Santiago stopped there.

After a moment, Brother Martaine, intrigued by the tale, pressed his hand on his friend's forearm and said, "Then what?"

Santiago put his finger to his lip. "It was then I noticed the train *had* no windows and that I was staring into black empty holes. I looked down and the train had no wheels, and the paint on the railroad car was peeled and faded. The tracks were scattered and the ground covered with weeds. The platform floor was decayed and rotted and missing several slats.

"I then saw that the acres of grasslands, bushes and trees that had surrounded us had become a hardscrabble wasteland. The station had clearly been abandoned for many years."

Father Santiago leaned back. "There was much more, but sadly, my friend, the details have begun to fade. However, two things remain sharp in my memory. One was a tattered sign just above the train station entrance that read: Dohesley Township, and the other, a big blue barn in the distance."

Chapter Eight

"Mom!" Virgil said enthusiastically to the large glass chamber of swirling gasses. "It's finished. All systems are up and running. We should have a clean line of communication now."

It had been a few days since their original conversation, and after considerable expense, crashes, meltdowns and near misses, all systems were go.

Inside the glass chamber the swirling gasses took the shape of his mother Lillian Vanderhill.

She eyed her surroundings. "This is amazing!" She looked at her arms, legs and at the dress that she had been buried in. "It's almost like being alive again! Oh look, Virgie, I can see my reflection in the glass!"

As she studied her figure in various positions, Virgil pulled a chair across the dirt floor to the ectoplasmic chamber. He hated it when she called him 'Virgie', her pet name for him, but he wasn't going to make an issue of it. This was too momentous an occasion to quibble over something so menial. "I'm so happy," he said as tears filled his eyes.

Over the next few hours Virgil cheerfully brought Lillian up to speed on the events over the last decade. During a break in the conversation he considered mentioning his money problems but decided that could wait for another day. For now he just wanted to enjoy being with his mother again.

While he was explaining some of the details of the machine, she interrupted. "Oh Virgie, that reminds me. Get a pad and pencil. I need you to make a list of things I need."

Virgil gave her a puzzled look. "A list? What could you need?" He looked around, "Why is it always so damn cold in here?" He rubbed his arms, then his thighs.

Lillian expression immediately changed from genuine warmth to stunned sorrow. "Is it too much to ask for you to do me a few small favors?"

When he saw the effect his comment had, he blanched and vigorously shook his head. He jumped from his chair and pressed his hand to the chamber's glass wall. "No, Mom, of course not!" he said as sincerely as possible.

She pressed her hand against the glass to his. "Then you will do these little favors for me?"

He saw her pleading expression and after a moment said. "Well," he sighed, "all right, Mom." Wearing a put-upon look, he sallied to his desk and retrieved a pen and a writing tablet. When he returned and sat down, he said, "Fire away."

The list was extensive. Send a letter to this one. Get a hold of an old painting her sister had and what appeared to be the most important, go back to their old house, dig up a box of porcelain figurines in the back yard and bring them to the barn.

"Mom, why do you need those figurines now? And why in heaven's name did you bury them in the back yard?"

That sorrowful look returned. "You won't get them for me?"

He rolled his eyes. "I'm not saying that. It's just that..."

"Is it wrong for me to want to be surrounded by my pretty things just once more?"

"Well, no. Of course not, I'm just saying..."

"So when can you get them?" she asked.

"I... Soon, Mom, soon. Now can we talk about something else?"

"Sure, honey," she replied. She clasped her hands and her smile returned. "What's your mind?"

Virgil put the tablet in his lap, sat back and crossed his legs. "Well, there's this guy I know," he began. "His name is Jimmy McCracken. The guy's a real psychic, I've tested him extensively. He says talking to the dead is very dangerous and by doing it I'm only asking for trouble. Is there any truth in that?" he asked. "Am I putting myself in danger by talking to you?"

Lillian scoffed. "In danger? How could talking to me put you in danger? That's ridiculous; I don't even have a solid physical form. You know what I think? I think this Jimmy fella is jealous because you can talk to the dead and don't need him anymore."

Virgil nodded and shook his finger. "You know, that's exactly what I suspected!"

"I'm sure that's it, honey. Now, when can you get my things?"

Chapter Nine

"Okay, according to the directions, we just place this memory card into the computer and the pictures should pop up," Mary said as she ejected it from the camera. They were back at Mary's kitchen table and had just sat down. Mary opened her laptop and booted it up.

"Still want to go on record as saying this is nuts!" Jess replied as she settled in. "You were shaking like a leaf when I brought the camera to you. We should have high-tailed it then. But, no, you just had to take pictures. You know, this is exactly what that comedian was talking about. People poking around in dangerous places when it would be a lot simpler and smarter," she said, accenting the word *smarter*, "to let the government handle it."

Mary slid in the card into the computer and clicked the camera icon. "And where's the fun in that?" she asked. "Besides, we didn't get caught. We're not strung up in some dungeon by our ankles. We saw an interesting old barn, took some pictures and snooped around a little. That's all."

Jess eyed her sideways. "That is definitely not all. You said you saw a woman in a glass cylinder. But I didn't see any woman when I looked."

"And that's why I had to take the pictures," Mary replied.

Jess rolled her eyes and shook her head. "Mary, that land is owned by the government and dotted with big, easy to read KEEP OUT! signs. Frankly, I wouldn't be surprised if a SWAT team showed up, kicked down the door and wrestled us to the ground."

"Yeah, that would be terrible," Mary replied clasping her hands and adopting a wistful expression. "Just imagine, some young, virile, muscular twenty-something grabbing you, forcibly running their hands over your body looking for weapons, checking again and again just to make sure, then pressing his hard muscular chest against yours, forcing you to the floor before climbing on top of you as you tremble under his steely gaze."

Jess closed her eyes and grinned, "Okay... So when are we going back?"

32

Mary chuckled. "How about we have a look first and see if we need to?"

Jess nodded and skooched in closer.

A grid of 24 thumbnail photos appeared. Mary clicked on the first.

A full size picture of the inside of the Blue Barn appeared on the screen. After Mary enhanced the value with a few keystrokes, the details became markedly clearer. Still, even with the enhanced clarity, there wasn't anything of real interest, at least not to them. It just showed the Tesla Coil, the surrounding machinery and an array of computer screens and gas powered generators. It was the same with only moderate variations for the next twelve pictures.

"Well," Jess said, "looks like our excursion into the lair of the mad scientist turned out to be a big, fat goose egg."

"Hold on, hold on," Mary replied, fiddling with the machine. "I used the zoom lens for the next twelve, and because it is smaller, I was able to slide it inside the knothole."

As the thirteenth photo appeared, both women took note.

"Does the back of that lab coat hanging on the wall say what I think it says?" Jess asked.

"Look like it says Homeland Security," Mary replied. She turned to Jess. "So, Little Miss Smarty Pants, still want to contact the government and tell them what we've seen so they can stick us in some top secret government facility never to be heard from again?"

Jess leaned back and folded her arms, "I need more black friends."

Mary laughed. "C'mon. We finally got something worth looking at. Let's see what else there is."

The next ten provided nothing more than a closer look at what they had already seen. Machinery, computer monitors, wires, and the glass chamber with the illuminated gasses.

"See that?" Mary said pointing to the screen. "That was the thing I was looking at when I thought I saw a woman's face inside, then heard somebody whisper in my ear."

Jess thought for a moment. "Maybe it's one of those holographic generators they were talking about on the Science

Channel. But what don't make sense is if he *is* working for Homeland Security, shouldn't he be in some secure, secret place far from the prying eyes of two crazy old ladies?"

Mary considered it then said, "Yes, you're right! So Homeland Security lab coat or not, our boy is not working for the government. He's on his own; hard at work in a place that has a lot of bizarre energy. What we've got to figure out is why."

Mary clicked to the next to final picture.

As it filled the screen, it showed the glass canister in sharp detail, and the face of a desperate woman peering out from amid swirling gasses. Beneath it, spelled out in blue smoke were the words: HELP ME!

"What in blazes?" Jess asked.

Mary clicked on the final picture of the glass canister.

As it filled the screen both women saw it was completely empty.

Chapter Ten

"Yeah, Bob, what's up?" Alvin Trolley asked after answering his cell inside his Adirondack Light and Power truck. He had put in a long day and had just squeezed in a quickie with his girlfriend at a roadside motel. He dreaded the thought of possibly landing another assignment on his way home.

"Where are you now?" Bob asked.

"Just leaving Wheatfield out toward Titusville."

"Good, you're in the area."

Alvin moaned. "C'mon Bob, I've been out here since four this morning. Can't it wait till next shift?"

"Oh, relax, won't take more than a few minutes on your ride home."

Alvin huffed. "Fine, what is it?"

"Check the lines on Route 727 between Titusville and Wheatfield. We got several intermittent power drains we can't account for."

Alvin wasn't sure he heard him right. "Hold it, 727 between Titus and Wheat? That's the ass end of Dohesley. Ain't nothing there but dead trees and abandoned buildings."

"I know, but numbers match up in every other area but that one."

"Hmmm," Alvin said, clicking on his directional indicator and turning onto 727. "Think there might be a meth lab out in the brush?"

"Could be, but considering all the government warning signs, it's hard to believe anyone would risk his life in that toxic waste dump when he could just as easily hide in the mountains. Still, drive by and give a look at the wires and cables on the power stations. See if anyone has tapped in."

"Why not just call the cops?" Alvin asked, stifling a yawn.

"Because it's government property and a restricted area. If the feds are doing something out there and using our power to do it, we need to file for reimbursement. If it's a bunch of yahoos and a meth lab, *then* we call the cops."

Alvin rolled down the window and took a deep breath hoping his second wind would kick in. "All right. I'll check it out."

Alvin ended the call and continued up Route 727 just as the first raindrops splattered against his windshield.

With a high-beam lamp attached to the passenger-side mirror, Alvin illuminated the tops of the telephone poles. Slowing down to check each pole over the eight-mile stretch had become time consuming and tedious. A thunderstorm had swept in and was battering the truck with gusting winds and heavy rain. Flashes of lightning lit the dark skies and occasional hail made visibility difficult. Alvin would have missed the spliced wire at the side of the power station had a squirrel not panicked in the high beam and leapt away.

"Whoa, what's that?" Alvin said aloud as he slowed to a stop.

As he climbed out, he zipped his parka and raised his hood, then noticed the storm was heading out as fast as it came in and was displaying only random flashes in the distance. He took his flashlight, focused it on the power station, then raised his binoculars.

Oh that's spliced all right. Professionally done, too. Whoever did this knows his stuff.

With lightning still in the area, he didn't dare climb the pole. Instead, he used his flashlight to follow the spliced wire down and into the woods.

It led to some structure about a hundred yards in. He again surveyed the area. Not a car or van in sight.

That's probably because only lunatics and linemen come out in weather like this.

He followed the splice into the woods, illuminating his path with the flashlight.

It's most likely the government testing the soil, Alvin surmised noting the recent traffic and tire marks in the dirt. *It's been a couple of years since the last one and...*

In the distance, came a woman's voice. "Help! Help! Please!"

Startled, Alvin jumped back. "Hello...?" he said, looking around. "Hello!" he repeated, slowly doing a 360 on the shoulder of 727. "Where are you? Are you all right?"

"Help!" the voice called again. "I'm caught in something. And I'm bleeding. Please help me!"

Although the voice was clear, Alvin wasn't sure where it was coming from.

This part of Dohesley is miles from anywhere. If I call 911, they're going to ask what the emergency is and the extent of the injuries and I don't have a clue.

"Pleeeeeeease," the voice called out again, weakening.

"All right," Alvin replied, believing he now had some idea of its location. "Stay where you are. I'm coming!"

Alvin plowed through the thick brush and warped trees with flashlight in hand to the clearing made by vehicle traffic. He soon neared the barn.

"Hello? Where are you?" he called out. He felt sure the voice hadn't been this far in but knew sound traveled better in moist air than dry, so he kept moving.

"Please hurry," the woman replied. "I've lost a lot of blood!"

A momentary cold rain sprayed his face as he pressed forward.

I don't care how thick the moisture is, her voice couldn't have carried this far if she stayed put. Besides, what is she doing out here? It's dark, with heavy fog and rain, and I don't see a car anywhere.

Still, there was somebody out there. And should it be some kind of trap, well, they would soon discover Alvin Trolley wasn't someone you messed with.

"Where are you!" he called out in exasperation as he neared the barn.

"In here," she replied weakly.

"Are you alone?"

"Yes. Hurry!"

He cautiously walked to the barn door, turned and stood back against the wall under the eaves as the water from the roof dribbled down. He saw his truck's headlights beyond the brush and the side view spotlight trained on the telephone pole. Seeing no one in the immediate vicinity, he tried the white door. It gave but didn't open. He looked up, saw a padlock...

But the lock was open!

"Hold on. Wait a minute!" Alvin called out. "How did you get in there if there's a lock on the *outside* of this door?"

"My boyfriend locked me in and took off but the lock is broken. It won't stay closed," she gasped in a low voice.

This is nuts!

Still, if the woman was as badly hurt as she sounded, she might die if he didn't act. True, he wasn't responsible for her circumstances, but...

If I take off and they find her dead in the morning...

Alvin cursed under his breath, reached up, removed the lock, undid the metal flap, pulled open the door and entered.

"Where are you?' he called out, his voice echoing slightly.

A flash of lightning lit up the interior.

"Over here," the woman moaned.

Alvin followed the voice in a semi lit room. In the far corner he saw the reflection of swirling lights against the wall. Stepping between the machinery, he drew closer.

Then he saw it.

A woman. A nude woman encased in glass with incandescent vapor swirling around her.

In a kneeling position she pressed her hands against the glass. "Please," she said. "Please help me!"

Alvin approached the ectoplasmic chamber wide eyed. "How on earth..." He stepped back. "I don't know, lady. Before I do anything I have to know what's going on. I mean, look at you," he said. "You seem to be... I don't know. Part person and part smoke? I don't even know if you're real."

"Oh, but I am real!" she said placing her hands against the glass. "Feel the warmth of my hands. I'm as real as you are."

Alvin was hesitant. "Uh-uh," he said, edging back. "There's something wrong with this whole set up."

The woman slumped and bowed her head. "I see. I...I understand."

Alvin studied the chamber again, inspecting it from the left, then the right. "Lady, it's not like I don't want to help, but let's face it, this ain't adding up. First you call out like you're dying…"

The woman looked up. "I am dying. Look at me!" she shouted, extending her hands. "My body is disappearing into the ether. Won't you at least help me a little? Just enough so I can escape before my boyfriend comes back? That's all I ask."

Alvin eyed her carefully. "How little?"

"See those metal couplings on the sides of the glass?" she said pointing. "Place your fingers inside, grasp the metal bar and twist the cylinder to the left. That will open the lock."

Alvin decided to do it. Whatever the reason, no one should be imprisoned in such a manner. And this boyfriend of hers, what kind of psycho would build such a contraption? It was cruel, un-American and just plain wrong.

But as concerned as he was, he wasn't stupid.

He pulled a voltmeter from his belt and tested the couplings for current.

Nothing.

Checked the electrical connections.

Normal.

"Please," she begged. "I don't know how much time I have left."

Against his better judgment, he snapped the voltmeter back in its holder. "Okay, let's do this."

He stepped up, placed his fingers in the couplings and his hands on the glass. "Okay, so I twist this to the left?" he asked.

"No need," she said smiling as she placed her hands against his.

Her face suddenly transformed into Bert Langley's, then, as his hands sliced through the glass, he grabbed Alvin's wrists in a vise-like grip.

Alvin suddenly felt himself racing down a dark tunnel, while Bert established himself inside Alvin Trolley's body.

Bert/Alvin grinned as he looked down at his hands and the new body he had acquired.

39

"Well, I'll be doggoned!" he said, patting his chest then running his hands down his stomach and thighs.

"What's it like?" Lillian asked as she reappeared inside the chamber.

Bert/Alvin gathered his thoughts. "It's not what I expected," he said, scratching his head, "but to be alive again! Whew! I can't tell you how good it feels to breathe and feel the world around me. The strange thing is, although I'm inside this body..." he paused, trying to find the words. "Ah, nuts," he finally said, "I don't know how to explain it, but it's not me."

Bert/Alvin rubbed his fingers against his forehead. "All the memories are his. All the likes and dislikes are his. For example, I have a strong urge to drink a beer right now but as Bert, I never touched the stuff. It's like finding yourself behind the wheel of someone else's car. The seats are in the wrong position, the mirrors aren't set right, and the radio is tuned to stations you would never listen to. It's going to take some getting used to but, son of a gun, it worked! And I gotta say, great job luring that Trolley fella in."

"Well, the real trick was forming a younger version of myself," she replied. "I doubt a nude 66-year-old version would have done the trick, but me at 22? Let me tell you, at that age I could seduce any man into doing anything. Anyway, back to business. I'm thinking that you having that guy's memories might work to our advantage. You just pick up where he left off and lay low. If we play this right, we can use my kid's machine to bring us all back. All I need you to do is figure out how the damn thing works."

Bert/Alvin turned from side to side and eyed the machines as they performed their tasks. "Lillian, I've been dead fourteen years. My scientific knowledge is long obsolete. I don't recognize any of this stuff. Looks like it came from the set of *Star Trek*."

"Maybe *you* don't," Lillian said, "but the guy whose body you took probably does. Not as much as Virgil, but he works for the electric company so he's got to know the basics. And as a former science teacher, I'm sure you can piece together the essentials. In the meantime, I'll try to get Virgil to increase the power. More juice will make possession much easier."

Bert/Alvin stared at his hands with a look of pure joy on his face. "You really should be the next one over. I can't tell you what a kick it is to be alive again."

"Believe me," she replied, "I would like nothing more. But Virgil built the machine to talk to me. If I join the living, he just might shut it down. No, I'll stay here for the time being and get everything ready."

"Ooooh," Bert/Alvin said, "I just had a memory flash from our new friend Alvin. He was sent here to check on a power drain. I'll go back to the truck, call this Bob fella, and tell him I couldn't find anything. That should buy us some time."

"And I'll warn Virgil," Lillian said. "We can't have some stupid technical foul up ruining our plans. Oh, and one other thing. Some psychic named Jimmy McCracken is pushing Virgil to shut down this machine. Unfortunately, my son for all his smarts, can be terribly weak-willed so…"

Bert/Alvin's expression turned cold and hard. "Don't worry. I'll take care of it."

Chapter Eleven

Virgil discovered keeping his machines up and running demanded a considerable amount of his time. From what he could ascertain, the world or dimension or astral plane his mother existed on was in constant flux and had no fixed location. On several occasions he lost contact, which threw him into a panic until the link was reestablished.

Now, nearly three weeks since their original and static filled conversation, he was exhausted, depressed and in deep financial trouble. Each day Dora was either riding him about their finances, or on the phone trying to line up work at children's parties or other social events. "Someone needs to be the man in this marriage," she snapped as she stormed out the door the previous evening. Although delighted to be speaking with his mother again, the time had come to ask her for help.

Virgil dragged a chair over the dirt floor and placed it next to the ectoplasmic chamber; moments later the swirling gasses took form.

"Mom, I'm in so much trouble!"

She pressed her hand against the glass "What kind of trouble, Virgie?"

Virgil placed his head into his hands. "I made an enormous amount of money working for the government, but I've spent nearly all of it on this machine. I'm behind on the mortgage, my credit cards, the car payments, insurance, you name it.

"And I just got a letter from the bank's lawyers threatening to take me to court. If I'm forced into bankruptcy, my creditors will take everything. I told Dora I'm working on a project for the government, but that was just a stall so I could get this machine running. Anyway, they say that from where you are, you can see the future. Is there something coming along that I can use to make some money, some new invention or IPO?"

Lillian pulled her dress tight and sat on her heels. "Well first of all, only part of what those books say is true," she replied. "Our ability to see into your world's future comes in skips and jumps, bits and pieces. What we do is similar to what mediums do and there are many hidden dangers. To help you, I need a stronger conduit between our worlds."

Virgil brought his hand to his chin and nodded. "That makes sense. The chamber tightens the feed, but we're still far from achieving anything akin to digital communications."

"Digital?"

Virgil grinned. "Sorry. It's a fairly recent invention. But, you've given me an idea." Virgil pulled a note pad from inside his jacket and scribbled a quick note. "Mom, have you noticed any improvement in the transmission at any particular time, under any conditions, any…"

"Thunderstorms!" she blurted. "It's the lightning!"

Virgil folded his arms and tapped the pencil's eraser against his teeth. "Hmmm, that's odd. The amount of the electricity shouldn't affect the transmission. In fact, increasing it could theoretically damage the data stream."

"Well, you're the scientist, Virgie. All I know is during lightning storms my ability to interact with your world increases quite a bit. Maybe that's the key to help me find money for you. In the meantime I need you to do me a favor."

Virgil looked up. "Another one? C'mon, Mom, digging up those freaking knick-knacks you buried behind our old house should be enough. You know, other people live there now and if I had gotten caught…

Suddenly…

Lillian appeared deeply frightened; as her eyes widened and mouth dropped, her face disappeared into the swirling gasses, then another face formed. A man's face.

"My name is Alvin Trolley!" the man shouted with a fearful look as his eyes darted around. "What happened to me? I came out here on a job and …"

Before a stunned Virgil, Alvin's face dissipated and Lillian's reappeared.

"Disconnect Virgil! They're coming! Disconnect!"

Virgil complied.

43

As the machine powered down and the gasses sank to the bottom of the chamber, Virgil tried to make sense of what happened.

Alvin Trolley? Who the hell is Alvin Trolley? And how did he manage to get into the chamber?

When Virgil returned home he entered through the front door and found Dora waiting for him in the living room. She was dressed neatly, with little make-up and a stoic look on her face.

"Virgil, we need to talk," she said. She had her hands pressed together and stood perfectly still.

He rolled his eyes as he closed the door, removed his jacket, placed it on the ebony coat rack and said, "Dora, for heaven's sake, must you ambush me every time I walk in the door? I told you I'm working on getting the money for the bill…"

"It's not about the bills," she replied. Her lips tightened. "I…"

He dismissed her with a wave of his hand. "Well then, it's going to have to wait!" he said sharply as he picked up the mail and riffled through it. "I'm getting sick and tired of all your penny ante concerns. You know, I'm a very busy man, and I don't appreciate you wasting my time. Whatever the problem is, take care of it. And if you can't, then hire somebody who can, all right? Now are we done?!!" he asked flinging the mail onto the coffee table.

She stepped back, surprised at the nastiness of his tone. Her lips trembled momentarily and a single tear fell. "Yeah, I guess we're done."

After she raced down the hall and slammed the bedroom door behind her, he went to the kitchen, opened a can of ravioli, dropped its contents into a saucepan then set it on the stove to heat up. As he waited, his thoughts returned to what happened at the Blue Barn.

I don't get it. I was sure using the ectoplasmic chamber would filter out interfering spirits. So how did this Trolley jackass get through?

He banged his fist on the countertop. *Who is this guy anyway? Mom said the dead gather and talk, so if Trolley is one of them,*

44

why is he asking me where he is and why is he there? It doesn't make sense.

Unless...

Virgil leaned back against the countertop and tapped his fingers against the empty ravioli can.

Could he be someone who just died and doesn't know he's dead? Crap! That's all I need. It's bad enough McCracken knows about the machine, now I got to worry about some dead guy spilling the beans? If the military gets word they'll jump in, toss me some money and kick me out. I'll never get to talk to my mother again!

He snarled, tossed the ravioli can in the trash, shoved his hands in his pockets and determinedly shook his head.

No! I'm not going to let that happen. I'm going to find out who he is, where he's from and then unless he can be of some use to me I'm going to flush him out of my machine.

Virgil charged into the living room looking for the telephone directory. He found it opened and on the couch. He lifted it and was about to flip to the T's when he saw the TO—TR at the top of the page.

"Trolley...Trolley...Tro... Here it is! Alvin Trolley! 674 Mountainview Rd. Titusville!"

Virgil strode back into the kitchen, grabbed the simmering pot of ravioli and tossed it into the sink. He then returned to the living room, grabbed his jacket and charged out the door.

Virgil had a plan by the time he reached Mountainview Road. He would introduce himself and say he had gotten an e-mail from an Alvin Trolley but it was accidently deleted and since there was only one Alvin Trolley in the phone book, he decided he'd stop by on his way home from work and ask if he was the author.

Virgil kicked the story around for a little while.

Ahh, it's a little weak, but most people love to dump their tales of woe on others so once I mention Trolley's name I'm sure his wife or whoever will open right up and tell me everything I need to know.

45

When he arrived at the Trolley house there was an Adirondack Power and Light truck parked in the driveway. Virgil pulled to the curb, left the Volvo and made his way to the front door. As he was about to knock, he heard a woman giggling and the sound of bare feet running on linoleum. What followed was a thin shriek and a man laughing.

Virgil knocked anyway.

No response.

He knocked again.

A man's voice called out. "Yeah, who is it?"

"Excuse me, but my name is Virgil Vanderhill and I'm…"

"Virgil?" the voice answered, then said, "just a minute."

Virgil heard movement, then whispering and a low giggle from the woman.

The door opened but the porch light remained unlit.

A man wearing a red flannel bathrobe cinched in the center appeared from behind it. He appeared to be in good shape, in his early-to-mid-forties and other than his thinning hair, might have passed for a man a decade younger. When he saw Virgil, he studied him momentarily, then smiled.

"Virgil!" the man said with a grin and extended his arms in greeting.

Virgil pulled back. This man had the same face as the person in the ectoplasmic chamber, only this man was obviously drunk, as was the woman wrapped in a down comforter who came up behind him.

"Do you know me?" Virgil asked, eyeing him.

The man's expression suddenly changed. He dropped his arms and sobered up quick.

"Um, no, no. Just …uh, kidding around. What can I do for you?"

Before Virgil could reply, the woman, still giggling, opened the comforter to reveal her naked body. She pulled the comforter across her back from side to side like she was drying off after a shower and with a coquettish grin, bounced her breasts up and down, but quickly covered up when Alvin heard the flapping of fabric and turned.

46

Realizing he would have to lie and knowing it wouldn't be believed, Virgil said. "I made a mistake. Sorry to have bothered you."

Virgil turned and hurriedly walked to his car.

Chapter Twelve

"Although the Love Canal is probably the best known environmental disaster in New York, there is another location in that state that equals, and in many minds, surpasses it as an environmental catastrophe. The place is called Dohesley Township, in the Western Catskill Mountains. Throughout the1940's '50s and '60s, Dohesley was famous for its super sweet apple crop and fine wines.

"It was also a popular winter destination, featuring many ski trails and fine restaurants.

"In the early 1970's a rash of unexplained illnesses and new forms of cancer were diagnosed among the residents. In 1972, midway through the growing season, the apples turned black and the grapes fell from their vines. It took nearly a year before authorities discovered that Metronic Component Labs, an electronics firm, nearly 60 miles north, was leeching mercury into the soil. Following heavy rains, the mercury seeped into the Callacahochie River and traveled downstream to amass on the shores of Dohesley Township."

Father Santiago gestured to the screen. "Dohesley Township! Good heavens, it actually exists!"

He was sitting on the couch in the living room of the apartment provided to them by the Albany Diocese. It was attached to St. Albert's Church and was often used by visiting clergy. It was clean, properly stocked with the daily necessities and was comfortably furnished to make weary travelers feel welcome.

Santiago had just finished making his comment when Brother Martaine entered carrying two cans of soda. He placed one on the coffee table in front of Santiago and sat down on the couch next to him.

"What are you on about?" Martaine asked as he popped open the can.

"Remember that dream I had, putting my mother on a train, and the rotted abandoned station?"

"Yes."

"Well that place actually exists! I think it's a sign from God."

Martaine smirked. "C'mon, it's not a sign. It's a coincidence. Happens all the time." He took a sip of soda and placed the can on the coffee table.

Father Santiago shook his head. "I'm telling you, it's a sign. God gave me that dream so I would recognize the place when I saw it on TV."

Martaine turned to him. "You know I am just as devout as you are, and like you, I firmly believe God personally guides us and influences our daily lives, but coincidences do happen! They are as common as drinking water and our job, as clergymen, is to lead our flock to God, not solve mysteries. Such things should be left in the able hands of O'Hoolahan, Smythe and Rabinowitz," he added with a grin, referring to the television show where each week a priest, reverend and rabbi teamed up to solve crimes.

Although disappointed, Santiago eventually nodded. "Perhaps you are right. Besides, we are leaving tomorrow. And if our Lord wanted us to pursue this, He would certainly provide the time and opportunity."

Martaine spread his arms. "Precisely!"

The phone rang. Martaine walked over and picked it up. "Hello?"

He said uh-huh a few times, nodded and closed the conversation with, "Thank you for the information. I'll relay it to Father Santiago."

The television piece about the poisoning of Dohesley Township had resumed and the priest was following it closely. "So, who was on the phone?" he asked, not turning from the screen.

Brother Martaine sat down, shrugged and said, "It was our Lord, calling to remind me to keep my big, fat mouth shut."

Father Santiago's face lit up and he burst out laughing. "What on earth are you talking about?"

"The call was from Monsignor Fredricks. Said he received a call from home, advising him that a broken pipe has flooded our living quarters. It will take a few days to repair and would the diocese provide for us until the work is completed. The diocese, of course, said yes, so here we are here with nothing to do and a few days to kill." He placed his hand to his chin and said, "I wonder how we'll pass the time?"

"The Lord has cleared the way," Santiago said, rising from the sofa. "We need to borrow a car and head down there immediately."

Brother Martaine sighed. "As you wish."

Chapter Thirteen

The following morning Mary and Jess settled in at the kitchen table to read the Sunday paper. They could have gotten all the up-to-the-minute news they wanted on the Internet but Sunday morning with the paper, coffee and warm pastries was a long observed tradition.

As the sun streamed in the window, Jess poured herself a refill while Mary tore off a piece of bear claw and dipped it in her coffee.

"Still think we should just mail those pictures of the inside of the Blue Barn to the FBI, with no return address and let them handle it," Jess said.

"Yes, I know," Mary snapped. "You've made that clear several times but I just want to wait a bit. See how it plays out. We can get the FBI involved anytime."

Jess shrugged. "Well, anybody with that much electronic equipment in a barn in the middle of a toxic wasteland is got to be up to no good. We don't even know if..."

The women were startled by several hard wraps on the door.

They turned.

"Expecting someone?" Jess asked with a note of concern. She checked her watch. She couldn't remember the last time Mary had a visitor so early on a Sunday morn.

"No," Mary replied, rising from her seat, "but it happens. Sometimes people want to get a look at me before deciding on whether they want my services."

Jess eyed her sideways. "You know, if you had a video camera out there, you could see who it is. There're a lot of nuts in the world and they all seem to find their way to your doorstep."

Mary waved her off as she checked her hair in the hall mirror. "If there was trouble, I'd know it," she said reaching for the knob.

She suddenly pulled back as if she received a shock.

Jess saw this, leapt out of her seat, went to the kitchen counter drawer where Mary kept her gun and yanked it open.

Mary saw this and shook her head. "No, it's okay." She opened the door.

What greeted her was a shaggy-faced stoner with a friendly but goofy grin. He was wearing a dungaree jacket with his long brown hair pulled back in a ponytail. "Hi, Mary," he said, extending his hand. "My name is Jimmy McCracken, and I need your help to prevent the end of the world."

Jess put her hand on the gun. "That is one strange how-do-you-do, young man!"

Mary shook Jimmy's hand and studied him. After feeling his friendly vibes and seeing his positive aura, she invited him in. "This is Jess," Mary said gesturing. Jimmy nodded hello. Jess nodded back and took her hand off the gun, closed the drawer and went to join them at the kitchen table.

"I'll get right to the point," Jimmy said, as he sat down and pulled in his chair. "I've been told you led Virgil Vanderhill to his mother's spirit. No offense, but that was not a good thing."

"Damn it!" Mary said, jerking her fist. "I've been doing this for over 50 years and the only time I've ever felt something was wrong was when I took Virgil to that Blue Barn. Speaking of which," she added, leaning in "Jess and I had a look inside. What's he doing in there?"

Jimmy shrugged. "Not exactly sure, but..." he said leaning back, "it's got the spirit world fired up like never before and I've been talking to the dead since I was twelve."

"Really?" Mary said with some admiration. "That's amazing. I've never been able to, but I am pretty good at tracking down their spirits."

"Appears so," Jimmy replied, "but here's the thing: when a good person dies, their spirit usually goes straight into the light and they're gone. Well, mostly. In some cases, there are the occasional stragglers, people who died unexpectedly and unprepared. I used to help them but don't anymore. Too dangerous."

"Dangerous?" Mary asked.

"Very," Jimmy said solemnly. "That's why it's a good thing you can't talk to them."

"So where am I getting these images and impressions?"

"People have energy signatures, which is what you see. A scientist I know explained that people like us have..." He was

52

going to say 'abnormal brains' which is the term Virgil used, but decided it was too harsh. Instead he said, "…have brains that are wired differently. We can see and hear things others can't; which explains why you can feel the energy signatures in people's possessions."

"Okay," Mary said, "but go back to why it's dangerous to talk to the dead. I'd like to know why."

"Well, "Jimmy began. "Like I said, when a good person dies they go straight into the light and on to what I suppose, is the next world. Bad people fear the light and won't go anywhere near it. They're horrible people who led horrible lives. Lillian Vanderhill for example."

"Virgil's mother!?"

"Yeah. Not a nice lady."

"What's the next world like?" Jess asked enthusiastically.

"I don't know." Jimmy replied.

"But you said you talk with…"

"Oh, I better explain. Over the last ten years I've only spoken to one spirit. It's an old prospector that I don't particularly like, but since he's not one of the bad guys, I use him to keep my hand in, which is how I found out about you. You see he's not afraid of the light. The only reason he hasn't gone into it is because he wants to stay and watch the sinners get what's coming to them on Judgment Day."

"Seems like a swell guy," Jess said sarcastically.

Jimmy nodded and grinned. "Yeah, he can be a real pain sometimes, but like I said, he's useful. Anyway, the reason I came here is because Virgil has created a machine to communicate with his mother, and by doing so, well…" Jimmy scratched his head as he tried to find the right words. "There's a chance… What could happen is…"

Mary eyed him suspiciously. "Jimmy, your vibe is as hot as a country stove. What's the real danger here? I can take it."

"Holddddddd on a minute!" Jess announced, jumping from the table and frantically waving her hands in the air. "I'm 65 years of age, and before this conversation takes a nasty turn, I want to ask this kid some questions, find out if he's on the up and up." She

53

approached with her hands on her hips. "First of all, kid, you reek of marijuana, and I'm willing to bet you've experimented with a few other chemicals in your day. How do we know you're not on some crazy acid trip?"

"You don't," Jimmy said with a shrug, "but if you don't want to hear what I got to say, now would be a good time to bail because this is some horrifying stuff."

Mary reached across the table and took his hands. "Go ahead. I'm ready."

"Well, I'm not!" Jess said, placing her hands over her ears. As she turned her back to them and walked away from the table, she muttered to herself. "Crazy white people, can't leave well enough alone. Noooo! Gotta stick they noses where they don't belong. Can we do the stuff regular old ladies do? Nooooo! We gotta smack the dead around until they tell us how to save the world. Well, I don't know if I want to save the world! Every day I gotta deal with a whole new crop of morons with devil tattoos and metal rings and shit sticking out they faces. Break my foot off in they ass is what I should do. That would straighten them…"

At that moment Jess turned to see Mary's trembling hand fly to her open mouth and her eyes grow with terror.

Chapter Fourteen

Jimmy's boots thudded against the creaking wooden staircase as he made his way to his apartment. The air reeked of old wood and mildew and Jimmy reminded himself that as the building's only tenant, he needed to occasionally air out the place.

As he reached into his jeans for his key, he had second thoughts about telling Mary what they were up against. She seemed like a decent person, someone worth getting to know. And although Jess tried to come off like a tough nut, he could tell it was all show. He didn't want to drag either of them into this.

Unfortunately, he didn't have a choice.

When Jimmy discovered his ability to talk to the dead shortly after his twelfth birthday, it scared him, but, after the first week, he began to view it as a super power.

Often sought out by the recently dead, he was asked to do small favors. Mostly it was writing down specific information and mailing it to a concerned party. He wrote letters to the police, telling them where to look for certain objects, or what questions to ask, sent letters with safe combinations, the locations of Last Will and Testaments, and where to find hidden money.

And in return, the grateful spirits rewarded him. He once won a brand new bike by guessing the amount of jellybeans in a jar after a departee gave him the exact number.

In the beginning, doing these small and seemingly innocuous favors had no downside. Everyone seemed to benefit. What he didn't realize was that these conversations had brought him to the attention of truly evil people and far worse, to the attention of the daemons.

Significantly different and far more powerful than humans, daemons existed since the beginning of time in a dimension close to that ghostly purgatory, between our world and that beyond the light.

Hating all humans, they generally keep to themselves and remain on their own side. However, when the dead and the living communicate for any significant period of time, they take notice.

And should that communication remain open long enough, they will swoop in and take control of that living being, usually to force him or her to murder family, friends and fellow humans for nothing more than their own amusement.

After a month or so, Jimmy noticed his abilities were growing stronger. He was now able to see the dead and noticed that the latest requests for help were from spirits who were clearly shying away from the light.

Something was wrong.

Jimmy severed all contact and concentrated on just being a kid in high school.

His decision didn't go over well.

Over the following weeks and then months, Jimmy was besieged by countless apparitions all begging favors, some offering every delight a boy approaching his teens could imagine. Other spirits, realizing they were not going to get what they wanted, threatened violence.

He continued ignoring them.

It made them increasingly hostile. One night, as Jimmy lay in his bed about to fall asleep, he rolled over and saw an elderly man's face before him. As Jimmy leapt from his bed in panic, the old man cackled, "Ready to do what I tell ya?" Instead of answering, Jimmy grabbed his bedding and slept on the couch.

But that event and others like it took their toll. Jimmy lost weight, his grades fell, and he was showing signs of sleep deprivation.

Concerned, his mother brought him to the hospital thinking he might have some neurological condition.

He caused quite a commotion his first day when a young nurse bringing in Jimmy's meds saw a man in a dirty and ruffled black coat sitting in the chair beside him. When the nurse scolded the man for being there after visiting hours, he lunged at her, his hands racing toward her throat.

As she began to scream, he disappeared.

After days of observation and various IV's of psychotropic pharmaceuticals, Jimmy was given a number of prescriptions and sent home.

He expected the harassment to pick up right where it left off.

Strangely, it didn't, and with each passing day Jimmy became increasingly convinced that the meds had somehow put an end to his ordeal.

Two weeks later, however, Jimmy awoke from a very sound sleep to discover he was in the kitchen. He was wearing his pajamas and had pulled a twelve-inch butcher knife from the drawer.

Suddenly frightened, he looked down at his hand. "What the…? What am I doing with…"

As if coming from the bottom of a very deep well, a voice inside his head called to him. Growing steadily closer and louder, it shouted, "Go inside and kill her! Plunge the knife in and rip her open from tit to twat. Make her scream, make her beg! Make her death slow and painful!" it roared, "I want to see the terror in her eyes as she dies!"

Horrified and in raw panic, Jimmy began pissing himself. He tried to drop the blade, but his hand wouldn't open. As the urine pooled on the floor beneath his feet, his legs began to move. He tried but couldn't stop them. He was walking toward his mother's bedroom. He felt his hand tighten on the handle of the knife.

"No, no, please!" he begged, tears running down his face.

His pleas had no effect. Whatever was controlling him was merciless.

Forcing himself to breathe deeply to clear his head, he realized he couldn't turn from the hallway. He felt like he was encased in a metal suit under someone else's control. Fortunately, his movements were slow and deliberate, like an injury victim learning to walk again.

With his thoughts racing, he discovered that although he couldn't stop, he could slightly control the angle. This gave him an idea. He needed a disruption, something that would throw off his puppet master's concentration.

He remembered that on his way to the bathroom the previous night he saw the maroon carpet in the hallway had peeled back revealing a wooden strip with the points of small nails sticking out.

He angled himself into their path.

Two more steps…one more…

The nail strip pierced the bottom of his foot.

He opened his mouth and shrieked in pain.

But no noise came out; nothing more than a small, insignificant squeak.

But the pain had broken his puppet master's concentration. As Jimmy yanked his foot up, he lost his balance and with knife in hand, placed the heel of that hand against the wall to keep from falling. He spun around and tried to muscle himself away from his mother's bedroom, but the element of surprise was wearing off. Within seconds, this creature would have control again and force him to accomplish his goal.

With only one way left to save his mother, he pulled back his right arm and plunged the blade into his own chest.

The pain was excruciating. The room began to spin. He pulled the blade out and stabbed himself again….

The dark wrapped itself around him.

Fortunately, his collapse outside her bedroom awakened his mother who, after seeing her bleeding boy with a knife in his chest, called 911, then used a towel to compress and slow the bleeding.

He was rushed to the hospital and immediately wheeled into surgery. Although he had two punctures in his right lung, no other organs were injured.

After a week, Jimmy returned home, with a whole new regiment of pharmaceuticals.

Shortly afterward, while watching an episode about the Ancient Greeks on the History Channel, he discovered that in the early years of their civilization, the Greeks were reluctant to visit the remains of their recently departed for fear of being possessed by their dead spirits. In later years however, the Greeks began burning sulfur in and around the viewing area believing that would prevent it. Since the Greeks continued this tradition for centuries, Jimmy suspected it might have some validity.

So just before going to bed, Jimmy would light an entire pack of matches, blow them out then wave the sulfurous smoke throughout the room. He didn't like the smell but discovered none of the departed ever approached him while it lingered, including the monster that had possessed him. He continued the practice every night, (which thoroughly annoyed his mother, especially on those rare occasions when it triggered the smoke alarm) until he was old enough and got his own place. Shortly afterward the nightly tradition was abandoned.

As Jimmy placed the key in the lock of his apartment door, he wondered if, because of the Virgil's machine, he should resume the sulfur regimen. Since he never cooked, he didn't own any cutlery, or dishes, and the generic rum he purchased came in plastic bottles he didn't think it necessary. And when he was visited by the dead, he purposefully ignored them until they disappeared.

The only exception was Ike Seward, a fire-and-brimstone prospector and mountain man who considered people who talked with the dead to be the worst sinners of all. When Jimmy once asked Ike why he would visit a man like himself, a man he considered to be one of the most evil of the evil, he replied, "Just because the devil brought the water, doesn't mean you can't drink."

Although Jimmy wasn't quite sure what that meant, he found the old coot occasionally entertaining so he didn't bother with the sulfur trick.

Moments later, he would reevaluate that decision when, after entering his apartment and tossing the keys on the counter, he was yanked backward and felt something wrap around his throat.

Chapter Fifteen

Jimmy's first thought was that he had somehow slipped in the dark and was thrown off-balance, but as the thing tightened around his neck, he knew he was in trouble.

Years of contact with the dead—murder victims with gunshot wounds to their heads, burned bodies, stabbings, and the like—left Jimmy desensitized to knee jerk panic or sudden terror. The moment he realized what was happening, he kicked his assailant in the kneecap, then as Bert/Alvin buckled in pain, Jimmy slammed his elbow into Trolley's face.

As Bert/Alvin staggered backward, Jimmy raced to the kitchen table, grabbed the open bottle of rum and flung its contents at Alvin again and again until the bottle was empty.

Startled, Alvin looked down at his rum soaked shirt and trousers. When he looked up, he saw Jimmy approaching with a BIC lighter with its flame on 'full'.

"How about a little fire, Scarecrow?" Jimmy sneered in his best Wicked Witch of the West voice.

Bert/Alvin bolted out the door.

Jimmy ran to the doorway. "Yeah, you better run, chickenshit!" he shouted to the sound of feet rapidly pounding down the stairs.

Jimmy flung the door shut, walked back to his bedroom and slammed the lighter on the nightstand. "Damn it! I was going to drink that rum tonight. Now I got to wait till I get paid Thursday…"

He was about to call the police and report what happened when Ike suddenly appeared at the foot of the bed. He was bent over, staring into his lap.

Jimmy stomped around to where Ike was sitting. "Oh! You have so picked the wrong time old man, I swear if you…"

"Just came to say good-bye," Ike said. "And to…well…What I mean to say is…"

Ike looked up and Jimmy saw tears in the old man's eyes. "Well, what I want to say is, I'm sorry. I'm sorry for causing you all that misery. And for all that gloating and that 'there will be a reckonin' stuff. I was wrong and I just wanted to make my peace with you before I walk into the light."

Ike lowered his head and stared at the floor

Jimmy took a seat beside him.

"Why the sudden change of heart, old timer?" Jimmy asked as he bent down to catch Ike's eye. "Thought you wanted to watch all us sinners get our comeuppance."

Ike turned and faced him. "Thought I did. But it weren't until just now that I realized the extent of my own sinning. That guy who attacked you? I saw him break in. Saw him slip behind the door and pull that, whatever it was, tight. I could have warned you, but I felt vindicated that justice had finally arrived and heavenly retribution was at hand.

"When he attacked, well, it wasn't until that very moment that I saw what he really was. And what you really was. And well, what I really was.

"M'boy," he said with a look of deep concern. "What attacked you tonight was an abomination, a dead soul inhabiting the body of a living being. I never thought it possible, but there it was, right before my eyes!

"You see," he continued, "I've kept to myself all my life. The only company I thought I ever needed was the Good Book. I read it careful and followed the rules to ensure my own salvation. The problem was that I did nothing to ensure anyone else's. Never realized until these last few minutes what real evil was. I should have been out there in the world; meeting people and helping them. Instead, I got so involved pointing out other people's sins, I lost track of my own."

He shook his head with regret. "Well," he said standing up. "I was right about one thing: There is going to be a reckonin' and I've put it off long enough. Time to face my Maker and accept whatever punishment I got comin'. Hope you can forgive me, boy, but I wouldn't hold it agin' ya if ya didn't."

Jimmy wanted to say something. Wanted to assure the old feller there were no hard feelings, but before he could put something together, the old man vanished.

Suddenly, the words, 'A dead soul inhabiting the body of a living being,' echoed in his head.

Jimmy pressed his hands to his temples. *Virgil, what the hell did you let loose in this world?*

He rummaged through his jacket for his cell phone. If Ike was right then Mary and Jess had better keep away from that barn!

He found it, yanked from his jacket and flipped it open. He went to Mary's number in his contact list, but the cell failed to light up. The battery was dead.

Not that it mattered. It was already too late.

Chapter Sixteen

"That little sonavabitch tried to set me on fire!" Bert/Alvin shouted as he stormed into the barn. He strode up to the ectoplasmic chamber as Lillian was forming and said, "I was planning to stab him when he walked in but there weren't any knives or forks or even dishes in the apartment. Wound up having to use Trolley's wife's pantyhose, which I had stuffed in my coat pocket."

Bert/Alvin thought for a moment and chuckled. "Now there is one good thing that came from all this. Alvin's wife is one royal piece of ass! And boy, does she love to fuck! And so does the real Alvin, because according to his memory, he's also banging some other chick across town. Oh, and speaking of Alvin's wife, there was a problem."

Lillian stared at him coldly. "What problem?"

Bert/Alvin smirked. "Virgil showed up while we were drunk and playing grab ass. I was so surprised I almost let on that I knew him. Any idea what he was doing there?"

Lillian nodded. "That was my fault. I was trying to convince Virgil to increase the power when Alvin caught me off guard, overrode me and started peppering Virgil with questions."

Bert/Alvin made a fist and slammed it to his side. "Damn it! We're so close. Just another couple of days and you'll be free."

"Don't worry. All I have to do is give Virgil the old 'puppy dog eyes' and he'll do whatever I ask. We just need to make sure he doesn't find out that the chamber doesn't completely filter out other spirits. In any case, let's just stay focused and stick to the plan."

Bert/Alvin reached into his mouth and pushed up the loose dental bridge. "Going to have to get used to that," he remarked as he bit down. "Anyway, let's go back to what you were saying earlier about the Tesla coil extending our reach. From what I remember, the Tesla coil was invented to provide wireless electrical energy."

Lillian shrugged. "I have no idea about the science behind it, but Virgil said he uses it to run equipment. But it's also doing something else. Something I don't think he's aware of."

"What's that?"

Lillian paused, then said. "The power from the coil somehow makes it possible for me to travel outside this chamber. The more power, the further I can go. And I can sense when people come near the barn, and if I want, I can actually come up alongside them, force them out of their body and take over."

Suddenly Bert/Alvin's jaw dropped. "Wow!" He pondered Lillian's statement then said. "I think I understand what's happening. The Tesla coil's power is interacting with the mercury in the soil causing it to branch out beyond the barn like a spider's web. With power like that we don't actually need to touch a person to take over his body anymore."

Lillian nodded. "I think you're right."

"So now anyone who comes within say, 50 yards..."

"Maybe up to one hundred," Lillian replied. "But yeah, it's like you said. We can ride the current of the coil and force out the spirit before they realize what's happening."

Bert/Alvin smacked his thigh and grinned. "Well then, what are we waiting for? Let's get everyone together and..."

Lillian held up a cautioning finger. "Hold on a moment. We have to be careful, very careful! If the daemons even suspect..."

"Oooh," Bert/Alvin replied, concern quickly spreading across his face. "Good point. You're right. If even one of them..."

Lillian looked from side to side. "I think we're okay though, because the communication is being done through a machine, not mediation. Still, since we can't know for sure, we need to maintain a very low profile. Wait," Lillian said turning. "I just felt something." She moved her hands across the glass. "Someone... no make that two, two people have entered the area. They're coming here!"

"Who are they?"

The gases that formed Lillian dissipated momentarily then reformed. "It's those nosy old broads again."

64

"I'll get rid of them," Bert/Alvin said rising from his seat and turning toward the barn door. "My truck is outside so I'll tell them Adirondack P and L is investigating a power theft. That should shoo the old birds away."

"Fine," Lillian said, "but don't overdo it. We don't that McGuernsey woman running to Virgil with questions."

"Excuse me, ladies? What are you doing out here?" Bert/Alvin asked Mary and Jess as he stepped out from behind a group of twisted bushes and approached.

Startled by his sudden appearance, Mary was at a loss for words. Jess, however wasn't.

"What's it to you?" Jess asked, stepping toward him.

Bert/Alvin was startled. He hadn't expected such an aggressive response. "It's uh… We're doing a… We're testing…"

Jess put her hands on her hips. "Well, you go test all you want. Just don't pull any of that authoritative nonsense with me. Adirondack P & L don't own this land."

As Jess spoke, Mary thought she saw something moving toward them, a shimmer in the air, then felt something, something…wrong. Goosebumps spread across her arms; her hands trembled.

Very wrong!

She grabbed Jess' sleeve. "We better go."

Jess spun and shot Mary a 'have-you-lost-your-mind?' look, but the moment she saw Mary's expression, she switched gears. "Oh, so you want to go now? Fine! Let's go!"

She turned and with Mary by her side, briskly walked back toward Jess' Honda Accord.

Surprised to have won so easily, Bert/Alvin shrugged and headed back to the barn.

As the two women neared the car, the hairs on the back of Mary's neck stood up and her emergency warning instinct went into overdrive.

She grabbed Jess' arm, "Run!"

Thirty years of friendship had certain advantages. So when Mary shouted 'Run!' Jess took off like an Olympic sprinter. Experience told her that when the usually unflappable Mary panicked, it was time to haul ass.

In between gasps, Jess called back, "Why are we running? Is that guy chasing us?"

"No!" Mary replied as she came up alongside. "Something worse. Keep running!"

Breathing heavily, Jess slowed and reached out for her friends arm. "Can't!"

Mary took a firm hold of Jess' hand. "C'mon! C'mon! Don't give up."

"Mary, I... I..." Jess said, gasping for breath. "My allergies..."

"Just a little further! You can do it!"

"Too late!" Jess moaned and slowed to a stop. She bent over and placed her hands on her knees.

Mary stopped and turned. "It's not too late. We can still..."

Jess slowly looked up and grinned wildly. "Oh yes, bitch! It's way too late!"

One look and Mary knew it wasn't Jess. The being inside Jess' body lunged, grabbed Mary and attempted to yank her closer, but regardless of who inhabited Jess, her body was exhausted and covered in sweat.

"No!" Mary bellowed and pulled free. As she turned and ran, she took no more than five steps when she tripped and tumbled to the ground.

Within seconds, Jess was upon her.

Chapter Seventeen

Jimmy McCracken reached to the top of his closet and pulled down a shoebox marked Income Tax-2005-2010. He brought it over to the bed and opened it.

He drew a breath, peeled back the two federal tax forms that lay on top and removed the snub nose .38. He looked it over, popped the chamber, saw it was loaded, then snapped it closed. A moment later he slipped it into the inside pocket of his blue jean jacket and returned the box to the closet.

He shook his head and with a despondent look said, "This is going to get so ugly, so fast...

He called for a cab, then left the apartment and went downstairs. Minutes later, when it arrived, he climbed in and gave the driver Mary's address.

*

Mary looked up at Jess' face as she lay on top of her and saw an expression of confusion and surprise. One moment earlier it had been a mask of rage and venom. Now she resembled someone startled out of a bad dream. Jess sat up; looked around, then back to Mary.

"What just happened?" she asked as she climbed off Mary's chest. As she reached down and pulled her friend to her feet, Mary said, "No time to explain. We have to get out of here!"

They ran to Jess' Honda and once behind the wheel, Jess jerked it into gear and floored it.

As the car rocketed down the road, Jess rubbed her head. "I think I should see a doctor. I might have had a stroke or something."

"That was no stroke. You were possessed."

Jess' eyes widened. "Possessed?"

"Yeah, I've seen it before. Over time, your personality shapes your face. Not so much while you're young, but by forty, your life experiences have left their footprints."

Mary momentarily stopped there.

Jess threw her a look. "Aaannndddd??"

Mary ran her hand across her brow and continued, "When you grabbed me and said, 'Oh yes, bitch. It's way too late,' I could tell by the hate in your eyes it wasn't you."

Jess stared in disbelief. "You've been my closest friend for the better part of my life. No matter how mad I got, I could never talk to you like that."

"I know, but something inside you did, something sadistic and cruel. I'm just glad we got away before it set up camp."

Jess nodded in agreement; unaware that something had indeed 'set up camp.'

*

When the power suddenly went out and the generator kicked in, Bert/Alvin raced into the barn and yanked open the utility drawer. He grabbed a flashlight, checked to see if it worked, then headed for the door.

"What happened?" Lillian called out in the dimly lit barn

He pushed open the white door and swept the beam across the area. "Not sure," he called back. "I'm going to check the wires."

Bert/Alvin stepped outside into the twilight, turned the corner of the barn and saw the taillights of Jess' Honda disappearing down the road. He pointed the beam to the path they would have taken to their car and followed it. As he walked the wind picked up and sent dust and dirt into the air. Moments later, he found the splice and saw it had been pulled loose.

He crouched down and gave it a once over.

The electrical tape used to cover the wires had unraveled, and the wires themselves split in different directions. It looked as if it had been tripped over.

After a quick stop at his truck for the necessary tools, Bert/Alvin, using Alvin's technical expertise, repaired the splice and the power to the barn resumed.

"Did you find out what happened?" Lillian asked as he returned the flashlight to the utility drawer.

68

"Yeah, one of the old bats must have tripped over the splice.

"How do you know they didn't pull them apart intentionally?"

He stared at her dismissively. "Because any idiot knows you don't touch a downed power line. Anyway, I fixed it so there shouldn't be any more problems."

"Oh, there are problems all right," Lillian said. "Jolene found a way to slip into the Tesla web and attempted to possess one of the old ladies. She was halfway in when the power went out and she got yanked back."

"Shit!" Bert/Alvin growled, slamming the tool drawer shut. "At best we're only going to have one shot at this and we can't have psychos like Jolene mucking up our plans. He took a breath. "Look, we're going to have to speed things up. We're running out of time."

"What do you mean?"

"I mean I'm losing Alvin's expertise. My memories are beginning to override his. I noticed it when repairing the splice."

Lillian pondered the situation. Her plan was to have her fellow dead souls lure selected members of the living, especially those in authority, to the barn, where they would then be possessed quietly and carefully and with as little fanfare as possible. But word was spreading about Virgil's machine and if the daemons…!

Lillian shuddered.

"You're right," she said. "We're going to have to make our move in the next day or so."

"Good. What's next?"

"Search whatever's left of Alvin's memories and figure out a way to make the splice difficult to find. Then go back and report you found the location of the power drain but need a full crew to repair it."

Bert/Alvin lowered his head and considered Lillian's request. "All right, but remember, these are professionals and they're not going to be fooled for long. If they discover the splice and disconnect it before we can take over their bodies, they'll call in the cops, confiscate the equipment and Virgil will very likely go to jail."

Lillian nodded. "I'll make sure everyone is ready."

*

Jimmy McCracken's cab arrived at Mary's house at the same time she and Jess pulled in the drive.

He paid the driver then trotted over to join them.

"We got trouble," he said, as Mary stepped out of the Honda.

Jess rolled her eyes as she closed the driver's side door. "Kid, why is it you never bring any good news?"

"Pay her no mind," Mary said as they started toward the house. "She was momentarily possessed and is more convinced than ever that white people invite trouble into their lives."

Jess harrumphed as she slapped at the dirt on the knees of her slacks. "And drag they fine, honest, we-ain't-looking-for-no-trouble, black folk into it with them!"

Jimmy stood stunned. "So it is true. The old prospector said he saw a dead soul in a live body. Ladies, I think Virgil's machine has made it possible for the dead to take over the bodies of the living."

Mary sighed. "Ah, crap." She took a moment then said. "All right, let's all go inside and see if we can sort this out."

They had gathered at the kitchen table when Mary, ever the dutiful hostess, placed a cup of tea in front of Jimmy, "Here," she said, "this'll pick you up."

Jimmy said, "I'm not really a tea person, do you have any alcohol?"

The request caught Mary off guard but she nodded, went to the cupboard, pulled out a half full bottle of vodka and placed it on the table. After pouring a healthy amount into his tea cup, Jimmy said, "All right, here's what I think is going on. Virgil has created a machine to contact his mother, but has no idea the dead are using it to take over the bodies of the living."

Standing over him, Mary said, "So we have to destroy the machine."

70

Jess shook her head, "Nuh-uh. We can't get close enough. Remember we were nearly as far away as my car when that…well, whatever it was, tried to take over my body."

The possibility of an entire army of dead, predatory souls taking over caused Jimmy's anxiety to kick into overdrive. His blood pressure spiked and his stomach acid flowed like a waterfall. He placed his hands on his middle, groaned, then downed his vodka and tea in one gulp.

"What's the matter?" Mary asked, bending over to get a look at his face.

Jimmy's hands shook as he placed them on the table. "Just need a little air," he said, muffling a burp. "I'll be back in a couple of minutes." He left the table and stepped outside to the porch.

After he closed the door, Jess turned to Mary. "You trust this kid?"

Mary, sitting down, took a moment. "Yeah, I do," she replied, "but I'm getting the feeling Jimmy's more troubled than he's letting on. He's the most powerful psychic I've ever met but he needs self-discipline. He needs to stop getting high all the time and get his act together."

Jess considered Mary's comment, took a sip of tea, then tilted her head toward the door. "So what do you think freaked him out?"

Mary eyed the window and watched him pace. "I think the speed in which things are happening is starting to overwhelm him. Maybe he thinks it's too late to stop it."

Jess eyed Mary, "Well, if 'I see dead people' boy is spooked, don't you think he ought to tell us what to expect?"

"Yes, I do," Mary said determinedly. She took a gulp of tea, rose from her chair and went outside to join Jimmy.

She had just closed the screen door behind her when the smell of marijuana nearly overwhelmed her.

Seeing this, Jimmy, who was leaning against one of the wooden porch posts, waved his hand at the lingering cloud and dispelled as much as he could. Moments later, a stiff breeze took care of the rest.

71

"I'm sorry," Jimmy said, flicking the lit tip from the joint and crushing it out, "but in situations like this I've got to use every trick I know to keep from having a full blown panic attack."

Mary sat down in her rocking chair and gestured to the one usually reserved for Jess.

"Thanks," he said, "but I need to keep moving."

Mary shrugged and said. "For a person who's been doing this for as long as you have, you're awfully jittery."

He absentmindedly drummed his fingers against the railing as he paced. "Mary," he said, turning and staring hard at her. "Think of the other side as this huge dam Virgil drilled a hole into. Because it's been open a while, the area surrounding the hole is cracking and the longer this goes on, the bigger the crack is going to become until that dam bursts and sends everything on that side over here. Everything."

Mary let that sink in. "Meaning the daemons?" With a stoic look, she stood and put her hand on his shoulder. "Well, all the more reason for us to make sure that doesn't happen. Now let's go back inside," she said, directing him to the door. "You, me and Jess need to plan our next move."

Jimmy nodded and, as he and Mary went back inside, he made a solemn vow to be strong and to suck back his fear, so that if and when the time came, he could step up and kill them both.

Chapter Eighteen

The following afternoon, after Father Santiago and Brother Martaine exited the gold-colored Chevy Impala loaned to them by the diocese, they trudged through the heavy brush and thigh high weeds of Dohesley Township.

"Sure are a lot of signs that read 'Keep Out! Contaminated Area," Martaine said. "You don't think they're meant for us now, do you?" He gave Father Santiago a sarcastic look but the priest either didn't hear or ignored the comment as he was studying the area with considerable intensity.

As they approached the front of the first building, Santiago lit up and eagerly pointed. "There it is, exactly as I dreamed it!" He was pointing to the faded Dohesley Township sign hanging above the abandoned train station. "And look, there are the railroad tracks, scattered along the ground. I tell you Silvio, it's like I was actually here."

Brother Martaine bent down and inspected the debris. "But what does it mean?"

"To be honest, I'm not sure, but I believe we have been brought here for a reason."

As Brother Martaine rose he hissed his disapproval. "Hector, I've come along because I'm your friend and because you firmly believe our presence here has been orchestrated by God, but personally, I'm not convinced."

He removed a handkerchief from his pocket and scrubbed it across the rust marks on the palms of his hands. "Probably shouldn't have touched that. Anyway, if there were truly something that required our expertise it would have been brought to our attention through regular channels."

Father Santiago pushed against the paint-peeled railing to test its stability, then leaned against it and pleaded his case. "But with the television show and the call about the flooding at the residence…"

"Yes, I know, I know, but seriously," Martaine said, stuffing the handkerchief back into his pocket. "When we are called upon to serve our Lord, we usually have solid evidence, eye-witness

73

accounts, physical changes. All you have is a feeling and a disturbing nightmare."

"Sometimes we must rely on faith."

Martine responded with a subtle shake of his head. "There is a difference between having faith and convincing oneself that vague and obtuse occurrences are signs from God."

"So what do you require?" Santiago asked.

Martaine leaned against the railing post next to him and folded his arms. "Well, it's obvious we're loyal and true employees of our Lord and Creator, so what do you say we pass on the dreams and obscure signs and request a simple e-mail? Something direct like: *Dear Hector and Silvio, I want you to poke around Dohesley Township. I believe there may be some shenanigans going on, and you know how much I dislike shenanigans. So snap to it, boys. I'll expect a full report on my desk by the end of the week. Sincerely, your boss, G. Almighty, Creator and Master of the Universe.*"

Santiago eyed him disapprovingly. "I think you might need to make a stop at the confessional, my friend. That was a bit on the blasphemous side, don't you think?"

Brother Martaine's lips twisted as he considered Santiago's admonishment. "Perhaps, but I stand by its intent. Clear instruction is all I ask; no more of this…" Brother Silvio saw he had lost his audience. "What are you looking at?" he asked.

Father Santiago pointed to the Blue Barn in the distance. "That was in the dream as well. Come, let's investigate."

Father Santiago and Brother Martaine were walking toward the barn when a teal green Volvo, barreling over the dusty ground pulled alongside and slammed on the brakes. From the dust cloud a man appeared and stormed over.

"Excuse me, excuse me!" Virgil said, stepping into their path. "Just what are you folks doing on my land?"

"Your land?" Father Santiago said. He gave Virgil a curious look. "This land is owned by the federal government. Are you claiming to be a federal employee? If so, I will need to see some identification."

Brother Martaine nodded in agreement. It was something he always did when Santiago took his usual, I-don't-take-crap-from-anybody stance.

Virgil stepped in nose to nose. "You want proof?" he asked. "Hold on."

Virgil went to his car, reached in, opened the glove box and pulled out a wad of stapled documents. He walked back to Father Santiago and held them up to his face.

"See this?" Virgil asked tapping the top paragraph with his finger. "It says 'Access Permit for Soil and Water Testing.'" He flipped to the last page. "And see this? It's a government seal authorizing me, Virgil Vanderhill, temporary easement rights to conduct those tests." Virgil then lowered the papers. "You are on this land illegally, gentlemen," he said jerking his thumb toward Route 727. "So hit the road."

Having seen the documents and convinced of their authenticity, Brother Martaine reached for Father Santiago's sleeve and was about to say 'Let's go,' when Santiago pointed to the papers. "And I would comply," he said, "however, if you take another look you will see your permit expired yesterday. And so, you have no more authority over this land than I do. Now if you will excuse us, my friend and I would like a closer look at that barn."

Virgil checked the permit dates and was startled to discover the priest was correct. Still he grabbed the clergyman's arm. "You ain't going anywhere. This is government land and you are trespassing."

"As are you," Santiago replied with a cold stare. "And if you don't remove your hand from my arm, I will remove it for you."

Virgil's eyes blazed with rage as he considered his next move.

Brother Martaine stepped in. "I would do as he suggests, senor. Father Santiago is a man of his word."

Virgil glanced up at the very large Martaine, then at the barn. It was locked tight and he had the only key. Still, he wasn't going to let these two poke around and perhaps draw attention to his project. He dropped his hand but had no intention of backing off.

"I'm going to tell you one last time to leave this area or I will call the police and have you both arrested for trespassing," he said.

"Fine!" Santiago said. "While you make your call, my companion and I will continue to look around."

"The hell you..." Virgil thrusted his hand out to grab Santiago, but Martaine, responding with a speed unexpected for such a large man, grasped it and twisted, driving Virgil to his knees.

"Fortunately for you," Martaine said, easing the pressure, "I have taken on the responsibility of being Father Santiago's bodyguard. Not that he needs protection; it's just that while I use my physical abilities to merely subdue an assailant, the good father here tends to be, shall we say, overly aggressive? Too often he leaves his attacker a bloodied mess."

Martaine, having made his point, released him.

Virgil slowly climbed to his feet, rubbed his hand and eyed the clergymen with contempt. "You win this time but remember, I'm doing tests because this land is highly toxic. So, if you get sick and try to sue, I will testify in court with my hand to God that I warned you and you intentionally ignored me."

Before either man could reply, Virgil stormed back to his car and sped off.

As the dust cleared, Brother Martaine clapped Santiago on the back. "Well played, my friend. By cleverly outwitting that gentleman, we are now able to traipse around a toxic landfill without protective attire. Bravo, compadre, bravo!"

Santiago continued to stare at the dust cloud as it followed Virgil's car to Route 727. When it and the car disappeared, he turned to his friend. "I don't believe this area is as toxic as he would have us believe. For all his theatrics, that man is not concerned about our well-being. He is worried we will stumble upon something."

Brother Martaine made a fist and slammed it into his open palm. "Shenanigans, I'll bet!" he said with a conspiratorial glare.

Father Santiago laughed, patted his friend on the back and said, "Let's check out that barn. We're going to need to snap to it if we're going to have that report on His desk by the end of the week."

Under the blaring light and heat of a late June day, Santiago and Martaine hiked through the barren landscape. Now within yards of the barn's white door, they heard a faint buzzing, perhaps even indistinct whispering in their ears, accompanied by a prickling sensation on the back of their heads. Martaine was the first to mention it.

"I am experiencing the same thing," Santiago replied. "I suppose it is some electrical device, but there is something else, something unholy."

Martaine opened his mouth but suddenly chose to remain silent for nearly half a minute. "I was about to question your use of the word unholy," he finally said with a look of concern, "but I'm sensing it, too. Similar to what we encountered in Colombia."

The Blue Barn loomed before them, a dark silhouette against a pale ashen sky. The nearby trees resembled bony hands reaching up from unattended graves. The patches of black grass, the twisted and malformed bushes, the collapsing structures and hardscrabble landscape all testifying that there was something seriously wrong with this area.

The air had turned cold and malicious. The wind picked up.

"Its center is inside that barn," Martaine said, buttoning his coat. "And I apologize, Father, for my lack of faith. Our Lord has indeed sent us here to investigate whatever evil lives inside."

They continued stoically onward to the white padlocked door. They walked to the back of the barn hoping to find another opening but there was none.

Unable to pursue the matter, they decided to return at a later date.

As they walked back alongside the barn, Brother Martaine saw a business card tangled in the branches of a malformed bush. He removed it and read:

Mary McGuernsey—Psychic Detective 142 New Loudon Road, St. Lawrenceville, N.Y. 518-555-2313.

He flipped it over. There was a note scribbled, *Get memory card and batteries for camera.* He flipped it back. "Psychic Detective?" he asked handing the card to Santiago. "How does one become a psychic detective? And what precisely do they do?"

Santiago read it and smiled. "I don't know, but seeing that the card has not been touched by the elements, she must have been here recently and perhaps for the same reason we are. Let's find out what she knows."

Chapter Nineteen

Shortly after Santiago and Martaine left, four green and white Adirondack Power and Light utility trucks pulled to the side of Route 727 just outside of the lower part of Dohesley Township. It was a warm spring evening with high clouds and occasional cool breezes. In the distance, the trees of the Catskill Mountains were in full bloom, carpeting the area in various shades of green.

"I still don't know why you need all of us to find a simple power drain," Neil Newbury, one of the ten additional Adirondack P & L workers said as he climbed down from his truck. "It's not like we're investigating a massive grid drain in Manhattan or Boston. There are only four lines going from point A to point B. All we have to do…"

"I don't need a lesson from you on power lines" Bert/Alvin snapped as he yanked a small spool of coiled wire from the back of his truck. "So keep your yap shut until we find out who or what is responsible. And if it's no big deal, I'll personally crown you King Shit for a day. Satisfied?" After wrestling the spool to the ground, he reached for his coffee, took a sip, tipped his orange hardhat to his hairline and wiped his brow with his gloved hand.

Newbury stepped up, contrite, his face red with embarrassment. "Sorry, Alvin. I appreciate the overtime. Just a little tired is all."

Bert/Alvin nodded. He was more concerned about Lillian's plan succeeding than winning a meaningless argument.

He ran the spool to the utility pole, gathered his crew and pointed to the power station. "If you look closely guys, and er…ladies," he added, acknowledging the two female linemen, "you'll see the splice running down the inside of the pole and into the dirt. The problem is we don't know what direction the line goes once it disappears underground. And because this land contains mercury, you might get some false readings on your scanners. If we can't find the source, we're going to have to suit up in HazMat gear and do some digging."

Newbury hooked his thumbs in his belt, eyed the area and said. "How do you want to handle this?"

"I want you and your crew to fan out and scan for current along the east side. Move quickly, but not sloppily. I'll start scanning here and head to that blue barn. The rest of you head west toward those abandoned houses, then check and see if there's anything spiking in those old vineyards. Everyone ready?"

When they all nodded, Bert/Alvin turned on his scanner. "Okay, let's go. Meet me at the barn when you're done and we'll compare notes."

After a quick affirmative from the crew, the eleven linemen set out on their assigned paths.

Following Bert/Alvin's instructions, the female redhead walked into the field with a large flashlight and scanner, determined to prove that even though she was a newbie, she was just as good, if not better, than any of them.

As she walked west in the twilight, through the brush and malformed trees, she carefully watched her scanner for signs of electrical current.

No wonder there are 'Keep Out' signs all over the place. I've never seen an area so flat-out creepy. It's like an alien world out here.

Thirty yards in there was still nothing on the scanner, but she did feel a light buzzing on the back of her head. At first she thought it was a bug and ran her hand through her hair to send it on its way, but seconds later the feeling returned. Then she noted there weren't any bugs or animals in the area and anything that was alive was terribly misshapen.

Suddenly her vision telescoped.

She took a deep cleansing breath, and the sensation passed but before she could resume scanning it returned more powerful than ever.

She turned and bolted toward 727.

Unlike the others, the redhead was an avid yoga student. Having studied the ancient discipline for over a decade, she knew her body well enough to know when something wasn't right.

"Everybody out of the field!" she shouted waving her hands as she charged toward Route 727. "Hurry! Everybody back to the trucks!"

"What's the matter?" one of her fellow lineman called, out running toward her.

"Why? What did you find?" the other female asked as she too, raced toward her.

"Whoa! Whoa! Whoa!" Bert/Alvin shouted as he confronted the returning linemen. "What the hell is the problem?!"

The redhead stopped, gasping for breath. As the others gathered around she said, "I don't know what it is, maybe some sort of chemical, or some type of powerful outside current, but something is seriously wrong with the ground over there." She pointed toward the vineyards. "I felt like I was going to pass out. If it wasn't for my yoga training, I..."

Bert/Alvin smiled and raised his hand. "Now, now, there's no need to run around yelling 'the sky is falling', Chicken Little. I'm sure it's just a temporary thing. Or maybe you're coming down with the flu or something."

She shook her head. "Mr. Trolley, I'm not some scared kid out in the field for the first time. There is something..."

As she spoke, her co-workers, smiling oddly, moved toward her, causing her to slowly back up. "Guys?" she said eyeing them with a puzzled look. "What are you...?"

Another wave of dizziness swept through her. She pressed her hand to the back of her skull. "It's happening again! C'mon," she said grabbing Bert/Alvin's shoulder. "I'm not kidding. We got to get out of here."

When he didn't move, she turned toward the others. "Guys? C'mon, let's go! We...got to...to...get..."

A half hour later, with all the transfers complete, Bert/Alvin made a call to Bob, their supervisor at central.

"We got real problems here," Bert/Alvin explained. "We're going to need at least two more crews and a visit from Homeland Security."

Bob was startled. He had expected a meth lab or a survivalist camp, something of that nature.

But Homeland Security? What in blazes had they found?

Still with all the questions running through his head the only one that made it to his lips was, "Why?"

"We didn't find just one splice. There's a whole array of electrical connections leading to, well, we're not sure yet."

"Okay, but why get the feds involved? You suspect terrorists?"

"We found a giant Tesla coil in a barn in the middle of nowhere. What do you think?"

Bob needed a moment to let that sink in.

A Tesla coil?

"Wait," Bob said, rummaging through his desk. "I checked the permit list for Dohesley and a Virgil Vanderhill is doing soil and water tests in that area. Have you spoken to him?"

"We haven't seen a single soul," Bert/Alvin replied. "Besides, you don't need a Tesla coil for soil and water tests."

After some consideration, and the realization when something as obscure as a Tesla coil is involved, you play it safe and call in the government.

"All right," Bob said with a sigh. "I'll make a call. In the meantime, I'll send as many people as I can spare. I want you to gather as much info as possible, give it to the feds when they arrive, then terminate our involvement. I don't want to see Adirondack Power and Light's name in the same headline as Homeland Security and terrorists."

"All right," Bert/Alvin said, "but get on this ASAP. If this does turn out to be a terrorist operation, we don't want anyone saying Adirondack P & L dropped the ball."

"Good point and good job. I'll get on it right away."

Bert/Alvin disconnected. Gesturing for the linemen to join him at the back of his utility truck, he said. "Okay, listen up people. They're sending another crew and some feds and hopefully they'll bring in the local police. Once we get a sufficient number of our people in various positions of authority, we'll use them to call in more. By nightfall we should have enough to make the switch and enough clout to keep anyone from questioning our actions."

*

With an empty coffee cup and crumpled pastry wrapper on her left, Dora slammed the pen on the kitchen table. She had had enough. With a pile of bills spread out before her, and with their joint checking account rapidly approaching zero, she needed to know when Virgil was going to finish that damned government project.

If that sonavabitch drags me into bankruptcy...!

She tried to broach the subject with him several times but he always stormed out and didn't return until she was asleep.

Two weeks ago, she re-hired Donnie Pascal the PI to follow him.

He met with her twenty minutes ago.

Parked in the driveway, alongside Dora's pink Mazda Miata, Pascal handed her the detailed report of his investigation. "So, as you can see, Mrs. Vanderhill, he follows the same routine every day. He drives to the college and goes straight to the science labs. In the last two weeks he's only left them twice, and both times it was for lunch at the Wheatfield Diner. And as for those late night drives? Doesn't appear to be anything to them."

Dora sifted through the pages of the report. She shook her head. "You sure?"

Pascal nodded. "According to the GPS I hid in his car, and from tailing him, he spends his time driving around the surrounding countryside with his radio blaring. He occasionally stops for coffee. Then around 11:30, he drives home. Oh, and I stopped by that blue barn you mentioned. It appears the county is doing water and soil testing there according to the Adirondack P & L workers I ran into. So it could be they asked Virgil to calibrate their equipment."

Dora thanked Pascal and handed him a check. It was the last of her savings.

83

As he took the check, he placed his hand on hers. "Seems to me that Virgil's a jerk who doesn't see to his woman's needs." He stroked her hand. "Maybe it's time you hooked up with someone who knows how to treat a woman." He pursed his lips, jutted hid head upward and winked at her.

She'd known Donnie for years and was startled by his aggressive come on.

Something's wrong here.

"I'll keep that in mind," she said, pulling her hand away and stepping back from the car.

"Your loss," he said with a grin as he started the engine and backed out of the driveway.

She returned to the house.

Dora leaned back in the chair, something smelled rotten. And that something rotten was Donnie Pascal's report. True, she had hired him, paid him, reviewed his notes and watched as he drove away.

What she didn't do…

…was believe him.

After twelve years of marriage, Dora knew that Virgil NEVER drove with the radio on. When he went for a walk or a drive, it was to think. He became furious when his concentration was interrupted and had the dashboard clock removed from a vintage car he owned because the ticking distracted him.

Besides, she was sure Virgil was working in the Blue Barn and not at the science labs. His clothes had an odd musky odor when he came home and you didn't get that from working in a 'clean room.'

Late last week, because of Virgil's increasingly erratic behavior, and the fact she hadn't heard back from Donnie yet, she tailed him when he left for work. And instead of driving toward the university, he exited 727 and took an old dirt road that ended at a blue barn crowned with numerous satellite dishes. They were the large older type, like the ones Virgil removed from the house and put in the garage a few years ago, except they were no longer in the garage. Nor was the equipment he stored in the basement.

Water and soil testing? Bullshit! Virgil's an electronic communications expert. What the hell would he be doing calibrating water and soil testing equipment?

So, what *had* she learned?

Well, either Virgil paid off Pascal, or the government did, or...

It's something else.

That thought stopped and surprised her. Why? She wasn't sure, but, instinctively it made sense. But what *was* that something else?

She glanced down at the pile of past-due bills and sighed. It was clear if she really wanted to know what Virgil was up to, she was going to have to confront him once and for all.

*

As the Adirondack P & L possessed linemen waited for the new crew and feds to arrive, Bert/Alvin saw Virgil's car approaching. He immediately raced to the barn, cut off the power, then headed straight to Lillian.

"Virgil's here!" he shouted.

"Shit!" Lillian snapped angrily. "Always at the worst moment." She thought for a second. "Okay, do whatever's necessary, but for heaven's sake don't let him restore power. Those on this side are getting frantic about crossing over. Make sure Virgil comes straight in here. I'll calm him down. Oh, and lock the door when you leave, I don't want him to know you've been inside."

After Virgil parked his car behind the row of Adirondack P & L trucks, he shot out of his vehicle and demanded to know why they were there. He had the Water and a Soil permit renewed and wasn't going to tolerate any further outside interference.

When Bert/Alvin saw Virgil arguing with one of his linemen, his face turned ashen. He raced over to them.

85

"Get your hands off me you crazy bitch!" Virgil shouted as he yanked his jacket free from one of the possessed linewomen. "I have legal access to that barn; it says so, right here in this permit."

Bert/Alvin was rapidly approaching, waving his hands. "Mr. Vanderhill. Mr. Vanderhill!" he shouted.

When he got there, Bert/Alvin stepped up to his crew and said, "I'll handle this. You go back to the truck."

As they filed away, Virgil held up his paperwork and called to them, "See? I told you!" He turned to Bert/Alvin and wondered if he remembered they had met the other night.

Probably not. He was pretty drunk and the porch wasn't lit.

"Sorry for the inconvenience, Mr. Vanderhill," Bert/Alvin said, smiling and placing his hands in his pockets. "We were only recently advised of your testing permits. However, there is still an issue regarding your use of our power, so until that is resolved, your splice to our lines has been severed."

Anger flashed across Virgil's face. "What! But you can't do that! I'm at a very critical juncture in my experiments."

"Well, I assure you the matter will be resolved within the next 24 hours. Until then you're just going to have to wait."

Virgil considered trying to force the issue but remembered he had no legal right to the power lines, so instead he growled in frustration and strode determinedly to the barn.

After opening the padlock, he flung the door open and stormed toward the ectoplasmic chamber. "Mother, what's going on out there?" he demanded with a jerk of his thumb to the outside.

The swirling gases formed and Lillian replied. "The power company discovered the drain on their lines and sent out a crew. Virgie, I'm sure you knew this day would come."

"Damn it!" He kicked at the dirt floor and banged the heels of his hands against his head several times as he paced. "Always a problem, always something getting in my way!" He pulled over a chair and dropped into it as tears filled his eyes. He placed his head in his hands. "Mom, I can't take it anymore. I don't want to be here. I want to be with you. I want to come over to your side."

86

"No, son, no!" she said with a panicky look. "If you do that, they will never allow us to be together."

Virgil wiped his eyes with the sleeve of his jacket and looked up. "Who's they?"

Lillian shook her head. "Never mind who. Just get that terrible thought out of your head. Now listen, Momma has some good news. There's a summerhouse in Titusville. It's a small place just off Seneca Road. It's a blue cottage with a tin roof. In the basement is a brick wall. Behind two gray bricks is a strongbox with nine thousand dollars in cash. It's there for the taking."

"But that's stealing!" he said startled, as if he misheard.

"I know, but you said you needed money right away and frankly, that's the fastest place to get it."

"But Mom, what I was asking for was more in line of stock tips or lotto numbers."

"Be that as it may, stock tips, even the best of them, take time to generate earnings. You said you were desperate. I tried to find the fastest way to help. I'm sorry if I let you down."

Lillian lowered her head.

Seeing this, Virgil's entire persona changed. "Oh no, no, no. Don't feel bad. I do appreciate it." He got up, wrapped his arms around the glass container and placed a kiss near her cheek. "I should have realized getting a hold of a large amount of money legally would take time. Besides, once you locate a legitimate source, I can return it. No harm, no foul."

Lillian smiled. "That's right. Just think of it as a loan. And don't worry about the power company. When you leave, tell the head guy—I think his last name is Trolley—to send you the bill for whatever power you used and whatever paperwork they need you to sign."

"But isn't he going to want to inspect my equipment? The minute he sees it, he's going to know this is no water and soil testing facility."

"Virgie," she replied with a motherly smile. "Trolley and his crew will accept any excuse to pack up and get out of here. They're convinced the ground is still poisonous, so once they have a name and a place to send a bill..."

Virgil leaned back, sighed and smiled. Once again his mother had pulled him out of a tough situation. "Thanks, Mom," he said in an emotion-choked voice, "you're the best!" He stood, put the chair back, waved goodbye and slipped out the door.

Ten minutes later, after Virgil was gone, Bert/Alvin restored the power. Shortly afterward the additional P & L crews and members of the police, FBI and Homeland security arrived. They parked their vehicles on the shoulder of Route 727 and as they peppered Bert/Alvin with questions, he simply replied that a picture is worth a thousand words and led them all to the Blue Barn.

Chapter Twenty

Hours later, Virgil was sitting at the bar at the Wheatfield Bar and Grill. He had just knocked back his fifth rum and coke and smiled when he noticed the mounted deer head above the bar was wearing sunglass and a pink beret. Life was good, Willie Nelson was singing about being on the road again and several pretty girls had just stepped in to celebrate a birthday or promotion or whatever. He didn't care; all was right with the world. He had nine grand in cash in his pocket and all his troubles were in the rearview mirror. As he went to order another drink, Jimmy McCracken sat down beside him.

"Well, you seem in a pretty good mood," Jimmy said as patted Virgil on the shoulder and ordered a beer.

Virgil turned, saw him and pulled back. "I was, until you showed up. What are you, stalking me now?"

Jimmy pointed to the window.

Across the street was the parking lot for Lumberland. "They changed my hours so I thought I'd stop in for a quick one before going home, but you rarely drink. And when you do, it's usually a wine spritzer or some drink with an umbrella in it. What's the deal?"

Jimmy wouldn't have been surprised if Virgil snubbed him. It wouldn't be the first time. But on the rare occasion when he did drink, Virgil became a different person. When drunk, he liked to talk. Liked to show off just how smart he was.

"So you want to know the deal, huh?" Virgil said from behind increasingly droopy eyelids. "Well, I'm gonna tell you. And you know why? Because you're probably the only one in this whole freakin' town who has the brains to appreciate what I've accomplished."

Virgil fiddled with the top button of his shirt and leaned in. "Look at all these hillbilly morons," he whispered as he threw a glance from right to left. "I'm about to change the world and not one of them has a clue."

Seeing that Virgil was building up steam for a tirade, Jimmy raised his glass and said, "Here's to you, Virg. I don't think there's a man alive who could do what you've done."

When Virgil eyed him suspiciously, Jimmy took a sip and continued. "No, I'm serious. I've been talking to the dead since I was a kid, but I've never been able to choose who I talked to. But you can, and without any psychic abilities. But here's the thing," Jimmy took a swig, put the glass down and rested his elbow on the bar. "You've been at this since your mom died. You've must have tried a thousand different ways over the years to make it work. What made this one different?"

"You'd like to know, wouldn't you?" Virgil said. He stared at Jimmy for a moment with a drunken, sloppy look. A look that said, ha-ha, told you I was smarter. He grabbed a handful of peanuts and emptied them into his mouth as Willie Nelson left for the road again and Axl Rose stepped up to sing about November rain.

Although Virgil's question was rhetorical, Jimmy decided to respond anyway.

"Yeah, I would."

Virgil eyed him with a confused look that asked, 'would what?' But he managed to pull it together and said. "So you'd like me to tell you, huh?"

Jimmy smiled and said, "Very much."

"Well, screw you McCracken." He chuckled, then dropped his elbow on the bar and popped some more peanuts.

As the bartender passed, Jimmy ordered Virgil another drink. When it was brought over, Virgil was surprised. No one had ever bought him a drink before and his hostility lessened.

"You know what?" Virgil said as he took a sip. "I am going to tell you. I mean, why the hell not? You're right. Finding the key took fucking forever!" He slapped his hand on the bar. "I went years. Years! Beating my head against the wall, spending all sorts of money and getting nowhere. But," he added, shaking his index finger, "I didn't give up. That's something you should know about me McCracker. I never give up, especially, when my mother is involved."

Virgil drank a little more and wiped his hand across his mouth. "Did you know that fat doofus wife of mine had my mother investigated? The gall of that bitch!" he spat. "She ain't half the woman my mother is. Anyway, since I promised Mom I was going to find her after she died; I had to keep my word? I mean you can't promise your mother something and not come through, right?"

When Jimmy didn't immediately answer, Virgil got surly. "I said... *right*?"

Jimmy pulled back and quickly nodded. "Right!"

Virgil nodded back. "Damn right, I'm right. Anyway, after I finally figured out how to communicate with the dead, I had to find out where my mother's spirit was. The spooks I talked to at first were no help at all. They were always trying to get me to do things for them, like I'm their freakin' errand boy. Then I got lucky. I saw an article about Mary McGuernsey." Virgil grinned. "That broad's fantastic! I handed her my mother's old change purse and right off the bat she takes me to Dohesley Township."

With a confused look, Jimmy asked. "What's so special about that?"

Virgil stared, his eyes slightly crossed from the alcohol. "About what?"

Jimmy knew he'd better move fast before Virgil's brain became completely pickled. "What's so important about Dohesley Township?"

"That's where the Blue Barn was and she brought me right to it. When I walked in the door, the energy in the place! I just knew

90

Mom was there! And what makes it funny is, at the time, I didn't realize the importance of the barn or the location."

Virgil gulped down the rest of his drink and again ran his sleeve across his mouth. "When I finally contacted my mother, the transmission was weak, really, really weak. I knew right off I had to widen the field and focus the transmission. Focusing the transmission was easy, I already knew how to build an ectoplasmic chamber but I needed a large electrical net to widen the field, which meant dealing with a ton of state and federal assholes, but then it hit me!" He reached for his drink and saw the glass was empty. "What metal is one of the best conductors of radio waves? Mercury! Remember those stories about people hearing voices and it turned out the mercury in their fillings were picking up radio signals? Well, with all the mercury in the soil, that large electrical field was already there, right under my feet. And once I installed the Tesla coil… it all came together, 'cause the Tesla coil emits a wave of electricity and with the mercury already in the ground…"

Virgil suddenly dropped his head like an exhausted athlete who just completed a marathon. After several seconds passed, he sighed and looked up. "Want to know what the real problem is?" he asked from behind watery eyes. He paused, then said, "The problem is, now that I've done it, I'm not sure I should have." He turned pensive and melancholy. "I thought that by contacting Mom, it would be like it was in the old days, you know? And it is… kinda, but I forgot how pushy she can be. I thought she'd be happy to see me, thought we could talk and spend time together like we did when I was young. But all she does is order me around. Do this, get that. It didn't turn out the way I thought it would."

Jimmy leaned in. "Virg, I've got to tell you something you're not going to want to hear."

Virgil gave a half drunken smirk. "Frankly, Jimmy Crackcorn, and I don't care!" Virgil slapped his hand on the bar and exploded with laughter.

Jimmy had heard that joke about a million times but gave a half chuckle so not to piss Virgil off, then took his shoulder and said. "Your machine has done more than let you talk with your mother. It made it possible for the dead to take over the bodies of the living. Actually anybody who gets close to that barn."

Virgil continued to smile as if waiting for a punch line but when he realized Jimmy was serious, his face twisted as if he caught a whiff of a particularly nasty fart.

He shook off Jimmy's hand. "What are…?" He leaned in with an angry snarl. "Are you fucking with me? You're fucking with me, right? He bent his head down and licked his lips. "That can't happen. It's stupid, it's…" Virgil's face nevertheless became a lot less drunk. His brows creased like he was trying to force the wheels in his head to kick into gear. "Where did you get that idea? It's impossible, it can't…"

Virgil staggered off the stool. "Just like you, McCracken, to ruin the one good evening I've had in long time. And that idea of yours is stupid. Do you hear me? Stupid! You're not smart. You're just some stoner who likes to ruin people's good times. That's what you are."

Virgil picked up the coins, put the paper money under his glass and grabbed his jacket from the wall hook. "Next time you see me in a bar, or anywhere else, just leave me alone, got that!? And your idea is stupid. *You hear me!"*

He said the last three words loud enough to get the bartender's attention. He put down the glass he was cleaning, turned, pointed at Virgil and said, "Hey! We got a problem?"

Virgil spun back round to the bartender, ready to tell him off but the sudden movement made him dizzy and he had to grab the bar to steady himself.

Jimmy waved and shook his head. "Nope, no problem here," he said edging Virgil toward the door. "We were just leaving." He pulled out his cell and rang the local cab company. In less than a minute, a cab pulled up and Virgil stumbled into the back seat.

As the cab took off, Jimmy wondered if Virgil would even remember the conversation.

Chapter Twenty One

Although they were the same age, lived in the same town, and went to the same school, Aimee McFarland and Sula May Hockenberger never met. Although it would appear they had a lot in common, the truth was, they lived in two different worlds.

Seventeen-year-old Aimee McFarland was pretty, personable, and had a number of close friends. With arched eyebrows, caramel-colored eyes, long jet-black hair, and a nearly perfect figure, she was good-looking and knew it. In addition, she was a straight A student, president of her class, captain of the cheerleading squad and came from a wealthy family. Her parents owned a chain of car dealerships and had been happily married for 22 years. With all this going for her, Aimee realized early in life that she was dealt a winning hand and to show her appreciation, volunteered at the Open Door soup kitchen twice a week after school.

Seventeen-year-old Sula May Hockenburger's life was the exact opposite. Although pretty with blue eyes, blonde hair and an attractive figure, Sula May wore oversized shirts and baggy pants to hide her assets. When her mother died eighteen months ago she had no choice but to continue living in a dilapidated cabin just outside the hills of Wheatfield under the guardianship of her stepfather who had, over the last few months, become a violent alcoholic. When he drank, which was often, he would storm through the cabin with a loaded shotgun demanding the imaginary FBI agents hiding in the closets to come out and show their faces.

She also had 15 year-old twin stepbrothers who, now having reached puberty, were constantly trying to see her naked. As the "woman" of the house it was her responsibility to cook the meals, wash the clothes and keep the place clean.

With the bathroom door lock now conveniently broken, Sula could only take a shower when the house was empty, which was rare. Or after gym class at school which was only one day a week

At school, her lack of hygiene garnered her the nickname, 'Smelly Sula,' and as such, she became a social outcast. And with no money to buy new clothes, she resorted to stealing cast-offs from Salvation Army bins.

She began skipping school but faced growing sexual harassment at home. One morning as she served coffee to her stepfather and two stepbrothers, they ran out of milk. When she told them one of the twins replied, 'Well, then pop out one of them titties and squeeze us out some. When she complained, her stepfather dismissed the comment with a 'They's just funnin' you, Sula. Don't make such a big deal out of it.'

He might as well said, *'Go on boys and fuck yer sister. Ain't no big deal.'*

Because that's the way they heard it, and from then on the harassment got worse. Much worse.

On this particular evening, after the old man had drunk himself into unconsciousness, the boys, wearing their usual bib overalls, T-shirts and boots slipped out back and took a couple of belts from the old man's liquid courage. As the minutes passed and the liquor took hold, they decided today was the day they were gonna see their stepsister naked.

She was in her tiny bedroom, writing in her diary, when they burst in, grabbed her, threw her on the bed and started pulling at her clothes. At seventeen, she was bigger and stronger, and after kicking one of the twins in the chest and pushing the other to the floor, she charged out of her room.

"Paw! Paw!" she shouted, racing down the stairs, "the twins are trying to strip me bare!"

Seeing her stepfather passed out on the couch, Sula bolted out the front door. The twins, after carefully checking to make sure the old man was in no condition to stop them, tore out after her.

At that same moment, Aimee McFarland was enjoying her first ride in her four-year-old, low-mileage, blue Ford Mustang ragtop that she had just received from her parents as a high school graduation present. Cruising through the Catskill Mountains, she was wearing a former boyfriend's letter jacket, had her right arm draped over the top of the passenger seat and was singing along with the radio as it blared one of her favorite songs.

She had just reached the top of a hill on Route 727 when she saw a large number of cars—most of which had flashing lights and official government emblems—less than a quarter mile ahead.

Suspecting a roadside check point, she down-shifted and killed the radio.

With only a junior license, she wasn't supposed to be driving after dark, and although it was still technically twilight, if she got pulled over, the cops might ticket her anyway and make her parents pick her up.

"Shit!" she said under her breath.

She also knew if she suddenly turned around, one of the patrol cars would take off after her.

Then she saw it. The pink Mazda Miata directly ahead of her veered off onto a small dirt road, leading behind Lavender Hill, away from the police

"Yessss!" the teen said and followed.

About a minute into the ride, the pink Miata turned onto the road leading back into Dohesley. Aimee had heard all the stories, so she chose the fork in the opposite direction, figuring she'd ride a couple of miles and if it didn't lead to the main drag, she'd double back and get on 727, heading away from the police checkpoint.

Happy with her plan, she began to relax.

Whew, that was close!

Sula's step-father, half in the bag when their mother gave birth, named the boys Coffee and Tee. He thought it would be funny and told the nurse to put that on the birth certificate. When their mother later objected, he raised his hand and promised to smack that smart mouth right off her face.

So Coffee and Tee it was. Spelled T-e-e not T-e-a because Paw didn't know the difference. Although identical twins, there was a noticeable distinction between the two. Tee's teeth protruded and his eyes had sort of a vacant, dopey look, whereas Coffee's teeth grew in just fine but his eyes were that of a natural predator.

Despite those minor physical differences, both lacked any conscience, social or otherwise.

And right now, Coffee and Tee were liquored up and horny as a pair of jackrabbits. Although Sula was stronger and could run much faster, they were able to follow her tracks down the hillside, across 727 and into Dohesley.

"Why'd that dumb ass run into that shithole?" Tee commented as he and Coffee edged down the hill. "Ten minutes in there and her titties'll fall off"

They both roared with laughter but stayed on her trail like wolves following a scent.

Dohesley, with all its abandoned buildings and wells and even the old train station provided a number of hiding places, but with no other foot traffic in the area and an earlier rain, they had no trouble finding her.

Sula sat quietly in the living room in what she thought was the securest house to hole up in. It was a large, three-story white Tudor that at one time had been the home of a wealthy executive. There were no broken windows or missing doors. Everything was securely boarded except for a heavy three-paneled front door that had been locked, (Sula jimmied it open with a thin piece of plastic). The only other opening was a tiny window at the very top.

Now that she had slid the bolt lock into place from the inside, she felt safe and decided to remain there till morning. Then she'd go home and tell Paw what the twins did. She smiled. He'd take the strap to them for sure. He'd beat them black and blue.

She paused for a moment, then worriedly pulled her legs up to her chin.

Or would he?

Over the last few weeks, Paw's dismissive attitude toward the boys growing randiness and sexual remarks made her suspect the old man was getting a hankering to see her naked, too. Maybe decide in addition to the cooking and cleaning there was gonna be one more womanly duty to perform…

"We know you're in there, Sula May!" Coffee shouted from the front porch. "Your tracks are as fresh as paint. Now get on out here. We ain't done with you yet!"

"You better get on home, Coffee," she shouted from behind a boarded up window, "and take Tee with you, 'cause when Paw wakes up, you both gonna get a whippin'!"

Coffee thundered up the stairs and kicked the heavy oak door. "Yeah, well, we'll tell him you ran away again. This time he'll lock you in the basement for good."

"And you two drank Paw's liquor," she replied. "When he finds his liquor gone, and smells it on your breath, he'll skin you both alive!"

"I said, you get the hell out here right now, Sula May!" Coffee bellowed as he pounded on the door. "Or I swear we'll burn the place down!"

Sula wrapped her arms around herself and shivered in fear.

I'm done. If I go out now they'll surely rape me, maybe even kill me to keep it quiet. And who's going to miss ol' 'Smelly Sula' anyway? And if I'm not home when Paw wakes up, they'll tell him I drank his liquor and run off. Then they'll track me down, drag me back and lock me in the basement. Then when Paw and the twins get their blood up, they'll come down the stairs and...

Sula suddenly looked up. She smelled smoke.

She ran up the stairs to the top floor, into the attic and looked out from its tiny window. Below were her stepbrothers. Coffee was grinning and Tee was holding a fiery tree branch. Her heart skipped when she saw the underside of the rotting porch was on fire.

"You ain't got no choice, Sula May," Tee called out as he waved the branch, "lest you wanna get burnt up."

She wondered just how bad that would be, considering what the rest of her life was about to become.

"Last chance!" Tee shouted, "This fire is moving mighty fast!"

With the underside of the porch aflame, the fire was making its way to the inside sub floor.

In the basement were a number of cardboard boxes, various sundries and a 100 pound propane tank that was nearly full when the house was abandoned. Over the years the wooden pallet that supported it rotted, the cylinder fell and propane leaked onto the basement floor. When the heavy gas and the flames met…

Aimee McFarland was about to make a turn and head back to 727 when she heard a muffled explosion in the distance. She jammed on the breaks and saw a plume of black smoke followed by a burst of flame in the twilight sky

With the area illuminated by the fire, she saw two figures running from the inferno.

I hope everybody got out all right.

She was about to put the car in gear when, as the flames grew brighter, she saw someone trying to climb out of a small window on the very top of the house.

A faraway female voice screamed, "Help me, please! Tee and Coffee you come back here!"

Seeing the two figures ignoring the girl's call for help, Aimee revved the engine and launched the Mustang down the hillside toward the fire.

Unable to squeeze out the window, Sula ran back to the door and tried again to force it open. She pushed as hard as possible but it barely budged. After several attempts, she was convinced there was something propped against it and suspected one of the walls collapsed after the explosion and was pressing on the door like a buttress.

Exhausted from running and from trying to force open the door, she walked back to the window.

That's it, I guess. I'm done.

As tears filled her eyes, Sula sat down, saw the scattered broken glass from the window surrounding her and considered picking up one of the shards and raking it across her wrists. She felt her heart pounding. The thought of slowly burning to death terrified her. She got up, looked outside and saw Coffee and Tee in the distance tearing up the hillside.

They left me to die.

She got down on her knees and placed her entwined fingers on the window ledge. "Lord," she prayed, "I know you hate this sort of thing but I don't want to get burnt up and die screaming. I just want to go to sleep and never wake up."

She reached down, picked up one of the shards, looked up into the sky and said, "I'm real sorry," then placed it against her wrist and just as she was about to pull it across…

"Is there anybody up there?!" Aimee shouted. "Is anybody inside?!"

Sula dropped the shard, looked out the window saw a girl about her own age with long black hair sitting in a car parked next to the garage.

"Yes, yes!" Sula said sticking her head out. "The door's stuck and I'm too big for the window."

"Hold on!" Aimee called back. "I'll see what I can do."

The young athlete popped the trunk, raced to the back and grabbed the tire iron. After running to the building, she pried the wood from a side window and climbed in.

There was some smoke, but the fire was confined to the right side of the building and the attic stairs were on the left.

She charged up and when she reached the landing between the second and third floors, she heard fire crackling and saw the smoke gathering at the ceiling.

Then came that moment.

Aimee had already done more than could be reasonably expected. She had raced into a burning building to save a complete stranger. She wasn't a trained firefighter; she was a cheerleader. What more could they expect from her?

She was still struggling with that thought as she took a deep breath and vaulted up the stairs.

The heat hurt!

Her hand tightened on the tire iron as she dropped to the floor and crawled toward where she thought Sula was trapped.

I don't want to do this.

She turned the corner and saw the wall in front of the attic had collapsed. It was on fire and blocking the door.

A voice called out from behind it. "Help! Help! I'm in here. Please help me!"

Aimee started sobbing as she crawled toward the voice; the fire had spread to part of the walls and ceiling. She could smell the singed tips of her hair. She coughed and pressed her letter jacket to her mouth. She felt like she was being slowly roasted.

Still, when she reached the collapsed wall, she climbed to her feet, jammed the tire iron into the broken panel and pulled with all her might. As the wall panel inched back the door opened a little but not enough to free Sula. She needed Sula to push from her side.

"Push the door!" Aimee called out.

There was a moment's hesitation then, "I can't. It's too hot."

Aimee had an idea. "When the door opens a bit, stick your hand out, okay?"

"Okay,"

Sweating profusely, Aimee shrugged off her letter jacket, reinserted the tire iron, pulled, and as the wall panel drew back and the door opened a few inches, she pressed the jacket into Sula hand. It quickly disappeared.

A moment later Sula called out. "I got the jacket on!"

"Okay, put your shoulder to the door and push on three. Ready? One, two, THREE!!"

Aimee pulled the tire iron and Sula shouldered the door. It wasn't enough. That's when Aimee jumped up, placed her feet on the other wall and pulled with all her might.

There came a snap, Aimee fell as the wall panel split in half and dropped to the floor only inches from where she lay. Sula, with a face as red a stop light, muscled the door open just enough to squeeze out and after pulling Aimee to her to her feet, they ran down the stairs.

"My name is Sula by the way," she said. "And thank you so much. You saved my life."

As Aimee was about to reply, a billow of smoke partially blinded them which caused Sula to miss the last step, stumble and ricochet off the boarded window at the landing between the second and third floors. Unharmed, she and Aimee turned toward the next set of stairs...

And saw the floor below was completely aflame.

Chapter Twenty Two

As Dora's pink Miata turned at the fork that led to Lavender Hill, she looked into her rearview mirror and noticed that the girl with the black hair in the Mustang had chosen to go the other way. She sighed with relief. When she saw the girl follow her onto the dirt road, Dora worried the girl might be tailing her and reporting back to Virgil. But now it seemed more likely the girl was, like her, only looking to avoid a police checkpoint.

It was rapidly getting dark. She switched on her yellow fog lights so as not to drawn attention from the cars on 727. She also slowed to a crawl because the road had numerous potholes and ruts and she was not going to ruin her beautiful pink sports car just so she could confront her idiot husband.

It took nearly fifteen minutes for her to arrive at the back of the barn. She cautiously rolled down the window and looked around. Surprisingly, although the inside of the structure was lit as if a party were going on, she didn't see anyone nearby. She turned off the engine and snapped off the inside dome light. As she opened the car door and stepped outside…

There was a gunshot, and then another.

Chapter Twenty Three

Seeing the second floor on fire, Sula turned, looked up the stairs and saw the fire had now completely engulfed the third floor.

"What do we do?" Aimee asked, her eyes darting feverishly.

"I'm gonna bust this damn board from the window. Just give me room."

"Let me help. That board looks pretty thick."

Sula shook her head, then charged and rammed her shoulder against it. There came a noticeable cracking sound, but when it didn't give, she stepped back and kicked, then kicked again. The third time it flew from the building.

Sula leapt onto the window frame, turned and extended her hand to Aimee. "C'mon! The porch roof is just below! We can jump to it!"

There was a second explosion.

Sula was blown out the window.

Just before she slammed onto the porch roof, she saw Aimee drop from behind the window frame as if through a trap door.

Sula tumbled down the slanted porch roof to the garage roof, pelted by flaming and falling debris. A brick struck her in the chest just as she fell from the garage and slammed into the muddy ground. Gasping and out of breath, she raised her head

Save the girl! Save the girl! If'n God takes her to punish me for trying to cut my wrists…!!

Everything hurt. She was bleeding, coughing. There was so much smoke. She climbed to her feet and wobbled toward the house, then forced herself to run.

Save the girl! Save the girl! Oh Lord, please don't take that girl because of me!

Suddenly, a gust of wind cleared the smoke and she saw it.

The large three story house was now a pile of flaming rubble.

The wind gusted again, the heat increased and the flames grew. With a roar it shoved her off her feet to the ground.

She stared at the inferno, felt the heat though the soles of her shoes, saw the surrounding trees reflect its pale orange light, listened to the crackling, snapping and spitting of the burning wood.

What she didn't hear were cries for help.

Absolutely convinced her actions had brought about her rescuer's death, Sula curled into a ball and became hysterical. She pulled at her hair and screamed at the burning structure. "Noooooooooo! She can't die! It was supposed to be me! It was supposed to be me!" Sula slowly climbed to her knees. "I'm sorry! I'm so sorry," she wailed to the sky above. "Please don't kill her to punish me!"

With her grief overwhelming her, and with the firm belief that God had killed Aimee as punishment for her suicide attempt, Sula's sanity began to unhinge. She staggered to her feet and with her hands pressed against her head, began to run, screaming and screaming…"

The last thing Aimee remembered was seeing Sula falling toward the porch roof and the floor giving way under her feet.

She looked around.

Where am I? Why is it so hard to see?

She surveyed the area. Her surroundings were grey, dull and indescript with only a pale flicker illuminating her way.

Am I in the basement?

To her right was a hole, but with the poor light she wasn't sure if it was the entrance to a cave or a tunnel or what.

"Why are you still here?" she heard someone call out angrily.

When Aimee spun around, she saw the silhouette of a woman pointing at her. "C'mon!" she shouted. "We're the last ones. Everyone else is gone. Let's go! Let's go! Let's go!" She gave Aimee a shove, and the teen fell through the hole. She felt herself tumbling, as if down a hill.

In the distance she heard a woman screaming and the screams were getting louder.

Chapter Twenty Four

Lillian Vanderhill, having taken the body of a young and athletic female, peeked out from behind the white door of the barn and saw Bert/Alvin amid the flashing and swirling lights of the patrol cars and EMS vehicles parked on the road. Most of the crowd, she noted, had gathered there. She assumed it was due to concerns about the toxicity of the area.

She quickly slipped back behind the door.

Having successfully transferred all five-hundred or so of what she called 'purgatory's prisoners' into living bodies, she had powered down the machine and was anxious to destroy it. Although relatively confident the daemons were not aware of what happened, Lillian Vanderhill did not like loose ends.

When she looked again, she saw Bert/Alvin walking toward a tree stump.

While his back was to her, she raced from the barn, across the field and sidled up behind a malformed tree that had a wide base and gnarled veiny branches.

She didn't want him to spot her. She didn't like him when he was alive and came to hate him during the years they spent trapped in that shadowy void. And now that they had strong, healthy bodies and had worked so closely over the last few weeks, she was sure he was going to make a play for her. If she refused his advances, he might decide to kill her. She wouldn't put it past him.

With her back against the tree, she glanced at the open door of the barn. All the lights were on and with the transfers complete and crowds rapidly thinning, she knew time was running out.

She pressed her lips together. Although she still felt she should destroy the machine, she was afraid Bert might catch her in the act and put two and two together.

While Bert was momentarily distracted by someone offering him a celebratory drink, she made her decision. She was going to slip away, drive to Virgil's, tell him what happened and let him handle it.

She stealthily made her way to 727 avoiding all contact until she reached the vehicle of the woman whose body she had taken and drove away.

*

Dora clumsily dove back into the Miata, her heart pounding, praying that she hadn't been shot. Laying flat on the front seats, she noticed an odd reflection in the window. She eased her head up but dove down again when she heard more gun fire.

Then she saw it. Fireworks!

She shook her head and chastised herself for being so easily frightened. She sat up, stepped out of the car and stared into the sky.

What's this all about?

Now more determined than ever to confront Virgil, she cautiously edged her way along the left side of the barn, which was dark and on the far side of 727. After crunching through the tall weeds to the front, she waited until another round of fireworks were shot into the air and when the light and sound filled the air, she slipped around to the white door, peeked in between it and the frame, and seeing no one, slid inside.

The barn appeared empty. No voices, or the sound of people walking, just the steady buzz of the Tesla coil.

As she made her way down the aisles of machinery, she noted that everything appeared to be off line. The computers monitors were dark.

She made a right turn and saw a wooden staircase leading to a second level, probably constructed as a hay loft.

Maybe Virgil's up there?

She walked over and quickly, but quietly, vaulted the stairs, two at a time.

When she reached the top she saw only cables, gasoline generators and crates. As she turned to head back down, she spotted a vent at the front overlooking 727.

With all the lights and commotion out front it shouldn't be too hard to find Virgil's car.

She went over to it, looked out over the great expanse and saw that Virgil's car wasn't there. But Donnie Pascal's was. Then she saw him standing against the wooden fence talking to a police officer.

Pretty good, Virgil, you even got to my P.I.

I'd better get out of here.

She quietly padding down the stairs, then down the aisle leading toward the entrance, she turned and ran right into...

Alvin Trolley.

"Dora? Is that you?"

Alvin Trolley stood inside the ectoplasmic chamber; and although his body was not completely formed, Dora recognized him immediately. It was the man she had been sleeping with for the last few months and who, for reasons unknown, had suddenly cut off all contact.

She ran over, placed her hand on the glass and stared at the rows of machinery in disbelief. "Alvin, what in heaven's name is going on? What are you doing in that thing and... and what's that at the bottom?" she asked pointing to the colored smoke on floor of the ectoplasmic chamber.

He explained.

She stepped back. "Are you serious? Virgil created a machine that can communicate with the dead?"

Alvin nodded.

"And this machine makes it possible for the dead to take over the bodies of the living?

"Yes."

"So what happens to the people whose bodies are taken over?"

"They're sent to the Void. It's a kind of Limbo. There's no passage of time, or aging or needing to eat. It's hard to explain."

"But if Lillian and the others escaped, why haven't you?"

"I thought about it, but I just couldn't take the body of some poor unsuspecting soul. It's just not right and besides, I want my own body back."

She studied the dirt floor shaking her head, trying to grasp the ramifications. "Un-freaking-believable! So that's what he's been working on all this time. Some damn machine so he could talk to his mommy? That sonavabitch! He could have sold the design and made millions but no, it's… it's… I can't even begin to describe how pissed off I am." She growled and snapped her fists to her side. "He told me it was some government project." She turned back to Alvin. "Well, you know what? The hell with him. So, how do we get you out of there?"

Alvin told her how Bert had tricked him and how the former science teacher was working alongside Virgil's mother. "He's outside waiting for Lillian, but she doesn't want any part of him, so I'm betting she's going to try to slip away."

"Which means he'll come looking for her, right?" she asked, putting her finger to her lips.

"Yeah!" he said, surprised he had missed something so obvious. "If we can get him close enough for me to make physical contact, I can get my body back."

"Why don't you just take over his body, you know, like the others did?" she asked, hooking her thumb toward those milling outside the Route 727 entrance.

"That only works if you catch the victim by surprise. If Bert feels my approach, he'll fight me until he can get out of range. No, I have to touch him."

Dora looked around, then walked around to the back and crouched under the ectoplasmic chamber's platform. "Listen, Alvin," she whispered, "I got an idea."

As the crowds continued to thin out, Bert/Alvin stood on a tree stump searching the grounds for Lillian. He hoped she would see him and come over to show him the new body she had taken. She assured him they'd leave together once the process was complete.

But as more cars and official vehicles left the area, he became concerned and wondered if something had gone wrong.

He jumped down and strode to the barn to see what the holdup was.

He pulled open the white door and stepped inside.

"Lillian! Lillian!" he called out amid the blaring lights, "Are you in here?"

"Oh, Bert," Lillian cried out. "Thank God you've come! That lunatic Jolene tried to kill me by opening the chamber."

Bert rushed to the ectoplasmic chamber and saw it was partially open. There was only a small pool of gasses on its floor.

"Don't worry," Bert said, climbing upon the platform. "I'll fix it!"

He stuck his fingers inside the metal couplings, leaned up against it and gave the glass tube a quick jerk. As it slid into place he asked, "Did it work, Lillian?"

With the speed of an attacking cobra, two whip lengths of gas rose from the floor, sliced through the glass and wrapped themselves around Bert's hands.

Bert was pulled down into the dark Void as Alvin Trolley re-took possession of his body.

Wasting no time Alvin rushed over and yanked out the cables from the gasoline generators and turned off the Tesla coil.

"There, you sonavabitch," Alvin shouted as he threw the cables to the dirt floor and raised his fist at the empty glass chamber. "Now you're back where you belong!"

"Alvin?" Dora whispered, peeking out from behind the platform.

He turned toward her and grinned enthusiastically. "Sweetheart, it worked great!" He extended his arms toward her. "You sounded exactly like Lillian. He didn't suspect a thing. Look at me! I got my body back!"

She jumped out from behind the platform, ran into his arms and kissed him passionately.

"Oh, Alvin," she said, pressing her head against his chest. "I've missed you so much. I thought you didn't love me anymore. I..."

He kissed the top of her head. "It's over, sweetheart. Let's get out of here and find a place where we can be together."

The two then slipped out, made their way to Dora's car and drove away.

*

Aimee McFarland awoke on top of a hill, unsure and confused. The sun had gone down and clouds hid the moon making it hard to see. As she raised her body from the ground and staggered to her feet, she looked into the distance and saw in the shadows, what remained of the house. It had burned quickly and was mostly smoldering ashes, with glowing red embers occasionally hissing and popping. She rubbed her nose as the smell of burnt word permeated the air. A sudden breeze blew smoke from the ruins into her eyes. She turned away and in the distance recognized the dark silhouette of the blue barn she'd seen earlier from 727. There were still some police cars and utility trucks there but most appeared to have left.

"Ow," she said placing her hand to her head and saw she was wearing her ex-boyfriend's letter jacket again. She barely recognized it as it was covered in soot and dirt.

Sula must have put it back on me to keep me warm. How did I get out here? Where's Sula? And where is that woman from the basement?

Still unsteady, Aimee put her hand on the tree then leaned back against it. "Sula!" she called out. "Sula, where are you?"

Receiving no reply, Aimee, still dazed, started walking in the dark through the brush and smoke toward the fire ravaged building.

Maybe Sula's went back to my car.

She pressed her hand to her head. *Why am I so out of it? And who in blazes is Tee and Coffee?*

Minutes later she saw her car. "Finally!" she said and carefully made her way toward it. She gave the blue Mustang a quick inspection and other than a few pieces of rotted wood, a dusting of soot on the upholstery and an open trunk, it had escaped the fire and subsequent explosion unscathed.

She pulled an old tattered beach towel from the trunk, laid it on the driver's seat, tossed the wood and climbed in behind the wheel. She surveyed the area.

Where is Sula?

She scanned the area again and felt herself becoming annoyed.

You know, if someone rescued me from a burning building, I'd stick around to say thanks. I don't get it. Why would she take off and leave me on the ground, especially in Dohesley, for heaven's sake?

Aimee blew the horn several times. "Sula!" she called out. "Sula!"

No answer.

"Well, I just can't wait around," she said, taking the keys from her jacket and starting the engine. "I have to get home, have mom call Dr. Ackerson. My head feels so weird, I think I might have a concussion."

As she was about to drive away, she checked the rearview mirror and saw it wasn't set correctly. She reached up, adjusted it and jerked backward in shock when she suddenly saw Sula!

She was in the mirror looking directly at her.

Chapter Twenty Five

Jimmy McCracken opened the front door to his apartment, carefully checked the space between the door and the frame before entering and seeing no one, stepped inside.

But there *was* someone there.

It was Ike Seaward, the old Bible thumping former prospector who had, until recently, considered Jimmy the embodiment of evil. He was wearing his usual baggy jeans, red shirt and grey floppy hat.

"Hey there, old timer," Jimmy said, tossing his keys on the counter. "Thought you were heading into the light to meet the Big Boss?"

"Was gonna," the old man said as he walked the room with his hands in his pockets, "but somethin' bad's happened and I came back to warn ya."

Concern crossed Jimmy's face. "About what?"

Ike bowed his head and said, "Appears every one of them evil bastards the good Lord stuck in Dohesley and Wheatfield got out. Escaped, I'd guess you'd call it, and they's been replaced by a whole group of people that don't belong there, people whose time ain't up yet. I couldn't see how it coulda happened, but then I recollected that abomination that attacked you..."

"Holy shit!" Jimmy shouted, his hands wrapping around the top of his head. "How many escaped?"

Ike's face twisted as he continued pacing. "All of 'em! As best I can figure, about 500, give or take a few. And Jimmy, these folks is hard-core sinners. Not one decent soul among 'em. If'n your buddy got them back to the world of the livin'...Well, all I kin say is you folks is in real trouble."

*

"Well, I'm gonna head up to my room," Jess told Mary as she picked up the remote from the doily covered end table and shut off the television. She was quite comfortable sitting in the puffy, dark

111

blue recliner in Mary's living room but didn't want to fall asleep there.

Jessica often stayed the night if her visit lasted past sundown. At 65 she didn't like driving the twisting, country roads after dark.

She slid her feet into her slippers, stood up and shuffled toward the stairs holding the small of her back. "Following that little adventure with the evil dead yesterday," she said to Mary as she walked past the kitchen. "I would really appreciate it if we didn't go traipsing around that Blue Barn anytime soon."

"It's a deal." Mary replied as Jess climbed the stairs. "I'm just going to put these dishes in the dishwasher and head up myself. Sleep well; see you in the morning."

"Yep, see you in the morn..." Jess started to say when Mary dropped the dishes. As they clattered, Jess bent down and saw her friend staring gap-jawed at the kitchen window and backing away in terror. Mary had her hands raised in a defensive posture. "No! No!" she moaned in a trembling voice, "keep away!" Suddenly, she began to shake, her eyes rolled back and her teeth snapped together. She collapsed to the floor in front of the dishwasher and flailed as if having a seizure.

Jess ran down the stairs and pulled Mary into her arms. "Easy, hon, easy," she said softly. "I gotcha. You're gonna be okay." She looked at the window. "What did you see out there? What scared you so?"

Jess had no more gotten the words out when Mary started shrieking.

Jess gently lowered Mary to the floor, ran to the phone, picked up the receiver to dial 911, but it was dead. She pulled out her cell but it never worked inside the kitchen, never any bars, always searching for a signal.

Without thinking, she bolted to the door, shoved it open, rushed out and punched 911 on her cell. As she headed toward the porch stairs, she ran into a tall figure in black. It loomed over her

She screamed.

*

As Lillian Vanderhill settled into her new body, she drove by the several banks on the main drag and saw scores of people she recognized from the barn with ATM cards in hand. She couldn't fault them; she was planning to do the same thing. Empty the bank accounts, max out the credit cards and party till the money was gone.

But now she was having second thoughts. This new body was in top physical condition. The woman couldn't be more than 30 and was drop-dead gorgeous. Lillian believed if she could just avoid all the screw ups that landed her in so much trouble the first time, she could have a second shot at happiness. Besides, it wasn't like money was an issue. She had the ten one pound gold ingots, the ones she had hidden in her figurines, safely stashed in her purse.

She smiled as she drove away. She had buried those ingots eleven years ago just in case she needed to make a quick getaway, but suffered a stroke and died before telling anyone their location.

Yep! This new life is gonna work out just fine! I got all the money I need and can do whatever I damn well please and go wherever I damn well please.

She saw the lit Kirshman's Deli sign and pulled over to buy cigarettes. While at the register an idea struck, so she borrowed the counterman's cell phone and quickly made a call.

*

"Easy, easy," the tall man in the black coat said as he gently placed his hands on Jess' shoulders. "I will not harm you." He gestured to Martaine. "My friend and I have come to see Mary McGuernsey. Are you her?"

She looked into the man's warm brown eyes and after hearing his comforting tone, brought herself under control. "No," she said. "I'm…"

As he lowered his hands, Jess was interrupted by a voice on the cell phone. "911. What is the emergency?"

Jess steadied herself, leaned against the porch banister and said, "My friend is seriously ill, I need…"

As Jess explained Mary's condition, Santiago and Martaine heard screams coming from inside and raced in.

Mary was still flailing on the floor; only the whites of her eyes were visible and lathery foam covered her mouth.

Santiago dropped to the floor and cradled Mary in his arms.

A few moments later Jess reentered the house. "That don't work," she said. "I tried it. Just leave her be, an ambulance is on its way."

Santiago ignored her and continued reciting phrases in Latin.

"I said it won't work," Jessica repeated, "so leave her…"

Suddenly, Mary stopped flailing and her eyes returned to their normal position.

Santiago looked to Jess. "A wet paper towel, if you please, and some water."

"Praise Jesus!" Jess said placing her hand to her chest. She sprinted to the sink and quickly returned with the requested items.

After he wiped away the foam and had her take a few sips of water, the clergyman helped her to her feet and guided Mary to the living room.

As she cautiously lowered herself upon the floral-patterned couch, she said. "Thank you, mister. I…" Mary stopped. "Oh, are you a priest? I didn't see the collar. Hold it," she said, her eyes suddenly widening. "I'm not dying, am I?!"

The clergyman smiled. "No, you are not dying. My name is Father Hector Santiago." He gestured to his companion. "And this large fellow is my friend and fellow clergyman, Brother Silvio Martaine. How are you feeling?" he asked as he sat on his heels and gently held her hand. "Do you remember what happened?"

Before she could respond, they heard a metallic squeal from the kitchen followed by the screen door slamming.

Santiago stood and turned toward it.

"Mary," a voice called out. "Mary, Jess, are you in here?"

Jimmy McCracken burst into the room, but stopped short when he saw Mary laying on the couch looking ashen and frail.

He came over and crouched alongside her. "Mary," he said taking her hand, "Are you okay?"

Mary's eyes widened, "Jimmy," she said, reaching over and placing her other hand on his, "the worst possible thing has happened."

Jimmy nodded solemnly. "Yeah, I know, Lillian and her scumbag friends escaped into our world."

Still wide-eyed, Mary slowly shook her head and pulled herself up. "I think the daemons are aware of what happened! I saw them in my window. Horrible creatures, just horrible! So hateful and twisted. Their vibrations completely overwhelmed me."

Chapter Twenty Six

The cab had to stop twice on the way to Virgil's house so he could fling open the door, jump out and vomit on the road's shoulder. The first time he staggered from the vehicle and into the night air, he was met by the strong smell of charred wood and the acrid odor made him spew like a sewer pipe. The second time he held onto a wooden fence to keep his knees from buckling, and as he finished and shakily wiped his mouth with his handkerchief, he recalled Jimmy's comment about him not being a regular drinker.

He was right. I should know better.

He flung his handkerchief to the ground and got back into the cab, now sober enough to recall what Jimmy said was happening at the Blue Barn.

No, all my research clearly disproves....

He paused.

But why would he make up such a thing? Besides, even if it was possible, the personality change would be obviou...

Virgil recalled his run in with Alvin Trolley.

When Trolley opened the door, the guy acted like he recognized me, as if he were an old buddy. Yeah, and when I asked if we knew each other... And he had this odd look... Virgil stared off for a moment, trying to recall. *And then when we spoke at the barn. I know I've seen that look before...*

His face went blank and his eyes widened. *Bert Langley!?? That creepy old bastard from down the block? Wait. That was him in the background when I contacted Mom the first time.*

As the cab pulled into his driveway Virgil winced. It felt like there was something in his stomach trying to rip its way out.

He paid the driver and with his hand on his gut, slowly made his way up the walkway to his front door.

He glanced at the driveway as the cab sped off.

Where's Dora's car?

He checked his watch. 1:45 a.m.

Where would she be at this hour?

His stomach hitched and he quickened his pace, not wanting to vomit on his walkway.

116

He climbed the porch stairs, unlocked and opened the big mahogany door, then called out, "Dora?" He waited, but received no response. He pushed back his stringy black hair, stepped inside and closed the door behind him.

"Damn it!" he blurted in frustration as he walked into the living room. "Why can't anything ever be normal around here? Why can't she be home like a normal wife? It's 1:30 in the freakin' morning. Where the hell is she?"

He searched the house, going from room to room calling her name. Receiving no reply, he grew even more annoyed. As he returned to the living room, he saw the phone answering machine light blinking.

"Ah, there she is." he said pointing, then smiled at what he thought was a very clever remark.

Virgil pressed the button, expecting the hear Dora's voice.

It wasn't. But what the voice said triggered a full-blown panic attack.

Virgie, listen up, because I'm only going to say this once. This is your mother speaking. Because of your wonderful invention, I was able to find an inhabitable body and am now back among the living. That right, because of you I am alive again! This woman's body is everything I ever wanted. And so what I am about to say will surely hurt you but it needs to be said. Virgie, I appreciate everything you've done but I need to start a new life. One without any ties to the past. I made a lot of enemies over the years, and I don't want them to know I've returned. This is my chance for a fresh start and I'm sorry, but that means I have to cut all ties.

Also your machine made it possible for a number of others to get new bodies. So, to keep it from getting out of hand you better destroy it. Seriously honey, there are some incredibly dangerous beings from where I came from and if they make it over to this side, well, we're all as good as dead.

Have a good life, sweetie, good-bye.

When he heard the click, Virgil's heart almost stopped. His face was pale, his eyes glassy and his hands shook as he placed them on his knees. He had the look of a man who was just told he had inoperable cancer or that a loved one had died.

117

Over the next half hour he repeatedly played the message, thinking perhaps he missed something. Surely she wasn't abandoning him? She was his mother! And he had spent eleven years of his life, ruined his marriage and was facing bankruptcy just so he could talk with her again.

I stole $9,000!

Have a good life, sweetie, good-bye. That's it? I've sacrificed everything for her only to be blown off? Have a good life? That's how she repays me?

Suddenly, overwhelmed with rage, he grabbed the answering machine and smashed it against the table until it shattered into pieces, then sprinted to the bathroom in the master bedroom, kicked open the toilet lid and vomited again and again, and when there was nothing left, he dry heaved until the pain forced him into a ball under the sink. The phone rang and rang and rang.

*

By 1:30 pm. the Blue Moon Lounge, just off route 727 in Wheatfield was filled to capacity and not with their regular crowd. Both bartenders remarked that tonight was shaping up to be something very different.

And not in a good way.

Most of the clientele were carrying pistols. Many were police, still in uniform. Others appeared to be feds, with that button-down, dead-serious look and all of them were drinking heavily. They huddled in clandestine groups, eyeing each other.

Then there were the Adirondack P & L guys and the telephone workers, all of whom had buddied up.

Or so it appeared at first.

"Say that again and I will blow your fucking head off," one policeman shouted as he jumped to his feet and pulled his pistol on one of the men at his table.

Then everyone who had a gun pulled it and scanned the room. The bartenders dove to the floor behind the bar, while the wait staff charged out of the dining area and nervously waited for the

118

place to explode. Fortunately, a moment or so later, somebody called out, "Hey, guys, I don't want to go back. Do any of you?"

That seemed to work because shortly afterward, one by one, the guns were holstered and the tense, but cordial atmosphere resumed.

Later that evening, the police officers and several FBI agents gathered at a large table at the back of the restaurant. It was cluttered with booze-filled glasses and plates of half-eaten fried foods. The men were discussing plans for the future.

"In order for this to work, two things got to be dealt with right away," a large, square-jawed police officer by the name of Bertram Van Pelt said. "And those two things are Virgil Vanderhill and Mary McGuernsey, Vanderhill because he built the machine that brought us here and probably knows how to send us back and McGuernsey because she can point us out. The question is, how can this be done on the down-low?"

One of the police officers said, "We go on the offensive. We frame the broad for murder and she gets killed resisting arrest. Simple, clean and effective."

Van Pelt nodded. "I like that, but how's the frame going to work?"

The officer dug into his pocket, pulled out an ATM receipt and a business card. "With this," he said holding them up for the others to see. "Found them in the bushes on the side of the barn while I was taking a leak. We just make sure they're found near the body,"

"All right, let's make that happen. Now what about Vanderhill?"

An officer whose name tag read Pastore said, "I'll drive by his house. Maybe he's clumsy and fell in his bathtub."

The group laughed and continued drinking.

*

Mary pulled herself from the couch. "We have to go to the Blue Barn."

119

"Girl, you need to go to the hospital," Jess said sternly. "We got an ambulance on the way."

Jimmy looked at his watch. "Do we?"

Jess turned, "What do you mean?"

"You made that call 35 minutes ago. I know from experience that if an ambulance isn't immediately available, a patrol car is sent to assess the situation. The St. Lawrenceville Police station is 5 minutes away, the hospital even less. I don't believe anyone's coming."

Jimmy looked at Santiago, then at Mary. "Ike Seaward said over 500 have been taken over, and since first responders are just that, we probably lost a lot of police, fireman and EMS personnel and since the electric, phone and microwave tower technicians often work together, a lot of them are probably gone too."

Jess turned and eyed the phone. "Hmmm," she said. "That might explain why the landline isn't working. Let me try 911 again."

With Martaine accompanying her, she stepped onto the porch with her cell and dialed. This time she received a high pitched beeping sound. Just a she was about to end the call, she heard a siren in the distance.

Jimmy, Mary and Santiago joined her on the porch.

"We should get Mary ready," Jess said as a parade of flashing lights appeared atop the nearby hillside. When she noticed the number of vehicles, Jess added, "Looks like they're sending the entire hospital staff and the National Guard."

Jimmy stepped forward, placed his hands on the porch post, eyed the approaching vehicles and noted a faint whooping and caterwauling echo in the distance. "I got a weird feeling about this, guys. Let's step back inside until we know what we're dealing with."

The others gave the approaching vehicles a second look.

"I agree with Jimmy," Santiago said. "Caution is in order."

Once inside with the door closed and only the porch light lit, Jimmy, Mary and the others crouched behind the front windows and watched as the flashing lights drew near.

As the whooping and caterwauling grew louder, there was no longer any mistake that the people manning those vehicles were either shit-faced drunk or well on their way.

Jimmy instinctively jerked back when, as a fire truck raced by, an empty bottle of Jim Beam flew from the back and shattered against the porch post just below its single bulb.

A rousing cheer followed, and a barrage of empty beer bottles flew from the subsequent ambulances, police cars and utility trucks, all aimed at the same target but with much less accuracy.

Moments later the parade of vehicles passed and their blaring sirens and flashing lights faded.

"I don't know what that was," Mary said stepping away from the blinds, "but I think we better get a hold of Virgil right now!"

"But how?" Jess asked as she plopped down in the blue recliner. "The phones aren't working."

"Maybe just 911 is out. I'll try his home phone." Jimmy said as he turned on his cell and stepped outside. It was littered with beer cans and empty bottles. He shook his head and speed-dialed Virgil. "It's ringing!"

After ten rings with no answer, Jimmy gave up and walked back into the house. "There's no telling if the call went through. Probably not because the answering machine didn't pick up. We're going to have to go over there."

They climbed inside the clergymen's Impala.

*

As Virgil lay shaking under the bathroom sink, he heard the front door unlock, open and close, then footsteps across the living room floor. He quietly closed the bathroom door. A moment later that someone entered the master bedroom.

Dora.

"What am I going to say to her? I've lost everything, everything!" Virgil whispered with his face pressed against the cold tile, "just because I wanted to spend some time with my mother. All those years. All that hard work and sacrifice, for what?"

121

He rolled on his back and pressed his fists against his chest. "How am I going to tell Dora there was no government job, there's no money coming and that she'd been right about my mother all along? Oh, and $9,000!" He shuddered and wept even harder. "My own mother turned me into a thief!"

There came a sharp wrapping on the bathroom door. "Hello? Virgil?" Dora asked. "Are you in there? C'mon out, we need to talk."

Virgil cleared his throat. "Maybe later, I'm not feeling well."

"Suit yourself," she replied, "but I just stopped by to tell you that I'm leaving you. I don't love you anymore, I'm moving out and I'm only here to pick up some of my things."

She waited, fully expecting him to come charging out, demanding an explanation but all she heard was him panting. She waited a little longer, still nothing.

"So that's it?" she spat. "No so longs? No bye-byes, no live long and prospers? You know, you are such a gutless prick. Oh, and I found out about your little machine to bring mommy back from the great beyond." She took a moment, then began imitating Lillian's voice. "You're such a good boy, Virgie, momma's best little boy, and thanks to you, dearie, the living dead are parading up and down Main Street… great job, asshole!"

The door flung open and he met Dora with a crazed expression. "Stop it! Stop it!" he blubbered, his eyes red, his face wet with tears. "You've won, okay? You were right! She is a monster!" He wiped his eyes with the heels of his hands as he paced crazily before her. "She's everything you said she was, only worse. She never loved me. She never cared about me. She never cared for anyone but herself." He looked down, saw the suitcase in Dora's hand and sobbed. "And if you're going to leave, then, go!" he shouted, pointing to the door." Take everything, I don't care. In fact," he blubbered, rushing past her, "you stay and I'll leave!"

She turned and watched in stunned silence as he ran out of the bedroom, grabbed his coat and bolted out of the house.

"Virg, I…" she began. But the door slammed and he was gone.

Chapter Twenty Seven

After Jimmy, Mary, Jess and the clergymen stopped by Virgil's house and found both cars gone, no lights in the windows and no response after they vigorously knocked on the door, they decided to try the barn.

A half hour later, while on route 727, they saw the blue/gray structure in the distance standing eerily against the pale moon like an ancient mausoleum built by a long-dead civilization. There were no cars or trucks parked on the shoulder.

After pulling over, climbing out and walking across the field, they saw the white door partially open and bright lights beaming from inside.

"Think he's in there?" Mary asked.

"There is only one way to find out," Jess replied.

As Jimmy pulled open the door and they cautiously entered, Mary moved ahead, walking to the center with her arms extended and looking around. "There's nothing here. It's empty," she said, dropping her hands. "No vibes at all, and it's no longer cold. Whatever was here is gone."

"Let's look anyway," Jimmy said, touching each machine to see if it was warm. "In the meantime, maybe Virgil will show up."

"Or maybe we'll find his crazy ass hanging from one of the rafters," Jess commented with a tip of her head to the above beams.

When the others eyed her, she shrugged. "Well, I'm just saying!"

Jimmy heard something crunch under his boot. "What this?" he asked as he bent down and picked up a piece of broken porcelain.

"Looks like a figurine," Jessica said, lifting her glasses from her chest for a closer look.

Mary pointed to several others nearby. "Looks like they were all shattered."

Not knowing what to make of their discovery, Jimmy tossed the piece of plaster and they pressed on.

After they finished searching the barn from top to bottom, the group decided that leaving a machine this powerful unattended was too dangerous. To prevent the arrival of any future 'push-ins' they went from machine to machine disconnecting cables, unplugging outlets and draining gasoline from the generators.

During the several hours they spent breaking down the equipment, Virgil never showed; nor did they find him at the end of any rope. The Blue Barn was, as Mary said, "empty."

"What's our next move?" Mary asked, as she removed the last set of connector cables.

"I don't know," Jimmy replied, "but I'm starving. How about we grab something to eat and make that decision on a full stomach?"

That suggestion was quickly agreed upon and within minutes they left, locked the white door and set out on their way.

"Do you need some more time or are you ready to order?" asked the smiling middle-aged woman with a name tag that read Cheryl.

"Grand Slams all around, just like it's shown in this picture with coffee," Jimmy said handing the menus to the waitress. "There are five of us, total, with one in the ladies room."

"Got it," the waitress said as she tucked the menus under her arm and headed to the kitchen.

Jimmy yawned, then said, "Okay, I admit it. I'm beat, I'm hungry and I'm scared. Frankly, I'd like nothing more than to flop down on my bed, open a bottle of rum, fire up a bone and chill until the daemon's break down the door."

He smiled as Mary pulled up a chair and joined them at the table.

Santiago leaned in. "Can any of you describe these daemons? What do they look like? How does one recognize them?"

"I've been possessed by one, but I've never actually seen one," Jimmy replied, unrolling the silverware from his napkin. "Wound up having to stab myself to break its hold."

A look like she had just tasted something extremely sour washed over Mary's face. "They're monstrous!" she said with a shake of her head, "just monstrous! Such rage, such hatred!"

Santiago eyed Martaine who was also following the conversation very carefully, then returned his attentions to Mary. "How close are they?"

"Very close, although they are not yet in this..." she paused with a puzzled look. "I don't know what to call it. This dimension? This realm of existence? This is no..." she took a moment to think of an analogy. "...gang of outlaws riding into town, or pirates coming ashore to plunder and pillage. Judging from their vibes, I believe these creatures literally feed on human suffering. And come from a world where torture and evisceration are entertainment, where rape, mutilation and dismemberment are common. It's unsettling to even imagine such a place.

"And as for their auras, which, I got to tell you are so black, so indescribably dark, that any attempt to reason with them would be viewed as weakness."

The waitress approached with a tray filled with cups, saucers and a small pitcher of milk. "And here's your coffees," the waitress said placing each cup in front of them. When finished she put her hands behind her back and smiled. "Your breakfasts should be ready in a few minutes. Is there anything else I can get for you?"

She was standing behind Mary, and as Jimmy and the others looked at each other, Father Santiago smiled and said, "Apparently there is nothing more. Thank you."

As the waitress walked away, Mary raised her finger to indicate they should keep silent. When the waitress was out of earshot, she glanced around, leaned in and said in a low voice, "She's one of them."

Jess' face dropped. "One of the five hundred?"

Mary nodded.

For nearly a full minute, they started at each other, but no one spoke. Finally Jimmy grabbed his coffee and took a sip. "Nuts to this," he said, looking at his watch. "I've been up for thirty straight hours and I'm too tired and too hungry to care."

Jess blinked her eyes several times. "I was afraid I was gonna fall asleep before the coffee got here," she said pushing it away. "Doubt that's going to be a problem now."

Ten minutes later the food arrived and their waitress, affable as ever, said, "Bon appetite," as she finished placing their orders on the table.

After she left, Jimmy grabbed his fork and was preparing to dig in when Brother Martaine placed his hand on Jimmy's arm and said, "Wait, how can we be sure the food is safe? Especially knowing what she is?"

Jimmy shrugged, stabbed a piece of bacon and said, "Just because the devil brought the water doesn't mean you can't drink." When he realized he was quoting Ol' Ike, he dropped the fork and fell back in his chair laughing. "Sonavagun! I finally get it!"

Jimmy finished his meal before everyone else. He patted his stomach and exclaimed, "Well, apparently the food's not poisoned."

"Let's hope the same can be said for the coffee," Brother Martaine added, "As I sorely need another cup."

As the others cleaned their plates and Santiago handed the waitress payment for the check, Jimmy noticed a bedraggled man enter the restaurant and look the place over. A moment later he walked determinedly toward the cash register just as Cheryl was opening the drawer. Without warning, he shoved her aside and began pulling out cash.

Regaining her balance, she reached over to the busboy's bin, grabbed a steak knife and rammed it through the thief's hand, and when he yanked it back in pain, she stabbed him in his forearm.

"The next one goes in your throat," she growled and shoved him toward the door.

The man, grimacing in pain, jammed the bleeding hand under his armpit and bolted out the door to the parking lot.

It happened so fast that no one other than Jimmy and Mary saw it.

Instinctively Jimmy ran over to Cheryl and blurted, "Are you okay?"

Her face brightened. "How thoughtful of you to ask," she said, wiping the blade and tossing it back into the dirty dish bin as if stabbing a would-be robber was as common as serving pie. "It's nice to meet someone who cares about people."

"Did he hurt you? Do you want me to call the police?' Jimmy asked.

She looked at him as if he were kidding. "Nah, I'm fine," she said with a dismissive wave of her hand. "Besides, I'm not going to risk losing my morning tips yakking with the cops. No honey, but thanks for your concern. Now let me get your change." She rung up the bill, removed the money and handed it to Jimmy. "You folks have a nice day."

Stunned, Jimmy nodded blankly and with money in hand, returned to the others.

Once back in his seat, he handed Santiago the change which the clergyman placed on the table for a tip. Meanwhile, Mary stared at him with eyes as big as their coffee mugs. "What is with you?" she hissed. "I told you she's one of them!"

"It was just instinct, I guess," Jimmy replied, sheepishly. "Besides we don't know what she did or why she was in the Void. Maybe she was an embezzler or murdered her abusive husband. Besides, it pisses me off when I see guys pushing women around."

"Well, in any case," Mary snapped, let's wrap it up and get out of here."

As the others donned their coats, Jimmy casually leaned back in his chair and saw a small television hanging from the wall at the entrance area where—when the place was crowded—patrons waited until a table became available. Although the restaurant was nearly empty, the TV was on with the sound off and the closed captioning engaged.

Jimmy was about to turn away when Mary McGuernsey's photo appeared on the screen. He quickly called the others attention to it

A bizarre murder in Wheatfield has the state police puzzled, read the words at the bottom of the screen. *With no sign of*

127

robbery or struggle a Mr. Ellis Macawber was found dead outside the Wheatfield Lounge at 4:00 am this morning. The police are looking to speak with Mary McGuernsey, a self-described, "Psychic detective" whose bloody ATM receipt was found under the victim's body.

Anyone with information regarding this crime is asked to call TIPS at 555-2313. All information will be kept confidential.

On a lighter note…

Jimmy stood up. "People," he said in a low voice, "I suggest we hit the road. Now!"

"Agreed," Father Santiago said.

Jimmy followed the others to the door but slowed until he saw their waitress turn away. He then grabbed the remote and shut off the television.

As they hurriedly walked through the parking lot, Mary placed her hand on her chest. "I can't believe Ellis is dead! And they think I had something to do with it!"

Jimmy said, "You knew him?"

Jess nodded as she chewed on a toothpick. "We've known Mac for years. He was no fortune teller, but he was one heck of a showman! Once he conned you into his 'Room of the Occult,' ghostly apparitions would appear and candlesticks would fly, followed by weird sounds and tapping noises from the great beyond. A couple of minutes of that and most of his customers ran out screaming."

Jess chuckled. "Good old Mac. The Amazing Macawber he called himself. Everyone knew he couldn't predict a fart after a baked bean dinner but his performance was well worth the five bucks and no one ever asked for a refund."

Mary brushed back a tear. "And he was such a dear man, who would want to kill him?"

"The authorities," Father Santiago said as he unlocked and opened the door to the Impala. "As Jimmy said earlier, most have likely been corrupted. And since you can identify them, they will portray you as a dangerous criminal so there will be no inquiries when you meet a violent end while trying to avoid capture."

128

"Violent end? You mean they intend to kill her?!" Jess asked horrified as she skooched across the back seat.

Brother Martaine nodded as the others climbed in. "Sadly, yes. Father Santiago and I have been missionaries in many of the poorest Third World countries. Almost all were run by dictators or military juntas. And the first lesson one learns is to never draw attention to yourself or do anything that threatens the authority's power. Unfortunately Mary, you have done both."

"What about me?" Jimmy asked. "Why didn't they tie me in?"

"I would suspect for the reasons you explained earlier at Mary's house." Santiago said as he started the engine. "You have the power but don't use it so you are not viewed as a threat."

Mary looked over at Jess and said, "Look's like you were right. I never should have gotten you involved in this mess. I am so, so sorry"

Jess gently patted Mary's hand. "It's okay and please don't worry about me," she said. "I mean after all, nobody's looking to shoot my black ass."

Mary face blanched or a moment, then both women fell back laughing.

Seeing all eyes were upon them, Mary said, "Well, what did you expect us to do? Break down in tears?"

Chapter Twenty Eight

Now back on the road, the group decided they needed a place to stay, plan and most importantly, hide from the police. Since Santiago and Martaine were guests of the Albany Diocese and Jessica's house was probably being watched due to her friendship with Mary, it looked like Jimmy's was the only option.

Although a one bedroom apartment, it was relatively large and possessed certain advantages. The only entrance was halfway into a blind alley and was situated over an out-of-business restaurant. The area was rundown and rarely frequented so it was unlikely they would run into anyone on the street.

After they filed up the stairs, Jimmy pulled out his key and said, "Well, here we are!" He unlocked the door, led the group in and then after seeing the empty rum bottles and piles of dirty clothes scattered about, added, "Sorry the place is such a disaster, but I never have visitors. Uh, hang on."

Having lived such a solitary existence, Jimmy was only now realizing what a dump his apartment was. The few pieces of furniture he had were obtained from garage sales and probably would have been tossed had he not claimed them. He had bed sheets for curtains, a worn out recliner in front of an ancient TV that was the size of a small refrigerator, plus two full bags of garbage near the door. The only saving grace was that his bed was relatively new and the kitchen table was large enough and had enough chairs to accommodate his guests.

Quickly gathering the empty bottles, he ran into the kitchen, dumped them in the trash, then rushed back to the living room to pick up the dirty laundry. Once done, he tossed them to the floor of his bedroom closet and shouldered the door closed. He turned and grinned sheepishly as the group peeked in.

He walked over to the unmade bed.

"It's a queen, and I just changed the sheets," he said patting the mattress. "So if you want, Jess and Mary can take the first shift, then Father..." Jimmy yawned and shook his head. "Sorry," he said. "Anyway..."

Mary walked over to the bed, smiled, then took him by the shoulders and lowered him down into it. "You are dead on your feet and can barely keep your eyes open," she admonished. "You sleep first and I'll just…"

"Hold it! Hold the phone," Jess interrupted, waving her hands. "Now Mare, you know ol' Jess' got your back but this sister has been up since the crack of ass and needs her beauty sleep. If you are all bright-eyed and bushy-tailed, well, that's just fine, but as for me," she said as she plopped down on the crumpled sheets alongside the now horizontal Jimmy, "I'm done. And as for you little man," she said, leaning over. "Don't you be getting all hot and bothered just because you're sleeping next to a fine piece a Nubian womanhood. 'Cause if you do, I will rip off your arm and…"

She heard something, stopped, and peered over his shoulder. She sat up, grinned and shook her head. "Now don't that beat all?" she said with a chuckle. "He's sound asleep!"

"Hector," Brother Martaine called out, gesturing for him to approach. He was standing in the bedroom doorway, nearly filling it. When Santiago stepped over, Martaine said in a low voice, "Our young friend appears to have no food, dishes or silverware. We will need to do some shopping."

Santiago nodded and filed out behind Martaine.

After waving to Jess, Mary left and closed the door. When she reached the kitchen, she tossed her white jacket over the back of one of the kitchen chairs, then walked into the living room, sat down in the recliner and turned on the television. So not to disturb Jimmy or Jess, she engaged the mute button and closed captioning.

Brother Martaine quietly walked over to her and whispered, "Father and I are going out to purchase groceries. Is there anything in particular we can get for you or your friend?"

Mary shook her head. "I pretty much have an iron stomach, so does Jess," she said in a low voice. "We'll be fine with whatever you bring back. Here, let me put in my share," she said reaching for her purse.

Martaine shook his head. "Our treat," he said with a smile.

131

Nearly an hour later, Jimmy bolted up in bed. He looked around; saw Jess peacefully snoring away, then Ike sitting on a chair in the corner.

"Git up young fella," Ike said, then pointed to the window. "There's a girl out there in bad shape and she needs your help."

Still half asleep, Jimmy groaned, climbed out of bed and staggered into the bathroom to throw some water on his face. "What girl?" He looked in the mirror and opened the medicine cabinet. "Where did I put the toothpaste?" he asked, turning on the water.

"Wake up, boy, this is serious!" Ike shouted, clapping his hands.

Startled, Jimmy jumped and covered his ears. "All right! All right! What the big emergency?"

Ike put his foot on the toilet lid and leaned in. "The machine your buddy built changed the way things ought to be. One girl was supposed to die tonight and another was supposed to be heading on home. But due to the ruckus surrounding that dad-blamed machine, the girl on her way home got detoured and went down a road she wasn't supposed to. Now that poor thing is in a serious pickle and you need to stop her before she, well, before she does sumthin stupid. If'n you get my drift..."

"Some kid is going to kill herself because of Virgil's machine?!" Jimmy asked, after splashing his face and turning off the water.

Ike's expression told him that was a distinct possibility.

"Where is she?"

Ike told him.

The sun had come up over an hour earlier and Aimee was sitting under a tree shivering, but not because of the weather. Fear, confusion and panic had overwhelmed her.

She had cried herself out twice, first, in her car, now under the tree. All through the night she kicked around different scenarios and possible explanations for her present condition, but with the arrival of the morning light, she could no longer deny her predicament. She had checked all the mirrors, the ones on the car,

132

the one in her purse, even the one inside the passenger-side visor. She had studied her hands, her feet, even checked to see if her appendectomy scar was still there.

It wasn't.

It wasn't there because somehow, she, Aimee McFarland, was now residing in the body of Sula May Hockenberger and that new reality was pushing the boundaries of her sanity to its limits.

"I got to go home," she muttered, slowly climbing to her feet. "Talk to Mom and Dad. They're probably worried out of their minds by now." She stopped. "Maybe I should call first."

She realized both options were bad ideas. Her new voice sounded nothing like her old one and if she went home, how would she convince her folks she really was their little Aimee? They wouldn't buy it for a minute and would call the police.

Her heart was pounding and her hands shook as she unsteadily walked over to the Mustang, opened the car door and climbed in behind the wheel.

After taking a deep breath, she started the engine and took a moment to review Sula's memories. Moments later, a deep, all encompassing sorrow washed over her.

She sobbed and laid her head on the top of the steering wheel.

Those people are monsters. Vicious, stupid, inbred monsters. No wonder Sula was running away.

Aimee took several more deep breaths, ran her hand through her hair and discovered it was seriously matted. For the first time she gave herself a serious looking over and again a pang of sorrow bit her. There was so much smoke and confusion back at the burning house that Aimee never really saw Sula up close. Now in Sula's body she realized the poor girl was filthy, her clothes were stained and ill-fitting, her sneakers had holes in the soles and were stuffed with cardboard, and frankly, she smelled.

Aimee brought up the convertible's roof, locked it in place, slammed the Mustang into gear and raced off with no idea of where she was heading or what to do when she got there.

She also had no idea she was being watched.

A half hour later, on her way back to Wheatfield, Aimee saw her purse on the passenger-side floor. Inside was her cell, wallet, and credit cards. Seeing these small connections to her former life gave her a glimmer of hope. Now a little more in control, she pulled over to the curb and texted her parents with an explanation she hoped would convince them that she was all right.

Car broke in middle of nowhere No signal 4 phone Spent night in car, cell battery near ded. Walking 2 near town CUlater

Not great but good enough to ease their minds and buy her some time. She put the car in gear and pulled back into traffic.

Jimmy knew he had to time this right and talk fast or his half-assed rescue mission might land him in jail, especially if that old coot had gotten his signals crossed and he jumped into the wrong car.

He took a cab to the center of Wheatfield, where Ike told him that Aimee, driving a blue convertible with the license plate AIM E GRL, would stop at a red light just outside the Lumberland parking lot.

He waited patiently behind the bus shelter until Aimee's car came into view.

"Well, here goes," he muttered as the Mustang slowed, then stopped at the light.

Jimmy burst from the bus shelter, yanked the door open, jumped into the passenger seat and blurted, "Hi,I'mJimmyandI'mafriendandIknow you're really Aimee and not Sula!"

Startled, she grabbed the door handle and was about to jump out when Jimmy's words sunk in. "Wait," she said turning, "you know who I am?"

Jimmy nodded enthusiastically with his hands raised, palms out. "Yes! Yes! I'm not a nut looking to carjack you. I was told to come here and tell you we are aware of what happened."

Still shaken, she slowly let go of the door handle. Wide-eyed, she looked him over. "We...? Who's we?" But before he could answer the light changed and the car behind her blew its horn. "All right, all right!" she said as she put the Mustang in gear and started off. "So, why am I in Sula's body?"

Jimmy's face scrunched a little. "As you can probably guess, some seriously weird shit has happened and I don't think you should be driving when I explain it. What I can say is a scientific experiment went horribly wrong. I was told to bring you to my place. You'll get the whole story and what's being done about it. Now I know that sounds like…"

"No, that's okay," she replied, shooting him a quick look. "A minute ago I was on the verge of losing my mind. Now that I know there's a logical explanation and things are being done about it, I feel a lot better. But before we do anything I have to go to the ATM, buy some clean clothes and find a place to wash up," she said, glancing at her hands and arms.

"You can take a shower at my place," Jimmy began.

She shook her head. "And what will I change into afterward?"

"There's a laundry mat around the corn…

She shook her head determinedly. "I'm not spending another minute in these disgusting rags." She gestured to her clothing. "They itch and they stink!" she said with a grimace. "I wouldn't be surprised if the damn things had bugs! Ewwww," she groaned, shuddering at the thought.

"Okay. If you need clothes, there's a Handlemans two blocks over."

She eyed him. "Handlemans? No way. They're a cheap designer discounter who…"

Jimmy pointed at his watch and said, "Who is open 24 hours. Nobody else is open yet."

She took a second look at her clothes, sighed and said. "Okay, Handlemans it is."

"I still don't get it. Why do I have to wait until we get to your place?" Aimee said as she placed the money from the ATM into her silver-mirrored pocket book and stepped out of the car. "Why can't you tell me now? This shit is freaking me out, you know."

"Because there is a lot to explain. Seriously, it's very complex." he replied. "When we get to my apartment we can sit

135

down and go through what happened bit by bit. I need you to trust me on this."

As they walked toward Handlemans, she slung her purse over her shoulder and said, "All right, I'll grab something to wear for the time being and then we'll head straight to your place, okay?"

"Works for me," Jimmy said as they entered the store.

"Oh and remember we parked in row A-5, near the bank. I always forget where I leave my car."

"Car near bank, got it," Jimmy replied, pulling a cart from the rack.

She stopped and made a quick survey of their surroundings. Noting that no one was watching or was even nearby, she took a quick whiff of the area of her blouse between the underarm and breast. "Ewww, disgusting! Remind me not to get near anybody. I smell like a combo of B.O. and burnt wood!"

"C'mon," he said, pushing the cart. "Let's get this done."

As they made their way to the young women's section, they turned at the fitting rooms and saw three women about Aimee's age approaching with arms full of clothes.

"Hey, Sula," one of them said. "Finally decide to wear something new for a change?"

Her companions giggled as they passed. Then one who was waving her hand under her nose called back, "If you're trying something new, why not start with a bath?"

All three were laughing as they disappeared down the aisle.

Aimee's eyes welled with tears. "Bitches," she muttered. "Damn cruel bitches!" then stormed toward the clothing section. "They're bad mouthing Sula for being poor but they're here buying irregulars at a bargain discounter."

"Don't let them get to you," he said, trying to keep up. "Girls like that are sick in the head."

She wiped her eyes. "Those girls," she said, her voice trembling, "are my, well, maybe were…my best friends."

Some friends, thought Jimmy.

When they got to the clothing section, Aimee quickly and determinedly sifted through the racks. "So where are you from, and what do you do?" she asked as she pulled out a yellow blouse, placed it a few inches from her chest and turned to the mirror.

Jimmy shrugged. "Well, I was born here in Wheatfield. My parents split up when I was a baby so I never met my father. I work as a stock clerk over at the Lumberland at night and have my own apartment. The rent is pretty cheap because it's commercially zoned so... technically it doesn't exist."

"That's it?' she asked, checking the blouse's price tag. "All you have is a stock clerk job? I thought you were some kind of scientist."

"No, just a guinea pig. Me and a few others were used to test the machine that did this to you."

He almost asked her about her background but stopped when he realized just how unsettling a topic that might be. As it stood, she presently had no past, and judging by her ill-fitting, stained, hand-me-down clothes, not much of a future.

Fortunately, she had more questions. "How *did* you know I was Aimee and not Sula?" she asked as she returned the yellow blouse to the rack and selected a blue one.

Jimmy smiled. "Let's just say I got people on the inside and they told me to get a hold of you before you knocked yourself..." He stopped and reddened, suddenly realizing he had said too much.

She tossed the blue blouse and a similar burgundy one into the cart. "It's okay," she said with a shrug. "I admit it. I was seriously messed up and was considering plowing into a wall and maybe would have if you hadn't shown up. I... Wait..." She turned to him. "How did you know I'd be stopped at that particular light at that particular moment?"

He raised his hands. "Please, enough with the questions. Like I said, there's a lot involved and I'll explain everything when we get to my place."

She rolled her eyes, started off toward the jeans department and casually slipped her arm into the crook of his. "Well you got to give me something. You already know my deepest and darkest secret."

He looked down at her arm. "Aimee, just so you know, I'm not a relationship person."

Her face reddened and she immediately yanked her arm from his.

He put up his hands and quickly added, "No, I don't mean I'm a wham-bam-thank-you-ma'am kind of guy. It's just that I don't date. In fact, I spend most of my downtime drinking rum, playing video games and smoking pot."

She looked him over. "Easy there, Casanova, you're making me swoon. What makes you think I'd even be interested?"

"Absolutely nothing," he replied with a wave of his hand. "I just want to avoid any future misunderstanding, that's all."

She stopped and put her hands on her hips. "So even if, for some unforeseen reason, we became close, you would never ask me on a date?"

"These jeans look nice," he said pulling one from the rack.

"Look, if you're gay, just say so," she said as she brushed by him and rummaged through the display. "I got no problem with that. Probably be a good thing since I could use a gay man's opinion with these new clothes. I just realized what looked good on me before; has nothing to do with what might look good on me now."

Finding nothing, she turned, took the jeans from him, held them up and said, "You're right, these do look nice and they go with the burgundy. Oh, and look at this miniskirt!"

"Just for the record, I'm not gay," he replied, stepping back behind the cart. "It's like I said earlier. I don't socialize, I don't have friends and I don't go on dates."

"Why not?" she asked, tossing the miniskirt into the cart. "you're young, good looking. Don't you ever get lonely?"

With a sad smile he replied, "Unfortunately, that's never been an issue."

An hour later, Aimee climbed the stairs to Jimmy's apartment carrying several shopping bags.

"Before we go in," she said, "I just want to say that when it comes to shopping, you suck. I was in there for barely a half hour before you hustled me to the cashier." She held up the shopping bags. "Two blouses, two pair of jeans, a skirt, shoes, underwear, make-up and toiletries do not a wardrobe make."

"I was sent to rescue you, not spend the day dicking around the mall." He reached into his pocket for his keys. "I don't get it. First you badger me for explanations for why you're in Sula's body, then you give me grief for not giving you more time to shop."

"Well, I need clothes don't I? Besides, when things get straightened out, I think Sula should have some nice new things. I think she deserves it." A look of sadness washed over her. "It isn't her fault she has to wear these rags. And I'm going to talk to my parents about getting her away from those inbred psychos. Nobody should have to live like that."

When he saw the determination on her face, Jimmy's stomach tightened. He knew what he was going to reveal once they got inside was going to go down hard.

He put his finger to his lips as he unlocked the door. "I have guests and they're sleeping."

They entered and Jimmy noted the clergymen hadn't returned and Mary was asleep in the recliner.

"Is that your mom?' Aimee asked, placing the shopping bags on the floor.

"No. Just another person who got dragged into this mess."

"Is Sula here yet?"

"No, right now it's only Mary and Jess. I expect the others will be back in a little while."

"Well, we're here," she said gesturing to her surroundings, "how about that explanation you promised?"

He nodded and pulled out a chair from the kitchen table. Just as she was about to sit down, Mary, although still asleep, began coughing, grimacing and waving her hand in front of her face.

Aimee reddened and shook her head. "Oh that's it! That is freaking it!" she spat in a stage whisper. "I'm taking a shower and getting out of these disgusting clothes. Where's the bathroom?"

Jimmy pointed to the back. "Next to the bedroom."

Aimee grabbed the shopping bags and stormed down the hall.

139

Five minutes later, the clergymen returned. "Sorry to have taken so long," Santiago commented as he unpacked the grocery bags. "But since we are new in town we it probably would have been wise to ask where the supermarket was located before setting out. We spent over an hour driving around looking for one."

After everything was setup, they sat at the kitchen table and Jimmy explained what happened during their absence and Aimee's present situation.

"Did you tell her the whole story?" Santiago asked. "The part that Ol' Ike…"

"Not yet," Jimmy replied solemnly

Shortly afterward, Aimee emerged from the bathroom looking considerably different and considerably more attractive. Her long blond hair was untangled and her new burgundy blouse went well with the new miniskirt and red pumps. The makeup brought out Sula's natural beauty and she smelled like wildflowers. And with her baggy clothes replaced with better-fitting ones, it was obvious that Sula May regularly engaged in some serious physical labor.

As she approached she saw the groceries on the kitchen counter. There was a large plastic pot filled with coffee, a box of pastries, paper cups, plates and plastic utensils.

Aimee joined them at the table.

"I feel so much better," she said running the brush through her drying hair. She stuck out her hand to the clergymen. "Hi, I'm Aimee."

After Santiago and Martaine introduced themselves, Jimmy lightly tapped the table to signal he was ready to begin.

He started by telling Aimee what Virgil had created, what Ike told him, and what, under Lillian's guidance, the machine was doing.

"According to Ike…"

"Wait," Father Santiago interrupted. "This Ike person, if he knows so much should we not invite him to join us?"

Jimmy smiled. "Trust me, he not missing a thing," Jimmy said reaching back and twisting his shoulder length hair. "Ike is a ghost, died sometime back in the early 1900s. He was supposed to move onto the next world but chose to stick around to see Judgment Day.

He says that people who committed the biggest sins and refuse to enter the next world are condemned to remain in the area of their greatest wrongdoing. Ike claims there were about 500 in this area and thanks to Virgil's machine, they have taken over the bodies of police officers, federal agents, utility people and a number of your average everyday folk who; for whatever reason, happened to be nearby. That's all I know so far." He turned to Aimee. "Now it's time to explain what happened to you. Are you ready," Jimmy asked, placing his hand on Aimee's arm.

"Am I ready?!" Aimee replied pulling away. "You just said you've been talking to ghosts and that some guy has built a machine that is bringing dead maniacs back to life. Seriously," she said looking around at her new companions. "It's a bit hard to swallow. I mean, how do I know you people aren't just plain crazy?"

"You only need to look in the mirror to answer that," Jimmy replied.

She paused, took a breath and placed the hairbrush on the table. "Yeah... I almost forgot. Okay, fire away."

Jimmy rose and walked to the kitchen counter and the coffeepot. "Ike says you weren't supposed to save Sula. Her time was up and she was supposed to die in that building. But because of the commotion caused by Virgil's machine, instead of driving home, you turned off the main road, setting off a chain of events that was never supposed to happen."

Aimee shrugged and glanced over at him. "Yeah, but I managed to save Sula, right? I mean at least one good thing came out of this."

Jimmy nodded, poured two cups of coffee and walked back. "Well, there's more," he said, placing one of the cups in front of her. "After the second explosion, when Sula's body was blown out the window and with Aimee's body still being in the house when it collapsed, the universe was faced with a problem."

A concerned look came over Aimee's face. She eyed him suspiciously then said, "Which was...?"

Jimmy brought his hand to his chin. "Well, as Ike explained it to me, the universe suddenly found itself with a living soul inside a

141

dead body and a dead soul inside a living one so, the universe, with the assistance of Virgil's machine, switched the two. And so, here you are."

Jimmy sat down believing he had explained the situation clearly and as best he could but wasn't at all surprised when moments later, Aimee shot out of her seat.

"Hold it! Hold it!" she shouted, "a living soul in a dead body? Are you talking about me?" she asked, pressing her hands against her chest. "Are you telling me my body's dead? That Sula's dead?" Her face went white and her hands ran to her head. "And I'm stuck in Sula's body for the rest of my life?"

"Well," he began but with the answer being so obvious there was no way he could soften the blow."Yeah," he finally said.

"No! No! No!" she shouted, stomping her foot. "I'm just starting my life! Everything I worked so hard for is just beginning to happen. I'm going to Vassar in the fall."

She balled her hands into fists. "I'm going to find this Virgil and make him fix this," she growled with teeth clenched. She patted her jacket pockets. "Where are my car keys?"

Jimmy stood, grabbed her shoulders and eyed her hard. "Listen to me! Your old body, the body of Aimee McFarland is gone, dead, crushed under tons of concrete and metal debris!"

She grabbed his shirt and yanked him toward her. "No! That's not true. Look at me, I'm still alive. I'm still..."

He gently pried her hands from his shirt and sat her down. "I'm sorry. I really am," he said. "And if it's any consolation, you're a hero. And yes, because of Virgil's machine, your soul wound up in Sula's body. But the important thing to remember is you're not dead, and you should be thankful for that. Besides, from what I can see, Sula was about your age and was attractive, healthy and strong. You could have done a lot worse."

Mary winced as she climbed out of the recliner. She placed her hand on the small of her back and said. "Jimmy, do you have any aspirin?"

As Jimmy pointed to the bathroom, Aimee collapsed to the floor, wailing uncontrollably.

An hour later, Jess, who had amazingly slept though it all; woke up and saw Aimee in bed beside her.

She got up, walked over and opened the door. She motioned to the inside of the bedroom and asked the group at the kitchen table, "Okay, what did I miss?"

Mary rose from the kitchen table, went to the counter and poured Jess a cup of coffee as Jess padded over and sat down with the group.

After handing it to her, Mary explained Aimee's appearance and the circumstances behind it.

When the story was complete, Jess' brows knitted. "Oh, that poor child."

"She's been up all night and is very upset," Jimmy added. "When she finally stopped crying and accepted her condition, she just walked into the bedroom, laid down next to you and fell fast asleep." Jimmy's stomach felt as if there were a lead weight in it. The look of horror on Aimee's face when she realized her circumstances was something he would never forget.

Jess nodded. "Probably just as well." She took a sip. "Okay, now moving on. What's next on the agenda and more importantly, have the authorities offered any reward

They were all laughing when someone banged loudly on the door.

Jimmy reached inside his dungaree jacket to the pocket where he kept his snub nose .38.

A voice rang out. "Open this door. Open this door right now! I know you're in there!"

Chapter Twenty Nine

As police officer Myrrh Cavanaugh signed out her shift at the Wheatfield station, she turned and saw Police Chief, Greg Marris enter and gesture for her to come over.

The thirty-five-year-old, ten-year veteran smiled, nodded and approached but inside was thinking, *Ahh shit, just what I need.*

She pulled the rubber band from her hair, letting her dark chestnut locks fall upon her shoulders. "You want to see me?"

"Yeah, Cavanaugh. What happened out on Route 727 last night and why didn't any of your fellow 4-to-midnight officers sign out at shift's end?"

Myrrh took a moment then said, "I'm sorry, chief, but I don't know why the guys didn't sign out. I've only been here about five minutes myself. It's been a busy night."

Various voices of officers and dispatchers crackled loudly from the communications center. He motioned for them to go to the lower-level staircase. When they reached the stairs, he resumed the conversation. "Okay, then bring me up to speed on that big to-do on 727."

Standing rigidly, almost as if at attention, she said, "At approximately ten o'clock we got several calls claiming there were strange lights and power outages along 727 at Dohesley, so dispatch sent a car. An hour later I get a call to work traffic control. When I arrive, Route 727 looks like a tailgate party at the Super Bowl and I can't get anywhere near whatever is causing the traffic jam. But cars are leaving so I start directing them out of the area. Takes about an hour but eventually it gets cleared."

"Why were they there in the first place?" Marris asked.

Cavanaugh shrugged as she donned her jacket. "From what I heard, someone was tapping Adirondack P & L power lines but they couldn't figure out who, so they contacted the feds who called us for help. Like I said, I was over a mile away directing traffic so I have no idea what they found, if anything."

The chief took a moment to let the info sink in.

"Uh, chief?" she said trying to get his attention. "If there's nothing else, I'm beat and I'd like to head home. I've been on duty for fourteen hours straight."

Marris checked his watch then tipped his head to the door. "Go ahead. You had a long night."

Cavanaugh was relieved that Morris accepted her explanation because she knew a lot more than she let on. When her fellow 4-to-midnight officers didn't return to the station or answer calls following the scene at Dohesley, she was asked to stay on duty. She complied and while on patrol made some inquiries. She learned her fellow officers were at the Blue Moon Lounge, so she dropped by and told the senior officer, Bertram Van Pelt, that he and the rest of the crew had better report in.

She was surprised that Van Pelt didn't seem all that concerned, however having done her part to cover for them, she went back on patrol. When she drove by an hour later, the police cruisers were gone.

Still, she was the only member of the 4-to-midnight shift who hadn't joined in the festivities at the Blue Moon Lounge, which made her the odd woman out.

Not a good thing.

After she went home and slept for twelve hours, she woke midday and noticed a number of voicemails on her cell. They all featured disguised voices warning her to keep her mouth shut if she knew what was good for her. Others reminded her that cops often get killed while on duty. Still another said...

She pressed END—and ERASE all. She got the point.

After all these years and all I've done for those guy, this is how I get treated?

*

Jimmy turned toward the door of his apartment as the knocking continued.

"C'mon, open up!"

Jimmy rose from his seat, walked over and looked through the door's peephole.

"Well, isn't this interesting?" he said, unlocking and pulling the door open.

The visitor stormed past Jimmy and peeled off his jacket. "She's not getting away with this!" he shouted. "My mother's been pulling shit all my life and I need you to help me find Mary McGu..."

He stopped, startled to see that Jimmy was not alone. He stepped back unsure of what to do. "What's going on here?" he asked in a low voice.

Jimmy put his hand on the man's shoulder and said, "Ladies and gentlemen, may I present Mr. Virgil Vanderhill!"

After Virgil was convinced to join the others at the table, Jimmy said, "We spent half the night looking for you, even shut down and disconnected the equipment at the Blue Barn to prevent anyone else from using it."

"So it was you guys," Vigil said. "I was wondering who did that."

"Well, where the hell were you?" Jimmy asked, throwing his hands in the air. "Do you have any idea what happened while you were at the bar getting shit-faced?"

"Oh, I know what happened all right!" he snapped. "My mother left a message on my answering machine. Did you know she's abandoned me? That's right! I dedicated eleven years of my life trying to contact her and now that she's got a new body, she's cutting off contact with everyone who knew her before, including me. Me, her own son!" Virgil's voice was becoming shrill, almost panicky. "And then she ends the message by saying. "Have a good life, sweetie. Good-bye. Can you imagine that? The gall of that woman! Well, I'm going to find out who she is and then tell everyone. I'm going to put it on the freakin' Internet, take out ads and then..."

Jimmy took his arm and said, "We get it okay? Calm down, we got bigger problems."

Virgil took a breath and eyed Mary.

146

"Should have figured she'd be here." He turned to Jimmy and the clergymen. "You guys are as thick as thieves."

Father Santiago said, "You have much to explain, sir."

"I don't have time to explain," he said with a dismissive sneer. He pointed at Mary. "All I need is for her to point out my mother's new body."

Santiago was about to press further but Jimmy stepped in. "Listen, Virg, you're responsible for the biggest fuck up since Chernobyl. You get nothing until you tell us how to fix it."

"Screw you, McCracken," he said with a dismissive wave of his hand. He turned to Mary. "I'll pay you $9,000 in cash just to point her out. That's all you gotta do, just point her out."

Jess took her friends' arm. "Don't do it, Mary."

Mary turned to Jimmy who was shaking his head in disbelief, then Virgil. "No deal."

Virgil's eyes widened with surprise. "What? Why not? It's nine grand for a couple of hours work. And to make it easier," he said reaching into his pants pocket, "I have something she recently touched, something that with your ability, should lead us right to her."

With a scowl, Mary said, "I'm not interested in what you want or need. It's because of you that monsters have invaded our world."

Virgil fell back in his chair, smirked and rolled his eyes. "Oh stop being so melodramatic. Monsters? Are you for real? So, my mother and a couple of her dead cronies slipped over to the land of the living. Once we find her, we'll round up the others and then I'll send the whole kit and caboodle back over the River Styx. The end."

"Virgil," Jimmy said. "Over 500 people, police, federal agents and technical workers were pushed out of their bodies by formerly dead, crazed and violent criminals. All of who are presently walking our streets."

Virgil stared, again with a smirk, thinking Jimmy was joking, then took on a puzzled look when it became clear he wasn't. "Crazed and violent? What would my mother be doing around

147

those kinds of people? Besides, what are we talking about? Psychos, murderers, what?"

"All that and more," Jimmy replied, finishing his coffee.

Virgil paled. "You're not making this up?"

Jimmy leaned in and eyed him hard. "No, and I got this info from the same source who told me you made contact with your mother."

Virgil raised his fist to his mouth and bit down on his knuckle. A moment later he sprung from his chair. "I'm doomed," he said with a frantic look as he wandered the room. "I am *so* doomed. Five hundred violent psychos out on the streets? They'll kill me, you know," he said with a quick nod of his head. "They'll do anything to keep me from sending them back." He paused for a moment, dropped his fists to his sides and added with a scowl, "And I'll bet that's why my no-good, lousy, lying, stinking mother tried to get me to destroy the machine. All that crap about dangerous creatures." He bowed his head, "just another dirty, stinking lie!"

Mary got up, walked over and placed her hand on Virgil's shoulder. "Actually, that part is true."

He spun and eyed her. "So it isn't...? Oh thanks a lot! So it's even worse than I thought!"

He again bowed his head and slowly shook it. "Why is it always me who has to suffer? Why must all the world's misery be dropped on my shoulders?" He staggered back to the table, fell into his chair then, as his eyes filled with tears, buried his face in his hands.

As Virgil sobbed, Brother Martaine held out his hands, looked questioningly at the others and asked. "Is he for real?"

"Enough of this nonsense!" Father Santiago shouted as he grabbed Virgil's chair and spun it to face him. "Now listen to me," he said, pulling Virgil's hands from his face. "You tell us what we want to know right now or Mary and I will find one of those unholy monsters, bring it here and leave you at its mercy."

Virgil raised his head, brushed away the tears from his red-rimmed eyes and snarled. "You wouldn't dare!"

Taking it as a personal challenge, Martaine shrugged, got up, walked over, grabbed Virgil by his collar and waistband, lifted him effortlessly into the air and flung him across the room as if he were a bag of laundry. As he crashed to the floor and slid up against the wall, Martaine came over, sat upon him and said to Santiago. "I assure you he will be here when you and Mary return."

As Mary rose from her chair and reached for her bag, Virgil capitulated. "All right, all right, you win." He looked up at the clergyman and wheezed. "Let me up, you genetic monstrosity; I'll tell you what you want to know."

Reluctantly, Virgil returned to the table, sat down and began to explain. "I figured out what went wrong. To put it in terms you people can understand, what I designed was supposed to be a telephone to the dead, but like early phones, I had a problem with what used to be called a party line. So I created the ectoplasmic chamber to filter out unwanted interference. But my mistake was I continued to think of it as a telephone long after the addition of the chamber changed it into a transporter. I forgot that the dead are not physical beings, but forms of energy. A telephone can't transmit physical objects but it can transmit energy. And so it became possible for the dead to use my machine to push themselves into a living body and force the original occupant out before they realized what was happening."

Jimmy quickly nodded. "We figured as much. The question is can you put everyone back where they belong?"

"I'm a freakin' genius, McCracken," Virgil replied smugly. "You leave that to me. Now first thing, we find my mother and…"

"Nooooo," Jimmy replied shaking his head, "out of the question. First we ask Mary to track down one of the…well I guess 'push-ins' is as good a term as any, and take him or her to the Blue Barn. Then you show us how to reverse the process. Once we can do that, we'll go after Lillian."

Virgil folded his arms and snarled. He was not used to being told what he could or could not do, especially by some long-haired, hippy, dipshit. But right now Jimmy held all the cards.

149

"Fine!" Virgil spat. "But we still need to go to the Barn. I got to set up the equipment again and make a number of adjustments to the hardware and software for it to work. I'm also going to need a flashlight or candles until I can get the power running."

"Don't have a flashlight or candles but I got a box of matchbooks," he said as he rose from the table, opened the cupboard and pulled one from the shelf. "There are forty packs inside," he said placing them on the table. "That should hold you."

As Virgil took the box, Santiago stood and said, "Brother Martaine and I will accompany Virgil while Mary and the rest of you track down one of the 'push-ins' and bring him to the Barn."

"You two clowns will just get in my way," Virgil snapped.

"Perhaps, but we will keep you honest," Martaine replied, grabbing Virgil's shoulder. "Now let us go."

"Aimee, honey, it's time to get up."

Feeling the hand gently shaking her shoulder, Aimee grunted and slowly rolled on her back. A moment later she rubbed her eyes, groggily sat up and swung her legs over the edge of the bed. She held out her hands then studied her bare feet. She let out a sigh and looked up at Jess.

"I was so hoping this was a dream," she said solemnly, "but I guess I got to face it. I'm Sula now."

Jess sat down and placed a comforting hand on her arm. "My name is Jessica, but everyone calls me Jess. The others told me what happened. I came in to wake you and hopefully say something comforting." Jess' deep brown eyes were warm and her gentle voice helped soothe the teen's rattled nerves.

Aimee slid over beside her and said, "Thank you."

Jess nodded. "You're welcome and believe me, I won't give you any of that be- thankful-you're-alive nonsense because I know how important the quality of life is to a person. I saw those raggedy-ass cast-offs and worn out shoes. Judging by the stylish clothes and make-up you're wearing now, you not only lost your body, you lost your family and future and inherited someone else's sad and unhappy past."

With tears in her eyes, Aimee hugged her. "Yes! Yes! That's what I've been trying to say. You're the only one who understands."

"No, child," Jess replied as she returned the hug, then let go and gently took Aimee's hands. "We all understand, but I'm the only one who lived it. I wore raggedy clothes, too, and well into my early twenties. My father was a poor, uneducated, hateful man who was mad at the world and took it out on us. My childhood…"

Her father's voice suddenly reverberated in her head.

Jessica Jean Maldonado, what deviltry are you up to now?!

Jess stiffened in terror.

How many years had it been since he mouthed those hateful, crazed accusations? Decades at least, but those words still filled her with fear.

Jess coughed to cover her momentary loss of concentration and continued.

"…my childhood was filled with violence and poverty. I had to accept the most horrible abuses. Things no child should have to endure. Figuring that a good education was the only way out of that hell, I worked two jobs, studied hard, went without and sometimes even slept on the streets. But in the end, I succeeded. I graduated college with a degree in architecture, went on to get my Master's and taught for 31 years."

Jess patted Aimee's hand. "To this day, so many years later, just the thought of that horrible life fills me with a dread that I couldn't possibly put into words. All I can say is, do what I did. Fight your way out. These people you suddenly find yourself related to have no legal hold on you. Once we all get through this, Mary and I will help you get your life back on track."

Aimee hugged her again.

Jessica Jean Maldonado, what deviltry are you up to now?!

Jess shivered and Aimee felt it. She leaned back, "Jess, are you okay?"

"I'm as right as rain, child," Jess replied, steadying herself.

Aimee was skeptical and changed the subject to give Jess a moment's respite.

151

"Just before I came in here, Jimmy told me that you and Mary have been friends for a long time. How did you meet?"

Jess placed her hands on the bed and leaned back, "Well if you really are interested, I suppose I got time to give you the short version."

"I'd like that."

Jess took a moment then said. "We met back when I teaching. One day, I saw a flyer announcing a guest lecturer was coming to campus. It was Mary. She had written several books about the occult and spiritualism and had come to give a talk on "The Scientific Importance of Avoiding Sin." At first I dismissed the event as New Age nonsense, but there was something about that title that spoke to me, probably because of my father's mental issues, so I signed up and attended."

"The scientific importance of avoiding sin," Aimee said. "Hmm, so what did she say?"

"In a nutshell, she said that although much of religions do's and don'ts were created thousands of years ago, they continue to prove invaluable."

"How?"

"Well, once a people form a civilization, one of the first things they do is form a code of conduct. The earliest civilizations believed that the human mind needs a strong moral core to function properly. Without it, the brain loses its ability to differentiate between right and wrong, and can't tell what behavior will bring positive results and what will bring negative results. She theorized that was why the criminal's lifestyle almost always deteriorates into perversity, deviance and self- destruction.

"She quoted several studies on criminal behavior and in nearly every one, the criminal said there had been a tipping point in their lives. A point where they intentionally chose to go against their conscience and do something they knew was wrong. In nearly every case is the more they violated the constraints of conscience, the more they lost their grip on reality. She said that although not all mentally ill people are evil; all evil people are mentally ill."

Jess smiled. "When the lecture was over, I was so impressed I invited Mary to dinner. She accepted and we immediately hit it off.

152

"And that's how we met," Jess said gently slapping the teen on the knee.

"Thanks, Jess."

Jess smiled but didn't mention the main thing she had gotten from Mary's lecture. Her father wasn't a victim of a disease. He wasn't a good man overwhelmed by madness.

He was evil, and the words…

Jessica Jean Maldonado, what deviltry are you up to now!!?"

…were once again echoing inside her head.

Mary popped her head into Jimmy's bedroom.

"Ahhh," she said, "our new friend is back among the living I see."

Aimee nodded and wiped her eyes. "Yeah, for the time being, anyway."

Jimmy, who had been watching television and working his laptop, entered wearing a concerned look. "It's getting bad out there. Violent crime is increasing by the minute. There was a big shoot-out in Wheatfield and an armored car has been stolen. We've got to find a 'push-in' and get him to the Barn before things get to the point where the cops have to use deadly force."

"Okay then, let's go," Mary said.

"Aimee," Jimmy said, "we're going to have to use your car."

"That's okay," Aimee said. "but I don't want to drive." She pulled out her keys and tossed them to Jimmy. "You can drive a stick right?"

Jimmy nodded.

So with Jimmy at the wheel, Mary riding shotgun and Aimee and Jess in the back, they set out to abduct a push-in.

"So where do we start?" Jimmy asked, as he turned onto the main drag.

"We go back to Denny's," Mary replied

"That's right! The waitress! The waitress is one of them!"

Jess checked her watch. "It's ten to ten, people. Odds are the night shift's over."

153

"Or it's just midway through the day shift," Mary replied. "A lot of restaurants open at five am. for early shift workers. This way, women with kids are finished in time to pick them up from school."

Aimee said, "If she's one of them, she had to be at Dohesley last night."

Mary thought for a moment and said. "Then our waitress *wasn't* working."

Jess shook her head. "How are we going to convince a crazy bitch to go to the Blue Barn with us? You know what I'm saying?"

"Uh, guys?" Aimee said as she turned and looked out the back window. "We got a bigger problem. That cop we just passed going the other way just made a u-turn and is coming right at us with his flashers on. He must have seen Mary."

A moment later they heard the siren.

Chapter Thirty

"I should have known you two morons would be a thorn in my side when I ran into you the first time," Virgil grumbled sullenly from the passenger's seat. Father Santiago was driving and Brother Martaine sat in the back.

"Shut up you braying jackass!" Martaine said, smacking Virgil in the back of the head.

Virgil spun around, "Owww! Why you, sonavabitch! I ought to…"

When Martaine snarled and raised his hand a second time, Virgil cowered and fell silent.

The clergyman lowered his hand and said, "Senor, since your actions may yet bring about the end of the world, I suggest you keep your snide comments to yourself and focus your energies on the task at hand."

"Oh, bullshit! You're just trying…" Virgil began but jerked in surprise when Father Santiago reached over and gently placed his hand on Virgil's shoulder.

"Mr. Vanderhill," Santiago began with a friendly pat, "my friend, Brother Martaine, is a former wrestler as you may have suspected when you were flying through the air back at Jimmy's apartment. And as a young man I was the light-heavyweight boxing champion of my native Spain. Both of us have considerable physical strength and could very easily remand you into a wheelchair for the rest of your life."

"Yeah, well…" Virgil began but stopped after noticing movement in the back seat.

Santiago continued. "We are not your enemy. We have no intention of harming you. We are only here to make sure you correct the very, very dangerous situation your shortsightedness has created. You see, our main concern is the daemons, not the push-ins."

That got Virgil's attention, "Wait!" he said with noticeable confusion. "You don't care about the 500 criminals walking our streets? What kind of clergymen are you?"

"Funny you should ask," Brother Martaine said smiling grimly as he leaned forward and placed his meaty elbows on the backseat partition. "We're a very special breed of clergy. Although we are members of the Catholic Church, we often assist people of other faiths when one of their own falls prey to the daemons."

Santiago took over. "What we are about to tell you, we have not told the others. We don't want to frighten them."

"Oh, but it's okay to frighten me?" Virgil asked sarcastically.

"Actually, yes," Santiago replied. "But only so you can understand the consequences should you fail." He drew a breath. "Brother Martaine and I travel to the most violent countries in the world because that's where the most horrible creatures reside. On occasion, daemons slip into our realm and take over the bodies of those who frequently communicate with the dead. Our friend Jimmy mentioned having been possessed by one as a child. Our job is to track down these daemon spirits and destroy them. To do so takes incredible self-discipline, restraint, and an unyielding belief that good must always triumph over evil. To destroy just one daemon, just one, can take days, even weeks and has often physically and emotionally crippled a clergyman. Your machine is a door, a door wide enough for them all to come through, and Virgil," Santiago said with all sincerity, "if they do, the phrase Hell on Earth will become a reality."

Virgil smirked. "So you're nagging me to get the job done. I get it. And you don't care about the 500 because that's small change compared to the bogeymen you're worried about. Fine, I get your point. But what if these daemons come through during the transfer? Huh, how about that smart guy? What do we do then?"

Santiago grimaced. "Mr. Vanderhill, if that should happen, there won't be any 'we'. Because of what you've accomplished, you will no doubt be first on their list!"

*

"Oh shit, we are so screwed!" Aimee said as the police car pulled up alongside them.

"What do we do?" Mary asked.

156

Jimmy looked to his left and saw the officer motioning for him to pull over.

"That cop's aura just turned black!" Mary shouted. "If we stop we're dead."

Jimmy jammed on the brakes and the police officer, not expecting the move was caught unawares. As the police car barreled forward, Jimmy jerked the wheel to the left, cutting off a pick-up truck that swerved to avoid them. Jimmy jumped the curb and floored it down the ramp to the highway. The pick-up couldn't stop in time and back-ended the police car.

The police officer jumped from the vehicle, drew his pistol and took aim at the Mustang.

Fortunately, a large van started down the ramp behind them, blocking the patrolman's view

As the officer holstered his pistol and the Mustang went under an overpass, they let out a collective sigh.

"Talk about dodging a bullet," Jimmy said, easing off the gas.

Mary took a handkerchief from her pocket and wiped the sweat from her hands. "This is way too risky," she said, stuffing the handkerchief back into her purse. "We can't be tooling around when every cop in the county is either a push-in or a regular who has been instructed to bring me in at any cost."

"So what do we do?" Jimmy asked, rubbing his stomach. His ulcer was biting at him, so he reached into his pocket, pulled out a small pack of antacid tablets and popped one into his mouth.

"First, let's get off this highway," Mary said. "The cops will be trolling the main roads, so let's take the back roads to the Blue Barn."

"But we haven't grabbed a push-in yet," Aimee said

"I know," Mary replied, "but I'm sure that cop called the others and told them I was in this car, but if we go back to the Barn I can ask Santiago and Martaine to let us borrow the Impala while I lay low and look for push-ins from the back seat. Plus, considering the circumstances, I think any push-in would think twice before stopping two clergymen."

That made sense to Jimmy, so he exited the highway and drove toward the countryside. He was no more than a few blocks away when they all heard the screaming of sirens as patrol cars raced down the highway. Fortunately, the police continued on past the exit.

"We are playing this way too close," Mary said nervously.

*

Although still early afternoon, the inside of the Blue Barn was almost pitch black. With a fully lit pack of matches lighting the way, Virgil cautiously led Santiago and Martaine over the dirt floor to one of the gas-powered generators. Since they had all been emptied, Martaine showed Virgil where they hid the siphoned gas and they quickly refueled them. Virgil started the engine.

Other than the engine running, nothing else happened.

"What did you lunkheads do, disconnect everything?" Virgil asked as he searched for the connector cables.

"Well," Martaine replied as he folded his arms and leaned against one of the computer tables. "Perhaps we were a little overzealous in packing things away. Probably would have been unnecessary had not some..." he paused, placing his hand to his chin, "Now how did he describe himself? Oh yes, some 'freaking genius' put us all in peril."

Virgil opened a box, found the cables and pulled them out. "Cute!" he sneered.

A half- hour later with all three men working together, the lights were on, the computers up and splice reattached. Virgil hit the switch and the Tesla coil began to hum.

As the clergymen continued connecting the cables, Virgil sat down at his computer, booted it up and began rewriting the software. He had a fairly good idea on how to reverse the process, but was still feeling an ominous chill from what Santiago had said earlier. He was not a religious man, but having scientifically proven there was life after death, the possibility of these 'daemons' really existing now seemed plausible.

As he typed, he reassessed his situation. He had stormed over to McCracken's to see if he knew where Mary was; now he found himself shanghaied in this Holy War or crusade or whatever it was.

They said if the daemons come though, I'll be their first victim.

As the computers reconfigured the data, Virgil nervously rubbed his hands.

They said they don't care about the 500, but I do! As long as the bad guys are on this side, they are going to try to kill me and destroy the machine!

Virgil then considered the possibility that Santiago and Martaine might be planning to do the same but for a completely different reason.

I wouldn't put it past them. Religious zealotry is the most dangerous form of crazy.

He eyed the clergymen who were pumping the gasses out of the ectoplasmic chamber.

I gotta get out of this mess.

Almost as if reading his mind, Santiago lifted the containers, approached and placed them down at Virgil's feet. "The chamber has been drained as requested," he said, swiping his forearm across his brow.

"Good," Virgil replied, "but I think I may have to get some extra equipment."

"No problem. I'm sure Brother Martaine will be glad to accompany you."

Virgil shook his head. "I don't need a baby sitt…"

"Mr. Vanderhill," Santiago said sharply. "If I were you and possessed your startling lack of concern for anyone other than myself, I would, at this very minute, be searching for a way out of here. But, being a 'freakin' genius,' I would remind myself that my two companions have extensive experience dealing with daemons and would know how to ward off an attempted possession by an outside spirit. Whereas I, not possessing those skills, would succumb almost immediately, regardless of where I attempted to hide."

Virgil's expression revealed his utter contempt. "But as holy rolling, do-gooding, self-righteous pains in the asses, you would

159

use all the weapons in your holy arsenal to free me from its evil clutches, right?"

Martaine smirked as he approached and placed his canisters alongside the others. "We're servants of God, not idiots," he said with a chuckle. "If a daemon took possession of your body, I would snap your neck like a Thanksgiving wishbone."

Virgil eyed them both and grinned. "Oh, you're so full of it. You couldn't kill me even if I was possessed. That would be breaking one of the commandments, one of the Thou Shall Nots."

"True," Brother Martaine said as he stepped up alongside Santiago. "Fortunately for me, my good friend, Hector, is a priest." He turned. "Father, if I gave you my confession after snapping this 'freakin' genius's puny little neck, would you grant me absolution?"

Santiago took on a pensive expression and folded his arms. "Hmmm, well," he said stroking his chin. "I suppose, but the penance would be considerable. At least 500 Our Fathers and 200 Hail Mary's."

Martaine thought for a moment then stuck out his hand. "It's a deal!"

Virgil returned to his keyboard. "You guys suck! And about your snotty references about me being a freakin' genius? Well, get your apologies ready gentlemen, because I just figured out a way to reverse the process."

"Bah!" Martaine said with a dismissive wave of his hand. "More lies. I'll tell you what, you egotistical windbag, If you actually succeed, I will personally, in front of the others, acknowledge that you, Virgil Vanderhill, are the freakin' genius you claim to be."

Virgil smirked. "Yeah well, start loosening up those vocal chords, chubby, because after we make a quick visit to the electronics store, the spotlight's going to be on you."

Chapter Thirty One

"This is where you say she ran off to?" Paw said as he looked over the Dohesley area and the building the twins had set fire to. He rubbed his nose in response to the smell of burnt wood.

"That's right Paw," Tee said. "She got into your sour mash and went all crazy. We locked her in her room but she busted out this morning while we was choppin' wood. We followed her here and saw her drive off in some blue car."

Paw turned and stared hard. His eyes were blood red and swollen. The purple capillaries in his nose stood out like a road map and the headache that accompanied it could drop a rhinoceros. When he got his hands on Sula, he promised himself, she was gonna rue the day she was born.

"Where'd she get a car?" he asked, eyeing both boys suspiciously. "And how did she drive it when she ain't got no license?"

"Derned if I know, Paw. I just know what we saw," Coffee replied.

"If'n you boys are lyin' to me…"

Both boys stood fast and shook their heads.

Paw rubbed his stubble and studied the road. "Hmmm. You think maybe she got herself a fella? Maybe one that owns a car?"

"Sounds right to me, Paw," Coffee said.

"Me too," Tee echoed.

Both hoped Paw wouldn't ask any other questions. They had seen what happened, saw Sula get blown out of the window, onto the porch roof, then onto the garage just as the house collapsed. Watched as she hobbled back to the flaming structure and screamed at the sky when the second girl didn't come out.

They ran home expecting Sula to follow.

But she hadn't.

Come daybreak, they rushed back to the burned down remains just in time to see Sula climb into the blue convertible and drive off. They went back home and when the old man finally woke up, told him their version of what happened. They knew it would be a hard sell, particularly since Sula hated the smell of sour mash, but with her gone, it was their word against...nobody's.

"Paw, why don't you go on back to the house and have some breakfast while Coffee and me look around. See if we can find some clue to where she was headin.''

Paw winced and rubbed the side of his head. "She's probably somewhere sleepin' it off. All right," he said, taking one last long look at the area. "You scout around, but do it from the road. This area is filled with poison. Can't have you two getting sick, ya hear?"

The boys nodded

"And another thing," Paw said. "Don't come home without her." With that he lumbered off.

Both boys sighed with relief but that was only the first hurtle. Now they had to find Sula and that car at all costs. Finding a single blue convertible in all of Wheatfield, not easy, but they had a clue: A license plate that read AIM E GRL

They set out.

*

"Will you stop following so closely!?" Virgil barked at Martaine as they trudged over the brush toward the Blue Barn. They had just completed their trip to the electronics store and Martaine was loaded down with an armful of their purchases. The trek was considerable as they had parked the car in the high weeds to avoid detection.

"If you wanted to lug all these items yourself you should have said something," Martaine replied as he hefted the boxes of neon tubing, switches, antennae, cables, video cameras and various related supplies.

"That's not the point!" Virgil spat. "If you tripped and fell on me, you'd have to scrape me off the ground with a spatula!"

Martaine chuckled as Virgil opened the white door and the two stepped in. "I just want to be ready should one of the daemons come through." He crouched down and placed the items on the dirt floor, then stood, laced his fingers, extended his arms and cracked his knuckles.

Martaine leaned in and eyed Virgil closely. "Do you feel any evil trying to sneak in?" he asked, extending his hands toward Virgil's neck. "Because, if so, I'm ready…"

"Ha-ha, very funny," Virgil said dryly as he pulled out his notepad and checked off the items from his list.

As Santiago joined them, Virgil got down on one knee and started opening the boxes. "We'll only need about twenty minutes to get everything up and running," he told the clergymen. "When we do, call McCracken, find out if they grabbed a push-in and tell him we're ready."

*

As Jimmy drove the Mustang through the dirt roads that ambled through the high corn stalks and wheat fields on the outskirts of Swinton Mountain, Mary's breath hitched in her throat as she stared out the window.

They were there, all along the road: daemons.

She could taste the bile rising in her throat and suppressed a scream, although the sight of them ran terror through her like a high-voltage current. Her only advantage was they no longer had the element of surprise.

Their faces and bodies were continuously morphing in and out of what appeared to be a silky black liquid, as if struggling to create a form that could penetrate the thinning barrier between the two worlds. Red eyes bulged from dark sockets, spiky bones poked out through skin and raked the barrier; some had huge mouths without lips, others hulking muscular torsos atop strands of probing tentacles; others had teeth like railroad spikes which gnawed at the divider. All were constantly changing.

Mary began rubbing her arms as if bugs were alighting on them. She desperately clung to the one thing that prevented her from succumbing to blind terror; they were still on the other side!

The daemons were close, very close, but not in this world yet. She comforted herself with the knowledge that they could look, but couldn't touch.

Also unsettling was the fact that, since daybreak, the sky had been losing its aquamarine hue and taken on a shimmering red-orange color, as if reflecting a massive forest fire miles in the distance. Mary took another deep breath, cursed her psychic ability and looked away.

Aimee had her head buried in the road map she had taken from the glove compartment and was giving Jimmy directions. Her father had placed it there (as well as an emergency kit in the trunk) because the farm service roads in and around Wheatfield, St. Lawrenceville and Swinton Mountain were a virtual maze.

Mary had nearly regained her composure when one of the daemons pressed its face through the closed rear window and came nose to nose with her.

It eyed her and the more she trembled, the more it seemed to enjoy it. It tried to touch her, but couldn't make physical contact, which at first confused, then infuriated it. Mary pressed her back into the seat and closed her eyes, trying to calm her breathing, blocking out the horrors visible only to her.

Five minutes later, the legions of daemons were left in the distance and Mary's ordeal was over, at least for now.

"Aimee," Jimmy said, "I think we made a wrong turn somewhere. We're supposed to be heading west but according to the sun we're heading southeast."

Aimee studied the map. "I think you're right. Stop the car for a minute. I'll get out on the hood and see if I can spot anything we can use as a point of reference."

Jimmy nodded and slowed the Mustang to a stop. "Well, here we are!" Jimmy said as he shut off the engine. "Smack dab in the middle of nowhere."

"This will only take a minute," Aimee said as she opened the door and stepped outside. As she climbed on the hood, Mary and Jess stepped out too. "Just need a little air," Mary commented.

Aimee lowered the map, climbed down and looked around. "I... I know this place," she said. "It wasn't too far from here when I woke up in Sula's body."

Jimmy also stepped out, and seeing a pale and shaken Mary, went over and took her arm. "You all right?

She wrapped a frightened hand over Jimmy wrist. "The daemons are closer than ever. I saw them back there along the road."

Jimmy scanned the hills and dirt roads.

Mary looked around. "They're still back there. And..." she pointed upward, "doesn't that seem odd to you? I've never seen a sky like that in my life."

Jimmy looked but decided to downplay it, their situation was difficult enough. "Yeah, it is kind of weird," he replied with a shrug.

"Well the good news is I know where we are," Aimee said. "See that ridge over there? That's Lavender Hill and right behind it is the Blue Barn."

Okay, good," Jimmy said, reaching for his cell. "Let's see how Virgil's doing."

A moment later, Jimmy ended the call. "Virgil said another ten minutes or so but it won't make any difference if we don't have a push-in to test it. Also he needs Santiago and Martaine to lug the heavy equipment. "So," he said, slipping the phone into his pocket. "What's do we do now?"

Jess replied. "We don't do nothing till we swap the cars, can't take a chance on the cops grabbing Mary. Besides, I can drive the Impala. We don't need the clergymen to..."

Aimee suddenly looked up. "Wait. Do you hear that?"

They stopped and a moment later, they did. They scouted the area trying to figure what it was and where it was coming from when a black twin-blade helicopter appeared from behind the hillside and raced toward them.

"Oh this ain't good," Jimmy said, backing up toward the car.

"Let's get the hell out of here, people!" Mary shouted

They jumped into the Mustang and sped off.

165

The copter quickly caught up and took position directly overhead.

"This is the FBI," came the voice from the copter's loudspeaker. **"Stop your vehicle and step out with your hands up!"**

The chopper dropped down and was flying almost alongside.

The wind from the rotors raised dust all around, its low-base thumping sound was deafening.

Aimee bit her lip and yelled to Jimmy. "What do we do now?"

Jimmy reached into his pocket and pulled out his cell phone. Just as he was about to tap the keys, two police cruisers appeared from behind and joined the chase. He hit redial and tossed the phone to Aimee.

*

"Shit, they're heading toward the Blue Barn," the FBI agent in the helicopter spat in frustration. He called the police cruisers. "Can you catch up before they reach Dohesley?"

"I don't think so!" came the reply. "We keep bottoming out on the furrows. And there're tarped mountains of cow manure everywhere. Can you force them to a regular road?"

"No, not with all these hills, look, I'm going to try and shoot the driver, so fall back a bit!"

The helicopter pilot turned. "What did you just say?"

"Just keep us alongside that Mustang," he shouted back, then removed his pistol and approached the door of the chopper. "Hold her steady until I can get off a couple of rounds."

"What?!" the chopper pilot shouted. "What are you doing? Get back in your seat and buckle up!"

*

It was Jess who saw the helicopter's door suddenly open and a man take careful aim.

"Look out!" Jess bellowed, pointing toward the chopper.

166

Jimmy saw the man in the doorway raising a pistol. Remembering a trick he'd seen a stuntman use on TV, he pulled the parking brake and spun the wheel. The helicopter quickly sped ahead and a huge dust cloud formed from the skidding tires.

Now pointing northeast Jimmy released the brake, floored it and, amid the smoke and dust, tried to figure out a way to lose his pursuers.

"Virgil says he needs a couple more minutes," Aimee said holding the cell.

"Tell him we don't have a couple of minutes!"

As Aimee relayed the message, the helicopter reappeared directly in front of them and two shots rang out. The first struck the ground directly in front of the Mustang; the second struck the convertible top, punching a hole through it and the floorboard, barely missing Mary.

Mary screamed and before Jimmy could react, the chopper suddenly veered sideways and pulled out of range. They heard another report but whatever the bullet struck, it wasn't anywhere near them.

*

"What the hell are you doing?!" the FBI agent screamed. "I had them directly in my sights!"

The chopper pilot turned. "Firing on a moving vehicle without provocation is a direct violation of federal law."

The agent turned the gun on the pilot. "You turn this damn thing around or I'll…"

The pilot yanked the joystick and the chopper wildly jerked from side to side sending the agent slamming against the walls. Without a seat belt, he was quickly battered into unconsciousness. After momentarily switching to auto pilot, the pilot grabbed the agent's pistol and headed back to base.

*

167

Although Jimmy and company breathed a sigh of relief when the chopper disappeared into the distance, the police cruisers doggedly followed.

Jimmy continued to fishtail the Mustang leaving a huge plume of dust and dirt in its wake. And with 12-foot high tarped mounds of cow manure dotting the fields, the police didn't dare race in blind for fear of plowing into one.

Jimmy sped across the asphalt covered Route 727 and into Dohesley township. Fortunately, the KEEP OUT signs, scattered trees and bushes made it difficult for the police to get a clear shot, but when Jimmy slid the Mustang to a stop in front of the white door of the Blue Barn and they all charged into the building, the police opened fire. Wood chips and splinters flew from the structure but luckily no one was hit.

The two police cruisers pulled up alongside the Blue Barn.

"Okay, they're trapped inside," Officer Van Pelt said as he stepped from the vehicle. "Dunne, go around the back. Warring…"

Two shots rang out barely missing the police cruisers. Several more followed and as the volley drew closer; all three officers dove inside the white door for cover.

Chapter Thirty Two

While out on patrol, Officer Pastore's cell phone rang. He reached into his pocket, pulled it out and read the caller ID. It was Van Pelt. He showed it to his partner Rodriguez who shrugged. "Maybe he's got good news."

He tapped the screen. "This is Pastore."

"Hey, chickenshit!" Van Pelt said jokingly. "You two feel like making an easy couple grand?"

"Hey, I never turn down easy money," Pastore replied. "What's the deal?"

"Well, me, and two of our friends from last night decided to take care of the Blue Barn and when we got there we ran into one of our other buddies. Turns out, the equipment inside is very valuable. So we worked out a deal on a first come first served basis. The white door is open. You walk in, grab some equipment and take off. This way none of us knows who got what or who sold what to who. The machine get scattered across the country, our problem is solved and we each walk away with a little extra dough."

Pastore considered the offer. A couple grand would come in handy since he had no intention of remaining a cop. Still..."

"Are you sure the machine is shut down? The door is open. Anybody could..."

"Oh cut it out, you whiny pussy!" Van Pelt said. "If you don't want to go, then don't. I'm just trying to solve the Barn problem and give our people a little taste at the same time."

"Ahhh, you're right. I don't know what..." Pastore began.

Van Pelt cut him off. "Look, I don't care," he said. "I got mine and I'm calling the rest of the crew to give them a heads up. In or out, don't matter to me. Now, did you take care of Virgil?"

Pastore replied. "No, we checked his house and he wasn't there."

"Well, with a little luck maybe he'll do himself in and save us the trouble," Van Pelt replied and hung up.

*

"Say it!" Virgil demanded. "I want to hear you say it!"

Martaine gritted his teeth and had his fists clenched at his side. His face was red and the clergyman would have clearly preferred a firing squad rather than comply. Still, pride goeth before a haughty spirit, so Martaine reluctantly swallowed his and said, "I, Brother Silvio Martaine do hereby affirm that the Virgil Vanderhill is indeed a freaking genius."

"Damn right I am!" Virgil said swaggering before those in attendance which now included Jimmy, Aimee, Mary, Jess, and the real officers Van Pelt, Warring, and Dunne.

They were all standing on the second floor of the barn having transferred all essential equipment to that level. First, to avoid being seen and second it gave them the opportunity to see who was approaching from the vent in the front.

"I'll say it too," Jimmy offered. "That was clever as hell, Virgil, using the white door's frame as the conduit. How were you able to do it so quickly?"

"Easy," Virgil began as he sat down behind the computers, crossed his legs, laced his fingers and laid them on his stomach. "Once I realized what the machine was doing, all I needed was to reverse the process. But since none of the bad guys would willingly give their stolen bodies back, I had to trick them. So I transferred the ectoplasmic gasses from the chamber to the neon tubing I installed on the inside of the door frame. It's a simple process really. By having the computer match the body entering through the white door with its original signal, the transfer is virtually instantaneous. By the time the bad guys realized what's happened, it's over."

Van Pelt turned to Jimmy with a look of begrudging respect and said. "You took a big chance firing at the push-ins to drive them through the white door. All Wheatfield police cruisers carry high powered rifles in their trunks. If they pulled them on you, well, we wouldn't be talking now."

Jimmy removed the snub nose from his jacket and poured the empty casings to the dirt floor. "It's not like I had a choice," he replied as he reloaded. "I knew the push-ins intended to kill us, so

170

my only option was to force them through the door where Santiago and Martaine could ambush them and force them back where they belonged."

The officer nodded then asked. "But can you trick all 500 into walking through that door?"

"And can you do it before the daemons get through?" Mary asked.

"Knock it off," Virgil said. "Let me enjoy my triumph for a minute or two."

Jimmy eyed him sideways. "She's got a valid point."

"Wait a minute, asshole!" Aimee shouted. "Because of you and this stupid machine, my real body got crushed. So instead of me going to Vassar this fall, I'm stuck in the body of some hillbilly chick who has a bunch of violent inbred relatives looking to drag her, meaning me, back to some ramshackle hellhole."

Virgil casually dismissed her complaint. "Well, being alive certainly beats being dead, doesn't it?" He grinned as if he made some amazingly clever remark.

Aimee grabbed a pry bar from the top of the utility chest. "Interesting theory, this dead versus being alive thing," she said as she raised it and approached Virgil. "Let's put it to the test!"

She had taken only two steps when Brother Martaine gently disarmed the young hothead.

"Not that I don't wholeheartedly support your plan," he said in a low voice, "but we may need this 'freaking genius's expertise later. However, should that not be the case, I'll leave this right here on the cabinet for easy access."

"What we really need is a fail-safe," Santiago said, taking center stage and addressing the others. "Should the daemons find a way to start breaking through, we'll need a device that will destroy the machine and abort the process."

Hearing this, Van Pelt immediately spun toward him. "Wait one damn minute! We're not destroying anything until all 500 are back."

With knitted brows, and an expression that made it clear this position was not negotiable, he stepped up to the clergyman.

171

"Daemons or not, I'm not going to abandon 500 of my fellow human beings to that horrific dark existence. These are my brother and sister police officers, firemen, EMS, technicians, as well as everyday hard working people. If the daemons break though we'll find some way to deal with them but all 500 are to be returned, end of discussion!"

With his lips pressed together into a thin gash, Santiago replied. "You need to listen carefully," he said matching the police officer's no-nonsense tone. "You're talking like there is a choice." He stepped in closer, so they were nearly nose to nose. "There is no choice! I don't want to sacrifice 500 lives any more than you do, but 500 is miniscule compared to the hundreds of millions who will be tortured and killed should the daemons make their way into our world. Whatever concept you have of these creatures from Sunday school, or the History Channel or whatever, is dead wrong. These are not criminals, they are not humans. They are biblical abominations, and for want of a better description, evil incarnate. They are superhuman, nearly indestructible and committed to the torture and evisceration of all mankind."

Van Pelt stood his ground. "Yeah, and how do you know all this?" he asked in a sarcastic tone. "I spent time in that hell hole and I never saw any of these so-called daemons. Frankly padre, I think these daemon nonsense is just so much mumbo jumbo, cooked up to scare half-wits into giving money to your church."

"Mumbo jumbo?! Believe me, officer, I've *seen* them, and have spent the better part of my life traveling the world to confront and destroy them. And for you to simply dismiss their existence because of that small amount of time you spent in Limbo, indicates not only a lack of knowledge but a lack of intelligence! And another thing…"

"Whoa! Whoa! Whoa!" Jimmy said, stepping in-between. "I'm all for voicing an opinion, but you guys need to cool down. Apparently we need a third option. So," Jimmy said, motioning toward the door, "it's time for the officers, clergymen and all nonessential personnel to leave so the psychics and the scientist can figure out a way to bring home our friends while keeping the daemons in their own back yard."

172

"I'm not going anywhere until this thing…" Van Pelt began.

He was interrupted by Officer Dunne. "Bertram," he said taking Van Pelt to the side, "we're still on duty and because those idiots who took over our bodies didn't sign out at end of shift, we still have to file that report on what happened that night. We're looking at possible disciplinary proceedings as it is, so we've got to get back out on patrol and keep a low profile until this all blows over."

Officer Warring agreed with Dunne. "Yeah, 'cause if we get suspended we won't be able to help anybody. Besides, what can *we* do here? We'd be far more effective convincing the guys we know are push-ins into coming here and getting sent back than arguing over what *might* happen."

Van Pelt was seething, but capitulated, and the two clergymen, seeing the logic of Jimmy's earlier proposal, also prepared to leave.

Impatient, Virgil stood up, clapped his hands several times and then motioning as if shooing chickens said, "C'mon, hit the road, I have work to do."

As they began to file out, Martaine looked back at Virgil and said to Santiago, "Why is it our Lord so often blesses the least competent with the most talent?"

"I do not know, my friend," he replied, then glanced at Van Pelt, "Nor do I know why he often places great authority in the care of small minds."

*

While Virgil adjusted the now idle machine to increase its processing speed, Jimmy stepped outside to smoke a joint. Minutes later, suddenly feeling anxious and edgy, Mary followed.

She was still wearing the thigh-length white parka with the big square pockets from the other night. She stuck her hands inside them, smiled at Jimmy, leaned against the barn door and asked, "You're out here because you feel it too, don't you?"

The wind whipped through her long silver hair. She pulled her coat tight.

173

He stared out over the fields as he took a hit. "I'm not the right guy for this job," he said. "The He-men should be handling this. You know, Santiago and Van Pelt. If the testosterone got any thicker…"

Mary shook her head. "That is precisely why they shouldn't be in charge. Alpha males always vie for dominance regardless of consequences. Hell, we'd be up to our asses in daemons before either one of them would admit they made a mistake. No, you're the one who has to run this show and don't let anyone tell you different."

Jimmy paused. "I don't know." He took another long pull on the joint and stared off into the distance. The wind picked up and emitted a low howl as it raced through the crooked trees.

Mary took Jimmy's arm. "Listen, people's vibes are easiest to feel during times of trouble. And back there, I felt nothing but an our-cocks-are-bigger-than-your-cocks contest without any regard to the danger. It was more important to Van Pelt and Santiago to win the argument than address the problem. In fact, to them, addressing the problem would be a sign of weakness."

Jimmy giggled. "You said 'cocks.'"

Mary rolled her eyes, took the joint and said, "You've had enough." She took a hit as Jimmy watched in wide-eyed surprise.

She continued to smoke until the joint was officially done. "Whoa," she said, blinking her eyes several times. "This shit is a lot more powerful than it was in my day."

Mary, now equally high, glanced at Jimmy and said, "Don't give me that look."

"I'm not giving you a look."

She smirked. "Oh yes you are! I've seen it before. That look that says, 'but my grandma never smoked pot,' my grandma was a sweet old lady who was always nice and baked cookies and disapproved of scantily clad young women… Well," she continued, "I'm not your sweet, cookie baking grandma. I'm a sixty-seven year old woman who drank hard liquor at biker bars, smoked pot at music festivals, snorted coke at Hollywood parties and fucked and sucked whatever man caught my fancy and sometimes, more than one."

"Whoa," Jimmy replied from behind bloodshot eyes.

"And as for me saying 'cocks', just so you know, I was referring to this," she said as she reached over and placed her hand on his crotch.

Having stunned Jimmy into silence, Mary removed her hand and placed both behind her as she settled back against the barn door.

"Now back to my original question," she said. "You came out here because you felt it too, didn't you?"

It took several moments before Jimmy answered and when he did, his face tightened and his hands trembled. "I feel like I'm being dangled over the edge of a volcano. I can't see them, but I feel their presence. They're getting closer."

He bowed his head. "I just want to go home."

"Jimmy, listen to me…" she began.

"No, maybe it's time you listened," he snapped, his face as tense as a cornered animal. "You think all I have to do is muster up my courage, march stoically into the breach, and be the hero that Van Pelt and Santiago can't be You know, do what a man's gotta do.

"I've spent most of my life buying into that crap, facing my fears and all that rah-rah shit. All I got for my effort was duodenal ulcers, high blood pressure, OCD and chronic anxiety. I might look like a typical twenty-three-year old, healthy, strong and ready for action, but inside I'm on life support. Your ability lets you track the spirits of the dead; my ability lets them track me! And all I get are people crying in torment, begging for favors, offering access to any pleasure I want, threatening when I don't help, and taking form during my most private moments."

"Taking form?" Mary asked curiously.

Jimmy began pacing. "Imagine being in the shower, and suddenly finding an eighty-five-year-old man standing next to you begging for help. Or having sex and a group of people only you can see, lines up and watches. Imagine looking out over the top of a tall building only to turn and see someone charging at you with arms extended. As your heart jumps into your mouth, that

175

someone runs right through you and disappears into thin air. That shit happens to me all the time, even though I never talk to them."

Mary's put her hand to her mouth. "I'm sorry. I had no idea."

He gave a sardonic laugh then slipped his hands into his dungaree jacket. "Let's make a deal," he said solemnly. "I'll stop thinking of you as my sweet old grandma and accept you as the worldly woman you really are if you stop thinking of me as a gutsy young hero ready to take on the world. See me as I am: a mentally damaged person twisting in a psychological wheelchair with a gun to my head praying for the courage to pull the trigger."

Jimmy didn't wait for Mary to comment. He turned, walked over to the white door, opened it and went inside.

"Hey, McCracken," Virgil said, elbow deep in wires and processors as Jimmy reentered. "Can you give us a hand here or are you too fucked up on the wacky weed?"

"Blow me, Vanderhill," Jimmy replied and walked into the portable toilet.

Mary overheard Virgil's request as she stepped in. "I can take care of it," she called to him. "What do you need done?"

Virgil pointed to the white door. "There's a series of small lights behind the frame. Let me know when they go on."

Mary nodded. As she walked back to the frame, she passed Jess who looked her over and said, "Wow, why are your eyes so bloodshot?"

Mary stopped and said, "I had to finish Jimmy's joint so he wouldn't get too high."

"How thoughtful of you," Jess commented with a smile.

As Mary reached the frame and inspected the lights, she was close enough to the portable toilet to hear Jimmy vomiting inside.

Fucking fairy! He'll probably shit his pants if we have to confront any real daemons. Shit, Aimee has more balls than that whiney cunt.

Mary stopped, astonished at her sudden insensitivity and lack of compassion.

I don't talk like that! I don't even think like that!

176

What surprised her even more was she enjoyed it. Enjoyed mocking Jimmy's fragility; enjoyed referring to him as a whiney cunt.

She snapped out of it when the series of lights blinked on one by one. Once completed, she called out, "They're all lit!"

"Great," Virgil said as he closed the lid on one of the laptops. "All finished."

As Jimmy exited the bathroom, Mary called for all to gather around. As they approached, she said, "I don't know if it's the toxicity of Dohesley or the proximity of the daemons, but I'm beginning to feel its effects."

Virgil started down the stairs "What's the problem?"

"As this group's canary in a coal mine, you should all know I'm getting increasingly strong feelings of hostility and with each burst of anger, I get an endorphin rush. Which is dangerous because…"

"Because like Pavlov's dog, you will begin to associate hostility with reward," Virgil said. He looked over at Jimmy. "How about you, McCracken? You feeling the same vibe?"

Jimmy didn't, but said he did, not wanting to complicate the issue.

"Very well then," Virgil said taking a seat on the bottom of the stairs. "This is something I'm going to have to address quickly. As a scientist, I have the mental discipline to control my emotions and keep myself in check but as for the rest of you…"

Jess, with her index finger wagging, stormed over and said, "You talk to us like that one more time and I will rip out that flappin' condescending tongue of yours and beat you senseless with it!"

"Easy, easy!" Virgil said, leaning back and raising his hands. "I didn't mean anything personal. But you're obviously feeling the hostility, too. How about you, kid?" he asked addressing Aimee. "You feel anything?"

Aimee took a moment, then replied. "Not as far as I can tell."

Virgil nodded. "That's probably because you're new to this area and because you're younger and stronger." He momentarily studied the floor then said. "Okay, Mary, Jess and McCracken, you

177

hit the road. Get some sleep. Come back when you feel better. Me and the kid will hold down the fort."

Jimmy eyed Virgil with some concern and stepped up to the staircase. "I don't like that idea. You've been working in here longer than any of us, and you're fifteen years older than me. Maybe me and Aimee should stay?"

"And what if something goes wrong with the machine, huh?" Virgil asked, motioning to the equipment. "What are you going to do then?"

Without waiting for an answer, Virgil waved his hand, "No, it's got to be me and the kid. She says she's fine so it's settled. Keep your cell phones on. If we run into trouble, we'll call. Besides Van Pelt and the others will be sending more of their buddies through the door, so if we need help, we'll ask them to stick around."

Something about that plan felt wrong, but Jimmy was too exhausted to argue. Mary didn't like it either, but with her growing hostility, getting away from the area was becoming a necessity.

As they prepared to leave, Aimee walked over to Jess who was putting on her coat. "Here are the keys to my car," she said, holding them out to her. "You're not too tired to drive are you?"

Jess reached over and folded Aimee's hand over the keys, "Oh, honey I'm just fine. Those few hours at Jimmy's place were all I needed. Besides, we called a cab. You guys will need that car if something goes wrong."

Aimee nodded, slipped the keys back in her pocket, then stepped up and in a low voice said, "But what about the anger? Will you be able to keep it under control? You did slam Virgil pretty hard."

Jess' eyes lit up and she had to cover her mouth to keep from laughing. "Honey," she said biting the inside of her lip, "that had nothing to do with this place. I've been waiting to chew out that windbag for a while now!"

Aimee chuckled and patted Jess on the arm.

Minutes later, Jimmy, Jess and Mary walked out to Route 727, soon after, the cab arrived and they were on their way.

Chapter Thirty Three

Although Virgil hadn't mentioned it, he had been awake as long as Jimmy and now, with the excitement over and with everyone but Aimee gone, the need for sleep hit him hard.

He was sitting alongside Aimee at the consol stifling a yawn. "Just keep your eye on those two computers," he said, pointing to the control panel. "They both read the data coming from the white door sensors. If more of the 500 push-ins show up, and I'm pretty sure they will, the first monitor will read the subject then send the data to the second which will initiate the transfer."

"What if something goes wrong?" Aimee asked.

He tilted his head to the corner where he had piled several canvas mats. "I'll be resting right over there. If you even *suspect* a problem, let me know. Got it?"

She nodded. "Got it."

He got up, shuffled over to the bedding and dropped down into it. "Don't be nervous; everything is preset. You don't have to do anything but stay awake, watch the monitors and make sure no one sneaks in. Do you think you can do that without screwing things up?"

"Yeah," she snarled, making it clear she didn't appreciate his condescending attitude.

He was about to lay down, but stopped, looked at her, sighed and said, "Look, kid…"

"The name's Aimee!"

He raised his hands, "Okay, okay!" he said. "Believe me, I'm not looking to piss you off. It's just that, well, I just wanted so say I'm sorry about what happened to you. I really am. Believe it or not, this whole…" he took a moment to search for the word, "*miserable* turn of events occurred because I just wanted somebody to talk to, somebody who liked me and would reassure me. I've been in a bad place for a very long time."

You've been in a bad place?! I'm in a different person's body, you insensitive wad!

But realizing he was trying to reach out, she pushed back her resentment and offered to listen. "Well, everybody needs a friend."

Virgil nodded. "But that's the point," he said wistfully as he bundled the canvases. "I never made any friends. I'm not exactly a social person." He shrugged. "I thought my mother was my friend, but she only used me, then abandoned me after I spent eleven years and every dime I had just to talk with her again. My wife took off. Says I'm self-absorbed, insensitive and too wrapped up in my work." He looked away and sighed. "Maybe she's right, but I find it so painful explaining to some fathead a basic concept that even a well trained dog could comprehend."

He then laid down on the stacked canvasses. In less than a minute, he was asleep.

Virgil was certainly right about more of the 500 push-ins showing up. Intrigued by Van Pelt's ruse of easy money, every 15 minutes or so, a car or van approached, studied the barn, then after determining it was safe, left their vehicle and slipped inside.

And not only was the ruse working, it was multiplying geometrically, because as each push-in was pushed out, the body's original owner called other push-ins touting the Blue Barn as a gold mine.

Halfway through the third hour, the entire police 4-to-midnight shift, nearly all the utility workers and a number of federal agents had been returned to their bodies.

At the fourth hour, Aimee heard the 'beep-beep-beep of a truck backing up. She ran over to the vent and saw a police paddy wagon with Van Pelt at the wheel.

After placing the rear of the vehicle near the white door, Van Pelt and three other officers opened it and waved to Aimee. Van Pelt said, "Just stopped by to drop off some push-ins and some coffee and donuts. Are all systems go?"

Aimee grinned, "All systems are go."

With that Van Pelt and his two associates opened the back door of the wagon.

"C'mon, let's go you body-snatching bastards," Van Pelt said as the three officers gathered the push-ins and one by one physically hurled them screaming and kicking through the white door.

There were fifteen in all and once the conversion was complete they jumped back into the paddy wagon. "We'll be back with more, later," Van Pelt called out as he and the others started back to town.

Aimee watched as they drove off but felt increasingly anxious when she noted that the sky was still a shimmering, blood- red crimson, even though it was well past midnight.

Hours later, seeing that a 17 year-old girl was running the operation by herself, two returned FBI agents, Dave Miller and Matthew Strom, joined Aimee upstairs on the oft chance that she might need protection. They sat on boxes at the vent, watching and making sure everyone who entered did not pose a threat.

The night continued to be very active and the hours passed quickly. All through the night cars pulled up, push-ins snuck in, and the machine returned them to the Void. Their victims, now back in their own bodies, often ran up the stairs and hugged Aimee before driving off and resuming their normal lives

Later that evening, agents Miller and Strom saw an attractive woman wearing tight slacks, a T-shirt and a leather jacket, park her car near the telephone pole on Route 727 and make a quick inspection of the area. She dashed toward the Blue Barn and when she reached the white door, she opened it a crack and peeked inside. Seeing all the laptop computers and high end electronic equipment, her eyes lit up and she slipped inside.

Following the transfer, the woman fell to her knees and began sobbing hysterically. "No! I don't want to live!" she wailed. "I don't want to live!"

Leaving his partner at the vent, Agent Dave Miller charged down the stairs and ran toward her. "Amanda? Amanda Bogdasian? It's me, Dave, the FBI guy. We spoke earlier this morning. When we were both back in…"

"Don't you understand?" she screeched. "I'm alone. That bastard… that filthy bastard!"

181

As she struggled to pull herself together, Agent Miller brought her a cup of coffee from the thermos left by Van Pelt and led her to the computer table in the back and out of sight from the doorway.

As they sat, Miller asked, "Who's this person you're referring to? Your husband?"

"No, not Steve," she replied in an emotionally choked voice. She took a sip. "He made everyone think Steve did it. But Steve was with me!" She began sobbing again.

She breathed deeply and forced herself to stop crying. "I'm going to tell you what happened so you can clear my husband's name."

She wiped the heels of her hands across tear-stained eyes.

"It started when me and Steve heard what sounded like gunshots and saw flashing lights in the reflection of our bedroom windows. As I went over, fireworks exploded across the sky.

I turned to Steve and asked what the celebration was all about."

He shrugged and suggested we go have a look since the fireworks were coming from Dohesley. And that was strange, because nobody is allowed inside that area."

"So we left the kids with our oldest, Theresa and drove down 727.

"We saw a group having a tailgate party on the side of the road, so Steve asked what the celebration was all about. The guy pointed to this barn and said, "Why don't you go have a look?"

"And that's when you and Steve were taken over by push-ins?" Miller asked.

"Yeah, we parked the car and were barely fifty feet into the Dohesley area when we suddenly found ourselves in that horrible place."

Miller pressed his hand on her shoulder. "Well, you're out of it now."

Her eyes welled up and she hurriedly wiped them.

"Yeah, but as we were sent there, a lunatic named Johnny Oswald and a grifter named Jennifer James came here.

Concern washed over Agent Miller's face. "Calling Johnny Oswald a lunatic is like calling the devil mean-spirited. Oswald

182

was the only pure psycho I have ever encountered and believe me; no one shed a tear when he was gunned down."

"That's sounds like him," Amanda said, pulling a handkerchief from her purse and dabbing her nose. "Anyway, we discovered that whenever the machine transferred people, we could see what the push-in was doing with your body."

"What did Oswald do?"

"He took our car and drove to Morales and Hart Construction Supply and Demolition, pulled into the parking lot, then ran into the building.

Miller said. "That's the place where Oswald was killed."

Morales was behind the counter when Oswald entered, headed down the first aisle, grabbed one of those carpet cutters and returned to the front. Morales had no idea he was in danger until Oswald came up behind him.

When Morales turned, Oswald held the canvas cutter to his throat, reached down, yanked open a drawer, pulled out a revolver and said, 'You don't get to pull that trick on me twice.'"

Miller nodded. "Yeah, Morales shot and killed him in the parking lot after Oswald shot Morales's cashier. What happened next?"

"He made Morales load a shopping cart with demolition supplies then shot Morales in the head. But that's when the machine shut down and Steve couldn't see what happened next. It wasn't until he…" She collapsed into sobs and it took nearly five minutes before she was able to speak again.

"Then… then Steve began to glow!" she said, still sobbing. "A crowd of glowing policemen appeared and just as quickly disappeared into the light."

"I asked Steve if he was all right. He pressed his lips together, and with an expression of pure sadness, pointed to my right and said, "Look."

"I did and saw Johnny Oswald appear. I turned back to Steve and said, 'He got you killed?!' And Steve nodded.

"I ran over to Oswald and screamed. 'You bastard! You got my husband killed?!'

183

"Then… then he… he smiled at me! This real smug grin, you know, then he said, "It couldn't be helped, cutie. But the good news is ol' Stevarino here is going to go down in history as one of the most famous murderers in history, so instead of giving me attitude I think you should be gratef…""

"He didn't get to finish because dozens of other victims, all of whom were as furious as me grabbed him and carried him toward the light.

When he saw what they were planning, he started kicking and struggling, but it didn't do him any good. They threw him in and he immediately disappeared.

Agent Miller nodded. "My grandfather used to say if you spend your life breaking the law, eventually, the law will break you. I'm glad he got what was coming to him."

Amanda began sobbing again. "But that's not all of it. I told Steve I couldn't imagine raising our girls without him. That I couldn't imagine Christmas, or birthdays or…

"That's when he stopped me, took my shoulders and brought me to arm's length. He looked so sad. I was about to tell him I felt the same way, when he said, "Amada, I'm so sorry."

He turned me around and there were, Theresa, Mandy, and Sophie, my three children, all glowing like their father.

"They ran to me and hugged me tightly. Theresa said, 'We didn't make any noise, Mom. Not a sound. After he locked us in the attic we held hands and quietly prayed that you wouldn't get hurt.'

Amanda shook her head and continued.

"As I wrapped my arms around them, Steve said he now had the memories of what Oswald did. He told me that after Oswald locked the girls in the attic, he filled the house with the dynamite he took from Morales' place then called the cops with Morales' cell and said he was our next door neighbor and that he saw Steve shoot me and herd our girls into the basement. So the police snuck in through our basement window and when they didn't find the girls they rushed up the stairs and into the living room where Oswald was sitting in the recliner, pointing a .45 revolver at his head. He told the cops that if they wanted to find the children alive,

184

everyone had to lower their guns to show good faith, then, eyeing them carefully, he slowly lowered his gun to his lap. He then let go of it and held out his hands

"The police cautiously lowered their weapons and crowded around him. Then Oswald said, 'I'm going to reach into my pocket and remove a single key.' But he didn't remove a key, he took out and pressed the detonator and blew up the house, the police and… and my husband and children."

"I'm so sorry, Mrs. Bogdasian." Agent Miller said.

"Thank you." She again wiped her eyes. "But it wouldn't have been so awful if it had been all of us together. I told the girls that it wasn't their fault and that we'd all walk into the light together. So I took my girls hands and started toward the light but they wouldn't move. I said, 'C'mon girls, there is no sense staying in this miserable place.' But then with tears rolling down their cheeks they shook their heads.

"I asked them why.

"Steve looked at me and said it wasn't my time.

"I freaked out and shouted, 'No! It's not right,' then spun around and marched into the center of the light…

"…and right out the other side. I was so upset but then Steve took me in his arms and the girls placed their arms around us. I told them I was going to stay there with them for as long as was allowed, but a short time later there was a flash and, well, here I am."

Ten minutes later Amanda Bogdasian left the barn with several returned federal officers.

Upstairs, Aimee remained quiet but had listened carefully, doing all she could to hold back her own tears. She knew Steven and Amanda and their children very well. She had been the Bogdasian's babysitter throughout high school.

185

Chapter Thirty Four

"This is a waste of time, Coffee," Tee said as they shuffled along Route 727. Cars and trucks raced by blowing gravel and dust. The sun was strong and both boys were sweaty, hungry and tired of walking. They had spent the night sleeping under an overpass and only had a couple of bucks between them.

"We've been out here for two days watching cars and not one of them was the one Sula took off in," Tee continued. "We need to go to the mall; I'll bet that's where she's hiding."

Coffee shook his head, opened a tin of chewing tobacco and stuffed a plug in his cheek. "Nope. She's holding out here in Dohesley."

But..." Tee began.

"Think about it," Coffee said as he offered his twin some chaw. Tee turned it down. "Sula got no money and her clothes are for shit. So why would she go to the mall when she knows all the other girls will make fun of her? No, Sula's betting we think she's dead. That why she hid out in Dohesley the other night instead of coming home. She figured we'd come back, see the house all burned up and reckon' she burned up with it."

"But she got a car," Tee protested. "She could be half way to California."

Coffee stopped for a moment, spit and nodded. "That's true, but Paw made it plain that we wasn't to come home without her, so we got to track her as best we can or he'll suspect something. Or even worse, imagine if'n she slips by us and tells Paw what really happened."

Tee paled. "What? That we drank Paw's liquor and tried to strip her bare?"

"No nitwit. That we set a fire and left her inside to die."

"But we didn't mean to, I was just looking to scare her, make her come out and let us see her naked."

Coffee pressed his hand against Tee's chest and shoved. "Don't lie, I'm your twin. I know what you was plannin'. Once she ran out you was gonna chase after her, knock her down, rip off her

186

clothes and fuck her. Fuck her hard. I know because that's what I was plannin to do."

Coffee ran his hand across his brow then raked it down the side of his face. He spit, then eyed his brother coldly. "And I also know what was gonna happen when we was finished."

Tee didn't protest or deny. He continued walking.

Coffee took his brother's shoulder and said, "And all that can still happen, 'cause everybody knows you don't go searching for bodies in Dohesley soil."

*

After leaving the barn, Santiago and Martaine returned to their apartment at St. Albert's and headed directly to their respective beds.

Back at Jimmy's place, Jimmy and Mary slept on the queen size as Jess occasionally dozed on the recliner with the TV's sound off and the closed captioning on.

Following nearly twelve solid hours of uninterrupted sleep, Jimmy was awakened by Ike, who was on the edge of the bed staring at him.

Jimmy turned, "For shit's sake!" he whispered firmly. "Will you stop doing that?"

The old man bowed his head. "Sorry, boy, but I just don't know any other way to keep your buddies out of it." He tilted his head toward the sleeping Mary. "But when we gets these small moments we's gots to make hay while the sun shines."

"All right, all right," Jimmy said, rubbing his eyes as he threw his legs over the side of the bed. Although it was midday, the closed blinds and curtains kept the room dark. "What's the big emergency this time?" he asked, padding to the bathroom. Still groggy, he didn't bother turning on the light or closing the door.

Ike followed Jimmy to the bathroom but stayed at the door frame. "They is certain rules I gotta follow. May not make all that much sense to you, but they gotta be followed nonetheless."

Jimmy began urinating, "What rules?"

187

"Well, for one," Ike replied, "it don't make no never mind that we talk, 'cause I'm not afeared of the light, so it's all right. But Virgil's been talking to his mother, and she's terrified of the light. And when those type people talk with the living, the daemons take notice, as you know yerself back when you was a boy."

"So you're saying should the daemons come through, Virgil's almost certain to be possessed." Finished, Jimmy flushed the toilet and went to wash his hands.

The old prospector shook his head. "No, I came to tell ya he's already possessed. He jus' don't know it yet."

*

"There's a black SUV parking outside," said Agent Dave Miller. "Looks like we're going to have a few more customers."

Aimee gave a casual nod from behind the control panel. Over the last twelve hours the sight of official vehicles pulling up and push-ins entering the barn in the hope of grabbing some hi-tech equipment was common, but now, as they entered their second day, she was eager for someone else to take over.

She considered waking Virgil but...

No.

After he explained the reasons behind the creation of his machine, Aimee didn't think he was all that stable. She wanted Jimmy.

But Jimmy was very likely still asleep.

She decided to give him another half hour, then call. Tell him she was done and needed him to take over.

"That's odd," Agent Miller remarked, studying the new arrivals through the slats of the vent.

"What's odd?" Aimee asked.

"Usually they park, take a quick run to the white door, see the equipment and slip right in. These guys... I don't know. I don't like it."

Both agents drew their guns.

"Wait, they're getting out now," Agent Miller said with a sigh of relief. "That's right, boys. Just come on over and everything will be all…Hold on! What is he pulling from the back seat?"

Aimee felt a sudden chill. Some primitive instinct was screaming for her to take cover. Without knowing why, she slipped out of her chair and slid under her desk.

"Holy shit, that's a rocket launcher!" Dave Miller shouted as both agents started firing through the aluminum vent.

"Shit! My gun jammed!" Miller said.

"Hit the deck!" Strom yelled.

The words had barely left his lips when the rocket stuck the barn and the lower level blew out in all directions. Aimee heard the roar as huge beams snapped, then felt the force of the explosion as it rocketed the desk and her to the other side of the barn. As the desk flipped, Aimee was flung into the air just as the floor dropped several feet. She managed to grab one of the satellite cables and used Sula's considerable upper body strength to slow her descent. She swung to the floor as flames seared her jacket and flying debris pelted her from all angles.

As she dove into an empty wooden crate for protection, she saw Virgil, seemingly unaffected by the blast, climb to his feet, pull his arms back then launch himself upward and through the roof as if propelled by a catapult. It was then the floor gave way and fell the remaining eight feet the ground.

Thirty seconds later, amid the smoke, ash, dust, dirt and a few small fires, she peeked out from the top of the battered crate. "Argggh!" she groaned and pulled her burgundy shirt tail up and placed it over her face. She gave herself the once over and saw that other than a few minor burns and bruises she was relatively unharmed.

Thanks for being in such good shape, Sula. I don't think I would have survived in my other body

As she climbed out and surveyed the damage, she saw her good fortune hadn't extended to her FBI companions. Both were dead. Dave Miller was crushed by the ectoplasmic chamber platform and Matthew Strom's neck was completely twisted around.

As the man from the black SUV opened the back door and placed the rocket launcher in, his partner congratulated him. "Excellent shot," he said as he eyed what remained of the barn through his binoculars. As he lowered them he added, "C'mon, let's get out of here before anyone shows up."

As he reached for the door handle, something vaulted toward them

.

*

"Shitfire, what was that?!" Tee exclaimed as he jumped, covered his ears and looked around. Surrounded by tall weeds and mountain terrain he wasn't sure where the sound was coming from.

"Look," Coffee replied, pointing to an emerging dark cloud in the distance. "It was another explosion. See the black smoke yonder?"

Tee lowered his hands and took a step back. "Yeah, I wonder what it was. Maybe we... Wait! You hear that? Sounds like screaming. C'mon," he said tugging his brother's arm. "Let's get out of here. They's probably gas pockets right under our feet. I'll bet that's what set off the house Sula was in."

Coffee pulled loose. "I ain't going nowhere until I see what exploded. For all we know Sula's behind it."

Tee's face scrunched up. "What? But that don't make no sense."

Coffee ignored him and set out toward the pluming smoke. Not comfortable being alone, Tee followed.

*

As Aimee took stock of her surroundings, she heard ear-piercing screams outside. Pleading, beseeching, begging, more screams. Dazed and in no condition to fight, she frantically sought another place to hide.

190

Burrowing deeper into what remained of the roof, she saw several match books scattered on the floor. She grabbed a handful, lit one pack, stuffed the rest into her miniskirt pocket and continued her search.

She came upon a secure fortress of overturned electronic cabinets and hid inside until the screams subsided.

As the minutes slowly passed, all remained quiet other than the occasional creak and snap of settling wood.

*

When Coffee and Tee turned the corner atop Lavender hill, the carnage below stunned them both.

"Thundernation!" Coffee said, using Paw's favorite expression. "Will ya look at that?"

Tee did and shook his head, awestruck. "That barn looks like someone lopped off someone's head and placed its hat on its shoulders."

The roof was nearly at ground level with the remains of the first and second floors spread out in an almost circular pattern beneath it. Tee gestured at the gaping hole in the roof. "Looks like sumthin shot through the top like a cannon ball!"

The boys edged down the hill, walked the perimeter and studied the debris. Unlike the building Sula hid in, this one hadn't succumbed to the flames. There were a few small fires that were, for the most part, concealed by a thick layer of oily smoke.

Coffee surveyed the area.

This don't make sense. According to Paw, Dohesley ain't had so much as a small wildfire since it was closed off forty years ago and now two explosions in two days?

He shook his head with an 'I ain't buyin' it' expression, then grabbed Tee and went to the front. He looked out over the highway and saw a black SUV with what appeared to be men's clothing lying on the hood.

He nudged his brother and pointed. "What in tarnation is that all about?"

Tee took a quick glance then turned away. "I don't know and I don't want to know," He had his shoulder raised in a defensive position and was ready to break into a dead run at the slightest provocation.

Coffee grabbed him and yanked him closer. "Stop being such a pussy! C'mon, I want a closer look."

When they were just a little more than ten feet away, Tee held out his arm to block Coffee from getting any closer.

Coffee stopped. "What's up?"

Tee pointed to the clothes lying across the hood of the SUV. "You tell me if'n I'm crazy but there 'peers to be hands attached to the ends of those sleeves and if'n I get any closer I'm afeered we'll see a head attached to that collar."

"What? That's stupid. There's..." Coffee began to reply dismissively but then saw them. There *were* hands at the ends of...

"They's got to be gloves!" Coffee snapped with a hard glare. "Someone's pulling our leg. Look for yerself." He motioned to it. "Nobody real is so thin they look like clothes laying near flat. And look at the way they's bent backwards. C'mon," he said, taking his brother's shirtsleeve. "We gonna get to the bottom of this right now!"

They approached.

On this particular day the sun was center stage and beat down hard. The cicada buzzing rose and fell and the occasional breeze whipped through the sparse grass. When the boys neared the road, they could see the air shimmering above the asphalt.

They were convinced that once they got close enough, it would all make sense.

But when they *did*...

"Laud a' mighty!!" Coffee barked in stunned terror. He shuddered, and stumbled back on rubbery legs. Embarrassed, he quickly gathered his courage and forced himself to press forward.

Tee grabbed his arm. "Don't do it! Sumthin mighty awful happened here. Look around, t'ain't even a drop of blood!"

Coffee pulled free, stepped to the hood of the SUV and after careful study, came to the conclusion—with the help of scores of flies hovering above the bodies— that what he was looking at was two human being whose insides, muscle, organs, bones and blood had been sucked out, Leaving only the skin and the black suits they were wearing.

He also noticed that neither man was wearing shoes. Steadying himself by placing his hand on the SUV's side panel, he reached down, grabbed the calf end of the pant leg and lifted it up.

The foot had neither sole nor heel. What remained was the inner layer of skin, hollowed out to the outer layer, all the way up the leg.

Tee cautiously edged his way alongside, rolled his hands, then nervously raised one to his mouth. "What do you suppose happened?"

Coffee dropped the pant leg. "Don't know. But something sucked the innards out of these fellas like they was eatin' crawdads."

With a look of disbelief, Tee placed his hands to the side of his face. "That is so fucked!"

With his hands inside the pockets of his bib overalls, Coffee cautiously studied the area looking for signs of who or what was responsible. But other than the bodies themselves, everything seemed calm and still. He felt the occasional wind that rippled the dead men's clothing, almost lifted one of the suits from the hood. Saw the honey bees at work; heard the cicadas sing. There wasn't another soul in sight.

Nothing.

With a small shake of his head Coffee said, "Whatever did this is gone. Maybe its best we got gone, too."

Tee was halfway through nodding when Coffee stiffened. "Laud'a'mercy!" he exclaimed.

Thinking his brother spotted the creature that savaged the remains on the car hood, Tee grabbed the door handle and was about to dive inside when he saw his brother smile.

"Well, looky there." Coffee said pointing to the area behind the debris where the smoke had just cleared.

Tee looked and saw a blue Mustang with the license plate: AIM E GRL

193

Aimee sat back in her make-shift fortress of wooden crates fully intending to wait a full hour before hazarding a look outside. With time to kill, she lit another pack of matches and used the flame to examine her hideaway and see just how sturdy it was.

It appeared to be plenty sturdy, having been constructed to house and protect large electronic equipment. Feeling safe, she began to relax.

A second later her fortress suddenly blew away as if struck by a tornado.

She gasped and leapt back in panic and confusion when the heavy wooden crates slammed into the floor several yards away.

From the smoke and dust a figure emerged.

What the hell is...?

She tried to focus, get a better look.

Is that Virgil? But what happened? He's bigger, taller by at least a foot...

It approached, leaned down and studied her.

The dying light of the matchbook made it difficult to see. As she brought it in for a closer look, most of the lit matches died out and the stench of sulfur filled the air.

It recoiled and hissed at her.

It doesn't seem to like the smell.

Working purely from instinct, she pulled out another pack, intending to light them with the dying flames of the one in her hand. But she miscalculated: the flames had burned down far enough to reach her hand. When the fire touched her flesh, she jerked in pain and the lit matches flew through the air and struck the floor

A sudden flash of light swept throughout the collapsed structure like the expanding ring of an atomic blast. Aimee heard a screeching, ear piercing howl. When she finally lit the other matchbook, the thing had gone.

I have to get out of here!

*

194

As Coffee and Tee trotted to the Blue Barn, a heavy plume of black smoke, fueled by several flaming plastic covered wooden crates, wafted throughout the area. The air stunk of burnt wood and rubber and a soot-like covering coated everything in a thirty-foot radius

As the two jumped upon the angled roof and started climbing, Tee said, "If'n she was in there when it collapsed, she's dead for sure." He momentarily coughed from the fumes. "Flatter than a flapjack!"

Coffee edged his way across, using the cables from the satellite dishes to jump toward the hole.

As he waited for Tee to follow, he said, "All the more reason fer us to find what's left of her and have the cops haul her away. Paw will be satisfied and nobody has to know nothin' about what happened previous."

Soon they were standing over the ragged edges of the opening. "Well, you goin' down?" Tee asked as he pulled a rag from his pocket and wiped his face.

Coffee stared into it. "We's both goin down!"

Tee put the rag away, raised his hands and stepped back. "But we still don't know what hollowed out those guys."

Coffee shook his head. "I tole you, whatever it was, is gone. Plus, it sure didn't shimmy up the side of a collapsed roof and swing acrost using cables like we just did. Now quit yer whining and help me climb down, once I'm in, I'll help you."

"But…"

"But nothing. We ain't leaving till we find Sula, got it?"

Reluctantly Tee nodded.

*

Aimee slowly made her way back to the hole in the roof and stood under it. As she looked for materials to create a makeshift ladder, she heard footsteps above.

Jimmy? Oh please be Jimmy!
But what if it's that Virgil thing?

195

She quickly back stepped and hid behind the large crates and watched the intruders lower themselves to the floor.

Chapter Thirty Five

Jimmy's eyes widened. "Virgil's possessed? So it's started?" he asked. "The daemons are breaking through?" He turned and approached the bathroom doorframe, but Ike was already fading into the darkness.

"Ike wait!"

Ike frantically clawed at the air as if fighting against a strong sea current, but the darkness quickly enveloped him.

The doorframe was empty.

Jimmy stood motionless, staring, gap-jawed, his alarm clock ticking in the background, the bathroom's florescent bulbs humming overhead.

There was a nervous twinge in his stomach. His pulse accelerated as that twinge grew and expanded from his stomach to the rest of his body. He began to shake. *No, not now. I can't deal with this now!*

But it was too late. Panic pounced on him with the savagery of a wild animal. Within seconds, sweat poured down Jimmy's face. His hands trembled and his stomach acid turned his insides into boiling magma.

He knew the routine.

Over the next few weeks, crippling anxiety attacks would ambush him at every opportunity, his blood pressure would go through the roof, adrenaline would routinely flood into his system and spike his heart rate. And, once the stiffs saw his physical and mental deterioration, they would converge upon him mercilessly.

No, please, no! I'm barely functioning as it is. I'm going freak out at the wrong time and get somebody killed.

Outside the bathroom door he saw his blue-jean jacket hanging on the wall hook. He stepped into his bedroom, put it on and felt the weight of the gun as his heart thundered against it.

He stepped back into the bathroom.

He could feel his pulse inside his ears, his throat tighten, his hands tremble. He had an overwhelming urge to run. To run anywhere, to run until his heart exploded, until his head blew off his shoulders like a bottle rocket on the 4th of July.

197

The clock continued to tick away and the above light continued to hum, but to Jimmy, all was silent with the exception of a searing white noise that came from everywhere and yet nowhere at all. It was as if time had stopped. He placed his hands on the cold tiled wall to steady himself. Then with glassy eyes and shaking hands, he reached inside his jacket, wrapped his fingers around the revolver.

He slowly placed his foot against the bathroom door and closed it.

It's better this way. Santiago and Martaine can handle this. They're trained for it. I'll only get someone killed.

He removed the gun from his jacket, sat on the toilet and raised the snub nose to his head, felt the cold steel against his temple. Perspiration stung his eyes. His stomach felt like that thing from the movie *Alien* was trying to tear its way out.

What do I have to live for anyway? My life has been nothing but misery. Constant panic attacks, constant harassment from the dead. No money, no career, no family. No one gives a shit about me and I don't give a shit about....

He thought of Aimee.

If Virgil's possessed...

He was suddenly back in the world again. Time resumed. He lowered the gun.

No. Not yet.

He slid it back inside his jacket, wiped the sweat from his eyes, took out his cell and called her.

No answer, same result when he tried Virgil.

Oh, God!

Still shaking, he leapt up and yanked open the bathroom door. "Everybody wake up!" Jimmy shouted as he clapped his hands. As Mary sat up in bed and Jess stirred in the recliner, Jimmy dialed the clergymen and announced they all needed to get back to the barn *now*.

Santiago and Martaine said they would leave immediately and as Jimmy ended the call, the ladies, like seasoned battle veterans quickly got ready to go.

Ten minutes later, as the three exited the apartment, Jimmy locked the door and said, "Ike told me Virgil is possessed but the daemon hasn't taken control yet. We need to get there before it does."

Minutes after they assembled in the foyer, the clergymen pulled up. They left the building, filed into the Impala and set off to the Blue Barn

*

Once they climbed inside the remains of the Blue Barn, Coffee and Tee discovered it reeked of burnt plastic and solder. Fortunately, there was more head room than expected. It took a while for their eyes to adjust to the dark, but the explosion left several nickel to quarter-size holes in the roof so they were able to explore without flashlights. As they moved forward, their feet snapped the shards and splinters that covered the remains of the floor.

"Sure is a lot of busted up machines," Tee commented as he scanned the area. "Sheooot, look at all that stuff over there. Must be three or four of them computer TV screens!" He turned to his left. "And I have no idea what that thang is," he said, pointing at a thoroughly mangled piece of electronic equipment. "I wonder if'n we could use any of this stuff back at the house. You know, maybe hook up some of that satellite TV I've heard tell about. Wouldn't that be cool?"

Coffee popped a plug of chaw into his mouth and said, "Watch where yer walkin', asshole. There's a body right behind yer left foot."

Tee jerked and spun around. "Ugh!" A moment later he bent down for a closer look. "Yep, he's dead all right. I wonder who he… Hey, looky here!"

Tee reached down and picked up a 9mm pistol with a laser sight, its thin red beam still working.

Coffee came over. "Let me see that!" he said, yanking it from Tee's hand.

"Hey!" Tee protested but Coffee ignored him.

199

"Hmmmm," Coffee said as he inspected it. "Ain't seen a gun like this before. Ain't nothing like the rifles we got back home."

"Maybe it's one of them space-guy ray guns!" Tee offered.

Coffee rolled his eyes and said sarcastically, "Maybe it is. Here, let me shoot you and see if'n you disappear."

Tee jumped out of the way. "No wait... hold on," he bleated with his hand outstretched.

"Oh relax, lame brain," Coffee said, examining the gun. He spit black tobacco juice to the floor. When it landed it resembled a silhouette of a flattened tarantula. "Besides, I ain't gonna shoot ya. I just need a little time to figure out how this works is all."

The boys resumed their search and had reached the far side of what remained of the roof when...

Suddenly, a sound rang out, like something clattering to the floor from the area where they entered. They turned, looked at each other then quickly, but quietly, raced to the opening.

When they arrived, the sun had disappeared behind another wave of heavy smoke. Still they were able to make out an upended office desk and several crates loaded on top of each other. Midway up, a figure in silhouette was climbing toward the gaping hole.

They moved in.

"Hey, you!" Coffee called out. "Where do you think you're goin'? Get on down here!"

As they angled in to get a better look, it turned. Tee leapt up upon the stacked boxes, reached up and grabbed its leg. As he did he was greeted by a burst of flame right in his face.

"Sheeeeeit!" Tee exclaimed as he let go and tumbled to the floor.

"Didn't like that, did you?" the figure asked, moving the fire back and forth. "Bet you're going to like this even less!"

The flame suddenly disappeared and the pungent odor of sulfur permeated the area.

When a sudden gust of wind dispersed the clouds of smoke above, the sun burst through and illuminated the inside of the roof for several yards in all directions.

"Well, well, well," Coffee said waving the gun at Aimee, "looks like our step sister is alive after all!"

200

Tee came alongside his brother and placed his fists on his hips. "Sonavagun, Sula, you got more lives than a cat."

Grinning, Coffee said, "Now you just git on down here. That's right, girl, nice and easy."

With her eyes trained on the pistol, and knowing the laser light was pointing at her forehead, Aimee reluctantly complied.

Coffee looked around and with the sun beaming in, grabbed one of the nearby overturned chairs and dropped it in front of him, Tee copied him. They both eyed her like lions in the tall grass.

"Okay, I'm here," she said defiantly as she leaned against the upended desk. "What do you want?"

Straddling the chair with his arms draped over the back, Coffee said with a grin, "What we want is for you to start taking off them clothes, all of them, every single stitch, and do it nice and slow."

Tee was guffawing and bouncing up and down. "Yeah, yeah, nice and slow, nice and slow!" he said echoing his brother.

Her expression was that of both dismissal and disgust. "In your dreams, retards!" she scoffed, then turned back to the stack of boxes and took a step toward them.

Coffee jumped to his feet. "Do it!" he bellowed, raising the gun, "and do it right now or so help me I will blow yer damn head off and fuck ya anyway!"

Her eyes widened when she saw Coffee cock the hammer and take aim.

Chapter Thirty Six

As they headed toward the Blue Barn, Jimmy, Mary and Jess got comfortable in the back seat of the clergymen's Impala. They noticed a large black box in Brother Martaine's lap. His arms were draped over it and the usually jovial Brother appeared stoic and deep in concentration.

"What you got there, bro?" Jimmy asked, tapping Martaine on the shoulder.

"Oh, this," Brother Martaine said patting the black box, "contains various articles we've acquired over the years to help and protect us during exorcisms. I only hope our situation hasn't deteriorated to the point where our defenses prove inadequate."

"Why didn't you tell us you did exorcisms when we first met?" Mary snapped. "When I told Jimmy what brought about my seizure, you looked at me like I had a screw loose."

"I know and I apologize," Santiago replied contritely. "We were being cautious. We weren't sure if we were dealing with true daemons or people with mercury poisoning. When a human body becomes toxic, for whatever reason, the effects are very similar to daemonic possession. They experience hallucinations, hear voices, interpret so-called signs from above, feel imbued with special powers, like controlling the weather or predicting the future. So following our first meeting we revealed our background to Virgil only, so not to frighten anyone. We hoped our knowledge and experience could assist him in bringing the situation under control."

Jimmy scrunched up his face. "Well, if this is what you guys do for a living, then why all the mystery and suspense? It seems simple enough: Crack open the black box, take out the Holy Hand Grenade, lob it at the bad guys and we all go out for pizza and beer."

Mary chuckled. "Yeah, let's go with that plan!"

Jimmy saw Santiago's solemn expression reflected in the rearview mirror. "Jest if you wish, but exorcising daemons is a very difficult process," he said as he clicked on the directional signal. "While the victims of the push-ins wait in that most uncomfortable and melancholy place, they are not in pain, they are not in fear and they are not in danger, because that void is a timeless waiting room."

"However," Brother Martaine interrupted, "the daemons come from a place of eternal punishment, misery and pain. And woe be the soul whose body has been possessed by one of them because that soul doesn't go to the void, it takes the daemons place in hell."

Jess leapt forward, her face filled with terror as she elbowed Jimmy out of her way. "Please tell me you're kidding!"

With a noticeably painful expression, Brother Martaine slowly shook his head. "I wish I were."

"But you've gotten them back right?" Jess continued, her eyes begging for a positive response. "That's what you do as exorcism guys' right? You drive out the daemons and..."

Santiago interrupted. "Yes, we do, unfortunately, never without a steep price. Sometimes when the daemon is destroyed, and the soul is released from its hell-ish prison, the body is too damaged to receive it back."

Jess took a moment, then slid into her seat with the words...

Jessica Jean Maldonado, what deviltry are you up to now?

...echoing in her head.

*

As Aimee stared down the barrel of the 9mm, and seeing Coffee and Tee's insatiable lust had overwhelmed any sense of right and wrong, she reluctantly began to carry out their demands.

They said, nice and slow, Well then, it's nice and slow they're gonna get.

She slowly slid out off one red pump and watched as Tee's eyes lit up. When the other shoe rolled to the floor she saw Coffee unhook the top of his bib overalls and slide his left hand down his pants. His right, however, still pointed the gun at her.

The twin's minds may have been focused on their increasing sexual excitement but Aimee was using this slow strip tease to plan an escape.

After sliding off her panty hose and noting the lust in Coffee and Tee's eyes, Aimee knew if she was going to make her move, it would have to be soon. All that was left was the real stuff, the blouse, skirt, bra and panties and there was no guarantee the twins would contain themselves until the end of the show.

Having run the events following the explosion through her mind several times, there was still one thing she wasn't sure off. Which one of the two FBI agent's guns was Coffee holding? Was it the jammed one, or the other?

If it was the jammed one, Aimee was pretty sure she could fight them off long enough to escape. At five-foot six and a half, she was taller, heavier and in top physical shape. The boys were 5 foot 3 and barely 100 pounds, but like her, lean and muscular. Aimee supposed living out in the woods and working the fields would make even the smallest guy a formidable opponent.

Still, she had taken a few self defense classes at the Women's Center with her mother and was convinced that if she kept her cool, and acted at the right time, she could get out of this in one piece.

But there was still the issue of the gun. She didn't have the luxury of assuming Coffee had the jammed one, because if she guessed wrong, she'd be dead. So to even the odds she had to get a weapon.

"Take off that damn skirt!" Coffee shouted, waving the pistol. "It's time we got to the interestin' parts."

Tee nodded vigorously and continued to bounce up and down in his chair.

Aimee reached for the button on the side of her miniskirt, opened it and started lowering the zipper.

Any kind of weapon, just something to give me an edge.

She looked down.

And there it was, only a few inches from her feet, a broken shard of wood amid several others from the roof. This one however, was special. It was approximately 2 inches wide, a foot long and came to a sharp point.

But when they attack, could I really use it to kill them?

Aimee suddenly felt something she wasn't familiar with. It was a sense of raw animal instinct. A sense of kill or be killed. She felt a quickening of her pulse, her intuition sharpening, a sudden adrenaline rush, but most of all a sense of rage and empowerment.

How dare these little bastards do this to me!!

Aimee slowly lowered her skirt and saw Coffee eye her, lick his lips then toss a glance from side to side

Aimee's breathing grew shallow, remembering side-to-side eye movement is one of the first 'tells' one learns in a self-defense class. If you're alone and about to be attacked, your assailant will almost always look from side to side to make sure there aren't any witnesses.

Once that happens, you have only seconds to react

With gun in hand, Coffee smirked and rose from his chair.

With a feigned smile Aimee, holding the edge of the mini skirt, seductively removed one leg from it and as Coffee drew closer, bent down and stepped out of it. Then in one deft move, she tossed the miniskirt with her left hand at Coffee's face while picking up the wooden stake with her right.

She lunged at him.

As the miniskirt fell from Coffee's line of vision, he saw Aimee and the wooden stake racing toward him.

"Bitch!" he bellowed, and pulled the trigger.

The report of the gunshot echoed throughout the barn as Aimee's eyes widened and her body shook.

He fired again and again.

Chapter Thirty Seven

As the Impala with Jimmy and company neared the barn, Santiago noticed a thin plume of black smoke in the distance. Soon afterward, as the car reached the top of the hill and the desolate landscape of Dohesley Township came into view, Jess cried out, "Oh, dear Lord!" She immediately pressed her hands against the window. "The barn! It's destroyed! What happened to Aimee and Vir…"

Jess' question died when they saw someone climbing out of the collapsed roof but the figure was too far off to make a positive identification.

Santiago gunned the engine and they raced toward the scene.

Moments later, the Impala pulled up behind the black SUV.

As they exited, Martaine saw the bodies on the hood. He immediately stepped in front of them so they would not be seen by the others.

Meanwhile, Jimmy, Jess and Mary leapt from the Impala and charged toward the structure. Jimmy pulled ahead hoping to catch whoever had climbed from the smoldering remains. Unfortunately, when he reached the barn, that person had disappeared into the woods.

Noting the concern on Martaine's face, Santiago did not join them.

With their companions well into the distance, Martaine slowly stepped aside.

Santiago's face tightened, then saddened.

What appeared before him told him one thing…

The daemons had arrived.

Aimee lay on the floor, her body shaking, her hand pressed against the wound hoping to stop the bleeding. Her breath came in short, sharp gasps as the adrenaline surged through her. The sun beat down from the hole in the roof and stung her eyes. As tears rolled down her face, she considered just letting go and slipping into the arms of eternity. Her real parents would never accept her. All the hard work, study and preparation for college was now meaningless. She had no home, no family; her supposed stepbrother had just shot her.

And it had happened so fast! When she had charged and saw her miniskirt fall from his face, she realized Coffee would get off at least one shot, so she twisted to the side.

He fired. She felt a burning sensation just below her rib cage.

She rammed the stake into his stomach and grabbed his wrist with her left hand.

Using her superior size and strength, she forced the gun upward causing him to fire into the roof as she twisted the shard deeper into his torso. Any second she had expected Tee to charge into the fray.

He didn't. Instead, as his brother succumbed and the gun fell to the floor, Tee leapt to the upended desk, then boxes and yanked himself up and out the hole.

As Coffee dropped to one knee, he snarled and with his last breath, spit blood and tobacco juice in her face, then collapsed. Moments later, as the light faded from his eyes, she kicked the gun away, then reached down, grabbed her miniskirt, pressed it against her wound, and laid down among the dust, wood and splinters.

Suddenly, that same feeling she experienced earlier, the one that made her angry and determined to fight, kicked in.

Sula! That's what it is. I may have my own thoughts and memories but this is still Sula's body, and I'm figuring you don't live long in the hills if you aren't tough and willing to fight.

She looked at the miniskirt pressed against the bullet wound. With her heart pounding, she gently peeled it back, expecting to see a large gaping hole and a pool of clotting blood. What she saw, however, was a two-inch-wide gash and blood spot that was quickly drying. With a sigh of relief she further examined the wound.

It's almost stopped bleeding.

She slowly climbed to her feet.

Now at a better angle she gave the wound another look and saw the bullet had only grazed her side and probably wouldn't require anything more than a tetanus shot.

She looked down at Coffee as he lay in the dark. The jagged shard rammed deep into his abdomen, the blood pooling beneath, the glassy dead eyes staring into nothingness.

She began dressing. As she did she noticed her shaking hands and light-headedness but figured that was to be expected after coming so close to being killed. As she finished, she heard a voice.

"Aimee?! Oh Aimee, thank God! Are you all right?"

Aimee looked up and saw Jimmy staring down from the edge of the hole. She had expected Tee to return with some type of weapon, but seeing Jimmy brought tears of relief.

"Yeah, yeah, I'm okay, I guess," she replied as she stepped onto the desk and started to climb. As she neared the top she reached out. "Give me a hand."

He did and when she cleared the hole, he pulled her into his arms and hugged her. She returned the hug, sought out his lips and kissed him deeply and passionately. Not surprisingly, he returned the kiss. He caressed her face and said, "When I saw what happened, I was terrified. I thought you had been killed."

They kissed again.

"I don't know why," Aimee said laying her head on his shoulder. "But I feel some kind of connection to you, like the way I just hooked my arm into yours back at Handlemans. I didn't think about it. It just seemed like the thing to do."

He hugged her again.

When they felt the structure shake and heard wood snap, they angled their way down the tilted roof and jumped the remaining three feet to the ground.

Jess and Mary cheered and came over to join them.

As they ambled across the fields on their way back to the Impala, Aimee took Jimmy's hand. Shortly afterward, Mary came up alongside and asked Aimee what happened.

"As far as I can tell," Aimee replied, "someone fired a bazooka or a rocket launcher and blew up the barn." She stopped,

208

let go of Jimmy's hand, gave herself a once over and shook her head. "I can't believe I wasn't killed. During the night two FBI guys were returned and they stuck around. Dave Miller and Matthew Strom. Nice guys, but they were at the front of the barn when it was hit. And when we were hit, it was like being in a hurricane. Everything was flying everywhere."

"What happened to Virgil?" Jimmy asked.

Aimee shrugged and shook her head. "I don't know. I thought I saw him jump through the roof but that's crazy. The roof was twelve feet high at least. I think I saw him after the explosion, but I was confused and scared. All I remember was something big, real big. But then it was gone."

Jimmy put his arm around her. "I'll have a look after we get you back in the car."

"Okay," she said, placing her arm around his waist. "So anyway..." She was about to give more details when she saw the two bodies on the hood of the black SUV.

She stiffened. "What the fuck is that?!!" she squealed.

Jimmy, Jess and Mary were equally startled.

Santiago, with his hands clasped behind his back, approached. "First, let me say that I am very happy to see you, Aimee. For a moment we thought we lost you."

With the sight of two hollowed out bodies on the hood, Aimee was speechless.

"The daemons have broken through," Santiago said, then gestured to the remains. "What you see here is typical of the mutilation these creature inflict upon their victims. How many have crossed over into our world, I cannot say, maybe only the one that possessed Virgil. Then again, it could be many, many others. It's too early to tell."

He turned to Aimee, "Do you have any idea how many push-ins were returned to their bodies before the machine was destroyed?"

Aimee slowly nodded but kept her face turned from the bodies. "Actually, I have an exact number. Out of the five hundred and six who were pushed out, four hundred and four got their bodies back.

Jimmy's jaw dropped. "Wow! What did you guys do, set up an assembly line?"

Aimee gave a sad smile. "Actually, it was Agent Miller who made it work. Right after the machine returned each victim to their body, Dave insisted they contact as least two push-ins and tell them about the huge amount of free equipment inside the barn. And to make sure it worked, he wouldn't let them leave until the two they called walked through the white door."

Aimee smiled. "What got me was that they were all such greedy bastards! For a while we were getting a new carload of push-ins every ten minutes. Some were even bringing pickup trucks. And of course, just as they pulled up, Dave and Matthew would 'just happen' to be exiting the barn with an armload of goodies.

"Where is Virgil?" Martaine asked.

"Like I told Jimmy," she said as a sad expression covered her face, "I don't know. I really don't. This might sound strange, but I feel so bad for him." She bowed her head. "I know he was an egomaniac but he did his best. He just had a lot of problems."

Jess eyed her suspiciously. "That's very forgiving, considering what his machine did to you."

Aimee shrugged. "I'm not saying I'm not still pissed. It's just that before he fell asleep we got to talking and he said this whole mess came about simply because he was lonely. His wife constantly bad-mouthed him; he had no friends, no kids, nobody to cheer him up. So he became obsessed with contacting the only person who ever encouraged him, his mother. And look how it turned out. He lost everything. His mother betrayed him, his wife left him, his career fizzled, and he ran out of money. Now, it looks like creating the machine got him killed."

"Fuck him!" Mary replied, then instantly placed her hand over her mouth. With a startled look she said, "I'm sorry! That's not what I intended to say. It's just that this area has a very negative effect on me."

"We saw someone slip out through the hole in the roof just before we arrived," Martaine said, "Who was that?"

"Probably just some lookie-lou," she lied, not wanting to tell what really happened. "I was on the other side when the rocket hit."

"Can we just get the fuck out of here?!!" Mary bellowed. "What, are you assholes deaf? Didn't you hear what I said?"

Jimmy could barely keep from laughing. He placed his hands on his hips and said, "Yeah! What's wrong with you assholes? Didn't you hear the lady?"

Aimee said, "Let's go back to Jimmy's. I'm sick of this place." She handed her car keys to him.

Santiago studied the smoldering wreckage of the barn. "Considering your ordeal and Mary's anxiety, I suppose that is best," Santiago said. "But Brother Martaine and I need to remain and find out what happened to Virgil. We will rejoin you as soon as possible."

Chapter Thirty Eight

Jessica Jean Maldonado, what deviltry are you up to now?!

Even with the Mustang's top down and with the sound of traffic all around, Jess could still hear her father's accusations. After originally startling her in Jimmy's bedroom, it was now occurring with increasing frequency. What's more, it was becoming so clear she was afraid the soul of her late father was in the car with her.

Perspiration beaded on her brow and her hands felt clammy. She had told Aimee her father, Jacob Maldonado was a hateful man. What she didn't say was that he was a truly evil man. A man totally bereft of any sense of right or wrong.

Jessica Jean Maldonado, what deviltry are you up to now?!
Stop it! Please stop it!

Aimee sat quietly and expressionless in the passenger seat. The adrenaline had worn off and the reality of what she had done was setting in.

That little fuck was about to rape me at gunpoint. He got what he deserved, she told herself, again and again.

However the more she recalled the event, the more misgivings she had. He hadn't laid a hand on her, or forced himself on her and she now wondered if she overreacted.

What if it was all a bluff? He was only fifteen, probably never saw a girl naked in his whole life. I bet the little bastard would have cum all over himself if I took off my bra. And Tee, that idiot probably would have passed out.

Her face tightened. *Still…*

No! I've got to stop this. I've got to stop obsessing. I'm the victim here, not them.

She felt tears welling in her eyes. She turned to the window so Jimmy wouldn't see.

I just want to go home.

Mary, wearing a scarf on her head, large sunglass and her collar pulled up, was doing all she could to control the rage welling inside her.

What the fuck is going on? We're miles from the barn, I should be calming down, not getting angrier.

She leaned forward and noted that Jimmy was carefully observing the speed limit even though all the other cars were barreling by. She leaned back and said nothing, but the urge to tell him to get a fucking move on was nearly overpowering.

Jimmy was curious as to why, after having undergone a severe anxiety attack only a short while ago, his panic hadn't spun him out of control.

Maybe because our situation is so serious my crazy brain is being forced to react normally.

He wasn't sure if that was it, but what he did know was that for the first time since early adolescence, he was experiencing an emotional attraction toward another human being.

Aimee.

She had said that, although she didn't understand why, she felt a connection with him, felt he was the person she was supposed to be with.

Jimmy was only now realizing that he felt the same way.

He had told her he wasn't a relationship person, but that was because the dead rarely left him alone. And what he had explained to Mary back at the barn was only the tip of the iceberg. His experiences throughout his teen years made him seriously paranoid. His digestive tract was in ruins, his blood pressure was far above acceptable levels and his frequent panic attacks left him exhausted and reeling from adrenaline overload. And more frighteningly, there were times when he couldn't tell the dead from the living.

And I'm considering bringing this sweet, good-natured girl into my daily horror show?

He glanced at her, but she had turned away.

*

213

After Santiago and Martaine lowered the bodies from the SUV to the ground so they would not be seen by passing cars, they walked toward the barn. They said nothing for a considerable amount of time.

They had seen such atrocities before. Over the years, they had viewed numerous violent deaths, even massacres all orchestrated by daemons in human form.

But this one was familiar. This one had all the earmarks of one daemon in particular!

D'Shaid, a creature whose taste for violence and sadism had no bounds.

A stiff breeze rattled the trees and the clouds of smoke dissipated from the barn area. The smell was subsiding and the fires had gone out.

As they continued walking, Martaine suddenly started whistling and strode in a very casual and relaxed manner. "I wonder, do servants of our Lord like us get to retire? You know, pack away their robes and sandals and hop on down to Florida?"

Santiago eyed him as they trudged over the hill and dales of Dohesley's toxic landscape. "My friend, we are in our thirties. Why would you ask such a question?"

Martaine shifted the black box from his left hand to his right as they drew closer. "Well, I just was wondering if after a lifetime of service, would one's golden years be rewarded with sun-soaked beaches and tropical breezes? I hear many people flock to Florida after retiring. And I can see why. There's Sea World and ..."

"Stop thinking about such nonsense," Santiago chastised. "Whatever reward we have coming, God willing, will be received in heaven, not Disney World."

Martaine however, persisted. "What have you got against Disney World? From what I hear, it has many amazing attractions from around the globe. In fact, I...I kind of feel a song coming on. Join me won't you?" Martaine cleared his throat and sang; "It's a small worl.."

"Will you shut up?" Santiago barked, "What has come over you? Do you not know what we are about to face?"

Martaine stopped and took Santiago's arm. "I do," he said solemnly. "The question is, why do you fear it so?"

Startled by the question's directness, Santiago's eyes widened and his face paled. The wind had stopped and an unexpected calm fell over the area. The clergyman dropped his head to his chest, bit his lip and moments later, slowly looked up at Martaine. "I am deeply sorry, my friend," he said, reddening with humiliation. "And I beg both the Lord's and your forgiveness. I succumbed to fear and should know better."

Martaine clapped him on the shoulder. "Yes, you should. But," he said, then shrugged, "what's an occasional crisis of faith between friends?"

A thin smile crossed Santiago's lips as they continued on until they reached the edge of the barn. "I am very fortunate to have you here. However, it's time to begin our preparations. Mary's intense reaction to this area should be taken as a warning. The daemons are very close."

Martaine nodded, placed the Black Box on the ground, opened it and removed a bottle of holy water. It was a special bottle once blessed by Saint Padre Pio, a modern day priest who reportedly physically battled the devil himself. Together the clergymen dipped their index fingers in the water and drew the sign of the cross on their foreheads.

Martaine closed the bottle and put it away. "Well," he said, "are we ready?" They stood side by side on the edge of the Blue Barn's collapsed roof and took a momentary glance at the blackened grass, the bare and knotted trees, the shimmering red sky and the orange sun as it descended into the horizon.

"As ready as we will ever be," Santiago finally replied, then climbed upon the wooden surface.

Because of the varying circumstances the clergymen faced in their previous battles, Martaine's black box contained a number of items that had proven necessary over the years. In addition to the religious artifacts were heat-resistant gloves, flashlights, matches, drinking water, two sanitized towels, road flares (for their sulfur content) and pen and paper.

They descended into the hole and onto what remained of the floor. The inside was dark and smelled of burnt wood. They took only a few steps when they came upon Coffee's body and saw the wooden shard jammed deeply into his upper abdomen, as well as the pool of blood surrounding his torso.

"Apparently this poor boy didn't survive the explosion," Martaine commented as he removed the flashlights from the black box and gave one to Santiago. "I wonder why Aimee didn't mention him."

Santiago turned on his flashlight and swept the area. The light soon illuminated the bodies of the two FBI agents and then further over on the cracked and splintered floor, the gun whose laser light was no longer working. The priest moved in for a closer look.

He knelt down and examined the two men, then walked over to the gun and sniffed the barrel. The smell of burnt gunpowder was noticeable. He then returned to Martaine.

"Those men were killed by the explosion," Santiago said as he removed a handkerchief from his back pocket and wiped his hands. He pointed the flashlight beam on Coffee's face. "The boy, however, was murdered."

"Murdered?" Martaine replied. "That's a serious accusation. What led you to that conclusion?"

"Actually we have our good friends, O'Hoolahan, Smythe and Rabiniwitz to thank."

"The TV show? How so?"

Santiago crouched down and closed Coffee's eyes. "On a recent episode, a murderer used a gas explosion to cover having stabbed his business partner. What gave him away was that the explosion occurred on the ground floor which blew out the sides of the house. The victim's body was found on the second floor with a perpendicular chest wound." Santiago stood and swept the flashlight. "In order for the victim to receive that particular wound, he would have to have been lying on the floor. But the blood splatter pattern clearly proved otherwise."

Martaine looked down at the young boy. "So young, such a pity. Who do you think is responsible?"

"I believe the murderer is either the figure we saw running away earlier or…"

"Aimee…?" Martaine asked as his brow furrowed. "Hmmm, there was blood on her clothes, but I was under the impression it was her own."

"Or the murderer is still hiding in here," Santiago said, surveying the area. "Nevertheless, we have our work to do and I am only mentioning it as a possibility."

As Martaine and Santiago ventured into the far corners of the barn roof, they came upon a section where physical objects—items like wooden posts, roof panels and computer stands—were fading in and out of existence.

"It is as bad as I suspected," Santiago said. He took the Black Box from Martaine, laid it on the floor, opened it and removed a spray bottle of Holy Water.

When Martaine first suggested the use of such a modern convenience, Santiago rejected it as inappropriate and disrespectful, but, when it proved far more efficient than the customary sprinklings from one's fingers, Santiago chose effectiveness over tradition.

The priest recited the prerequisite prayers as he sprayed the affected areas. As in the past, the shimmering and fading objects immediately regained their solidity. One could almost hear the rage and frustration from behind the veil.

Santiago stepped back and inspected the area. "It appears we have arrived before a complete collapse occurred. Perhaps there is still hope."

After Martaine nodded in agreement, Santiago gave the area a cursory examination and said. "It appears we've done all we can. We've looked from front to back and there's no sign of Virgil." He pointed the flashlight at a group of boxes piled in a corner. "Let's check that out, just to be sure, then we'll join the others."

The two walked toward the boxes in single file because of all the scattered debris. A few moments later, Santiago heard a strange gurgling behind him. He turned and saw Martaine wrapped head to toe in what Santiago first thought was a black cloak. As the priest ran to him, there came a hissing, like something wet being thrown on a hot skillet. Slowly the area covering Martaine's forehead began to peel back. The hissing grew into a cracking sound, like someone snapping dry twigs.

Slowly the cross symbol Martaine had applied to his forehead appeared and was glowing with a green ethereal light. Still Martaine was struggling, clawing at the covering, unable to breathe.

Seeing this, Santiago pressed his hand to the wet outline on his own forehead and charged. "Release him, D'Shaid! Release him now or feel the touch of he who vanquished your master in the name of our Lord."

The black covering instantly transformed into talon-like claws and pressed against Martaine's throat, but when Santiago raised the spray bottle of Holy Water, the darkness, which resembled a liquid shadow, retreated and slithered down the clergyman's robe. Like an arc of black fluid, it leapt into a chair. Santiago had seen this before but each time his brain objected, unable to fathom what was happening.

Holding the bottle steady, like a gun on a prisoner, Santiago rushed over and edged Martaine away from the shadowy figure. He propped up Martaine until he was able to steady himself and breathe normally.

A mouth-like opening appeared at the top of the shadow and a dark voice resonated from it.

"You may have your companion back, Santiago, for I have no need of him, or you. We have outgrown your mastery and our servitude. The days of our fleeting inhabitations of your world are about to come to an end. One of your own has opened a doorway and we are preparing to enter en masse. Human Science is about to free us and relegate you and your crude incantations to the graveyards of history.

"Within twenty four hours the lords of hell shall walk the Earth. So make your entreaties to your cold and uncaring God, my dear Santiago for the thousand years of darkness is at hand."

The shadow swirled then slithered into the earth with a speed too fast for either to follow. What came next was the sound the winter wind makes when howling through dead and dying trees.

Suddenly a voice echoed through the structure.
"Hello? Hello? Who's out there?"

Chapter Thirty Nine

Everyone was quiet as Jimmy drove through the valleys of the Catskill Mountains. As they approached Wheatfield and Jimmy's apartment, he took in the scenery and with his elbow on the open window frame, enjoyed the fresh country air.

Beyond the shoreline, Swinton Lake sparkled as if filled with tiny mirrors, with its sailboats in the distance and the setting sun glistening on its surface. Lavender clouds framed the horizon and the lush greenery surrounding the lake provided a cooling shade.

As Jimmy returned his attention to the road, the car in front of him, a blue Ford Taurus with a cracked taillight, suddenly squealed to a stop. Jimmy jammed on the brakes to avoid a collision as two other cars pulled alongside. Another loudly braked behind him and lightly tapped the Mustang's rear bumper.

"What the…!" Jimmy shouted as he opened his door and squeezed out to confront the driver of the Taurus who had stopped short for no apparent reason.

"Jimmy wait…!" Mary called.

He had only taken a few steps when five men brandishing guns leapt from the surrounding vehicles. "Police," one shouted, holding out a badge from a chain around his neck. Two more exited the car behind his, yanked open the passenger door of the Mustang and pulled Aimee out. When they saw the blood on her blouse and miniskirt, they forced her to the pavement and handcuffed her. Both Mary and Jess were soon on the ground beside her.

Jimmy quickly raised his hands as one of the plainclothes police officers grabbed his wrists and placed them behind his back. He turned to the officer. "What's this all about?" he asked, his eyes darting from side to side.

Two police cruisers with their flashers on pulled up. The officers quickly joined the plainclothes policemen who had pressed Jimmy's face to the hood of their car and were going through his pockets. Discovering the snub nose, they yanked it out, handcuffed and Miranda-ed him, then arrested him for carjacking, gun possession and for being a person of interest regarding the disappearance of Aimee McFarland.

All four were hustled into the two police cruisers, Jimmy and Mary in one, and Jess and Aimee in the other. It had all happened in less than two minutes and not a single car passed while the arrests were being made.

The police cruiser containing Aimee and Jess raised a cloud of dust as it pulled away the plainclothes officers' cars followed.

Mary and Jimmy had been placed in the back of a second police cruiser and handcuffed to a metal bar that ran across the back of the front bench seat. With the officer still outside the car, she leaned over and whispered, "These cops are legit. This isn't a set up by the push-ins."

"So I am really being charged with carjacking?" Jimmy asked with a look of stunned surprise.

"Seems so," she said. "Aimee's only seventeen and has been missing for nearly forty-eight hours. You can bet her parents filed a missing person report."

Jimmy gently closed his eyes with the realization of just how serious his situation was. He pulled at his cuffs. "Ahhh, crap!" he muttered. "Of course, we're driving around in Aimee's car. How am I going to explain that?"

A moment later, Jimmy and Mary's arresting officer opened the driver's side door and called the precinct to request a tow truck to pick up Aimee's car. He was told one had already been dispatched and should arrive any minute.

He ended the call and said to Jimmy and Mary. "I'm going to flag down the tow-truck driver. Once he arrives, I'll take you in."

Aimee and Jess were taken directly to the Wheatfield Police Station. Once inside, Jess was seated at a detective's desk and questioned about the Ellis Macawber murder.

Aimee was hustled into processing to be fingerprinted and photographed.

"State your name!" the police matron said as Aimee was shoved into a chair and handcuffed to it.

221

Aimee stared at the cuffs as they closed on her wrists.

The matron banged her fist on the desk. "I said, state your name!"

Startled, she looked over and said, "Aimee McFarland."

The officer eyed her hard. "You think you're funny?"

Aimee gave her a confused look, then remembered. She momentarily considered giving Sula's name but realized dragging Sula's family into this would only cause more problems. As she tried to decide how to answer, the matron resumed typing and said, "You're going to be difficult, huh? Fine, I'll just list you as a Jane Doe."

Once the procedure was completed, a female officer brought in a prison jumpsuit and told Aimee to remove her blood stained clothes as they were going to the lab to be tested. When the officer saw the blood clumped gash caused by the bullet, she asked if she needed to be transported to the hospital.

"No," Aimee replied, thinking that would only complicate things. "But if you have some gauze and some bandages."

Following some preliminary questioning—during which she claimed to know nothing about Aimee McFarland's disappearance—her wound was properly dressed and she donned the orange jumpsuit. She was then photographed and ushered into an interrogation room. As the door opened, the smell of pine-scented cleaner nearly overwhelmed her. Inside was a heavy oak table and two metal chairs. She was shoved inside and told to sit and wait.

She shuddered when she heard the heavy clank when the door locked.

Sometime later, she had no idea how long, the door opened, a bald detective with a red mustache stormed in, eyed her and slammed his fist on the table.

"Where is Aimee McFarland?!"

Terrified, Aimee jerked back, raised her hands defensively and began sobbing. She couldn't answer that question, at least not in any way that would be believed.

He eyed her hard, then snarled and pounded the table a second time. "I asked you a question. Where is Aimee McFarland!?"

Wide-eyed, Aimee shook in her seat.

The detective, reading her reaction as someone ready to crack, poured it on. "I don't think you have any idea the trouble you're in, young lady," he said, pressing his hands on the table. "Either you start talking or we're going to charge you with first degree murder and in New York, that gets you the death penalty. Is that what you want, huh, is it?"

When Aimee continued to shake, yet say nothing, he lifted the edge of the table and slammed it against the concrete floor, "Well?"

"I... I," she stammered, but didn't know what to say. She couldn't say, *'I'm* Aimee,' or say 'Aimee's body is at the bottom of a burned down building in the middle of Dohesley Township', at least not without implicating herself. She also knew she had the right to an attorney but couldn't see how one could help.

To make matters worse, she already made two major incriminating mistakes. First by giving her name as, 'Aimee McFarland,' and second by denying she knew anything about Aimee's disappearance.

"Lying ain't going to help your case, little girl," the detective said, "We got the video from the bank's ATM. He produced his smart phone and after giving it a few taps, showed her behind the wheel of Aimee's blue Mustang and withdrawing money with Aimee's debit card.

"Want to try the truth this time?" the detective asked as he slipped the phone back into his pocket.

Aimee fought the urge to vomit. Her stomach hitched and she felt lightheaded. She began panting and rolled her shaking hands.

"Can... can I talk to Jimmy? Just for a minute?"

The detective pulled over a chair, slammed it down in front of her, smirked and waved off her request. "You want to talk to your boyfriend? Well, you can't," he said leaning in. "You get nothing! You hear me? Nothing, until you tell me your name and where I can find Aimee MacFarland!"

Still sobbing, Aimee shook her head.

The detective tossed up his hands in an I-give-up gesture. "Okay, the hell with you! But you should know this Jimmy fella is saying Aimee McFarland's kidnapping was your idea and he only came along for the ride. He's selling you out, little girl. He's making a deal and letting you take the fall."

Confused by the statement, she was about to say, 'The fall for what?' then realized the detective had pieced together a probable scenario and hoped to bluff her into a confession.

Seeing he had no idea what really happened, and that Jimmy hadn't told them anything, she sat back, folded her arms and turned away.

"Okay, if that's the way you want it." He got up and left the room.

Twenty minutes later, he unlocked the door, stuck his head in and said, "I have two people who would like to talk to you."

Fearing Tee had gone to the police with Paw, Aimee paled and braced for the worst.

The detective opened the door wider and in stepped John and Nancy McFarland, Aimee's parents.

Worn out, frazzled, frightened and on the verge of hysteria, the sight of her mother and father caused Aimee's face to light up as if she had received a last minute reprieve from the governor.

Beaming, she leapt from her chair and before the detective could stop her, wrapped her arms around Nancy McFarland, sobbed and hugged her tightly. "Oh Mom," she blubbered, "Thank God you're here! This has been such a nightmare! I've been so…"

Nancy McFarland forcibly pried off Aimee's arms and shoved her away. The detective pushed Aimee back into her seat.

"How dare you! How dare you!" Nancy shouted in tears as she stood over her. "What have you done with my daughter? What have you done with Aimee?"

Aimee was horrorstricken. She tried to speak, but nothing came out. Then her body went limp. Her mother's fierce and total rejection was more devastating and painful than learning her body had been destroyed, even worse than being forced to strip at gunpoint.

224

Aimee bowed her head. The transfer was now complete. She was Sula May Hockenberger, inheriting all the pain, misery and horror that came with it.

A police officer suddenly burst in and shouted, "Detective, we need everyone front and center. There's an officer down, two escaped prisoners and a stolen armored car!"

"Unbelievable, this town's become a madhouse!" the detective replied.

As the detective hustled the McFarland's out of the interrogation room, he turned and said to Aimee, "This ain't over young lady."

Aimee stood and called out, "Mom! It's really me, Aimee. Please don't leave me here. Please!"

The response was the slamming and locking of the interrogation room door.

*

As they waited for the tow truck to arrive, Mary leaned over and said, "Don't tell them anything until we get a chance to talk to Officer Van Pelt. He knows what really happened. Maybe he can figure out a way to get us out of this."

Jimmy was about to reply when an armored car flew over the nearby hill at high speed and headed right for them.

Seeing the sudden look of panic on Jimmy's face, Mary turned.

"Holy shit!!!" she bellowed and flung herself toward Jimmy.

She was nearly sitting in his lap when it plowed into the rear door causing the cruiser to flip several times. Fortunately, the side curtain airbags deployed and the reinforced door panels absorbed most of the brunt of the collision.

The back and front windows shattered as did the flashers when the police car landed on its roof and slid onto the small dirt road that led to the lake's pier and boat dock. As it came to a stop and slowly wobbled from side to side, Jimmy pulled at his cuffs to no avail. He was scuffed, but sustained no real physical damage.

"Mary, you all right?!"

225

"Ahhh!" she growled as she placed her feet against the front seat and like Jimmy tried to pull free from the metal bar. "Damn it!"

The police officer opened fire on the armored car as it burned rubber in reverse and made a second charge. The bullets had no effect and the armored vehicle struck again. When the patrol car, after rolling several times, landed on its side, the armored car pushed it toward the pier.

Wood splintered and flew in all directions as the battered police cruiser plowed through the pier's posts on its way to the end of the deep water fishing dock.

A moment later it was airborne, slammed into the water, flipped several times and began to sink.

The armored car charged back across the pier as the lone police officer continued firing. He tried for the windows, for the tires, for the gun sights hoping that at least one of his bullets would get through and put an end to the assault.

But it was hopeless and the officer, having miscalculated his opponents speed, was struck in the hip and went flying. The armored car exited the pier, spun around and took off.

*

With the news of the assault on the patrol car now widespread, everyone at the Wheatfield police station was scrambling. Jess had been released shortly after their arrival because there was nothing to connect her to Aimee MacFarland's disappearance or Ellis Macawber's death. She asked to see Aimee but was told she'd have to wait until bail was set. Not knowing what to do next, she left the station and placed a call to the clergymen.

*

In the precinct's lower level, the McFarlands were being hustled to the stairs by the detective who was reassuring them that, should there be a break in the case, they would be the first to know.

226

Nancy McFarland thanked him then asked for directions to the ladies room. As the detective hurriedly placed the interrogation room keys back on the peg board, he said,

"Upstairs to the left." He turned and pointed to the landing. "It's right next to the Processing Room."

"Thanks," she replied and began putting on her coat.

The detective intended to walk them to the front door, but when the public address system repeatedly called for all personnel to report immediately to the main hall, he gave a quick wave and charged up the stairs.

This was exactly what Nancy McFarland was hoping for.

Ignoring entreaties from her husband to 'leave it to the authorities,' she walked back to the peg board, removed the keys for Interrogation Room #2 and strode toward it.

As she slipped the key in and turned the lock, John McFarland again pleaded with his wife.

She shook her head determinedly. "I'm not leaving until that girl tells me where Aimee is!"

Aimee looked up when her parents reentered the room and again took the seats across from her.

"Where's the detective?" Aimee asked.

"He's right outside," John bluffed. "So don't try anything."

Aimee gave a small smile. For a car salesman, her father was one of the world's worst liars.

Nancy reached over and took Aimee's hand, her pleading expression broke the Aimee's heart.

"Young lady, please," Nancy said. "Where is my daughter? If you want money, I'm sure my husband and I can..."

Aimee slipped her hand from Nancy's then raised it in a stop gesture.

She eyed them both. "Look, Mom, Dad, I'm at my breaking point. I can't take anymore so just listen. I'm going to tell you the absolute truth, and... and you're not going to believe a word. Probably call me a liar and make all kinds of threats. But here's what really happened." She steadied herself, placed her hands back on her mother's and said, "This whole thing started when a guy named Virgil Vanderhill invented a machine..."

Deke Esterhaus witnessed the entire event.

Minutes earlier, he had received a call from the Wheatfield police requesting a tow truck. He was less than a mile away.

Easy money, he had said to himself.

It would be anything but.

He knew the area, was born and raised there and was one of the very few fortunates who, after receiving a second chance in life, was smart enough to take advantage.

Now almost a decade and a half after serving 8 years for armed robbery, Deke was an upstanding citizen with his own towing company, was happily married, a proud father and a respected member of the community.

He had his arm propped against the open window of his tow truck as he turned onto the main road. He was enjoying a country & western tune and nearing the reported location when, about a quarter mile ahead, he saw an armored car catapult over the hill and slam full force into a parked police cruiser. The car tumbled and bounced like a die on a craps table. He heard the police officer open fire.

Deke floored the accelerator and charged toward the scene. As he drew nearer he saw there were people in the back of the cruiser as the armored vehicle plowed into it a second time.

"Holy shit!" Deke said in astonishment as the police car rattled against the slats of the wooden pier then plunged into the lake.

As the police car slowly sank, the armored car raced backward toward the shore, clipped the police officer, spun around and took off.

Deke hoped he could get there in time.

*

Dazed but still conscious, Jimmy noticed the cruiser had righted itself and felt the cold water rushing in. Mary too, was awake and her frightened expression told him she knew how desperate their situation was.

Jimmy's teeth chattered as the water rose up his body.

The cruiser was sinking faster now and the available air was running out. With damage to the side panels and the front bench seat, Jimmy hoped the metal bar had snapped or broken away.

No such luck.

Jimmy turned to Mary. With the water up to their chests and their hands still manacled to the metal bar, it looked like their time had run out. Jimmy glanced to the side and saw that he and Mary were no longer alone.

Several of Jimmy's dead provocateurs had settled in beside them, their pale, sallow faces grinning. They nudged and pointed. One held his nose and held up his arm in a 'goodbye cruel world' gesture, another held his throat, crossed his eyes and stuck out his tongue, thoroughly enjoying the pair's final minutes.

*

"You really expect me to believe that *you* are my daughter?"

Nancy McFarland pulled her hand from Aimee's and sat back in her chair. "What do you think I am, young lady, an idiot?"

John took his wife's shoulder. "C'mon," he said, "we're wasting our time."

Aimee bowed her head. She was emotionally and physically drained. "I didn't believe it at first," she said in a low voice. "Sat out in the woods all night trying to figure out what happened. But just think about it. I know everything Aimee knows and proved it by answering every question you've asked. I even know your maiden name. If I'm not Aimee, how would I know that?

"I don't know," Nancy replied.

Aimee thought for a moment then said, "Remember the time I came home from school and saw you standing on the coffee table and said, 'Mom, why are you stand... then I saw the rat and jumped up on the table with you?"

229

Nancy paled. "How could you know that?" She reached over and grabbed Aimee's hands, there was a look of terror in her eyes. "What did you do to my daughter to make her tell you that?"

Suddenly realizing how shrill and threatening her actions had become she forced herself to take control. In order to find her daughter, she needed this girl to keep talking.

She released Aimee and changed her tone. "Well, you seem about Aimee's age. You could have heard about it at school or forced Aimee to tell you our family history."

Aimee gave her a puzzled look. "Forced? Why would I do that?"

"I don't know. They told us you had blood on your clothes when you were brought in."

"Don't worry, it's not mine...well not Aimee's. Anyway, you want more proof? Well, just look around. You must have noticed how strange everything has gotten. We've lived in Wheatfield all our lives. It's a quiet and peaceful, right? So how do you explain the recent gun battles, bank robberies, rapes, and murders? That sound like Wheatfield to you?"

"And for heaven sake, look at the people being accused of these crimes," Aimee continued. "Dad, you've known Steve Bogdasian for twenty years. He was my softball coach and I babysat his kids. Do you really think he would blow up seven state troopers and his own daughters?"

"I'm not your father!" he snapped.

Aimee exhaled. "Just think about it, okay?"

Nancy didn't resist when her husband coaxed her from her chair.

As they walked toward the door, Nancy suddenly turned. "So if you're Aimee, why did you text us and say your car broke down and you spent the night sleeping in it?"

"Because I didn't have any choice! How could I come home in this body or call with this voice? Still, I knew you'd be worried so I texted. At the time I had no idea what had happened." Her eyes welled with tears and her hands shook. "Can you imagine what it's like to wake up in someone else's body? Can you? Do you have any idea how horrifying it is to look in a mirror and see a completely different person staring back at you? And to tell you the truth," she added, sobbing, "I probably would have killed myself if Jimmy hadn't shown up and told me about Virgil's machine. The thing is, I thought it just made me and Sula switch bodies and that it could switch us back," Aimee replied. "It wasn't until later, at Jimmy's apartment that I learned my body had been crushed when the building collapsed."

Startled, Nancy fought to keep her emotions in check.

Aimee's dead? My little girl is dead?

Nancy refused to succumb. For Aimee's sake, she was going to get to the bottom of this and any breakdown would have to wait until she learned the exact location of her daughter's remains.

She steadied herself and said, "Okay then, let's say that is the case… So what happened to the person who belongs to the body you're in now?"

"Sula? She was the one who died, not me." Aimee explained.

"So where is your body now?" Nancy asked.

A tear fell from Aimee's eye. "It's at the bottom of a burned-down building in Dohesley, buried under tons of rubble."

Nancy became tight-lipped. "That's pretty convenient, young lady, especially since it's nearly impossible to get a permit to dig in or anywhere near Dohesley."

Aimee bowed her head and wept. As she did, John motioned toward the door and Nancy nodded. After they exited the room, Nancy returned the keys to the peg board.

While climbing the stairs, John said, "You didn't believe any of that hogwash did you?"

Nancy hesitated for a second and said, "Of course not. But at least now we have an idea where Aimee's remains are and the names of three people who were involved, a girl named Sula and two guys, Virgil Vanderhill and Jimmy. With any luck, when she gets out, she'll head right back to them and the police can arrest every one of those bastards."

*

231

Jimmy and Mary pressed their faces against the roof of the cruiser and desperately sucked at the little air that remained. When Jimmy looked down, he could see the dead laughing and pointing as he and Mary struggled for what were soon to be their final breaths.

And if that weren't enough, still another appeared outside the cruiser and was waving at them. Jimmy wanted to flip him off but was too busy trying to pull the bar loose.

However when Mary elbowed him and tiled her head toward the figure, Jimmy realized this person was real and had jumped into the lake to save them.

The man pointed to a large metal hook in his hand then disappeared behind the trunk. Moments later there was a tug and the cruiser was pulled upward.

Just as they had drawn in the last pocket of breathable air, the vehicle broke the surface and the water quickly poured out.

The battered cruiser was slowly pulled onto the dock.

Deke ran over, grabbed the window frame and poked his head in. "You people all right?"

Mary and Jimmy were soaking wet and gasping for air. "Yeah, thanks… thanks to you!"

Deke saw the handcuffs and the metal bar. He left and a few minutes later returned with a bolt cutter.

"That cop is out cold," Deke said as he pulled the cutters open. "But his pulse is steady and I called an ambulance. Now listen, I'm gonna cut you both lose, but only because there was a time I needed a break and got one, so I'm paying it forward. And in return, I expect you to make right whatever you did that got you in this mess."

Deke slipped the bolt cutters between Mary's cuffs and wrist and snapped them off, did the same for Jimmy.

"Now you folks better skedaddle," he said as he stood up.

Mary climbed out of the battered cruiser, placed her hand on Deke's arm and said, "Mister, you've just saved more lives than you will ever know."

Deke smiled as he walked to the back and unhooked the tow chain. "Glad to hear it."

Jimmy and Mary dove into Aimee's Mustang and sped off.

Chapter Forty

"I said, is there anybody out there?!"

Santiago and Martaine raced over to where they thought the voice was coming from. After removing several crates, they found Virgil lying on the floor in ragged and dirty clothes. They were, however, the same clothes he was wearing when they left him the previous day, only now torn and covered in ash.

Martaine quickly checked his vitals.

"He is exhibiting the signs of having undergone an exorcism," Martaine said as he gently helped Virgil to his feet.

Santiago quickly grabbed the sprayer of Holy Water, aimed at Virgil, and pulled the trigger.

"Nominee Patris et Fili…"

As Virgil's face was spritzed again and again, he waved his hands and said, "Hey, knock it off! What are you trying to do, drown me?"

Startled, Santiago and Martaine stepped back and stared at each other.

"My apologies," Santiago said, taking Virgil's left shoulder and lowering the Holy Water bottle. "In our experience, survivors of a daemonic possession are very fragile, both emotionally and physically. We meant only to assist."

"Yeah, well," Virgil replied as he wiped his face, staggered over to a nearby crate and sat down, "I guess I understand." He looked around. "Hey, wait. Where's the kid?"

"If you are referring to Aimee, she escaped unharmed," Santiago replied.

"Well that's good news. Anyway, you were right about those daemons. They're a lot more dangerous than the 500 crazies I let out."

Martaine crouched down and studied Virgil. "But how is it you are unharmed? Those possessed by those abominations are usually left emotionally devastated and deeply troubled."

"That's because they were not trained scientists!" Virgil said smugly as he brushed ash from his forearm. "And stop referring to them as abominations and monsters. Makes them sound supernatural and all powerful. Yeah, they're violent all right and have the strength and hide of a rhinoceros, but keep in mind, there are microscopic bacteria and viruses capable of inflicting months of unrelenting agony on the human body. When you consider what the micro-verse is capable of, these bogeymen are strictly minor leaguers."

Santiago pulled up a crate and sat in front of him. "But their domain is hell itself."

Virgil shivered momentarily, inspected his tattered clothes with a puzzled look, then replied. "Yeah, I'm pretty sure it's the place you holy rollers call hell. If not, its damn close. Unbelievable heat, and a blinding light that never sets, and smoke from sulfur fires surround the area."

"Were you not afraid?" Martaine asked.

"At first I was terrified," Virgil said. "But then saw that D'Shaid, with all his bluster and fury, didn't know what to make of what I had accomplished, and realizing he might need me somewhere down the line, saw to it that I wasn't harmed. I held tight until the spilled ectoplasmic fumes from the chamber ignited. The blast forced D'Shaid out of my body and somehow, I got sucked back into it."

"Amazing!" Santiago said.

Virgil shrugged. "D'Shaid and his buddies might be physically powerful, but they aren't all that smart and to survive, they need whatever pheromone or vibe or whatever ethereal compound human misery produces as sustenance. Pretty twisted, huh? But as science tells us, if you require fuel to survive, you can be killed."

"You're talking in circles. Please get to the point," Santiago said.

Virgil rolled his eyes and smirked. "Oh yeah, *I* talk in circles, parable boy. Anyway, bottom line? The only thing you guys know about daemons is when they show up, people get killed in horrible ways, so you think they're supernatural because regular weapons don't affect them. Our ancestors felt the same when they ran up against animals like the grizzly."

"Surely that is not the same," Santiago said dismissively.

"Sure it is," Virgil replied. "Think about it. A grizzly can grow over ten feet tall and eats live meat. If it decides you're on the menu, that's pretty much it. They can outrun, out climb and out swim you. And they won't hesitate to jam their six inch claws into your back, hold you in the air and tear the skin off your bones like string cheese."

"Your point being?"

"My point is when our ancestors finally stopped thinking of them as supernatural monsters, and took the time to study them, they were able to invent weaponry capable of killing the sonsabitches."

Santiago smirked dismissively. "So are you suggesting the next time a daemon appears, we pull a gun?"

"No smartass, what I'm saying is that they made a major mistake letting someone like me take a peek under the hood. They don't understand how my machine made it possible for them to enter our world, but I do, and I'm going to use that knowledge to send them back."

"But…"

"Listen," Virgil said as he stood and began pacing. "I've already figured out most of it. Religion and science are not all that different. The reason Holy Water and blessed articles work against these things is because they are infused with…well, to put in simple terms, positive energy. That positive energy cancels out the negative energy generated by these creatures. That's basic science 101. But since you don't fully understand how your weaponry works, you don't know how to improve it. I do."

"My friend," Martaine replied, "we have battled D'Shaid before. He is one of the most powerful daemons. He is ruthless, savage and merciless."

"Like I said, so is a grizzly. Just give me 24 hours and I'll have D'Shaid and his buddies high-tailing it back to the River Styx. Now all I need is for Jimmy and Mary to…"

Santiago's cell rang.

He opened it, said hello and listened carefully. After a few moments, he nodded and said, "I understand, Jess. Just sit tight and we will be there direc…"

A scream echoed from the cell phone. What followed was the squealing of tires, the breaking of glass and the sound of gunfire.

Chapter Forty One

As Aimee sat in the holding cell it suddenly occurred to her that she hadn't heard that nerve-jarring CLANK that resounded throughout the room every time the door was locked.

Curious, she got up and cautiously walked over. She discovered that not only was it unlocked, it was slightly ajar.

She slowly pressed against it, eyed the hallway and seeing it was empty, slipped out.

She saw the keys on the pegboard and quickly checked the other cells. She expected to find Jimmy and Mary, but neither was there.

Upstairs she could hear people running, phones ringing, and printers spitting out documents. She peaked up the stairwell, saw no one and considered making a break for it.

An innocent person doesn't run, a voice in her head said.

"Yeah, well this one does!" she muttered.

She looked at her clothes.

Shit!

She knew she wasn't going to just slip by in that bright orange jumpsuit.

Ahh, what's the worst that can happen? They grab me and drag me back.

She quietly climbed the stairs, pressed herself against the wall and peaked out.

There were heavily armed police everywhere. Each one was holding a rifle of some sort, tear gas containers, bullet-proof vests, and Tasers, Just when Aimee was about to dismiss her escape plan as a lost cause, an armored car burst through the front doors of the precinct and opened fire.

*

As Jimmy drove the Mustang off-road, he pulled his cell from the pocket of his soaking wet clothes. "Please work, please work!" He hit the on button and his heart momentarily sank when the screen remained dark.

"Ahh, shi…" he started to say when the phone slowly came to life.

"All right!" he said as he pressed Contacts, scrolled to Santiago's name and pressed SEND.

"Where are you?!!" Santiago shouted having answered on the first ring. He switched the phone to speaker so they could all hear.

"Me and Mary were picked up by the cops but got away. Can't take a chance of getting grabbed again so we're driving up Swinton Mountain's snowmobile trail. It's closed this time of year but we moved the sawhorses and slipped in. We're heading back to the barn. Since it's rubble, I doubt if they'll bother looking for us there."

Virgil leaned over from the back seat and said, "When word gets out about the explosion that place will be crawling with cops. Jimmy, this is Virgil. Go to my house and put Aimee's car in my garage so it won't be seen from the street. We'll meet you there."

"How long till you get there?" Jimmy asked.

"About forty-five minutes."

"Oh, and another thing," Jimmy said. "The cops are holding Aimee and Jess."

"I know. I spoke with Jess. She was released and is waiting outside the station house. Says an armored car just smashed through the front doors. We're heading there now. Hopefully Aimee is all right."

"An armored car!? We were nearly killed by one not fifteen minutes ago."

"What happened?"

"I explain later. In the meantime we'll head on over to Virgil's. Word of warning, though, I think that armored car is being driven by push-ins, so be real careful."

"Will do."

Jimmy ended the call and turned to Mary. "Jess has been released and the Rev is going to try to get Aimee out on bail."

"Jimmy, look at that!" Mary said pointing.

He did. Now three-quarters up the side of Swinton Mountain, the view was clear in all directions. And even without binoculars they could tell from the smoke, the sirens and the sound of distant gunfire that the Wheatfield police station was under siege.

*

When the armored car crashed through the walls and bullets, grenades and smoke bombs started flying, Aimee—frightened, exhausted, overwhelmed and maybe just a little bit crazy—saw that the thick clouds wafting down the stairs had created a smoke screen between her and the police. Seeing the hole created by the armored vehicle, she dashed for it.

She expected to be shot and when she wasn't, became giddily euphoric. With rapid gunfire and explosions shaking the ground beneath her, Aimee leapt through the hole, jumped over the railing to the landscaped grounds below and sprinted behind the bushes toward the side street. As she vaulted from the grounds to the sidewalk, she collided with…

"Jess?" Aimee said after they ricocheted off each other and narrowly avoided tumbling into the street.

"Good Lord, child!" Jess said grabbing a stop sign pole and steadying herself. "What are you doing in prison clo?"

Aimee didn't let her finish, instead she grabbed Jess' shoulders and whipped off her knee length raincoat.

As Jess watched in surprise, Aimee slipped it on, buttoned it, then reached down and folded the jumpsuits pant legs up over her knees. She then twisted her hair into a knot and pulled the back of her collar over it. She took Jess' arm and said, "Let's go!"

*

Five minutes later, the clergymen plus Virgil approached the spot where they were supposed to rendezvous with Jess. The police however had set up a detour for regular traffic and were hastily setting up a blockade in front of the police station.

The Impala was next in the line of cars and Santiago would have been forced to follow the detour except at that very moment, the armored car burst from the hole and rumbled down the stairs toward the assembled police cruisers.

In the commotion, Santiago slid the Impala between the sawhorses and headed down the blocked-off street.

As they slowly ambled along, passing the surrounding buildings and alleys, a pebble struck the side window. When Martaine turned, he saw Jess and Aimee emerge from behind a dumpster. After telling Santiago to stop the car, he flung open the back door and waved them in.

"Whew!" Aimee said as she joined Martaine in the back. "I was afraid you guys wouldn't make it. I tried to call but was sent straight to voicemail."

"The Lord is obviously keeping an eye out for us," Santiago said as Jess climbed in alongside him. "We are all presently free from imprisonment. Let us hope we may continue in that regard."

Aimee's eyes lit up, "All free? You mean Jimmy and Mary got away?"

"They're on their way to Virgil's house as we speak," Santiago said as he turned the car at the light and took the road out of town. Jess sighed and said, "That's a relief!"

It was then Aimee saw Virgil behind Martaine and jerked in surprise. "Hey! You're all right. I was afraid you got killed in the barn."

Virgil smiled. "Same here, kid!"

Aimee leaned toward the driver's seat. "Father, before we go to Virgil's, can we stop at Jimmy's place? I have to change out of these prison clothes."

Santiago considered the request for a moment then made the turn to Jimmy's. "I will swing by but should I see any suspicious vehicles, I will not stop."

"Fair enough," Aimee replied, "but I think it will be all right. When me and Jimmy were shopping, he told me his apartment is considered part of the downstairs restaurant, so there shouldn't be any record of him living there."

Aimee had completely forgotten that Jimmy locked the door when they left. Fortunately, it was only a door knob lock so Aimee stepped back, muttered an apology, then slammed her shoulder against it.

With Sula's considerable upper body strength it gave easily. Aimee quickly gathered the shopping bags, pulled out jeans, a blue blouse, bra and panties, her new white-canvas sneakers and quickly changed. After collecting her toiletries and Jimmy's, she tossed them in a bag, exited the apartment, jammed the front door closed with a wad of cardboard from Sula's old shoe, then headed down the stairs and waited in the shadows until Santiago's Chevy Impala, having circled the block, picked her up.

*

"What in Sam Hill was that all about?" Detective Hutchins, the bald, mustached man who had interrogated Aimee asked as he climbed to his feet, holstered his gun and pressed through the debris and the smoke.

Officer Myrrh Cavanaugh, who had come in an hour early to answer questions regarding what happened on the night of the Dohesley incident, shook her head as she wiped the plaster dust from her uniform. "I have no idea, but I'll tell you this: after the armored car crashed through and took out the communication center and the ceiling caved in, I saw a guy jump out of the back and race downstairs to the holding cells. When he came back, he yelled, 'The bitch ain't there!' then jumped back in and the truck took off."

After hearing the words 'the bitch ain't there' the detective turned and charged down the stairs to interrogation room #2.

When he arrived and saw the door open, he balled his fists and shouted, "Sonavabitch!"

Chapter Forty Two

Virgil's house was situated on three acres of land. The expansive McMansion was painted light gray with white trim, was two stories high, with seven bedrooms, two gas fireplaces (one was in the center of the expansive deck) and a three-car garage.

He and Dora purchased it when things were good and Lillian was alive. Virgil made top dollar in those days and he bought that particular estate to show everyone (especially his mother) how well he was doing.

When Santiago and company arrived, they pulled into the garage and closed the door. After they exchanged hellos with Jimmy and Mary, Virgil looked them over and said, "You two look like drowned rats."

"Does it look like I'm in the mood for jokes, numb nuts?" Jimmy replied sullenly.

Virgil shrugged, opened the side door and they entered the house.

Once inside, Virgil went to his bedroom and scoured his clothes closets and dresser drawers for a shirt and pants to replace Jimmy's wet ones. It took a few minutes since Jimmy wasn't as tall or thin but eventually some were found and Jimmy was able to toss his into the dryer.

Finding something for Mary was harder, as Dora was heavier and not as tall. But a recently laundered sweat suit was found and fit well enough for Mary to toss her wet clothes in with Jimmy's.

Realizing they all needed a break from the roller-coaster ride that had become their lives, Virgil went to the back deck, fired up the gas grill and invited everyone to come out to sit in the sun and relax for a while. As they took him up on his offer, he took hamburgers and franks from the fridge, as well as rolls, salt-and-vinegar potato chips, macaroni salad, potato salad and iced tea. With the high walls surrounding the deck, they were safe from prying eyes and, for at least a little while, could enjoy this momentary break in the action.

As the food was served and after both Mary and Jimmy put on their dried clothes, they talked among themselves and compared notes. They listened intently as Santiago spoke about D'Shaid, then to Virgil as he spoke about the netherworld and finally to Mary, as she described the daemons on the side roads. Aimee however, said nothing about her experience at the Blue Barn, other than there had been an attack and she had survived.

After the sun set and the deck lights came on, they continued to chat, had more drinks and another round of food but after such an exhausting day, it was clear it was going to be an early night.

After the food was gone, Mary and Jess helped with the clean up and, having endured a little too much excitement for people their age, camped out on the living room's black, plush, wraparound couch. They fell asleep on it shortly thereafter.

Santiago and Martaine were given adjoining rooms just off the kitchen and Jimmy and Aimee told Virgil they'd pick theirs from one of the three on the second floor.

"Fine," Virgil replied. "Just remember I'll be in the one with the beige door." With that he said "Goodnight," and stepped back into the house.

Too wound up to sleep, Jimmy and Aimee remained on the deck, side by side on the padded lounge chairs and gazed at the flames inside the brick fireplace. The neon blue bug zapper sparked to life as it incinerated an alighting insect.

"This is an awfully big house for just two people. Well, one person now," Aimee said as the firelight shimmered across her face. "This deck alone is bigger than the basement in my house, and our house is the biggest on the block."

"That's nothing, the master bathroom is bigger than my apartment," Jimmy remarked and they both laughed.

After pouring a glass of iced tea for them both, Jimmy sat back down and took a sip. "Man," he said, smacking his lips, "I would really prefer something stronger right now but I don't want to be half in the bag if the bad guys show up. What a day!" he said shaking his head in disbelief.

"That's for sure!" Aimee replied. She stared off, took a sip of her tea but wore a solemn expression when she placed the glass down. In a very soft voice she said, "I've never been so frightened." She paused for a moment then added, "Or heartbroken."

Jimmy sat up, reached over and placed his hand on hers. "Heartbroken? Why heartbroken?"

Aimee bit down on her lip as tears welled. "The cops surprised me by bringing in my parents. I was so happy to see them. But when I tried to hug my mother, she shoved me away. Screamed at me! My father wouldn't even look at me."

She wiped her eyes with her sleeve. "I'd been through so much, I was so shaken. All I wanted was for them to hold me and tell me everything was going to be all right."

She started to sob. "But when I saw all that hatred and anger, it finally sunk in. I no longer have a home, or parents, and I'll probably never see my little brother again. I can't even describe what it's like to be considered a monster by the people I love. I can't get over how wrong this is. All I did was try to help, that's all. And what did I get for it? I got abandoned by my family, damn near raped by two psychos, then arrested and charged with my own murder."

Startled, Jimmy leaned in. "Wait. You were nearly raped?"

She waved him off. "I don't want to talk about it," she said as she bowed her head and continued weeping.

Several moments passed then Jimmy said, "Looking back, do you know what scared *me* the most?"

Unable to speak Aimee looked up and shook her head.

"Knowing that I wasn't there when you needed me," he said. "When I think of you being there alone when Virgil was possessed, or when the Blue barn was destroyed. I... I..."

He stood, took her hand and brought her to her feet. He kissed her and she wrapped her arms around him. She ran her hand up the inside of his leg and he placed his hand on her breast. She moaned and leaned her head back. He nibbled her ear and kissed the side of her neck.

"Let's go upstairs," she whispered.

He smiled, turned off the fireplace flames then took her hand and together they left the deck, closed and locked the door, then raced up the stairs to claim an empty room.

Seeing a blue door, they entered, quietly locked it and wrapped themselves in each other's arms.

"I want you so bad," Aimee moaned as they kissed and began removing each other's clothes.

"Me, too," Jimmy said as he slipped off her blouse and bra. He saw the gauze covered wound. "Where did you get that?"

"Don't worry about it" she said as she leaned back, eyed him, then lowered his zipper and slipped her hand down the front of his pants. "Hmmm," she moaned.

He unzipped her jeans and slid them to the floor. As she kicked them aside, he slipped both hands inside the back of her panties and grabbed her ass.

She pushed his pants down, then his underwear.

As he started to remove her panties, a figure appear on the edge of the bed, then another and another. It was the same group who had watched and cheered as he and Mary nearly drowned in the back of the police cruiser.

She noticed the change in his demeanor. "What's the matter?" she asked as she gently ran her hand over his erection.

He stepped back and scrunched up his face in frustration. "The reason I don't date, is... well because there isn't a single moment that I'm free of the spirit world. Since I refuse to do what they ask, they taunt me by showing up whenever I need a private moment."

"A private moment?" she asked with a confused look.

He grimaced. "They're here right now." He tilted his head to the side, "sitting on the edge of the bed, watching our every move."

"Oh," she said startled. She covered her breasts with her hand and forearm, scoured the room and eyed the bed. After a moment, she took a deep breath and gazed deeply into Jimmy's eyes. She smiled, stepped back, slid her hands into the sides of her panties, stretched the elastic and let them drop to the floor. Naked, she placed her hand on his chest and pushed him onto the bed.

"Let 'em watch!" she giggled and dove on top of him.

Chapter Forty Three

"That was wonderful," Aimee said as she pressed her body against Jimmy's. It was early morning and the two had just finished making love for the second time in ten hours. She gave him a squeeze, sat up and noted for the first time how very feminine the room was. Lace curtains, pink and peach-colored pillows, lavender walls, floral paintings, everything most women would desire in a room of their own.

Except there aren't any women living here.

She recalled what Virgil said about his wife, his mother and his life. He had lost everything, just like her.

Must be very hard to live in such a beautiful home and have no one to share it with.

Jimmy sat up and slipped his arm around her shoulder. She turned, kissed him and asked. "Are the ghost perverts still here?"

Jimmy smiled. "No, they revel in whatever makes a person unhappy. When they realized you didn't care, they lost interest."

"Good," she replied. "Oh look, it's six o'clock. Turn on the morning news. Let's see if there's any word on the daemons."

Jimmy nodded as they both skooched back against the headboard. Jimmy grabbed the remote from the lace covered bedside table and clicked on the TV.

"...Good morning and welcome to On The Spot News, I'm Dave Braverman. New DNA evidence taken from the fingernails of murder victim Ellis Macawber has eliminated Mary McGuernsey, whose ATM receipt was found beneath his body, as a suspect. Autopsy reports indicate Macawber was stabbed repeatedly by two assailants, both of whom were male and at least six-feet tall. Mary McGuernsey is a sixty-seven-year-old female and is five-foot six. Police are asking that anyone with information on the slaying call 555-0154.

"In other news, drivers using Route 404 are advised to watch out for stray pigs wandering the hillsides. It is believed they escaped from the Little Piggy Hog Farms, located several miles north of Titusville. Little Piggy has been a mainstay in the area for

over twenty years and employs over 100 people. Phone calls to their business offices have not been returned.

The company suffered a power outage when a still unexplained electrical surge nearly fried the power stations along Route 727 just outside of Dohesley Township several days ago. Officials believe the incident may have shorted the magnetic locks on the pigsties. Further information on this story as it becomes available.

Power has been restored to the Swinton Mountain Lake area, meaning Saturday's speed boat race will commence as scheduled. Adirondack Power and Light reports that residents of Titusville should have their power restored by the end of the day and that the sodium arc lamps on Route 727 have been repaired.

"In sports, the New York Mets..."

Aimee leaned forward and was watching intensely. When the story changed to sports, she quietly muttered. "Damn! I wish I could read people's auras over the TV."

It was the phrasing that caught Jimmy's attention. He turned toward her. "You can read auras?"

Unaware that she had spoken aloud and startled when she realized she had, Aimee frantically tried to backpedal. "Oh! Well... uh, what I meant to say is that I wished I could read auras...uh...like Mary."

Jimmy eyed her suspiciously and muted the TV. "Then why add 'over the TV?'"

She looked away. "I... I don't know."

Her face reddened as he studied her. "Okay, okay," she finally said. "Yes, I can read auras."

Jimmy swung his legs over the side of the bed, reached down and picked up his underwear. "Now it makes sense."

"What does?"

"I was wondering why the armored car crashed through the police station after they tried to kill Mary and me. Now I understand. Believing they had finished us off, they went to take care of the only other loose end: you. Why didn't you tell us?"

Aimee climbed out of bed, gathered her clothes and started dressing.

"Because at first I didn't know what it was. Remember the first time you took me to the Blue Barn? Well, during the ride I saw shadows along Route 727, scary shadows. It freaked me out so I buried my head in the map. Then I saw Mary, she had this gray light surrounding her. I thought it was some kind of side effect from being in Sula's body, and it wasn't until Jess told me about Mary's abilities that I realized I had them, too. I don't think mine are anywhere as strong, but I got them."

"I still don't understand why you didn't say anything," Jimmy said as he finished dressing.

"Because I didn't know if it was permanent or just temporary. Besides, the push-ins tried to frame Mary for murder because of her abilities and I sure didn't want them coming after me." She sat down in the chair and put on her white sneakers. "Not that it did a whole lot of good. Apparently, they knew anyway."

"Well," Jimmy said. "It probably doesn't matter. This thing is coming to a head and I figure by the end of the day, it will be resolved one way or the other. With that, he took the remote and unmuted the TV.

After Aimee finished dressing and sat down beside him, Jimmy noted that Braverman said they'll be back after commercial with the world news.

"That's all the local news?" Jimmy said.

"Guess it was a slow night."

He turned to her.

Her eyes widened. "You're right!" she said. "No crime means the push-ins are laying low."

"And," Jimmy added, "they're working as a team."

"Why do you think that?"

"Well according to the cop shows, when guys break out of prison they usually split up. This way if one guy gets caught, the rest still have a chance. If they haven't gone their separate ways, it means someone has taken control and is a person who can make 100 hardcore criminals do what he says."

"D'Shaid!" Aimee said.

"Exactly! The question is, where are they and what are they planning?"

249

Just then, they heard Virgil charging down the stairs calling Mary's name.

Chapter Forty Four

Virgil got up at five a.m. that morning. He'd forgotten to close the blinds and the glare of the morning sun rousted him out of bed. The room with the beige door was just an ordinary room he had converted into an office.

Inside was a twin bed, a small refrigerator and a microwave so he could rest or have a bite to eat while working on a project. On the professional side, the room also had a large, steel and glass, black-lacquered desk, a state-of-the-art desktop computer, a drafting table and various electronic accessories. Still half asleep, he climbed out of bed, booted up his computer and had it download the information from the Blue Barn.

Anticipating the possibility that the barn may be attacked or destroyed after his mother and the push-ins escaped, he programmed the computers there to continuously upload its information to an online data storage company.

In addition, he set up digital cameras in the rafters. As he installed them, Martaine quoted the old saw about locking the barn door after the horse was stolen, but Virgil—convinced it was the *not knowing* that caused all the problems—was determined not to make that mistake a second time.

By the time the data and the videos were retrieved, he was fully awake and ready to get to work.

As he reviewed them he was thoroughly impressed with Aimee's devotion to duty. She never left the control panel (except for the occasional bathroom break) and made sure all the technical information regarding the transfers was properly categorized and uploaded by the computers.

He was pleased that everything had worked so well. The data was detailed and complete; the videos clear and steady and the audio recordings were hiss and echo free. A self-satisfied smile spread broadly across his face.

Then he saw Amanda Bogdasian enter the barn.

And as the story of losing her family unfolded, Virgil's smile was replaced with mute horror. His hands fell from the keyboard and dangled limply at his sides. His eyes filled with tears. Twice he stopped the video. Twice he had to grab the comforter from his bed and press it against his mouth to muffle his sobbing. For nearly fifteen minutes he gazed at the motionless screen, staring at Amanda, seeing her despair. Her eldest daughter's comments echoed in his head. "We didn't make any noise, Mom. Not a sound. After he locked us in the attic we held hands and quietly prayed that you wouldn't get hurt."

It's my fault. I'm responsible. My God! I got that family killed!

He again pressed the comforter to his face and bawled uncontrollably.

It took a half hour before Virgil was able to continue. After wiping his tear-stained face, he returned to work with a new resolve

No matter what it takes, no matter what I have to do, I will put an end to this.

When he went back to watching the videos, he was amazed by the amount of push-ins they had conned into returning. It was like a going out of business sale. Eventually however, the videos of push-ins entering the barn grew monotonous so Virgil sped up the film to the part where the barn was hit by the rocket.

He pressed his hands to the sides of his face in horror when the saw the explosion and the ectoplasmic chamber's platform rocket into Agent Miller's back and nearly snap him in two. In the now shaking background and growing smoke, he saw Aimee get thrown from the underside of his cartwheeling desk and deftly grab the satellite cables in mid-air and slowly she lowered herself to safety.

Suddenly, a monstrous figure stepped into the frame.

"What the hell is…Holy shit, is that me?" he said aloud when he saw himself grin malevolently then leap right through the roof as the building collapsed and the video terminated.

"That was D'Shaid in my body," Virgil murmured.

D'Shaid.

Virgil fell back in his chair and ran his finger over his upper lip.

Abomination, Santiago had called him.

He thought of what had happened to the Bogdasian family. With a cold and determined look, he leaned into the screen.

Well, abomination or not, get ready for round 2, you sonavabitch, because I'm going to put an end to you and your friends once and for all.

Virgil opened the schematics to what he originally called his 'Telephone to the Dead, machine', but had shortened the file name to the Dead machine, then opened his notes on the ectoplasmic chamber's gasses, hoping that somewhere in those powerful and unstable chemicals was a clue on how to destroy the daemons. They were powerful but not indestructible, and fed on human suffering.

But how does the process work?

He put his feet on his desk, leaned back in his chair and tapped his pencil on his thigh. A minute or so later he returned to the keyboard and created a new file.

Is misery and unhappiness something concrete? Does it emanate from a person like an odor or pheromone? If so, can it be re-created and used as bait, the way hunters use lure to attract…?

Virgil shook his head and dropped his hands into his lap. It was all well and good in theory but he needed something tangible, a way to view and analyze the emissions so he could re-create them.

Shit!

Virgil stared at the blinking cursor.

Double shit!

He slammed the pencil on the desk.

If I could just hook a daemon to a MRI, I could see what organs activate when he absorbs this human emission. Then I could block…

He shook his head. Such thoughts were merely wool gathering.

Maybe I'm looking at this from the wrong angle.

He folded his arms and placed his hand to his chin. *All right, what is the lowest common denominator? What exactly do they metabolize as fuel? Clearly it is something humans emanate…*

Vibrations?

253

Vibes! Mary feels vibes! I can use her to figure out what is attracting the daemons and create a similar vibe or pheromone or whatever, to draw them in.

He shot out of his chair, raced to the door and ran into the hall. "Mary!!"

Receiving no reply, Virgil vaulted down the stairs—taking several at a time—and burst into the living room. When he called out again Mary jumped and Jess stirred. It had also alerted Jimmy and Aimee who, after making sure no one was nearby, slid into the hall and down the stairs.

Seeing Mary, Aimee quickly came over, took her hand and pulled her to the side. "I got good news," she said. "You're no longer a suspect in the Macawber killing."

Mary's face brightened. "Really? Where did you hear that?"

"When Jimmy and I woke up this morning, we put on the news and the reporter sa…" Aimee stopped, and realizing she had just let the cat out of the bag, blushed.

Mary leaned in. "Honey, we may not get through this day in one piece. So as for you and Jimmy…Well," she said with a sly smile and a wink, "if he had made a play for me, we'd still be at it."

As Aimee chuckled, Virgil summoned the clergymen and within minutes everyone was gathered in the living room. Once they were all seated on the couch, Virgil pulled up a chair and began.

"The first thing I need to know, Mary, is what is it about a suffering person that alerts you to their condition?"

She yawned, then blinked several times to clear her vision. "You mean their vibe?"

"Yes. If three people, with their faces completely covered, are lined up in front of you and one of them is suffering emotionally, could you pick that person out and if so, how?"

Mary thought for a second, then crossed her feet and pushed her long silver hair from her face. "I could probably feel their vibe," she replied, "if not, then certainly by reading their aura. A person suffering, for whatever reason, is surrounded by a gray aura. It resembles the sky on a cold, overcast day. A healthy, normal person's aura is bright and airy. A violent and brutal person's aura is like tar, black and thick. But those are extremes. Most people's auras change with their circumstances. We are generally attracted to people with strong, light, positive auras, repelled by those with dark, negative auras and we try to help and comfort those with troubled gray ones. It's human nature."

Virgil quickly scribbled in his notepad. "But why are the daemons attracted to people with gray auras?"

"Because they have no faith," Santiago said matter-of-factly.

Virgil spun toward him "What? Explain."

"Misery is a by-product of fear," he replied. "A person with strong faith knows God will get them through life's many trials. And since they are aware that every obstacle is merely temporary, they do not fall victim to despair or misery. Those who lack faith however, see no escape and are overwhelmed by their concerns."

"Which attracts the daemons, which in turn creates more misery," Virgil mused. "Interesting, but I'm looking for something tangible. Something I can re-create in a lab to use as bait."

Santiago gave a bewildered look. "Why would you want to do that?"

Virgil rolled his eyes, then glared condescendingly. "Because in order to stop them, we have to make them come to us. Try to keep up will you." He turned to Mary. "I need to run some tests on you, I know a guy at Wheatfield's Medical labs and…"

"Whoa, wait a minute!" Jimmy said. He rose from the couch, grabbed Virgil by the arm and pulled him aside. "If you think I'm going to let you do to Mary what you did to me…"

Virgil snarled and yanked free. "The tests I did made it possible for me to build the ectoplasmic chamber. If we're going to stop these sonsabitches, we have to know what attracts them, what they feed on and how to destroy them and I need Mary to get that information."

Hearing her name being bandied about, Mary got up, walked over and joined them. "Listen boys, any decision made about me will be made by me. Got that?"

"I don't like the idea of him doing tests on you," Jimmy snapped and gave a cold eye to Virgil.

255

Virgil placed his hands on his hips and matched Jimmy's cold stare with one of his own. "Yeah, well without the tests, we don't have a chance."

"What kind of tests?" Mary asked.

After Virgil explained and Jimmy pointed out the side-effects and emotional trauma involved, Mary decided to get Jess' opinion.

Jess was sitting on the edge of the couch staring into the hallway. When Mary took her arm, she felt a chill. She assumed it was the air-conditioning.

"I need your advice, Jess."

"Mary!" Aimee said, suddenly concerned.

That's when Jess turned, and what Mary saw nearly brought on another seizure.

Whatever it was, it was not Jess behind that face and the others immediately noticed it, too.

"Stand back, everyone!" Santiago shouted as he ran toward Jess and pushed Mary aside.

Jess began to shake and fell from the couch to her knees. She sobbed as her face morphed from one of fury to one of fear. "I ain't up to no deviltry, Daddy!" she blubbered. "I swear, I ain't up to no deviltry!"

"Everyone get into the bathroom," Martaine called out as he grabbed the black box, opened it, removed one of the road flares and tossed it to Jimmy. "Get in, lock the door, light this and place it in the tub. The sulfur will smell terrible but it will protect you until we can free Jess."

As Virgil backed away, and Jimmy and Aimee hustled Mary from the room, Mary called out. "Free Jess? Has she been…"

Suddenly Jess leapt to her feet and backhanded Santiago across the face with enough force to send him sailing across the room.

"Go!" Martaine shouted.

As Jimmy and company ran down the hall, Martaine helped Santiago to his feet.

The priest wiped the blood from his nose and with Martaine by his side, charged.

Meanwhile, as Jimmy ushered Mary and Aimee into the bathroom, Virgil suddenly chose not to join them.

"I gotta go back and watch those guys in action," Virgil said, starting back. "They're using 2000 years of passed down experience and I need that data."

"But you were already possessed once," Mary said. "What makes you think they won't do it a second time?"

"Because nobody fools *me* twice!" Virgil snapped and raced down the hall.

Ten minutes later, Santiago knocked on the bathroom door. "You may come out, my friends," he said. "The danger has passed."

Aimee and Mary, with towels pressed against their noses, opened the door a crack, confirmed it was Santiago and filed out. Jimmy stayed just long enough to toss the still lit flare into the toilet, where it extinguished.

Mary took the priest's hand. "How is Jess?" she asked, clearly concerned.

"We have driven the unclean spirit from her body," Santiago replied as he patted her hand, then stepped inside the bathroom, unrolled several squares of toilet tissue and pressed them against his bloody nose.

Santiago heard footsteps, turned, and saw Virgil approaching.

"The daemon who possessed Jess' father has been attempting to possess her," he continued. "Fortunately, we were able to drive it out, but our situation is grave."

Virgil stepped up alongside, eyed the clergyman sideways and twisted his lips. "You're a big fan of drama, aren't you, padre? Just tell her what the deal is!"

Santiago's face tightened. "If you are so knowledgeable, why don't you tell her?"

Virgil exhaled in exasperation. "Fine! Bottom line? Another daemon has broken through which means the barrier is starting to crumble. So unless we do something soon, they're all going to break through and possess whatever they can get their hands on."

"Whatever?" Jimmy asked. "Don't you mean whoever?"

Virgil shook his head. "Nope. So keep your eye on Fluffy, she just might push your clock radio into the tub while you're taking a bath."

Aimee eyed him. "Well, Virgil, since the worst that can happen is already happening; you seem to be in a good mood. I'm guessing you found what you were looking for?"

Virgil reached in and turned off the bathroom light. "Not exactly, but after watching these guys in action, it confirms my theory that the daemons can be hurt. And if they can be hurt, they can be killed."

Virgil was about to go into detail when he saw Mary look away. He turned to see what caught her attention.

It was Martaine with his arm around Jess' shoulder. She looked dazed but in considerably better condition than when they last saw her.

Mary and Jess exchanged heartfelt hugs, then Mary stepped back to look her over. "How are you doing, hon? You had us all scared."

Jess took a deep breath and exhaled. "I was pretty scared, too. I could literally feel myself being forced out of my body. But just when I thought I was a goner, someone grabbed me and pulled me back. That was Father Santiago here," she said, placing her hand on his shoulder.

"Good job, holy guys," Virgil said sarcastically as he placed his fists on his hips. "Now let's get back to the Halls of Justice so we can continue our never ending battle against the forces of evil."

Jimmy's snarled. "You're a douche bag, you know that?"

"Oh lighten up, I …" He turned and sniffed the air. "Wait! What is that stink?"

"That would be your bathroom," Jimmy replied, with a grin and a tilt of his head.

"Geez, McCracken, see a proctologist."

"Uh, guys?" Aimee said with her arms extended.

She didn't have to say anything else.

After they returned to the living room, Virgil said, "Okay, so, here's my theory. I believe the reason Padre Pio's holy water is so effective against daemons is because he was continuously channeling a more formidable power."

"God and the angles," said Santiago.

"Let's keep religion out of this for the time being," Virgil said. "I want to take a scientific approach."

Santiago shrugged. "As you wish." He stood up, walked over and leaned against the fireplace mantle. As he glanced down, he noticed a collection of silver-plated fireplace hardware inside an ornate holder, in particular, a poker, metal tongs and a brush. He grinned when he saw that the logs weren't really logs at all and the fireplace itself ran on natural gas.

Such affectations, he said to himself.

Virgil tapped his finger to his lips and continued. "We know from Jimmy that those who channel the dead are often possessed by daemons, so conversely if one channels those on the positive side, they would be infused with the power of... uh... inter-dimensional beings with, uh..."

Martaine smirked and slapped his knee. "Oh for heaven's sake, just say angels, jackass!"

Virgil made a dismissive wave of his hand. "Fine, fine, angels, whatever. Anyway, my scientific point is Padre Pio contacted this inter-dimensional force several times a day and so was able to channel that positive force into that water the daemons are so afraid of. What I need to do is construct a chemical that is as powerful as Pio's holy water."

"I don't see how that's possible," Santiago said as he ambled over to the window. "One is of God and one is of man."

"But the results are the same," Virgil replied. "The laws of physics aren't being breached here. Whatever Padre Pio's water contains is a tangible element that has an adverse effect on the daemons.

Aimee raised her hand and waved it. "Guys, guys, I really think we ought to take care of the remaining push-ins first." she said as she began rummaging through her purse. "We know how to get rid of them and we should do that before taking on the daemons, even though the daemons are more dangerous. Oh, here we go," she said, pulling out her makeup kit.

Her comment stopped the conversation.

Finally Virgil spoke up. "You know, I think the kid's right. Push–ins can pass as regular humans, disappear into the crowd then attack at will. And judging by what I became after being possessed by D'Shaid, daemons are far too different looking to pass. The problem is, I haven't figured out how to get the push-ins to come to us.

"And even if you did," Mary added, "we no longer have the Blue Barn or the equipment to send them back."

Virgil shook his finger to indicate he didn't quite agree. "Technically, that's correct, but I have an idea for a new device, one that could possibly take them all out if we got them in one place."

Having just finished peeking through the blinds, Santiago eyed him sideways. "How?" he asked. "The Tesla coil is gone, as is the ectoplasmic chamber, not to mention the power necessary…"

Virgil waved him off. "That was for the original, which was big, awkward and to be honest, very inefficient. The second machine, the one I installed in the barn's doorway, was better. This new one, a third generation device, can be just as effective yet powered by something as simple as a car battery and detonated like a hand grenade."

"Really?" Jimmy said, clearly impressed.

Virgil thought for a moment, then slowly nodded, "I'm almost sure of it."

"But that still leaves the problem of getting them all in one place," Mary said.

Aimee snapped the cap back on her lipstick and said, "I think that problem's already been solved."

Jimmy turned and with a confused look said, "Really? I got to start paying more attention."

Aimee smiled and said, "Earlier, Jimmy and I were watching television. During the news the reporter said that pigs were wandering the hillsides off Route 404. Said the Little Piggy Hog farm employs about 100 people, but had a power outage on the night Lillian and the push-ins took over and their business isn't returning calls even though their product is running around loose. I bet that's where the remaining push-ins are hiding."

Mary turned to the others. "You know, that's a real possibility. Dohesley Township is between Wheatfield and St. Lawrenceville and Little Piggy is just 5 miles north of that, right over the hill. If they were let out early because of the outage, they may have seen the fireworks and gone to Dohesley out of curiosity."

They kicked around that possibility for several minutes until Jimmy stood and replaced Virgil center stage.

"Okay, folks," he said, looking at his watch. "We're running out of time. Virgil, can you build this device or not?"

For once, the supremely confident Virgil seemed unsure. Theoretically he was confident his new, smaller version would work, but technology-wise, the device would be a considerable leap of faith. There would be no time to test it or even to make sure it wouldn't blow them all to Kingdom Come when detonated.

Martaine studied Virgil as he struggled with the answer. During their time together he discovered that Virgil was terrified of failing at a critical moment, so he decided to challenge him, in the hope of igniting his enormous ego.

Martaine rose, gestured to Virgil and said in a dismissive tone "You're asking if he can build the device? Of course he can! Why not too long ago, I stood before all of you and declared him to be a freakin' genius!" With that, he reached down and placed his hand on Virgil's shoulder. "And to prove I truly believe it, I will be the one who detonates the device."

Startled, Virgil's eyes widened and his face reddened. "Wha...wha...Wait!" Virgil said as he removed Martaine's hand. "Since it is my machine, I should be..."

"Au contraire," Martaine interrupted, waving his finger side to side. "If you are truly a freakin' genius, the device will work. Of course," he added with a grin, "if you wish me to retract my statement..."

That conniving S.O.B, Virgil thought to himself. *He's doing this so should the device fail, I'll still be around to construct another with hopefully better luck...*

261

"Then it's settled," Martaine said. "Virgil will construct, and I will detonate. How much time do you need to design it and for us to retrieve the components?"

Out maneuvered, Virgil reluctantly capitulated. "At least to mid-afternoon," he replied, placing his fist to his lips. "And another thing. We may have to force our way into Little Piggy, so we're going to need a powerful vehicle with a heavy duty battery to charge and calibrate the new device. None of the cars in the garage fit the bill."

"Looks like our luck is holding out," Mary said. "I own a brand new Ford F-350 dually V8 diesel with a hybrid battery to keep the fuel from thickening on cold nights. Believe me, it's got all the bells and whistles. I use it for plowing snow and pulling my trailer when I'm out on tour," she said reaching into her pocketbook and pulling out the keys.

Jimmy looked around. "I guess that does it. Brother Martaine, when Virgil completes the design, you two get the equipment. In the meantime, me and Aimee will google Little Piggy and find out as much as we can, then we'll get Mary's truck and Mary, since you know Jess better than any of us, why don't you and Father keep her company?"

When no one objected, they began their preparations.

*

"Look at this mess," Officer Van Pelt commented, gesturing toward the inside of the Wheatfield police station. He and the other officers on the 4-to-midnight crew arrived fifteen minutes early to plan their next move before leaving on patrol.

To enter, they had to climb over piles of twisted metal, wallboard, broken desks and other debris. The inside was crowded with repair crews and structural engineers. The sounds of hammering, sawing and drilling filled the air.

Van Pelt picked up a brick, eyed it, then tossed it into a nearby wheelbarrow. He shook his head. "Un-freakin-believable!"

As they waded through the smoke and over broken brick and mortar, they saw the collapsed ceiling above the communications center and the mangled antenna that had once stood on top of it.

Van Pelt felt sure the push-ins were responsible. It was the only scenario that made sense. What possible reason would ordinary criminals have to crash through the front entrance of a police station, open fire, toss grenades, then speed away without having accomplished anything?

So the question was, *why* had they done it?

When Van Pelt checked that day's police blotter he believed he'd found the answer. Jimmy, Mary, Jess and Aimee (who had been booked as a Jane Doe), had been arrested earlier and the armored car that crashed through the front of the station house was the same that had pushed the police cruiser off the pier. It wasn't the police the push-ins were going after, they were out to get Jimmy, Mary, Jess and Aimee.

After signing in and receiving their assignments, Van Pelt and his fellow officers went to the downstairs parking garage to plan.

Under the garage's rows of florescent lights, Van Pelt folded his arms and leaned against one of the parked patrol cars. "Okay, I think I know what happened," he began. "When the push-ins learned that the people who could identify them weren't killed when the barn blew up, they stole an armored car to finish the job. Amazingly, Jimmy and Mary survived the attempt on their lives, as did Jess and Aimee. The way I see it, our job is to run interference until Virgil can free the remaining victims of the push-ins."

"But is Virgil is still alive?" Pastore asked, eying Van Pelt. "The last time we were at the Blue Barn, Virgil and Aimee were alone."

"True, but Aimee's still alive. I saw her mug shot listed as a Jane Doe from earlier today. I figure if she made it out, so did Virgil. At least I hope so."

"So how do we find him?" Pastore asked.

Van Pelt pushed himself up and onto the driver's side front panel, just behind the headlights and said, "Since no one is answering the phone at his house, one of us will have to stakeout

263

the place. With all the commotion, He'll need to stop there sooner or later to grab some things."

"I'll do it," said the person standing at the open door to the staircase.

Everyone turned.

It was Myrrh Cavanaugh. She let the door close as she casually walked toward the group. "Aren't you boys here a little early?"

Van Pelt lowered himself to the floor and took a step to greet her. "I appreciate your offer, Myrrh, but this is an ongoing investigation and too much is involved to bring you on board now."

Cavanaugh shrugged. "Sounds simple enough," she said, joining her fellow officers. "You need someone to watch the Vanderhill house and report if Virgil shows up. I can handle that."

"Wait," Van Pelt said. "You know Virgil Vanderhill?"

She shook her head. "Not personally. He came in the other day to pick up that stoner, McCracken. But I know his wife, Dora. I met her at the gym. She's got a bit of a weight problem so she comes in often. I've worked the stair machine with her a couple of times. She lives in one of those McMansions, on Crestview."

"So you know the address?" Van Pelt asked.

Myrrh nodded. "Yeah, every so often I'd see her and Virgil drive by or Dora huffing and puffing her way up Darlington Hill."

"All right then," Van Pelt said. "Take an unmarked, swing by and let us know if he shows up."

"Sure," Cavanaugh replied. "What's he done?"

"Look, if you want in, you can't ask questions," Van Pelt replied. "Although Virgil's probably not armed, he's going to be extremely edgy so don't approach him. If he shows, call me and do nothing until I get there."

Yeah right, she said sarcastically to herself. *I don't trust any of you bastards.*

*

Later that day, Virgil turned to Martaine and said, "You know, you're not as smart as you think."

They were on their way to Filaments Electronics with Martaine at the wheel of the Volvo. Virgil sat beside him leafing through his notes and blueprints on his electronic tablet.

Martaine grinned. "Perhaps, but I am often as smart as I need to be."

Virgil gazed out the window. "Yeah well, our chances aren't all that good. " He started tapping his fingers on the side of the pad. "There is an awful lot that can go wrong, probably resulting in you getting your fool head blown off."

Again Martaine grinned. "My friend, you worry too much. Let us take a moment to assess our situation." He took a breath and began. "As in any battle, the first priority is to lessen the amount of enemy combatants, and we have been very successful so far. Of the 500 or so push-ins who originally crossed into our world, over 400 have been returned, leaving a mere 100. It also appears they have gathered in one place which gives us the opportunity to dispatch them all at in one fell swoop."

"But!" Virgil said, holding up the tablet, "I still have no idea if this ectoplasmic bomb, for want of a better word, will work."

"Virgil," Martaine said, taking his eyes off the road for a moment to turn and face his companion, "I don't know that much about you, but I'd be willing to wager that your entire life has been an exercise in fear, loneliness and futility."

Virgil smirked. "This coming from a man who parades around in a brown dress with a rope tied around the middle."

"Enough with the snide comments and just listen for a change, will you?" Martaine chastised. "You know I'm not your enemy, nor am I trying to insult you. It's just that your enormous ego, combined with your fear of failure, causes you to panic and retreat when you clearly should muster your faith and courage. As for your loneliness, anyone can see you mistrust and anticipate betrayal from anyone who dares befriend you. Clearly your many years of fruitless endeavors are the result of egotistically pursuing a goal every instinct told you was wrong."

Virgil sneered but did not contradict. "You mean contacting my mother?"

"Judging by the results it would appear so. However, it is never too late to make amends. Our inevitable confrontation with the push-ins will be your greatest challenge and hopefully your greatest victory."

Virgil eyed him suspiciously. "Push-ins? But you guys said taking on the daemons would be the hard part."

"Yes we did, but I now believe eliminating the push-ins will sabotage D'Shaid's plans."

"What plans?"

"Well, knowing him as I do, I'm sure he wants to remain the only daemon who has entered our world in true daemonic form. Not only does it make him stronger and far superior, it gives him the power to select which daemons will possess the bodies the remaining push-ins now inhabit. It also explains why, when Father Santiago and I were inside the barn following the explosion, D'Shaid waited until we sealed the cracks in the barrier before attacking us. Had he not, those daemons would have broken through in daemonic form, as well."

"But I thought that was the whole idea."

"Their plan, yes, but daemons are the most untrustworthy of creatures. They possess no sense of loyalty and only follow orders when forced. So I suspect D'Shaid might wish to keep the barrier intact, at least for the time being, so he may personally select the daemons he knows will do his bidding."

"What about the one that tried to possess Jess?"

Martaine slowed then stopped for a red light. "Father and I believe that one came through before D'Shaid. Remember Mary telling us how Jess had almost been a push-in victim at the Blue Barn? Well we think that daemon piggy-backed the push-in who tried to possess Jess. The daemon was successful; the push-in was not. And like D'Shaid's possession of you, that daemon waited until it could do the most damage."

"So if we send the remaining push-ins back to the Void, we may only have to fight D'Shaid?"

266

"I believe that is a real possibility." Martaine said as the light changed and they continued on.

"But, what if my device doesn't work?"

Martaine reached over and patted Virgil on the shoulder. "Then I'll be safely in the arms of our Lord and you'll be rotating on a spit over D'Shaid's campfire. Oh look, there's Filaments. Get out your list; it's time to go shopping."

Chapter Forty Five

"I wish we were back in bed," Aimee said as she rubbed Jimmy's hand and stared out the Mustang's window. The temperature had fallen over the last few hours, so before starting out, Jimmy put the top up.

He took her hand and squeezed it. "Me too. I only wish we didn't have to take your car to Mary's. If the police see us..."

"Yeah, well, since Father Santiago and Brother Martaine can't drive a stick, they'll need the Impala in case Jess flips out again and they have to take her to the hospital. Besides, we should be okay. When my dad was teaching me to drive, we often took this road. He said it was only built to connect the miles of farmland between St. Lawrenceville and Wheatfield and as a delivery route to Little Piggy. He also told me the state troopers rarely bother with it because other than delivery trucks, there isn't much traffic other than those big commercial tractors and other farm machinery. If our luck holds out, we shouldn't have a problem."

Jimmy burst out laughing, catching Aimee by surprise, "Yeah, we've been real lucky so far," he said.

When Aimee recalled how amazingly unlucky they had been, she started laughing, too.

As they continued their drive, the shimmering orange sky slowly dulled to a murky maroon, the clouds thinned and ere resting on the horizon. The trees along the mountainside were so closely cropped, they resembled broccoli florets.

The conversation soon petered out to dribs and drabs. It wasn't because there wasn't anything to talk about; there was too much.

Aimee was still trying to cope with her life changing situation and Jimmy was concerned that their little group was falling apart. Over the last few days, he had considered suicide, Mary had suffered a seizure, Jess had been possessed, Aimee was arrested for murder, Virgil had an emotional meltdown and Martaine had volunteered to trigger a device that just might kill them all.

Jimmy noticed his white knuckles and his unnecessarily tight grip on the wheel.

Calm down, Jimmy boy, calm down.

He considered turning on the radio when he heard the approach of a vehicle clearly in need of a muffler. He checked the rearview mirror and saw an old pick-up truck chugging and wheezing up from behind. Jimmy checked the speedometer and saw he was doing 58 in a 55 MPH zone.

The old truck however appeared to be doing 80, maybe more judging by the smoke, the occasional spray of sparks coming from its undercarriage and the speed in which it was gaining on them.

Aimee noticed Jimmy's fixation on both his rear and side view mirrors. She also heard the approaching racket.

"How do old wrecks like that pass inspection?" she asked. When Jimmy again checked the mirrors, she turned and when she saw who was behind the wheel…

"Holy fuck! That's Sula's stepfather and brother!" she squealed in terror. "Hit the gas, Jimmy. Get us out of here! Hurry! Hurry!"

When Jimmy saw the raw panic on her face, he reached for the stick shift, pressed the clutch and…

They were both violently thrown back against their seats when the old truck slammed into their rear bumper.

Jimmy downshifted and floored it. The Mustang pulled away but with an increasing vibration from the back. When Aimee lowered the window, a metallic scrapping sound barked at them followed by the smell of burning rubber.

She stuck out her head and saw the wobbling back tire and the large dent in the right rear panel.

Jimmy saw a road sign. **St. Lawrenceville—12 miles**

The wobbling intensified and he was forced to slow down or risk losing the wheel.

"How bad is it?" Jimmy called out as he veered from lane to lane to stay out of the truck's reach.

Aimee pulled her head in, closed the window and said. "Really bad. We might make it to town if we dropped down to thirty but at eighty…" A worried look crossed her face.

"What do they want?"

Aimee hesitated for a moment then said, "Sula's brothers tried to rape me at gunpoint back at the Blue Barn. And the only reason

269

I'm not dead is because I stabbed one of them as he shot me." She pointed to the area where she had been hit.

"You killed him?!"

She took a worried breath and pressed her knuckles against her lips. "I didn't have a choice. These are hill people, Jimmy. They're fucked in the head. I'm telling you, those little freaks were going to rape and kill me. Their auras were black, tar black!"

"Shit!" He eyed his rearview and pressed down on the accelerator to maintain distance. The wobbling in the back became more pronounced.

Aimee said. "We've got to do something. If they catch us, they'll kill us."

Jimmy's eyes widened as he looked into the rearview mirror. He grabbed her shoulder. "Holy shit, duck!!"

*

"I'm tellin' you, Paw," Tee said. "She's in that car!"

"You damn well better be right, boy!" Paw thundered as he turned and scowled at him. "If'n it turns out you're wrong, we's both goin' to jail. Now I'm askin' you agin. You sure that's the car, and are you sure Sula's inside?"

"I swear, Paw!" Tee bleated. "I jes saw her check the back tire after we rammed them. It's her all right."

"And are you absolutely sure she kilt yer brother? 'Cause I got a real problem with yer story. I jes cain't believe Sula overpowered Coffee, at least not while yer standing alongside him."

Tee reddened but with all the commotion, Paw hadn't noticed. "I tole you she surprised us!" Tee explained. "She was lyin' in wait, jumped out, stabbed Coffee and pushed me over the railin' before we knew what was happenin'!"

Paw eyed him again and sucked his teeth. "Well then," he said with a snarl as he spit out the window. "That little bitch is gonna answer to me. And if'n you're tellin' the truth, and she kilt my boy, I swear, I will strangle that girl with my bare hands."

Tee's stomach tightened. The last thing he wanted was for Paw to actually talk to Sula. His story was weak and he knew it.

Even if Sula had caught him by surprise, they both knew Coffee was as fast and deadly as a rattler, and no girl would keep the upper hand for long when dealing with him.

She'll tell Paw and he'll believe her, then strangle us both. Her for killin' Coffee and me for runnin' off.

When the Mustang suddenly sprinted ahead, Tee yelled, "They's gittin away!" He reached back to the gun rack, pulled the shotgun, jumped up, planted his ass on the open passenger side window and fired directly at the Mustang.

The ragtop's plastic rear window was obliterated as Jimmy and Aimee ducked into their seats. A second shot torn away more of the roof and most of the seat's upholstery. Two pellets of buck shot lodged into Jimmy's side.

From the floor, Aimee peeked out over the top of her seat and saw the damage. "Motherfucking shit!" she shrieked in panic. "There's nothing left! If he gets another shot off, we're dead!"

Jimmy winced and pressed his hand against his lower back. "I've been hit. Burns like a bitch!"

Aimee removed his hand and lifted his shirt.

"It's not too bad. No worse than what I got."

"Still hurts like hell!" he grunted as he again placed his hand to the wound.

"Keep both hands on the wheel!" she shouted, taking his right hand and slamming it back onto it. "If you lose control at this speed, we'll flip!"

Jimmy grunted and tightened his grip. "Listen, climb into the back and pull down the rear seats! Hurry!"

Aimee didn't ask why; any plan was better than nothing. As Jimmy jerked the car into the approaching lane, Aimee dove into the back, reached to the top of the rear seats, found the lock release, pulled and dropped them down. She slid into the trunk.

"Now what?" she called out.

His reply was drowned out when another blast disintegrated the passenger-side seat as well as the passenger-side mirror and front windshield.

Aimee screamed.

271

"For fuck sake, boy!" Paw bellowed. "I taught you to shoot better 'en that! Now either you blow out the tire with the next shot or I'll wrap that shotgun round yer damn fool neck!"

"They's hard to hit with all that wobblin', Paw!" Tee protested.

Suddenly the Mustang swerved back into their lane and slowed.

"I won't miss this time!" Tee shouted as he prepared to take his shot. When he saw Sula head momentarily pop up from the back seat, he grinned and began to squeeze the trigger.

"Good-bye, Sula," he whispered and fired.

"Ready?" Jimmy called out.

"Do it!"

Jimmy yanked the trunk lock lever and the trunk lid popped open. Buckshot pitted small holes into it as Aimee slid the spare tire out and directly into the path of the oncoming truck.

Jimmy downshifted and floored it.

"Ohh, shit!!" Paw bellowed and yanked the wheel.

The truck immediately took to the air. It flipped several times and when the roof flattened, blood sprayed from the cab like soda from a shaken can. When the vehicle finally righted itself, it creaked and shimmied nose first into the drainage ditch along the shoulder.

Jimmy hit the brakes and the Mustang squealed to a stop.

They got out and cautiously approached, eying the vehicle carefully. Aimee immediately took Jimmy's hand as he scouted the area. Not another car in sight.

Standing on an empty road in the middle of nowhere, they watched the smoke rise from the battered hull, almost expecting Paw and Tee to burst from it with guns blazing.

But that clearly wasn't going to happen.

The truck lay there like a KO'ed boxer with his face pressed into the mat and his ass in the air. They could hear one rear tire squeak until it slowly spun to a stop. Saw the blood splatter on the door panels trail downward in thick red lines; watched the fire as it grew and consumed the vehicle and its occupants. Could smell the thick black smoke as it rose like a dark ghost into the air.

"Should we do something? Contact someone?" Aimee asked, turning to Jimmy. Her eyes were frightened, her complexion sallow.

"No!" he replied coldly. "They tried to kill us. They got what they deserve. As far as I'm concerned, the world's a better place without them."

As Aimee began to sob, Jimmy placed his arm around her shoulder. When they walked back to the Mustang, Jimmy pulled the crushed rear panel free. Since there was nothing he could do about the bent axle, they got back into the car and drove off.

Aimee turned and looked at the ragged and torn material that had once been their back window and at the road behind them.

"It's like the end of the world," she said to herself as she fought to hold back the tears. "Everything is falling apart like it's the end of the world."

Chapter Forty Six

After completing their shopping at Filaments, Virgil pushed the shopping cart to his car. Once there, he popped the Volvo's trunk and placed the electronic and electrical supplies inside as Martaine put the four white lab coats, the four white hard hats and four clipboards into the back seat. After closing the trunk and back door, both men got in the car.

"I understand the need for the electronic equipment but why purchase lab coats and hart hats?" Martaine asked as he sat down behind the wheel

As Virgil put on his seat belt, he replied. "I spent years working in government research and development and noticed that people wearing white lab coats, hard hats and carrying clipboards are rarely, if ever, questioned. I suppose it's because they look like they're doing an inspection and you don't want to be the guy who gets grilled, so they get avoided like the plague. And since we'll need to get inside the Little Piggy Hog Farms facility and look around, the lab coats might help us pull that off."

"Quite clever," Martaine replied.

"Yeah, well I'm a freakin' genius, remember?"

Both men laughed.

Virgil was about to fold his change into his billfold when Martaine asked, "Why do you carry such a large amount of cash?"

"My wife just ran off with another man."

"And you carry a large amount of cash because of that?"

He turned to the clergyman. "Well, it's not like I have a lot to be concerned about. My wife left me. My mother betrayed me and now I'm trying to construct a device that will hopefully destroy the most powerful enemy the world has ever faced without killing us all in the process. At least that's the plan. So, my dear Brother Martaine, when we look at the big picture, does the amount of cash I carry really matter?"

Martaine started the engine and put it in gear as Virgil booted up his electronic tablet. "No, I am quite sure it does not," Martaine replied. "I suppose I have seen so much evil in this world that I fear for the safety of anyone who does not regard his fellow man as a potential threat." He sighed. "I am often appalled at the lack of humanity we humans possess."

Virgil pulled back with a raised eyebrow. "Well, that's one hell of a revelation. Imagine, a man who devotes his life to saving souls while hating the people they belong to."

Virgil expected Martaine to backpedal but the denial didn't come. Instead, the clergyman pulled out onto the road. For several minutes he remained quiet as they made their journey back to Virgil's house. Finally, Martaine said, "You've heard of Mother Theresa, right?"

Virgil nodded. "Little nun from India, helped the poor, downtrodden and thoroughly screwed. Yeah, I've heard of her."

"Well," Martaine continued. "After her death, they found her personal papers. They were supposed to be destroyed, but weren't."

Virgil rolled his eyes. "Please, if her papers went on about how she wished she could have suffered more, or done more, or gave more, or any of that super Holy Roller nonsense, I don't want to hear it. Frankly, I've never found those stories inspiring. People like her are so goody-goody the regular schmuck on the street doesn't have a chance at that pie-in-the-sky heavenly reward. I figure why bother trying if there's no pay off?"

"Interesting you should say that," Martaine replied. "Because it turns out that after establishing the Missionaries of Charity, she lost her faith." The clergyman nodded after noting Virgil's suspicious gaze. "It's true. She did what God asked and in return, the thing that meant more to her than life itself, the thing she based her entire life's work on disappeared. Just vanished. And for the rest of her life that faith never returned. Can you imagine? The world's most revered clergywoman, the person we all believed to be a living saint, actually died an agnostic."

"You're kidding!" Virgil said. "Is that true?"

With lips pressed tight he gave a quick nod.

Virgil folded his arms and solemnly said, "That's pretty sad."

"But you miss the point."

Virgil smirked. "Oh, and what's that?"

"The point, my friend, is; she did it anyway."

"Did what?"

"Don't you see? God took her faith. And so, like you, she believed there was no payoff. No heaven, no eternal life, no built up treasures in the afterlife, nothing. Nevertheless, she still spent her life helping the poor and downtrodden simply because it needed to be done and she was in a position to do it. And it is that very content of character that makes her a far better person than I will ever be."

"Oh c'mon," Virgil said, clapping him on his shoulder. "Don't get all weepy on me, Bro."

Martaine turned to him. "Call me Silvio. Considering what we have both gone through, I believe we should be on a first name basis."

Virgil leaned back. "Okay, Silvio."

Moments later, Martaine said, "So, now that we have the parts, how does this new device work?"

"Do you know what an electromagnetic pulse is?"

"I have heard of it, but to be honest, my comprehension of the sciences is limited. So if you will, in a condensed, easy to digest version?"

"Okay." Virgil placed his electronic pad in his lap, rolled his hands for a moment, gathered his thoughts and said, "The magnetic pulse was discovered when an atomic explosion generated a wave of gamma rays that lasted for only a microsecond. Yet because of the radiated field, it destroyed all the electrical devices it came into contact with. But that was back in the early 50s and we've learned a lot since then. Nowadays scientists are using magnetic pulses in a process called Transcranial Magnetic Stimulation, or TMS, to treat people with severe depression. It's been very effective.

"Now here's where my plan comes in. Since magnetic pulses affect electricity, and the human thought process is generated by the electricity inside the brain, a short concentrated blast should blow the push-ins out of the victim's body, as it did to D'Shaid when the fire ignited the pool of ectoplasmic gasses. And because the brain is naturally calibrated to host that which it was born with, my life-force or energy compound…"

"Just say soul, will you?" Martaine interrupted.

276

"Fine. The point is, my soul automatically returned to my body because my brain was constructed to house it, somewhat like a computer being restored to what it was before being attacked by a virus, well, not exactly but you get the point."

Martaine eyed him sideways. "This sounds pretty far-fetched. Does this theory have any basis in fact?"

Virgil shrugged. "None that I am aware of."

"Then why do you think it will work?"

Virgil pointed to himself. "Freakin' genius, remember? I am the first man to successfully contact the dead." Seeing the clergyman was about to contradict him, Virgil raised his hand. "I'm talking about strict science, not religion. And because of my success and the unexpected results that grew from it, I better understand that breakthrough. Don't you agree?"

Martaine's lips twisted sideways. "Well, I'm still having trouble with the freakin' genius part, but I am coming to realize that contention might very well be true. So, please continue."

"Okay, here's my theory. I have studied the effects of electro-shock and TMS therapy over the years, and although there is no hard evidence to back this up, I believe what electro-shock does is force all the…well for the lack of a better word, the malevolent influences that have possessed the brain, out. Unfortunately, it only works temporally.

"Due to what I believe are gaps in the brain's defenses created by either a malfunction in the womb or repeated contact with the dead, these defective and corrupt influences can and often do, slip back in."

"Interesting theory," Martaine said, clearly impressed.

Virgil shrugged, "I wouldn't submit it to any scientific journal, but judging by what we have seen so far, it certainly seems possible." Virgil wiped his brow and opened the window a little. "In any case," he continued, "we're only going to get one shot.

As for the device's effectiveness and the possible aftereffects following detonation, your guess is as good as mine. But if it works, the resulting magnetic pulse should compress the conduit between our worlds, sealing any cracks or holes brought about by

277

my first machine. So there you go. As dumbed down as I can make it. I hope you understand at least part of it."

Martaine ignored the insult. He now understood the more frightened Virgil became, the nastier he got.

*

Santiago was sitting in Virgil's kitchen drinking a cup of coffee. He positioned himself so that the light green, tall-backed, kitchen chair he was sitting in gave an unobstructed view into the living room. There Jess was sleeping on the wraparound couch with the blinds pulled and the chocolate-colored drapes drawn. She appeared calm and restful. Still, he kept a close eye.

The dome lights in the kitchen ceiling reflected off the stainless steel refrigerator, dishwasher and stove. The center island was butcher block with pots and pans hanging above and a wooden cutlery holder in the center. Santiago noted that Virgil's kitchen had the professional appearance of a television cooking show. That is until he saw the wall clock. It was designed to look like a dinner plate with fork and spoon as hands. He was pretty sure that purchase had been Dora's.

"Father Santiago?" Mary said as she entered.

He turned and smiled. "Hello, Mary."

She returned the smile, came over and sat in the chair beside his. "How's Jess doing?"

Santiago glanced into the adjoining room. "She's sleeping and appears to be all right."

"But you're still concerned."

"In these situations one should always be… well, let's say, vigilant."

She nodded. "I suppose." There was a pause. "What do you think our odds are? I mean, of us getting out of this mess in one piece."

Santiago bowed his head. "I suppose as good as any. Simply put, either we will be successful or become the slaves of butchering, sadistic abominations."

Mary paled and looked down.

Realizing his response was more fatalistic than intended, Santiago reached over and gently squeezed her hand. "I apologize," he said, attempting to catch her eye. "I am not usually a man who worries. It insults God and shows a lack of faith. The truth is I firmly believe we will be successful in overcoming these..." He smiled. "You know, I was going to say abominations, but have decided to erase that description from my vocabulary. From now on I will refer to them as enemy combatants."

Mary tilted her head. "Really? But I thought that's how the clergy described daemons."

Santiago gently squeezed her hand and sat back. "Yes, but Virgil has convinced me to challenge the fear we have of these creatures. In reality, they are merely deviant, violent, parasitical, megalomaniacal rejects. They refuse to contribute anything of value, and as punishment, have been relegated to the netherworld."

Mary pulled her beige sweater tight. "Father, do you hear confessions from non-Catholics?"

He folded his hands on the table and said. "As a priest, I am obligated to not only hear the confession, but to also offer penance and absolution to anyone who requests it."

Several seconds passed before she said, "Okay, so how do we do this? Do I have to kneel and do you have to get holy..."

Santiago shook his head. "Why don't we start by you just telling me what's on your mind."

"Well," she said, "since its possible we may all be dead tomorrow I'd like to square myself with God, just in case. You know what I mean."

"I do. Please go on."

Mary took a breath. "I guess it all started when I discovered my psychic ability in my early teens. Even at that age I could see the moneymaking potential, so I began offering my services as a professional.

"I did great. By eighteen I had enough money to go wherever I wanted, so I headed west and wound up in Vegas. Got a job there working security. With my ability to read auras and pick up vibes, I could scour the casino floor and inform the pit bosses who to watch.

279

"Most of the rip-off artists weren't clever enough to succeed, but enough were caught red-handed to put my career on the fast track.

"I loved Vegas; still do. There was always something going on. I'd spend one night rollicking in bed with some handsome Hollywood actor and the next reading Tarot cards for a Mafia don. And if some guy got rough in the sack, the next day I'd make some calls and have the bastard beaten senseless.

"Everything was going fine until I fingered someone with considerable underworld connections and one who had a lot more to hide than a casino rip-off scheme. When he heard, he put out a hit on me.

"Fortunately, my talents warned me, so I took off and joined a motorcycle gang. Spent a year with them, selling coke, robbing dealers and using my abilities to sniff out cops and feds.

"When I got word that the man who put the hit on me was dead, I left the gang and headed to Hollywood where I hooked up with the Hollywood A-list who were fascinated by my abilities.

"Life got good again. I went to red carpet movie premiers, ate at world famous restaurants, mingled with movie stars and traveled the world. For the second time I was on top.

"But I got stupid and developed a serious cocaine habit. After a few drug deals went bad, my world fell apart. Broke and in trouble with the law, I was sent to a Los Angeles rehab clinic in lieu of jail. I was there only three days when two orderlies slipped into my room and brutally beat and raped me.

"While in the hospital I vowed I would never again put myself in such a vulnerable position. So I cleaned up and turned my life around. I began writing books on ESP and Spirituality and with constant touring found a loyal niche of devoted followers.

"That's how I met Jess and why I decided to make St. Lawrenceville my home. This way, when I was in town, I could hang out with her. Well, I guess that's it."

Santiago recited some Latin phrases, made the sign of the cross, walked her through the Act of Contrition then told Mary her sins were forgiven.

She smiled. "So what's the penance?"

Santiago looked at her solemnly. "Your penance is as follows: Over the next 24 hours you are not to be afraid, you are not to be swayed regardless of the temptation and you are not to falter, no matter how difficult the trial. Do you understand and accept your penance?" he asked.

"I do."

"Then go in peace," he said and made the sign of the cross to indicate the confession was over.

Mary stood. "I'm going to make myself a cup of tea. Would you like something to eat?"

"No, thank you." Santiago replied as he again checked on Jess, who was just turning over.

Mary scanned the pots and pans but didn't see a tea kettle, so she filled a small saucepan with water, placed it on the stove, turned the burner on HIGH then took two cups from the cupboard and placed them on the island counter.

"The more I think about it," Mary said as she put the sugar bowl next to the tea cups and went to the fridge for milk, "the better I feel. I mean, about the push-ins and daemons. And Virgil's right," she added, pulling open the refrigerator door, "we shouldn't think of them as supernatural monsters but as enemy invaders. Ah, here we go," Mary said as she reached for the milk.

Santiago had just checked his watch and was reaching into his jacket for his cell when Jess charged into the room and swung the fireplace poker into the side of his head.

Blood spattered the wall as the clergyman stumbled from his chair. It toppled over as he fell against the wall and collapsed to the floor.

Hearing the commotion, Mary looked up and saw the bloody fireplace poker with its curved spike still lodged in the side of Santiago's skull.

Jess, with a crazed expression was trying to get at him but the overturned chair had its legs entwined with those of Mary's chair and—along with the table—formed a minor blockade.

Mary dropped the milk container and bellowed, "Jess!!"

Jess turned to her, looking confused. Then back to Santiago, who was struggling to get to his feet like a boxer trying to beat the

281

ten count. He muffled a scream as he slowly and carefully removed the imbedded poker from his head.

Jess yanked a carving knife from the wooden cutlery holder then wildly kicked at the entangled chairs, trying to separate them. Finally succeeding, she charged Santiago.

Santiago pressed himself against the wall and, blind in one eye, attempted to fend off Jess with the bloody poker.

Mary rushed over, "Jess, Please! My God, what are you doing?"

Jess swung the knife from back to front, first at Santiago then at Mary, unable to decide who to attack first. Her crazed look however, never abated.

"Jess, please, please put the knife down, look at what you've done." She motioned to Santiago. "We've got to get him to a hospital!"

As Santiago stumbled toward her with the raised poker, Jess turned and charged at Mary with the 12" carving knife. Mary quickly backpedaled to the stove where, in panic and desperation, she grabbed the pot of boiling water and flung its contents at her.

Jess screamed, dropped to the floor and grabbed her face.

But she didn't let go of the knife.

"Drop it, Jess! For heaven's sake" Mary hollered as she stood over her. "Let... go... of... the knife! Please!"

Although nearly blind, and with the skin on her face seriously burned, Jess got up on one knee, raised the blade and lunged at Mary.

With the butcher block cutlery holder as the only possible weapon within reach, Mary grabbed it and slammed it down on Jess' head. The crazed woman paused, but kept moving toward her, slicing the air with the blade. Mary struck her again, and when that didn't stop her, she hit her again and again... and again... and again...and

Jess finally collapsed to the bloody floor and stopped moving

Shaking, gasping and out of breath, Mary fell back against the stove with tears running down her face. She looked down at Jess' broken and crushed skull as the blood pooled around it. She dropped the cracked and bloody cutlery holder and was feeling light-headed when Santiago's troubled, rasping voice called to her.

"Mary... I need help." he said as he staggered to the nearest chair and fell into it. "I'm blind in one eye, I'm bleeding, and I can't feel my left arm or... leg."

Mary sniffed, ran her sleeve across her eyes and said. "I'll call an ambulance," She reached into her pocket for her cell phone.

Santiago held up his hand. "No, the push-ins are still looking to kill you, remember what happened the last time?"

"But all the police and professional people were returned to their bodies. The only push-ins left are on the hog farm."

"That's... that's what we *believe*," he groaned as he pressed his hand to the side of his head. "That is not what we *know*. And since all it takes is one, I... I refuse to risk your safety."

Having seen this adamant expression before, she knew there was no sense in arguing

"All right. I'll drive you, but first we have to stop that bleeding."

She grabbed a dish towel, wet it under hot water, and wrung it out, then, remembering alcohol prevents infection, searched and found a near empty bottle of whiskey in a side cabinet. She poured what remained of its contents over the wound.

After wrapping the towel snuggly on Santiago's head and tying the ends tight, she pulled his arm over her shoulder, lifted him from the chair and led him to the door. As they passed Jess' remains, Mary sobbed and blurted, "I'm sorry, Jess, I'm so sorry. I loved you so much!"

She wanted to say more but Santiago was pale and shivering. As she tightened her grip on the clergyman's waist, he pointed at the Black Box. "We must bring that," he said in between coughs.

Without comment, Mary grabbed the handle and they headed to the garage.

Moment later, she was behind the wheel of the Impala with Santiago beside her.

As they left and raced down the street, Mary didn't notice the woman sitting in the brown Buick parked on the side of the road.

283

Chapter Forty Seven

With the Mustang wobbling like a cartoon jalopy, Jimmy and Aimee's journey to St. Lawrenceville took far longer than expected but they did make it to Mary's house. After parking in front, they ran inside, took a quick leak removed the two pieces of buckshot from Jimmy back, bandaged it, then headed to the garage.

When they opened the garage door, they were readily impressed. This was no mid-size hauler. This was a mastodon of power and torque with huge wheels and tinted windows. "Wow!" Jimmy said as he walked alongside and looked it over. "Apparently our friend Mary likes to go first class."

Aimee nodded and said, "Guess so. You ready to roll?"

Jimmy and Aimee stepped up and into the sleek black powerhouse and snapped on their seatbelts.

Jimmy started the engine, pulled out of the garage, then stopped and jumped out. After a quick look around, he got back into the Mustang, pulled it into the space where the truck had been and closed the garage door.

Climbing back into the truck, he said, "Couldn't leave it outside. In that condition someone is bound to ask questions and call the police." As he put the truck in gear and started down the road, he said, "Amazing! This thing handles like a luxury car yet feels as powerful as a tank."

"Then open it up, handsome," Aimee said as she sat back and placed her feet on the dashboard. "Let's see what this baby can do!"

So Jimmy did.

"It's six p.m." Jimmy said as he clicked on 'Cruise Control' and turned down the radio, "and our friends at Little Piggy Hog farms will be getting out in two hours." He eyed her. "Are you scared?"

She flipped down the passenger-side visor and checked her make-up in the mirror. "Aren't you?"

He thought for a second. "A bit I guess, but not as much as I expected. Which is surprising because…"

She had just flipped the visor up when she suddenly pointed ahead and said "Shit! Look at that!"

He turned and saw a line of flashing red lights ahead. There was a police road block where Paw's truck overturned. They were stopping cars from both directions.

"What do we do?" Aimee asked and nervously started chewed her nails. "If we stop and they recognize us, we're going to jail."

Jimmy downshifted while frantically trying to come up with answer.

As he took the truck out of gear, Aimee grabbed his hand. "What are you doing? Didn't you hear me? If we stop, we'll be arrested."

He pulled his hand from hers. "I'm betting they haven't got their communication network back on line yet. From what I saw— and I was a good distance away—the station house was nearly demolished when the satellite antenna caved in with the roof."

Aimee sat back and nervously rubbed the sweat from her hands on her jeans. "You're right, it did. Okay," she said, sitting up, "let's do this."

As he slowed to a stop, two officers turned, then suddenly pulled their guns and charged toward them.

*

The original plan called for Virgil and Martaine to return to Virgil's house to assemble the device, then leave with the others for the hog farm, but upon reflection Virgil decided that was a waste of time. With all the necessary components and the tools for its assembly in the car, he instructed Martaine to pull into the parking lot of a half empty strip mall. Once parked, he retrieved the electronics from the trunk, climbed into the back seat and started assembling the device.

Nearly forty-five minutes passed without a word between Virgil and Silvio. Not due to tension, but rather the construction of what they were now calling the ectoplasmic bomb had Virgil deep in concentration.

Frustrated, Virgil slammed his hand against the armrest. "Balls!" he spat in disgust. "There is no way to tell if this thing is going to work without that big truck battery. Call McCracken and find out where he is."

Martaine made the call. After being automatically transferred to voicemail, he turned and said, "No answer, but I'll keep trying."

Virgil looked up. "No. I just realized we'll have to wait. Mary lives in St. Lawrenceville, and there are no microwave towers along 404, so they're probably still in the 'no service' zone."

"How do you know where the microwave towers are located?"

Virgil gave a dismissive glance. "Really? I created a devise to talk to the dead and you're surprised I know where the communication towers are?"

"Fine, Mr. Freakin' Genius. Do we stay here or head out to 404 to intercept Jimmy and Aimee?"

Just then, Martaine's cell phone rang.

Virgil sat up. "Finally! Tell McCracken where we are and that we should meet at the intersection of Routes 727 and 404."

Martaine nodded and answered his phone.

*

Seeing the officers draw their guns, Aimee jerked in panic. And just as Jimmy reached for the shift and was about to slam the accelerator to the floor, he heard a voice in his ear, one he instantly recognized.

"Don't worry, young fella," the voice said. "You jes' hold tight and everything will be jes fine."

Aimee stared hard at Jimmy but he simply patted her knee, lowered the window and raised his hands.

As he did, the officer's holstered their guns. "Didn't mean to frighten you, sir," the officer said as he climbed the step and placed his hands on window frame, "but you have tinted windows and since we couldn't see in…"

"I understand," Jimmy said, pulling the parking brake. "Things have been pretty crazy around here lately. So what's going on?"

The officer surveyed the inside of the cab and, seeing nothing suspicious, explained.

"Well," he said, "we found shotgun shells and a recently fired shotgun lying on the ground about twenty feet up and two burned bodies inside that truck so we're stopping all vehicles and asking if anybody saw anything."

"Oh," Jimmy replied, scratching the back of his head. "No officer. We just left St. Lawrenceville and are heading toward Wheatfield to meet with friends."

The officer nodded, climbed down and motioned to the other officer to let them through. "You folks have a nice day," he said with a tip of his hat.

"You, too," Jimmy replied as he took off the parking brake, pressed the clutch, put the truck into gear and drove off.

As they continued their trek along 404 and the flashing lights of the roadblock faded, Aimee heaved a deep sigh and rolled her eyes. "Man!" she exclaimed, pressing her hand against her chest, "When I saw you reach for the stick shift and press the clutch I thought we were going to do a Bonnie and Clyde. What changed your mind?"

"I've mentioned Ol' Ike before haven't I?"

Aimee nodded as she put her feet back on the dashboard. "Yeah, back at your house when we first met."

"Well, he told me it was going to be okay and not to panic."

Aimee smiled. "So there is a good side to your talking to spooks."

"It doesn't happen often, but yeah, Ol' Ike does come in handy once in a while. Anyway, take out your cell and let me know when we're back in a service area." He looked into the darkening crimson skies ahead. "Time's running out."

*

As Brother Martaine pressed CONNECT on his cell and said 'Hello,' he was startled to hear, not Jimmy or Aimee, but the panicky voice of Mary telling him she was taking a seriously injured Father Santiago to Wheatfield hospital.

"Mary, Mary, calm down," Martaine pleaded. "What has happened?"

She told him how Jess went berserk and nearly killed Santiago with the fireplace poker.

"Where is Jess now? Martaine asked.

"She's dead!" Mary cried out. "I… I killed her."

For the first time since their arrival, Martaine felt fear. "Can I speak with Hector? Can he talk?"

Father Santiago, overhearing the conversation, held out his hand.

"Here," Mary said and handed over the phone.

Martaine heard Santiago's labored breathing. "Hector, how serious are your injuries?"

"That is not the issue," Santiago rasped. "Now listen. D'Shaid must be aware of our intentions. Expect him to order the daemons to possess the farm workers. Tell the others daemonically possessed humans are far more powerful."

"I will," Martaine replied. "And if they are waiting for us, our only hope is that Virgil's machine works. If not, our cause is lost," Martaine paused, then added. "Still, D'Shaid has not unleashed his war on Mankind, Perhaps he is not as prepared or as powerful as he'd like us to believe."

Santiago replied, "You make a good point."

"Mary says Jessica is dead," Martaine said pulling out his handkerchief and dabbing his eyes. "Did that daemon again take possession of her body?"

"Yes, she attempted to kill us both," Santiago said solemnly. "Is Virgil's device ready?"

Martaine turned to Virgil. "Father Santiago wants to know if…"

"I heard. Tell him I need Mary's truck battery before I can go any further. Ask if they've heard from Jimmy and Aimee."

Martaine did, and was told they hadn't.

Santiago was about to ask Martaine their location when he suddenly experienced an epiphany, an unexpected moment of pure clarity. He realized now what had to be done.

288

I suppose this is the feeling a soldier gets when he realizes he won't survive the battle. Well then, I must do everything in my power to protect the others.

"Silvio," Santiago said with renewed vigor. "I have the Black Box. Mary and I will meet you at the intersection of 727 and Route 404. If God is with us, we will connect with Jimmy and Aimee on their return."

Hearing this, Mary shouted. "You can't be serious! If we don't go straight to the hospital, you'll die!"

Santiago ignored her. "Silvio, you have your instructions. I shall see you there, and if not, then as Jess used to say, 'We'll meet poolside at Jesus' house.'"

Santiago disconnected as Mary stopped at the red light.

"I wasn't kidding," she scolded. "You will die," she added pointing to the sign before them that read Left to Wheatfield, Right to St. Lawrenceville.

Santiago solemnly bowed his head. "There is far more at stake than the fate of an injured priest. This is a moment for strength," he said and gestured toward the right. "Let's not keep our friends waiting."

It was almost too much for her. Her best friend was dead and her companion seemed determined to join her.

With tears running down her face, she turned the Impala toward St. Lawrenceville and sped off.

*

Jimmy increased the truck's speed to ninety where it occasionally took to the air like a car in an action movie.

"I got signal!" Aimee shouted. She phoned Mary.

Before Aimee could say hello, Mary blurted, "Listen, there's been a change of plans. We're all meeting at the intersection of Routes 727 and 404. Get there as quickly as you can. Things have taken a bad turn. Father Santiago is badly injured and Jess is dead."

Aimee paled. Fighting to retain her composure, she pressed her lips together and held the phone in a vice-like grip. She wanted to ask what happened, wanted to know the details but there was no

289

time for that, she would have to wait until they met. Finally she said, "We should be there in a few minutes." She disconnected and turned to Jimmy with tears in her eyes. "I've got some really bad news."

*

Twenty minutes later, all three vehicles were on the shoulder of 404 with Virgil in the back of the pick-up using the truck's large hybrid batteries to calibrate the device.

Virgil stood and stared down at his construct. It was the size of a quart size propane tank. The one's that camper's use for gas grills. Inside were several vials filled with thick, ever-changing colored liquids and surrounding the vials were electronic gadgetry and wires. On top was a metal box the size of a child's building block. It had a red ignition button in the center.

Jimmy stepped out of the truck, walked to the back and eyed the device. He looked at Virgil and asked, "Is it gonna work?"

"I dunno!" Virgil spat as he flung the screwdriver to the floor of the pick-up and started pacing. "The entire concept is based on some cockamamie theory running around in my head. Technically, yeah, it should work but then so should cold fusion, anti-gravity and warp drive. The problem is not only has this never been tested, it's never even been properly theorized. My best... my best guess... my... my..." Virgil began hyperventilating. Seeing this, Martaine grabbed one of the paper bags from Filaments and gave it to him to breathe into.

As Virgil sat down on the edge of the tailgate, Mary, still in the driver's seat of the Impala, eyed Santiago and said, "Hold still, I need to replace that towel. After Santiago nodded, she carefully removed the bloody towel and replaced it with her scarf. After tightening it over the wound, she said, "The wound is clotting and the towel's absorbency is probably doing more harm than good. Just keep the towel around your neck. If you start bleeding again we'll switch back."

Virgil, having regained his composure, tossed the paper bag and said, "I'm sorry, but I don't think it will work. Most likely it will kill us all."

Aimee started biting her fingernails again. "Then what are we going to do?!"

The ashen-faced Santiago motioned for the others to approach.

As they gathered around the passenger-side door of the Impala, he said, "It is no coincidence that we are all here at this moment. It is no coincidence that we have been chosen. And it is certainly no coincidence that uncertainty plagues us. Twice I found my faith lacking, and the more I questioned, the more our fortunes worsened. Fifteen minutes ago, I was given the choice to go to the hospital or to bring the Black Box here. I do not know if I will survive this day but I am certain you will." He reached out the window. "Take my hand, all of you. Feel what I feel and believe what I believe."

"Yeah well…" Virgil began, but Martaine shot him a look that clearly said, "Shut up!" and Virgil, seeing the singular intensity in the clergyman's face, did.

After they all placed their hands on top of Santiago's and he placed his other hand on top of theirs, he recited a small prayer and when completed he let go and said, "Brother Martaine and I use that prayer when we perform exorcisms. It will protect you from possession."

As they stepped away from the vehicle, Jimmy said, "Well, since we're here and since the daemons will definitely break through if we do nothing, I say we take a shot. Even if Virgil's device kills us, it's still better than living in a world ruled by those bastards."

They all turned to Virgil who was staring at the ground shaking his head. Finally, he motioned for them to follow him as he walked over to his Volvo. Once there he opened the back door, reached inside and pulled out the four white lab coats, hard-hats and clipboards. As he returned and handed them out, he said, "Put these on. As I told Silvio earlier, people wearing lab coats and carrying clipboards are rarely questioned."

291

As Mary, Aimee and Jimmy complied, Virgil, after donning his lab coat, and jamming a blue canvas harness under his arm, went back to the truck and disconnected the diesel fuel battery. He opened the canvas bag and carefully placed the battery inside. Once secure, he added the device, then attached the wires from the battery to it. He slung the harness over his shoulder.

"I still feel there's something wrong with this," Virgil said patting the canvas bag. "But I haven't figured out what it is… yet. Hopefully, I will before we have to use it."

As he walked away he muttered, "I really hope I am a freakin' genius."

"Okay, how we going to do this?" Jimmy asked. "Driving three cars, one behind the other is going to look suspicious and I don't want to tip our hand before we're even there."

"We should leave Virgil's car behind," Martaine said. "It's very low on gas."

Jimmy turned and eyed Virgil. "Really? You didn't think to put gas in?"

Virgil jerked his hands into the air. "Hey, I had more important things to think about," he said, gesturing to the canvas bag. "Besides, I wanted to use my gas card. One more fill-up and I'll get a…"

"Forget it!" Jimmy snapped. "So I guess it's been decided for us. We take the Impala and the truck. Virgil, you come with me and Aimee and Brother Martaine you ride with Mary and Father Santiago."

He had barely gotten the words out when Mary shook her head. "The Impala's heater doesn't work and it's getting cold," she said. "Father Santiago started shivering on the way over so before we set out, let's put him in my truck. You could roast a chicken with the heater in there."

Mary's suggestion did seem to be the way to go, so he called over Brother Martaine and Virgil and the three gently lifted him out of the Impala, carried him to the truck and placed him in the passenger-side seat.

With Jimmy, Aimee and Father Santiago in Mary's Ford pick-up and with Virgil, Mary and Brother Martaine in the Chevy Impala they set out toward Little Piggy

With Virgil and Father Santiago having the most advanced cell phones, theirs were chosen to be placed in their vehicle's respective ashtrays, with the lines connected and on speaker.

How are you doing Father?" Mary asked over the cell.

Santiago leaned in and said, "As well as can be expected."

"Good, you keep hanging in there," Mary replied.

As Mary turned and gazed at the shimmering dark crimson sky, she thought of Jess and her eyes welled. She quickly brushed at them away not wanting the others to think she was losing her resolve. Actually, Jess' passing had made her stronger. Without Jess, there was nothing to go home to. She had no husband, no children. Her parents had passed long ago and she had no idea where her younger brother wound up.

Save me a chair poolside, Jess. I'll probably be joining you soon.

*

Because of the smells affiliated with hog farms, the county would only permit Little Piggy to construct their facilities in an area where their powerful odors would not drift into nearby towns. And so a special road was constructed for its employees that ran five miles from its Route 404 entrance to the company's parking lot.

Led by the Ford pick-up, Jimmy and company turned onto that entrance road and began their journey.

Ten minutes in, Jimmy saw, partially hidden by the tall grass, the armored car.

Jimmy leaned toward the cell phone. "Mary, you see that?" he asked.

"See wha…? Oh, yeah I see. Just more evidence that the push-ins are hiding out here. Fortunately I don't see anyone behind the wheel."

"I don't either, and the engine's not running," Jimmy replied. "But we might have to deal with it on our way out.

"Let's worry about that later," Santiago commented.

Seven minutes later, after crossing a metal bridge that was constructed over a considerably deep gorge, the black silhouette of the Little Piggy Hog Farm office building and slaughterhouses rose from behind the hills against a crimson sky backdrop. Surrounding it were scores of empty wooden pigsties. The gates were open and the occasional breeze gently rocked them on their hinges.

"Where are all the pigs?" Mary asked, peering out from the rear seat of the Impala. "My next door neighbor works here and I've given him a lift to work plenty of times. These pigsties are usually full. So where in blazes are they?"

"There are lights on inside the building," Martaine said. "Apparently somebody's there."

Hearing this, Jimmy checked his watch. "It's only 7:29. They don't close till eight."

Aimee said, "The parking lot is almost full; maybe we should get out and... Watch out for that pig!"

Just then a full size black and white pig crossed the beam of the pick-up's headlights and Jimmy slammed the brakes. The pig lumbered across the road toward a small hill.

Having stopped behind Jimmy, Martaine grabbed the high powered flash-light from the Black Box, left the car and shone its beam on the trotting animal. It seemed unfazed and slowed to a stop at the top of the hill.

As Jimmy prepared to leave the truck and join Martaine, he heard Mary call out to the clergyman. "Listen, be very careful out there. My friend told me that Little Piggy is doing research on feral pigs from the south. Some of them can grow to be the size of a small cow, weigh over 800 pounds and are particularly vicious."

Martaine acknowledged her, then, as Jimmy sidled up to him he shined his flashlight on the black and white pig but unfortunately, it has its back to him. "I saw something in its mouth," he said to Jimmy. "I think it was a rat, but I'm not sure. I'd like to get a closer look."

"Pigs eat rats?" Jimmy asked, shooting a glance at the pig.

Martaine nodded as he angled the flashlight for a better view. "Oh yes, pigs are omnivores. They will eat anything and more importantly, can eat anything. If hungry enough, they will chew right through a bone to get to the marrow. They will trample a skull to get to the brains. Believe me, I've been to villages where— after diseases decimated the population—herds of wild pigs overran them and fed on the corpses and when that wasn't enough, they attacked the ill and dying. Pigs will keep eating until nothing eatable remains, which is where we get the saying 'greedy as a pig.'"

"C'mon!" Virgil called out in a stage whisper. "Stop dicking around with Porky and let's do this thing. The smell is gonna make me puke."

"He's right," Jimmy said, "I'm sure that pig will head back when feeding time rolls around. I'd still like to know where the other pigs are."

Martaine nodded and switched off the flashlight.

Chapter Forty Eight

Officer Myrrh Cavanaugh had seen Mary McGuernsey lug the badly injured and bleeding Santiago from Virgil's house into the passenger side seat of a gold Chevy Impala and drive away.

She jotted down the license plate.

Myrrh had been staked out on the street across from the Vanderhill house for an hour in an unmarked brown Buick. But she hadn't arrived early enough to catch Virgil and Martaine as they left for Filaments or Jimmy and Aimee when they left for Mary's.

She considered calling Van Pelt, but with no sign of Virgil, decided against it. Something violent had happened in that house and as soon as the gold Impala turned the corner, Myrrh left her car to see what that was.

The garage door was open and after entering and seeing fresh droplets of blood on the cement floor, she eyed the outside area. Seeing no one, closed the garage door, then walked over and twisted the knob of the adjoining door to the house.

It was unlocked and opened easily.

Following the blood trail, Myrrh came upon Jess' remains. A cursory inspection plus a look at Jess' face told the story. That and the fact that the stove top's electric burner was still glowing, filled in the blanks.

But why?

She remembered that on the day following the commotion at Dohesley, her patrol car computer downloaded Mary McGuernsey's driver's license photo, stats and orders to bring her in for questioning. Later communiqués advised that unmarked cars had been dispatched to both Mary's and Jessica Maldonado's house due to their close friendship.

Now Jess was dead and Mary was driving off with a badly injured priest.

Myrrh searched the house. When she reached Virgil's office she attempted to log on to his computer but was unsuccessful. She checked his desk drawers but found nothing of interest. Even rifled through his garbage and after noting all the used paper plates, plastic cups and crumpled napkins, realized that a number of people had gathered here recently.

To do what? she wondered as she peeked out the window to the deck below.

There was clearly a lot more to this, and Myrrh was determined to find out what before contacting her superiors.

She exited the house, returned to her car and drove toward Wheatfield figuring Mary was likely bringing the clergyman to the hospital.

I just hope I can get there before she dumps him there and takes off.

When she got the intersection, Myrrh almost automatically made the left into town but suddenly stopped.

But, what if, instead of the hospital, she's looking for a place to bury him?

Suddenly considering that a real possibility, she placed a call to the Wheatfield hospital admissions office and asked if anyone had just been brought in with a serious head injury.

She was told no and that over the last 24 hours, things had been relatively quiet.

After instructing the admissions officer to notify her immediately should someone fitting Santiago's description show up, she made the turn toward Route 404 and floored it.

Ten minutes later, she came upon Virgil's teal green Volvo, parked just inside the entrance of the road that led to the Little Piggy Hog Farm. Shortly afterward, following that same road, she saw the armored car.

Myrrh decided she had gone as far as she could go without risking disciplinary action. She pulled to the side, called Van Pelt and reported Jess' dead body, then said she was enroute to the Little Piggy Hog Farm following a vehicle she believed contained the victim's assailants.

"Oh, and I found the armored car," she added.

"Good job," Van Pelt replied, then told her he would take care of the situation at Virgil's house and for her to wait at the intersection of 727 and 404 until back-up arrived.

"Hold on a minute," she replied, "I'm in active pursuit. I don't want to take the chance of them getting away."

"They can't get away," Van Pelt said. "There is only one road in or out. Sit tight until help arrives, understand?"

She signed off.

Great, now I get to sit around twiddling my thumbs while everyone else gets ready to swoop in and take credit for my hard work.

With clearly exhibited frustration, she shoved the gearshift into PARK, leaned back and folded her arms.

*

Minutes later, Jimmy and company arrived at the Little Piggy main office building, behind which was the slaughterhouse, as well as the cutting, wrapping and shipping facilities.

After parking on the road just outside the parking lot entrance, the group climbed out of their vehicles and surveyed the area. It was unsettlingly quiet and the lights surrounding the building and parking lot only added to its ghost-town ambiance.

"Why is it so damn quiet?" Mary asked. She had her hands clasped over her stomach and her arms folded at her sides.

"It does feel kind of creepy," Aimee added as she surveyed the area.

"Well, folks," Jimmy said, "no sense standing around." As he took a step toward the building, Santiago called out from the truck's passenger seat.

"I will remain here as a lookout. I can be of no value to you inside the building, but perhaps here," he said tapping the truck's open window frame, "I might be of some use. Virgil, keep your cell phone on. Should I see anything suspicious, I will bring it to your attention."

Seeing Santiago's ashen condition, Virgil had doubts about the clergyman's ability to perform even this meager task, but since having him come with them was out of the question, he simply nodded.

298

As the others filed off, Martaine, with the Black Box in hand, gently grasped Santiago's arm and with a reassuring look said, "We will get through this, my friend. We always do." He winked, then handed him the keys to the Impala. "It's the spare set," he said, "just in case."

Santiago, having learned through experience that anticipation of the worst is often the key to avoiding it, took the keys in hand, pocketed them and nodded. Martaine then joined the others.

"Ewww, there's shit everywhere," Mary commented as she weaved her way through the muck.

Aimee gestured to the lights along the pathway to the entrance, "Well, the lights are on, so somebody's gotta be here."

"Not necessarily," Jimmy replied. "At Lumberland, the parking lot lights activate automatically when it gets dark."

"This is nuts!" Virgil said, pulling up the strap of the harness. "I was scared because I thought the minute we drove up, a hundred or so push-ins would come charging out with butcher knives and meat cleavers. What's the deal? This place seems deserted."

"Disappointed?" Martaine asked sarcastically as they climbed the front steps.

"Ha ha, your timing stinks, you know that?" Virgil snapped.

"Guys," Jimmy said. "Virgil has a point, we got a parking lot full of cars but as far as I can tell, no people or pigs."

Mary tilted her head toward the front door, "I can hear machinery running."

"Could they have gone on break?" Aimee asked as she tied her blonde hair back with a scrunchy.

"It's almost quitting time," Mary added, checking her watch. "You don't have breaks just before quitting time."

"Maybe one of the machines broke and they're waiting for repairmen." Martaine offered.

Virgil turned with raised eyebrows. "That could be it."

"Yeah, that makes sense," Mary added.

Jimmy stopped at the top of the entrance stairs and from under the overhead lamp addressed the group. "If that's the case it could work to our advantage," he said as he tried peering through the opaque steel and glass doors. "If the remaining push-ins are together waiting for a repair crew, we just toss in the device and run like hell."

"Yes but there's still one problem," Virgil said, again adjusting the harness. "What if they aren't push-ins? What if they are just normal people sitting around drinking coffee and eating stale donuts and we detonate a device that instead of eliminating the push-ins, blows us all to kingdom come? What then?"

"How the fuck should I know, Vanderhill?!" Jimmy said with a furious glare. "And if you run your fucking mouth again I'm…"

"Whoa! Whoa!" Mary interrupted as she stepped in and separated them. "Guys, take a moment and calm down. Remember my language and aggressive attitude back at the Blue Barn? Well, now it's starting to happen to you. It's caused by the negative vibes the daemons give off."

As Jimmy and Virgil stepped away from each other, Mary said, "And I think the heavy concentration of vibes in this location answers Virgil's concerns about whether we are attacking the right group. Besides, the ectoplasmic device is supposed to drive out push-ins and daemons, not kill anyone right?"

Vigils tossed his hand dismissively. "I don't know. Maybe. Hopefully."

"So," Mary continued, "that being said, we're going to have to buckle down and keep a tight rein on our emotions."

"All right, enough talk," Martaine said gruffly. "We are here. Let's go inside and do what must be done."

Jimmy nodded, pulled open the heavy metal and glass entrance door and found the inside of the main office strangely lit, especially for a business during office hours. The corridor and reception area were partially dark and illuminated—for the most part—by the emergency lights whose batteries were clearly winding down.

As they entered, Virgil placed his hand on the air-conditioner vent and noted it was blowing warm, stale air. He gestured to the reception desk and the immediate area with an expression that asked, 'Where is everybody?' They noticed a picture window overlooking the slaughterhouse's packaging area and when they walked over and peered through it, saw the ramps and sorting machines working, heard their clanking and stamping but the shoots were empty. No product was being produced.

Jimmy looked away and shook his head "This gets weirder by the minute. C'mon, let's check out the rest of the place."

A cloying unpleasant odor followed them as they walked down the corridor. The corridor itself had green ceramic tiles from the floor up to the mid-point, then above that numerous motivational posters ballyhooing such traits as perseverance, teamwork and self–reliance.

As they passed each door, one of them would open it and check inside.

All were empty.

Frustrated, Jimmy said in a low voice. "Where the hell is everybody?"

"You think maybe they're in a break room or cafeteria?" Aimee asked.

"That's a possibility," Virgil said.

Mary stopped in midstride. "Wait, you hear that?"

They stopped, listened, then did hear it. It was faint, very faint but it sounded like people talking, then laughing.

Jimmy looked at Virgil and mouthed the words, "You ready?"

Virgil opened the harness, removed the battery clips from the ectoplasmic device, shrugged and whispered, "I guess."

As they continued down the hall, the sound of people talking grew steadily louder.

The smell also grew stronger. Aimee covered her nose as did the others. "How can people work in these conditions?" she asked.

They reached a wooden door with the word CAFETERIA on it but the constant entering and exiting had worn most of the decal away. Standing in front and judging from what they were able to hear, there were definitely people inside.

Jimmy turned to the others and spoke in a low voice. "Okay, I'll go in first and see what we're dealing with. If anyone asks, I'll say I'm with Albany Health Care Services and am checking the facilities for insurance purposes; meanwhile Virgil will set the device and hand it to Brother Martaine. Then I'll step out of the way, Brother will press the trigger, lob it in, and close the door before it detonates." He eyed them. "Are we ready?"

Virgil grabbed Martaine's sleeve, leaned in from behind and whispered, "Look, it's simple, just push the button, toss it and get your chubby ass out."

Martaine turned. "Thank you for your concern. I will do my very best."

Jimmy took a breath, nodded to Martaine and Virgil and turned the knob.

Chapter Forty Nine

Myrrh Cavanaugh looked at her wristwatch gritted her teeth and slammed her hands against the steering wheel.

"It's been twenty minutes!" she snapped. "I could be checking out that armored car, I could be searching for Virgil, or finding out what Mary McGuernsey did with that priest. But nooo, instead they got me sitting on my ass waiting for back-up. What do they think I'm stupid? It's not back up they got me waiting for, it's male police officers 'cause Van Pelt doesn't think a woman can handle a big case."

A dark countenance painted itself on Cavanaugh's face. "Enough of this!" she said determinedly. "I'm smarter than they are, I think faster and my ideas actually work!"

She rolled down the window and pantomimed hearing something by placing her hand behind her ear. "Was that a gunshot? Dear heavens, was that another? Well, it's my sworn duty as a police officer to investigate any possibility of gunfire. I just hope I'm not too late."

She shoved the shift into gear and sped off, burning rubber.

*

When Jimmy opened the door to the cafeteria, the smell overwhelmed them, then the flies. A dark buzzing cloud exploded from the room startling Jimmy who, using the door for leverage, flung himself backward. With the door now wide open, Mary leapt to the side and pressed herself against the wall while Aimee crouched, covered her head and waved wildly to fend them off. Once free, the flies quickly disappeared down the hall.

The cafeteria lights were on and what they revealed caused Mary's stomach to hitch, Aimee to squeal and Virgil to step back. There had been a slaughter here, but not of animals.

The slaughter had been of employees.

Strune across the floor were 35 to 40 of them. All dead, all killed by knives and slaughterhouse cutlery. Several were decapitated, others gutted like deer. Still others had their throats

303

slit. Legions of maggots feasted on the remains as the pools of drying blood thickened with decay.

Above it all, the TV, with a streak of crimson cutting through the screen, played a rerun of, *How I Met Your Mother*.

With his heart pounding, Jimmy continued to stare. "I wonder how long they've been dead."

"Several days at least," Martaine replied, eyeing the carnage from the doorjamb.

"Should we look for the others?" Mary asked.

Martaine shrugged and turned to her. "I would think that if anyone were alive they would have called the police or left the facility."

"But what happened here?" Mary asked.

"Is it not obvious? They killed each other," Martaine replied.

"We know that, chucklehead," Virgil said drolly as he stepped up and shot a glance inside the room. "She's asking *why* they killed each other."

Martaine took a moment. "I have seen similar scenes following prison riots in South America and Africa. In those prisons, rivalries accrue and fester over time and eventually come to a head. Extreme violence like we see here, however, is rare because, unlike in the United States, the guards in those countries routinely shoot to kill during prison riots. Still, even with that as a deterrent, it does occasionally happen."

Martaine removed a handkerchief from his robe and dabbed his forehead. "When you consider the push-in's situation, they are like longtime prisoners. Once they acquired a new body and saw the opportunity to settle old scores, they did and the violence escalated until there was no one left."

"Looky here," Aimee said. Having literally gagged when she saw the carnage, she moved to what she thought was the next office, "This door is open." When she reached it and looked inside, she shook her head and waved them off, "Never mind, false alarm, it's just a staircase."

With no one willing to step through the drying pools of blood to close the cafeteria door, they left it open and continued their search.

Father Santiago was listening to their conversation on Virgil's open cell line as he kept watch. He noted the sun had gone down but the sky remained a shimmering dark crimson.

There is something so unsettling, so... wrong about that.

He heard a grunt and turned to see a pig come around from the back of the building. Under the entrance's dim light it approached the black and white Virgil had christened Porky. Now closer and better illuminated, Santiago saw it was not a rat Porky had been eating— it was a human hand, chewed off just above the wrist. The interloper snorted, then charged through the mud toward Porky, letting out blood-curdling squeals that pierced the evening air.

Reet! Reet! Reet!

It attacked and the surrounding hills echoed with snorts, squeals and cries of pain. Moments later, bloodied and injured, Porky broke off and ran.

The other gave chase.

They squared off again under the trucks headlights and Santiago was startled by the physical appearance of the other pig. It was almost twice the size of Porky and more angular, its teeth longer and sharper. It had none of the roly-poly features most pigs have.

A wild boar perhaps or one of those feral pigs Mary warned about?

A similarly-looking pig appeared and joined the fray, then another and another, all from the back of the building. Santiago lost count at ten. Moments later, one pig dashed away with a bloody strip in its mouth, then another, then still more.

Santiago, straining to get a closer look, accidently pressed the horn. Startled, the pigs scattered.

That's when Santiago saw Porky's torn and scattered remains on the road.

The pigs again rushed into the beam and resumed savagely tearing and ripping strips of meat and entrails from it. Within minutes there were only scattered bones and a dark red stain as

Porky's blood seeped into the dirt. With the food gone, the pigs filed off into the dark.

One of them turned. It eyed Santiago with bared teeth then ran its tongue over its snout. Its eyes were that of a madman, wild and crazed, euphoric with the afterglow of the savagery. Apparently sated, it turned and trotted off.

The clergyman shivered and leapt forward to warn the others

As he opened his mouth to speak, he was startled by a trill of reedy musical notes from his cell phone, then saw the screen flashing LOW BATTERY and powering down.

His hands ran to his head. *What a fool! I should have given it a full charge when we were back at Virgil's.*

He looked for the charger and winced when he remembered it was in the Chevy.

I have to get it. I am of no use whatsoever if I cannot warn them of danger.

He recalled how the pigs savagely killed one of their own.

He paused and eyed the bones and blood glistening in the truck's headlights.

Or was it one of their own?

He looked into the truck's rearview mirror and saw the Chevy parked behind him.

Shouldn't be too difficult to turn the truck around so both vehicles are door to door.

As he slid over to the driver's seat, he saw the clutch and realized the truck had a manual transmission.

He gritted his teeth and growled. "Still more trials, Lord?" he asked as he looked upwards. "I have no idea how to work these pedals and I can barely move my left leg."

He again looked into the rearview mirror.

It can't be more than a few meters away.

He sat back and continued to debate. *The others are depending on me. What if something happens and I am unable to contact them? No! I need only open the door, walk the ten or so steps to the Impala, climb in and hook the cell into the charger. And if the walk is tiring, I can sit inside the car as easily as I can sit here, except I'll have use of the phone.*

He scoured the area. With the shimmering maroon sky, playing off the puddles of muddy water, his surroundings had taken on an otherworldly appearance.

Nevertheless, he still had a job to do. He placed the dead phone in his pocket.

The truck's high-beams illuminated his surroundings but didn't reach as far back as the driver's side door to the Impala, so he lowered the window and listened.

He remembered that many predators drag and hide their prey.

Do pigs fall into that category?

Porky did, or at least tried to. Besides the ones that attacked him are either full or still eating. Hopefully if there are any stragglers they'll be too far away or too busy to pose a threat.

He continued to listen.

Still quiet.

*

Virgil placed the ectoplasmic device back in the harness and reconnected it to the battery as the group caught up with Aimee and continued down the corridor. "Well," he said, "that adventure was a whole lot of nothing. Got anymore bright ideas fearless leader?"

Jimmy's growing anger at Virgil's snide comments had him seriously considering spinning around and punching him. But that brought another concern. If he was still feeling rage, presumably generated by their proximity to daemons, then where were they? All the employees of Little Piggy were dead, or so it seemed; therefore the push-ins should be back in that timeless Void. Plus the pigs had scattered, some as far as Route 404, 5 miles away. All of which begged another question: if the employees were dead for several days, as Martaine believed, wouldn't somebody have missed them? They must have had families, wives, husbands, and children. Surely someone must have called or stopped by to see where they were…

"Well, McCracken?" Virgil asked in a sarcastic tone as he closed the harness. "Got any more brilliant plans?"

307

Jimmy waved Virgil off and placed his finger to his lips. "Something doesn't add up," he muttered.

"Of course it adds up," Virgil snapped. "Push-ins take possession of the employees' bodies, then get on each other's nerves, eventually they snap and kill each other. Not hard. Even you should be able to figure that one out."

Jimmy turned away. "Will someone shut him up. I'm trying to think."

Virgil scoffed and hiked the harness further up his shoulder. "Well, I guess there's a first time for everythi..."

Jimmy spun and charged with a closed fist, but Aimee, anticipating this, grabbed the collar of his dungaree jacket and yanked hard.

Suddenly gagging, Jimmy jerked to a halt, coughed, and put his hand to his throat.

Aimee let go, raised both her hands and stepped in. "Listen everyone, do you need to be reminded a second time?" She gestured down the hall to the open cafeteria door. "Want to wind up the same way? Do you?" She looked around. "Didn't think so. So let's all calm the fuck down!"

"Aimee's right," Mary said. "Something has to be fueling this anger we're feeling and if all the push-ins are dead, then why would the daemons remain here?" She took a moment. "No," she said determinedly, "we're not alone. I just know it."

"I agree," Martaine said. "Let's continue searching. If we find nothing, we'll return to our vehicles and plan our next move."

Virgil's expression told everyone he'd like nothing more than to make some insulting comment but to his credit, he held his tongue, folded his arms and nodded.

"All right," Jimmy said, clearing his throat. "Let's check each room, and Virgil, keep that bomb ready to go. Bottom line, we either find and destroy the remaining push-ins or daemons, OR, verify once and for all that they're all gone. Agreed?"

Virgil began walking toward the next office. "Let's just do it."

*

The pain from his wound was flaring and Santiago gritted his teeth until it was at least endurable. Having sat quietly for fifteen minutes following his companions' departure, Santiago felt that perhaps, just perhaps, he might survive after all. The side of his head felt like there was a grapefruit tucked under his skin, but the bleeding had stopped and he had regained sight in his left eye as well as some feeling in his left arm and leg. He seriously considered the trek to the Chevy.

He put his ear to the slightly open window again and listened.

After nearly a full minute of nothing but rustling trees and wind-blown grass, he was convinced there were no pigs nearby.

He snapped on the trucks dome light and searched the interior.

Okay. I have the phone. Is there anything else I might need should I not be able to return?

He studied the insides. *The towel!* He reached over and grabbed it. *Just in case I begin to bleed again.* He tucked it under his arm.

After turning off the dome light, Santiago opened the truck's driver's side door and hearing no reaction, slowly climbed out.

Holding onto the door for support, he cautiously placed his foot on the step and eased himself to the ground. He scouted the area. The shimmering crimson sky provided some light but not as much as he had hoped. Instead, it gave a deep purple tint to the surrounding hills and trees. He turned and eyed the Chevy. It sat only fifteen feet away yet he was surprised at how far that small distance seemed now.

He closed the truck door.

"Here goes," he said softly and edged himself toward the back of the truck.

*

Having finished checking all the rooms on the ground floor and finding no one other than the corpses in the cafeteria, Jimmy and the others backtracked to the open staircase and trudged up to the second floor.

309

There, they came upon the break room. Inside were at least ten dead, all killed like the others, flies everywhere. There wasn't much blood, however and Virgil noted the floor had a drain a few feet in front of the vending machines.

He turned to Jimmy, shook his index finger side from to side and said, "No, this isn't right." Virgil then walked to the drain, saw it was wet, then sat on his heels, touched it and examined his finger. It was wet all right, not with blood, but with water. He looked up and noted there were no automatic sprinklers. He stood, stepped into the hallway, walked to the cabinet holding the fire hose, opened the door and felt the nozzle.

"Yeah, just as I thought."

Returning to the others he said, "At least one person's alive. The fire hose was used to wash blood down the drain and the vending machines have been vandalized."

Jimmy shrugged. "Maybe that was one of the issues that led to the violence."

Mary's stomach had had enough of the thick, cloying odor and she ran to the ladies room. Barely inside, she felt her legs wobble as she stumbled over and vomited into the sink.

Easy old girl, you've been telling everyone how tough you are. Now is the time to show it.

She pulled a paper towel, wiped her lips, turned on the faucet, cupped her hands and washed out her mouth.

"You okay?" Aimee asked, poking her head in.

Mary grabbed another paper towel, dried her hands and wiped the sweat from her forehead. "Yeah," she said tossing it into the waste barrel. "I can handle the blood and guts. It's the smell I can't take."

Mary followed Aimee out of the bathroom.

"So far we've found about fifty push-ins," Jimmy announced. "If our arithmetic is correct, there's got to be at least fifty more, so we keep looking.

"Maybe we should open some windows," Aimee said with a scrunched up nose. "If we get a little fresh air, maybe we won't have such a tough time."

A sneer washed over Virgil's face. He walked to the nearest window and motioned to the frame. "No hinges or latches."

He pointed to the ceiling. "See those vents along the top?" He was gesturing to the 3-inch high 12-inch long metal grates just below the ceiling. "That's where they pump in fresh air."

"So why aren't they working?" Martaine asked.

Virgil paused before answering. "I don't know. Everything else is."

"We only have one more floor to check," Martaine said. "If we move quickly we can be done and out of here in ten minutes. We'll take the exit at the end of the corridor."

Everyone scowled but Virgil, who surprised them all by merely nodding and proceeding toward the staircase door. When he reached it, he opened the harness and checked inside it to make sure the device was properly connected and that everything was set up as it should be. The possibility that there was something wrong with the device continued to gnaw at him.

If there is, then what the hell is it? I've gone over it a hundred times. I've checked, double-checked, triple-checked...

He had done all that was humanly possible. Still, he continued to be concerned.

*

Santiago momentarily stopped advancing toward the Impala when he saw the full moon break through the clouds and stare down on him like a bright white eyeball surrounded by a pool of clotted blood. The Catskill Mountains with their deep purple hues were topped with moonlight, making them look like giant cresting waves on a vast blue and lavender ocean.

He shivered.

He wasn't sure if it was because of the cold or because he had lost so much blood, but if he was going to reach the Chevy he had to keep moving. He took a step and felt a trickle of blood run down the side of his face and drop to the ground. It made a 'plip' sound when it struck a dead leaf.

He took another step and the vision in his left eye darkened.

311

I don't have enough blood to keep both eyes working.

He stood still for a moment and his sight slowly returned. The wind picked up and rattled the trees. His skin felt like paper. He took a step, heard the dried leaves crackle beneath him, then another and slumped at the tailgate. Still, he held on and breathed deeply hoping the additional oxygen would keep him functioning. He stared at the Impala's grill.

It seemed miles away.

Santiago continued to breathe deeply and staggered forward. The crunching of the gravel and the occasional snapping of twigs beneath his feet sounded louder than they should, but he suspected that was due to his weakened condition.

His knees wobbled but he managed to lurch forward and make it to the left headlight panel of the Impala and pressed both hands against it to steady himself. His shadow stretched before him beneath the pale moonlight.

He felt bugs crawling all over him.

He forced himself to ignore it.

Just another sign of blood loss.

He took a step and dropped the towel. As he was about to bend down and pick it up, he felt another droplet of blood fall from his chin to the ground.

Can't take a chance on passing out. I'll come back for it later.

He took another step and heard…

…something breathing nearby.

*

When Brother Martaine opened the gray door below the EXIT sign, they were again greeted by a swarm of flies. Inside, however, was not a staircase but a ramp that stretched from the ground floor to the roof. Looking up to the roof door, Martaine saw scores of bodies, slain in the same manner as the others.

"The rest of you stay here," Martaine said as he pulled the door fully open. "I will go up, inspect the remains and check the roof. No sense in all of us wading through this carnage."

The now strangely quiet Virgil shook his head, hiked the harness on his shoulder, stepped past Martaine and started up the ramp. Jimmy's face twisted at the smell, but he followed Virgil in.

"Looks like we're all going in," Mary commentated as she followed the others.

Aimee stamped her feet at having to further wade into the pools of blood and body parts. "I just bought these sneakers, you know!" she shouted. But she started up the ramp without another word.

There were at least fifty bodies strune upon it, probably more. The savagery in which they were killed startled even Martaine, who had seen such atrocities before.

The group held onto the railing as the ramp was thick with drying pools of blood. "I hate this!" Aimee snapped, "I freakin hate this!"

There was a bloody scrawl on the wall and Jimmy would have walked right past it had Martaine's flashlight's beam not lit upon it.

It read: ***the daemons are I n.***

"The daemons are in? What does that mean?" Virgil asked as he crouched for a closer look.

Aimee lips tightened. "The daemons are in... here?"

The roof door was slightly ajar, and as they stepped out upon the roof, they were greeted by cool air and a far less pungent smell. The area was lit by two spotlights attached to the outside walls of the roof landing. Jimmy and the others gathered and surveyed their surroundings.

Finally Virgil spoke. He had extended his hands in front of him, bewildered "This makes absolutely no sense. Why would they head up to the roof instead of out to their cars?"

"Maybe one group was more dominant and blocked the exits?" Jimmy offered.

"No! That's just..." Virgil paused. "If all the push-ins are dead there couldn't have been one dominant group."

"True," Jimmy replied, trying, like Virgil, not to let his anger taint the conversation. "But we haven't checked the entire roof yet. Maybe we'll come across something."

Virgil didn't think so, but agreed as it was the logical thing to do.

There were less than ten bodies on the roof, all apparently dead and covered in blood.

As they considered their next move, one of the 'corpse's eyes opened.

Chapter Fifty

Santiago, too frightened to draw a breath, slowly eased his way along the Impala's side panel to the driver's door. His heart pounded and he was bleeding again.

No longer able to raise his left foot, Santiago dragged it along the gravel as he passed the driver-side mirror.

The sound of the breathing grew louder, closer. Something was aware of his presence and was slowly moving toward him. As Santiago cautiously reached for the Impala's door handle, there came a squeal and something charged out of the dark. Panicking, he yanked the door open.

He was too slow and he knew it.

Everything seemed to move in slow motion: the opening door and pig's dash toward him.

Dear Lord forgive me.

However, the pig raced by him as Santiago half jumped/half fell behind the wheel and quickly closed the door.

"Dear God, thank you. Thank you!" he said as he struggled to catch his breath.

He looked out the window and saw what the pig was so interested in.

It was the bloody towel.

*

The group wandered the roof comparing notes and mulling options.

Mary was alone and thinking about Jess when Aimee suddenly grabbed her hand. As she turned, Aimee leaned in and whispered. "Over there, on the far side of the roof door. Green pants."

As Aimee walked away, Mary looked and saw the push-in's dark aura.

Realizing what Aimee was planning, Mary followed. When they reached the opposite side, and out of his sightline, they crouched down, grabbed butcher knives from the corpses and headed back to catch the push-in from behind.

As Aimee quietly strode toward the roof door alongside Mary, she looked down at the bloody knife and the thought of Coffee's lifeless eyes staring blindly into nothingness leapt into her head.

Her stomach lurched.

No, she said to herself determinedly. *No time for that.*

When they turned the corner of the roof's brick landing, they saw they'd miscalculated. The push-in was already on his feet and charging toward Jimmy, who was back on and staring at the moonlit crests of the Catskill Mountains.

Mary shouted in panic, "Jimmy, behind you!"

Jimmy turned but it was Martaine who took action. As the push-in charged with the blade extended, Martaine leapt forward and 'clothes-lined' the assailant. Upon contact with Martaine's meaty forearm, the man's feet flew out from under him and he fell with enough impact to make those watching wince with empathy.

The compassion was very short lived and before the man could move, Mary pounced upon him and pressed a 14" butcher knife tightly to his throat.

She stared down hard, her eyes red-rimmed from the daemonic fueled rage pulsing within her. "Just give me a reason!" she growled through clenched teeth.

"All right! All right!" the man said, dropping the knife and placing his hands up and alongside his head.

As Mary took his knife and climbed off, Martaine grabbed the man's hand and pulled him up. "Who are you?" the clergyman demanded.

"Ah geez, a holy roller," he scoffed as his brushed the back of his pants. "As if things weren't bad…"

Martaine grabbed his shirt and yanked him into the air with one hand. The clergyman, also feeling the effects of the rage, found himself fighting the urge to toss the assailant over the side. "Do not dare push me, little man," he said, eyes blazing, "for my patience has truly reached its limit."

Suddenly realizing just how life-threatening his situation was, he quickly bleated, "Okay, okay," and raised his shaky hands in surrender. "Please, just let me down."

After Martaine complied, the man said, "My name is Abner Bolo and I'm just trying to protect my own ass. You have no idea what it was like. Everyone was at each other's throats. Crazy I tell you. Absolutely crazy!" He shook his head as he recalled the events over the last few days. "As you can see, I'm a little guy and not built for hand-to- hand combat. When the killing started, I smeared myself with blood and dove under those three bodies over there and stayed put until everyone was dead."

"But why were they killing each other?" Jimmy asked.

"I don't know. One afternoon some of the guys just went berserk. Maybe something toxic got into them. Maybe…"

Martaine grabbed him by the throat and squeezed. "Stop your lies! We know you are a dead soul and are in league with D'Shaid! Now tell us the truth and start at the beginning!"

"All right! All right!" he gasped, prying Martaine's powerful fingers from his neck. "After that night at the Blue Barn, we were just happy to be in live bodies. To breathe, to feel, to taste, to touch!" he said wistfully as he ran his hand over his chest. "We even showed up for work the following day because it was payday and we were all looking forward to a big weekend with a wallet full of cash. Then, out of nowhere, D'Shaid bursts into the building, slithers down the hallways killing everyone who wasn't a dead soul, then made those of us who were his prisoners. Not that we didn't try to stop him but a human body is no match for a daemon who crossed into this world in full daemonic form. We didn't stand a chance.

"Days passed and tempers flared. Then other daemons showed up, eager to take over these bodies. But knowing where we would wind up if they succeeded, we fought them tooth and nail and with the barrier still largely intact, they couldn't force their way in."

Abner looked down as he recalled the event. "Fuckers!" he spat.

"Anyway as time went on, being trapped on this stinking pig farm, knowing the barrier was weakening and feeling the daemons' constant presence got to be too much. We started fighting among ourselves. Small fights at first, then big ones and soon people were getting killed. Then—and I swear I don't know why this was—we

317

starting enjoying the violence, the rapes, the mutilations, the tortures. We were addicted to it. And in this crazed state the daemons started taking over our bodies, but it was too late, we were out of control. The bloodlust overwhelmed us."

"But how could you overpower a daemonically possessed body?" Martaine asked, eyeing him suspiciously. "They are far more powerful."

"Yeah, but the physical change takes time, so when we saw one of us turning into a daemon, we tore him to shreds. And the more they tried to possess us, the more we killed each other. It was insane; we were literally wiping ourselves out.

"And when they realized their chance of inhabiting human bodies was slipping away, the daemons went berserk, and the angrier *they* became the more violent *we* became. That's when I realized that I'd better do something if I wanted to stay alive so I covered myself in blood and slipped under the stiffs."

"Where was D'Shaid while all this was going on?" Jimmy asked.

"He took off." Abner suddenly stopped and gave that fact some thought. "You know, thinking back, I'll bet D'Shaid planned it that way. I just don't know why."

"I believe I do," Martaine said turning to Jimmy and taking a seat on the wall surrounding the roof. "Remember what Ike said about the Void? He said God puts all the people who committed a crime in a certain area to be, let us say, 'chained' to the area where their crime occurred."

Jimmy nodded. "That's what he said."

Virgil stepped up. "So you're saying my mother committed her crimes in the area of the Blue Barn?"

Abner turned toward him. "Who's your mother?"

Lillian Vand..."

Abner's face lit up. "Lillian Vanderhill? Ha-ha, really? When your old man found out what she and Bert Langley were up to and threatened to go to the police, Bert killed him and buried him under the Blue Barn, knowing that nobody looks for corpses in Dohesley soil."

Virgil cocked his fist and probably would have hit Abner except the strap from the harness slipped and fell into the crook of his arm throwing him off balance.

Abner stepped back. "Easy pal, nothing personal, I'm just telling you what happened." He walked away. Virgil scowled and was about to follow when Aimee took his arm, shook her head and led him in the opposite direction.

Jimmy turned to Martaine. "So, you were saying?"

"Well, if Ike is correct, then hell is not one large facility, nor is purgatory. And if so, then there must be hundreds, maybe thousands of these holding cells where the dead wait until they are ready to face their judgment and where the daemons serve their eternal punishment. Now since there were only 502 dead souls in the Void, and since our Lord tends to keep everything in balance, I'm going to assume there were only a comparable number of daemons."

"But how does D'Shaid fit into all this?" Jimmy asked.

"Like Lillian, D'Shaid knew that in order for a plan to succeed, you need the support of those in authority. Fortunately for us, Virgil's machine returned the FBI agents, police and first responders to their bodies before D'Shaid's daemons could possess them.

"Left with only a hundred or so slaughterhouse workers, D'Shaid chose to use them as bait to attract the daemons, knowing their presence would spark unrestrained violence."

"I still don't see how that helps his cause," Jimmy said.

"That, in itself, doesn't," Martaine continued. "But D'Shaid knew when word got out that there was a brutal massacre here, all sorts of professional people would be brought in and as they arrived, he would have the daemons possess them."

And since he is here in true daemonic form he can control whom the daemons can possess. That form also makes him invulnerable to exorcism. But..." Martaine tipped his finger to his lips with the expression of a man who had just put the pieces together, "such a form would make him especially venerable to..." his voice trailed off.

"So bottom line, whatever happens we're still going to have to deal with D'Shaid?" Jimmy asked.

Martaine nodded.

"Hey guys?" Aimee said as she and Mary approached. "What about the writing we saw on the rampway. One of them wrote, 'the daemons are in here.'"

Abner overheard. With his hands in his pockets he stepped over and shook his head. "No, I saw him write it. What he was trying to say was, "The daemons are in… the pigs."

When he saw their puzzled look, Abner said, "Well, where else were the daemons going to go? All except me were dead, so they possessed the pigs."

Aimee said, "But the pigs are gone!"

"Nah, they're just in the back," Abner said hooking his thumb to the grounds below. "There are several hundred down there wandering around. After the blackout, the magnetic sty locks didn't come back online, so some wandered off but the majority stayed. They spend most of their time in the back because every so often I toss a body over to keep them from getting ravenous and busting down the front door."

"How can pig bust down a door?" Jimmy asked. "They don't have horns or raw power like a bear."

"Remember what I told about the daemons taking over people and how they would physically change? Well, that goes the same for pigs," Abner said. "Little Piggy is a pig *farm,* which means we got all kinds of pigs, including those wild, southern bastards. Some are the size of a baby hippo and twice as vicious. Lucky for you, I saw you guys approaching and tossed several stiffs over the side to draw the pigs to the back of the building. If I hadn't, you wouldn't have had a chance."

"So why didn't they possess you?" Jimmy asked.

Abner stared at him. "Didn't you hear me? I said the daemons are in the pigs and they're hungry as hell because I only feed them enough to keep them alive. And no daemon is going to possess me or anyone here when he knows that should the pigs get in, that person will be eaten, so it's a standoff."

"So why did you try to kill me?"

320

Abner sat on the ledge and placed his arms on his knees. "I wasn't trying to kill you. I just needed a hostage so you would have to take me with you."

"Wait," Jimmy said. "Why didn't you just drive away?"

"How? I've been dead for one hundred and fifty years. I have no idea how to drive and neither did the real Abner. He came in from Wheatfield on the company bus each morning."

Martaine jumped to his feet. "Santiago!"

*

Now behind the wheel of the Impala, Santiago found himself amid several daemonic pigs with dozens more approaching. When they arrived, some placed their front legs and snouts against the Impala's driver's door, staring with unblinking eyes, salivating.

The clergyman shakily connected the charger to the cell phone, started the engine, then turned and saw a blood-soaked snout smear the window.

He blew the horn, snapped on the lights, pressed his foot on the accelerator and revved the Impala's powerful engine. The pigs momentarily scattered.

Momentarily.

Suddenly, one huge pig snapped its powerful jaws on the driver's side mirror, crushing it. As the glass rained to the ground, the pig, eyeing Santiago closely, literally ripped it from the door of the car. Another charged head first into the driver's side door, then another.

Realizing the necessity of getting the car as near as possible to the front entrance, Santiago put it in DRIVE and floored it. Dirt and gravel flew.

One pig was knocked into the air and crashed into the windshield forming a large hole as pebbled glass rained onto the dashboard. Santiago's head swam with the sudden acceleration. Again he took deep breaths, trying to stay conscious. He could see the front entrance just ahead and angled the car toward it. His cell phone rang. He leaned forward and reached for it. His head swam; he couldn't remember what button to push.

He blacked out.

*

As Martaine and Virgil raced toward the part of the roof that overlooked the entrance, they heard the Impala's horn blow. When they reached it, Virgil looked out and saw the Impala speeding past the empty sties toward the building.

"What the…!? He yanked his cell from his breast pocket.

"Santiago! What's going on down there?" Virgil shouted into it. Hearing nothing he checked the screen. "He disconnected!"

Martaine became bug-eyed. "Why in heaven's name would he disconnect and who is behind the wheel of the Impala?"

Abner joined them and with a panicky look pressed his hands to his head. "Whoever it is, he just turned and is heading right up the road to the front entrance. If crashes through, the pigs will get in and… and…!" With hands shaking he turned away unable to look.

Martaine took the cell from Virgil and punched Santiago's cell number.

"It's ringing!"

It rang twice, then transferred to voicemail. He handed it back to Virgil

"I don't understand. Why won't Hector pick up?"

"He's probably dead," Virgil said matter-of-factly as he put his cell away. "I mean, let's face it. He was knocking on heaven's door when we left."

Martaine spun around, growled, and Virgil literally gasped when he saw Martaine's expression. "You will kindly shut your filthy mouth," the clergyman said in measured tones. "Or I will… permanently!"

They all felt a cold chill, then outright fear when they noticed Martaine's usual jovial countenance transformed into homicidal fury.

There came the sound of shattering glass and the squealing of twisting metal.

Everyone ran to the front and looked down. With a grim expression, Martaine turned and rolled up his sleeves to his biceps. His arms were the width of a normal man's legs and looked like they had been carved out of granite. "There is nothing more to be done here," he said solemnly. "The front doors have been shattered, the Impala is somewhere in the lobby and the pigs are rushing into the building. Our goal now is to try to escape with our lives."

Aimee turned to Jimmy. "What are we going to do?"

Virgil started shaking. "What can we do? We're screwed! We're finished!"

"Not yet," Jimmy said. "Follow me, I have an idea."

He opened the roof door and started down the ramp.

"This is your idea?" Vigil asked, grabbing his arm. "Leading us directly to the pigs?

"Shut up," Jimmy snapped as he pulled free. "You want to stay on the roof, go ahead."

Abner took Virgil's shoulder. "Just so you know there's no food or water up here and once the pigs make it to this side of the building you'll be trapped."

"Fine!" Virgil spat as he followed the others. "I just hope Brainiac here doesn't get us all killed."

As they angled their way past the bodies, Jimmy turned. "Abner, does this ramp lead to or connect to the slaughterhouse?"

Abner nodded. "Yeah, each week they bring a number of pigs up for routine medical and physical inspections. But you've got to cross the hallway on the first floor to get to it."

"What's the length?"

"About forty yards. Why?"

As Jimmy helped Aimee over a pile of bodies he said, "I'm figuring that the pigs will follow the smell and head to the cafeteria first, but that room can only hold so many, so the rest will keep searching."

"And smell the bodies on the second floor," Abner said.

"Right, and since the open staircase is pretty close to the cafeteria, those pigs should, hopefully, head up the stairs toward them."

"But what about all the stiffs here?" Virgil asked.

"This ramp is at the back of the building, and the dead are scattered near the roof. We need to get down to the first floor while the pigs head up to the second. Then we wait till the coast is clear and make a break for the slaughterhouse. We know there are no pigs in there because we looked through the slaughterhouse window when we first came in. Once we're there, we check the parking lot then make a bee line for the truck."

"But what about Hector?" Martaine asked. "I will not permit you to leave him to the mercy of these monsters!"

Jimmy gently pressed his hand against the clergyman shoulder. "We'll see what the situation is when we get down there."

That appeared to satisfy Martaine, so Jimmy and the others continued down the ramp.

But Martaine wasn't satisfied; in fact he was shaken to the core. In all their adventures, he and Father Santiago had never faced anything this serious.

Three years ago in Colombia, a 5-foot 2-inch, 98 lb. fifteen–year-old possessed girl nearly gouged out Martaine's left eye and broke his wrist. Had it not been for the quick actions of Father Santiago, she likely would have killed him.

In Tripoli, as he struggled to hold down a seven-year-old boy so Santiago could recite the exorcism prayers, the child lifted him into the air, all 345 lbs. of him.

In Jerusalem, inside an excavated temple dating back 3,000 years, they encountered a malevolent spirit that sealed the doors and dropped the temperature to 50 degrees below zero. It was Father Santiago's indomitable will and perseverance to complete the exorcism prayers that prevented them from freezing to death.

Now they were confronting a potential army of daemons, and although never discussed, both men knew there might come a day when one, or perhaps even both of them would fall in battle.

Martaine swallowed hard and ran to catch the others.

As they passed the second floor landing and continued toward the lobby, Virgil stopped. "Hold up! Hold up!" he said in a low voice.

"What's the problem?" Mary asked.

Virgil grunted and slid the harness from his shoulder. "The harness for the battery is tearing." He grabbed the bottom and held it for the others to see.

"Already?" Mary asked.

"Do you have any idea how heavy this damn truck battery is?" Virgil countered.

Jimmy thought for a moment, then said, "I wonder if we still need it."

When Virgil's jaw dropped, Jimmy continued. "Think about it. We brought the battery to keep the ectoplasmic bomb fully charged, but since all the push-ins, with the exception of Abner here, are dead, do we still need it?"

Virgil's surprise turned to confusion. "We do if we want to drive out the daemons."

"So they stay in the pigs, who cares? When we get out to the truck, you put the bomb on the ground and set the timer to give us enough time to clear the area. We get to safety, the bomb goes off, the daemons are forced back and we're done."

"Great, except it doesn't have a timer," Virgil replied.

"How long does the charge last?" Mary asked.

Virgil thought for a second. "Once disconnected, about thirty minutes. After that, it's just a cylinder filled with very unstable chemicals."

"Then let's take the bomb and leave the battery here," Mary said. "If we're not out in thirty minutes we'll probably be dead so it won't matter."

"Look, we got to get going," Jimmy said, eying Virgil and Mary. "So what's it going to be?"

"This harness is shot," Virgil said removing the device and placing the torn carrier and battery on the floor. "If we're taking the bomb, what are we going to carry it in?"

Mary opened her shoulder bag. "Put it in here."

Jimmy nodded. "Okay, drop it in and let's go."

325

Santiago awoke to the strong smell of gasoline. He coughed as the caustic vapors entered his lungs. As his head slowly cleared he looked up and saw the windshield had caved in and the driver-side window had shattered. Clearly vulnerable, he wondered why the pigs had not attacked. As he pulled himself into a sitting position, he saw them racing past and through the growing pool of gasoline beneath the car.

It's the smell and the burning effect the gasoline has on their sensitive skin that's keeping them away.

He coughed again, pushed the collapsed air bag to the side and assessed the damage.

The front end was crushed inward and the hood resembled an accordion. The steel and glass entrance doors were heavier and sturdier than they appeared and had snub- nosed the Impala.

Why is my head wet? Why are my clothes wet?

He placed his hand to his temple and when he brought it back saw it was covered with blood. The wound had reopened during the crash and was bleeding heavily.

He lurched for the cell phone and almost blacked out.

"No!" he shouted. "I will not succumb until the others are safe."

He called Martaine.

When Martaine picked up, he joyfully shouted, "Thank the Lord you are alive my friend! I was…"

Santiago cut him off. "Listen, I have little time. The pigs are in the building and throughout the first floor. You cannot come this way."

"We are heading toward the slaughterhouse by the back staircase," Martaine replied. "We believe the pigs will follow the smell of the deceased to the second floor. Once the first floor is clear I'll come and get you."

"You will do no such thing!" Santiago shouted and nearly passed out from the exertion. "I am bleeding heavily and will not survive. While the pigs search for food you must all escape to the truck."

"I refuse to abandon you!" Martaine bellowed. "I will not."

There was a pause then Santiago said, "Then, my good friend, I must leave you no choice."

"Hector! Hector!" Martaine shouted into the receiver. As he pulled it from his ear he saw the call was terminated.

"What did he say?" Virgil asked.

"Doesn't matter," Martaine snapped. "We have to get down there immediately."

"But…" Aimee said.

"No buts!" Martaine roared as he lowered himself until they were face to face. "Have I made myself clear?"

The red-faced clergyman had indeed made himself clear.

*

Santiago had figured out what D'Shaid was planning and why his injury hadn't killed him. It was simple: he needed to be here at this moment without any chance of survival. He also understood why circumstances forced him behind the wheel of the Impala, (the truck wouldn't have fit through the front doors.) And why he had to have that final conversation with Silvio. The possessed pigs had to be destroyed. If they were left for the authorities to round up, the daemons in the pigs would possess them and D'Shaid would once again have control over the people in power, which was his goal all along.

The oil light sensor chimed.

The oil pan must have ruptured with the gas tank.

As the sensor continued to chime-chime-chime its warning, Santiago imagined it as a countdown signal, telling him it was time to act.

He reached over and pressed the cigarette lighter.

*

327

"Hurry! Hurry!" Martaine shouted as they approached the first floor door.

"Keep it down," Jimmy scolded in a stage whisper. "You want the pigs to know we're here?"

Jimmy eyes widened when the powerful Martaine spun, pulled back his arm and...Aimee jumped in between. Startled, the clergyman jerked as if snapping out of a trance.

Ashamed by his uncharacteristic reaction, he slowly lowered his hand and said, "My apologies, I must not be thinking clearly."

Having reached the door, Jimmy placed his hand on the knob and turned to them. "Okay folks," he said. "Here's the problem. This door opens inward, so if I open it, even a little and the pigs are out there, they are going to charge in and we're finished."

"I don't care, I'm going through," Martaine exclaimed as he reached for the knob.

As Jimmy grabbed his hand, Abner said, "The pigs ain't out there. You can open it."

"How do you know?" Virgil asked.

"Cause the real Abner worked in a slaughterhouse and I have his memories. If there were pigs out there we'd have heard them."

Martaine yanked open the door.

*

Santiago heard the snap, reached over and removed the cigarette lighter. He looked at the glowing red coil for a moment then said, "Greater love hath no man than to lay down his life for his friends."

He tossed the lighter out the window and into the pool of gasoline below.

Chapter Fifty One

It was dark when Myrrh Cavanaugh drove the unmarked brown Buick past the empty wooden sties and through the parking lot of the Little Piggy Hog Farm. The area had an ethereal feel to it, especially when she saw how the silhouette of the office building was framed by the dark maroon sky and the cue ball moon.

Spinning the wheel to the entrance, she saw the twisted door frames and the shattered glass reflected in the overhead lights. She did not see the Impala as it was farther inside the now dark corridor, but did see the last few pigs squeezing their way in.

Something's wrong here. Where is everybody?

She noted the Black Ford pick-up parked outside the lot and scouted the area for signs of the Impala and the badly injured clergyman.

Perhaps they drove around back.

She snapped on the Buick's high beams and followed the path that led to the rear entrance. When she reached it she scanned the loading dock but she saw nothing of interest. She drove a little farther and noticed the road came to a dead end.

So where's the Impala?

As she made the u-turn to go back to the entrance, her headlights fell upon what she thought was an oddly shaped large bundle of rags.

Then got a closer look.

It was pile of skeletal bodies, almost picked clean. Entire sections of bones were missing.

What happened here?!

She thought of the bleeding priest.

Fearing that the group would take off before she could confront them, she burned rubber to the front entrance.

Once there, she killed the engine, jumped from her vehicle and was heading for the entrance stairs when…

*

329

Martaine stepped outside the rampway door, looked down the hall and to everyone's relief, saw no pigs. He immediately took off for the entrance

Jimmy shook his head. "All right, it looks like clear sailing all the way to the slaughterhouse. Everybody ready?"

A massive explosion shook the entire building.

Jimmy saw a bright flickering light illuminating the intersection at the end of the hall. The hall Martaine had just disappeared into.

Jimmy yelled, "It's the Impala!"

He pointed to the slaughterhouse entrance. "Everybody, go, go, NOW!"

They didn't need to be told twice.

But halfway to the slaughterhouse doors, Virgil turned and ran toward the illumination at the intersection. "Hey, Silvio! Are you all right?"

The words had no sooner left his lips when Brother Martaine reappeared running at a full gallop toward Virgil frantically waving and shouting at him to 'Run!'

Virgil took a couple of steps back, unsure why Martaine was so concerned. He picked up speed as the clergyman continued to ward him off, then he heard it

Screams?

No, not screams but...

Reet! Reet! Reet!

He saw the pigs.

A full herd, most of whom were on fire, barreling right toward them.

"Holy shit!" Virgil bellowed and fled toward the slaughterhouse entrance.

*

As Mary and Abner flung open the doors to the slaughterhouse, Aimee turned back to the hallway to see where Virgil and Martaine were. When she peeked around the corner she

330

saw Virgil and Martaine charging toward her. For a split-second she wondered why they looked so terrified.

Then she saw why.

"Look!" she shouted, pointing.

Jimmy turned, grabbed her hand and said. "C'mon, get inside. We're cutting it too close!"

That's when Jimmy saw the doors to the slaughterhouse entrance were swinging doors!

A set of swinging door won't stop them! And once they break through...

*

The explosion blasted through the opening to Little Piggy office with the force of a commercial jet engine. Myrrh, who had been approaching the entrance stairs, hurtled into the air and crashed into the asphalt ten feet back. As debris fell around her, she covered her head and rolled away as fast and as far as she could.

With a thunderous ringing in her ears, Cavanaugh staggered to her feet and assessed the damage. There was fire throughout the entrance hallway and a big hole had been punched through the right side of the front of the building.

The fire was spreading quickly. The flames were bright enough to permit her to see the outline of a car but it was impossible to tell if it was the Impala.

People are going to be heading toward the fire exits. I'd better get over there and find out what happened.

She took a step and her legs almost gave out.

"Whoa!" she said. "Looks like I'm going to need a little time to recoup." She staggered over to her car and leaned against it. "Oh shit!" she suddenly said. "I'd better call the fire department."

*

Jimmy had mere seconds to come up with a plan. The pigs were closing in on Virgil and Martaine as they raced down the hall

331

and the swinging doors of the slaughterhouse entrance offered no defense.

Jimmy quickly studied the area and noted that behind the doors was a circular catwalk which overlooked the area where the pigs were butchered. There was a 30 foot drop to the concrete killing floor. On the side of the door were shelves containing several pairs of boots caked with pig fat and dried blood. Above it was a sign that read: **KILLING FLOOR BOOTS ARE NOT TO BE WORN ON THE CATWALK. PENALTY IS IMMEDIATE TERMINATION.**

Jimmy could see why. The 4½-foot-high railing along the catwalk had only one horizontal bar halfway between it and the catwalk floor. If you slipped, you got a 30-foot fall. But that gave Jimmy an idea.

*

As Brother Martaine raced from the pigs he quickly caught up with Virgil and realizing the scientist would not be able to stay ahead of them, dropped the Black Box and literally scooped him up as he passed.

Although startled at being swept off his feet, Virgil was keenly aware of their predicament. "We're not going to make it!" he shouted, looking over Martaine's shoulder.

The pigs were gaining.

Hearing them thundering behind then, Martaine decided to return to the ramp entrance. It was closer and once inside, they could slam the door behind them.

What if there are pigs already inside? he wondered.

He almost grinned when he recalled the old saying, *Better the devil you know.*

As he banked toward the door to the ramp, he lowered Virgil to his feet.

Please don't be locked. Please don't be locked, Martaine prayed.

It wasn't.

They made it in and closed the door with less than a second to spare.

*

When Jimmy saw Martaine and Virgil race through the door to the ramp and slam it closed behind them, he was startled by the savagery with which the beasts rammed the door in their attempt to break through.

What startled him more was when the pigs suddenly stopped, turned and charged toward the slaughterhouse entrance.

"Everybody grab a boot and bash it against the floor behind the door. Try to get as much grease off as you can," Jimmy shouted as he grabbed one and demonstrated. "Hurry!"

Aimee, Abner and Mary immediately complied. In a few seconds, the floor behind the door was slathered in pig fat and blood.

The pigs thundering hooves were almost upon them.

Jimmy saw the fire extinguisher, grabbed it and sprayed it on top of the greased entrance for good measure.

He turned to Aimee and Mary. "When I say 'GO!' Yank your door open and stand behind it! Abner you stay with me."

He peeked in between the door hinge and the frame and raised his hand, "Go!"

Just as the pigs were about to burst through, the doors flew open and the pigs, unable to slow or stop on the heavily greased and foamed floor, slid across the catwalk, over the side and fell 30 feet to the cement floor.

The pigs were packed so tightly they never saw the edge of the catwalk railing until it was too late.

Nearly all the pigs had slid over the side when the last two pigs managed to stop.

As they turned, Jimmy slipped two boots over his arms and charged. Mary placed her pocketbook to the floor and did the same. Jimmy's quick response caught the first pig by surprise and sent him careening over the edge. Mary wasn't as lucky. her pig was fast and avoided Mary's attempt to shove him over the side.

333

As she came at him a second time the pig grabbed the boot with its teeth and yanked it from Mary's arm. As she stumbled backward, her shoe found a patch of grease. She slipped and as she fell to the catwalk floor, the pig lunged, bit into her calf and tore out a snoutful of flesh.

Mary screamed. As the pig greedily attempted to take another bite, Aimee charged with a mop handle and stabbed it in the eye. As it squealed in pain, Jimmy shoved it over the side.

It was over, at least for now.

As Aimee knelt and tended to Mary's wound and Abner went to the sink for water and towels to clean it, Jimmy pulled his cell and called Martaine.

"You guys all right?" he asked.

"Yes," Martaine replied, "but we don't dare look outside. Can you see the door to the ramp from where you are?"

"Yes, it's clear, but I can only see for about ten feet in the area surrounding it. Look for yourself and let me know what you intend to do. We got to move quickly. Mary's been injured."

"What happened?"

"Pig took a big chunk out of her leg. Aimee's trying to patch it but it's deep, so we've got to get moving."

"Understood," Martaine replied. "You three go to the truck. Virgil and I will follow as soon as possible." He ended the call.

As the clergyman opened the door and scanned the hallway, Virgil said, "Was it the Impala that exploded?"

"Yes, Father Santiago sacrificed himself so that we could escape. It is a gift we must not squander."

"What's our next move?"

Before he could reply, they heard a noise at the top of the ramp.

Hooves.

*

As Jimmy closed the doors, Abner returned with several clean, dry towels that Aimee fashioned into a bandage and tourniquet.

334

After Aimee tied it off, Mary gritted her teeth and climbed to her feet. "Okay," she said, pressing her hands against the railing. "What's next?"

Jimmy scouted the area. "Almost all factories have a fire exit that leads to the parking lot. Abner, do you know where it is?"

Abner nodded. He pointed to the side of a concrete beam. Peeking out from behind it was the first two letters of the EXIT sign. "There's a staircase that leads down to the Utilities section, then we go straight to the door."

"All right," Jimmy said, "let's go."

*

Virgil tapped Martaine on the back as the sounds of pigs trotting down the ramp grew louder. He whispered, "Uh, Silvio, we need to get out of here."

Martaine nodded and the two quietly stepped outside and closed the door behind them. They looked around and saw the corridor was filling with clouds of black smoke.

"It's hard to see," Virgil said softly, waving his hand in front of his face, "but it seems like the coast is…"

Virgil was about to say 'clear' when he saw streaks of flame ignite on the floor. It reminded him of the fire trails left behind by the DeLorean when it reached 88 miles per hour in *Back to the Future*. One by one these snakelike ribbons advanced toward them like someone unrolling long strips of carpet. He didn't understand its cause at first but then…"

"Oh shit!" Virgil said nervously. "The fire is igniting the trails the pigs left after they ran through the gasoline."

The strips of flame continued racing toward them. There came another explosion and flames crawled across the corners of the ceilings.

Virgil and Martaine charged toward the slaughterhouse entrance.

*

335

"Did you hear something?" Mary whispered. She was using the catwalk's metal railing to help keep the weight off her injured leg.

Both Aimee and Abner looked down to the killing floor. Aimee shook her head.

The staircase leading to the exit ended about sixty feet short of the door. At the bottom of the stairs was a series of aisles, separated by eight-foot-tall metal shelves stacked with equipment, chemicals and supplies. In addition, the aisle at the bottom of the stairs was flanked by two additional aisles running parallel. The one to the left led to the killing floor; the one to the right, to the main office but they all converged and ended at the exit door.

"Any suggestions before we head down?" Jimmy asked as he stood at the top of the stairs.

"Yeah," Abner said. He was clearly frightened and his complexion was pale, almost ashen. "Once we get to the bottom just move quickly through the aisle. It'll take us straight to the exit. We gotta move fast because pigs are pretty strong and I'm betting not all of them are dead. And once they come to and smell the blood," he motioned to Mary's leg, "they'll charge after us."

"So we gotta get to the exit before they do," Aimee said.

"Yeah, because if the pigs get there first, they'll just turn into our aisle and… well you get the picture."

"Got it. Let's go." Jimmy said and started down the stairs.

Holding the banister tightly, Mary followed. As she looked over the side, she saw the pile of dead pigs on the cement floor. Feeling wetness inside her shoe, she glanced down and saw the tourniquet Aimee had fashioned was unraveling, leaving a blood trail on the stairs.

Her breath caught when she saw one of the pigs stir and open its eyes.

Then another.

She tapped Aimee on the shoulder and motioned toward the pile.

Aimee looked, nodded, but said nothing.

Once they reached the bottom, they briskly walked one by one down the aisle toward the exit.

On the other side of the metal cabinets something grunted, then snorted. The dazed pigs started raising their heads. Slowly, they stood and looked for a way down to the cement floor. The first few took a few hesitating steps at the edge of the pile of pig carcasses and tumbled down. As others regained their senses, they followed. Once back on the cement floor they raised their snouts…

…and smelled Mary's blood.

Slowly, they started down the adjoining aisle. One clumsily knocked over a metal cart and it fell to the floor with a resounding clang.

Hearing this, Jimmy, Abner, Aimee and Mary took off.

There were now at least twelve pigs in the aisle alongside theirs and although Jimmy and crew were far ahead, the pigs were quickly closing the gap.

"Aimee!" Mary shouted as her blood-soaked makeshift bandages continued to unravel. "Run ahead and see if you can knock one of these metal shelves into their path!"

Although the pigs were still dazed and not yet able to run at full capacity, it was only a matter of time before they caught up. Aimee, aided by Sula's powerful physique, sped on ahead and leapt onto the middle shelf of a partially filled rack and forced it over.

But it only partially blocked the aisle containing the pigs. Falling at an angle, it left an opening just big enough so that when the pigs reached it, they could squeeze through one at a time and continue on.

Mary, valiantly hobbled along, refused Aimee's and Jimmy's offers of assistance. "I'm an old woman who had a good life," she said huffing and puffing. "Forget about me and get to that damned door!"

Aimee took off and tried knocking over another shelf, but they were stocked with machinery and too heavy to topple.

Abner stumbled and fell. As Mary limped alongside, she reached down and yanked him to his feet.

Without uttering so much as a 'thanks,' he sped off.

Jimmy and Aimee were already at the exit door and were trying to knock over the last shelf to block the pigs from getting through.

Pressing her shoulder against the metal shelving, Aimee grunted, "It's no use. They're just too heavy!"

As Abner pulled up alongside, it became clear Mary wasn't going to make it.

Abner grabbed the bar on the emergency exit door. "What are you waiting for? C'mon!"

"Mary, you've got to run faster!" Aimee shouted, then ran to help her.

"You guys are crazy. I'm outta here!" Abner shouted as he pushed the emergency exit bar, opened the door and raced outside. The door slammed behind him and the alarm sounded.

Jimmy grabbed a wheeled metal cart and shoved it down the aisle.

The pigs barreled past like it was made of Styrofoam.

"Go!! Go!! Get out!" Mary bellowed as Aimee drew closer. "I'm not going to make it."

With the pigs only seconds away, Jimmy backed up, desperately searching for something to stop them. A weapon, anything. He saw a paint can on the shelf above and as he reached for it, felt the bar press against his back.

Suddenly the door swung open, a figure entered and shoved Jimmy aside.

Just as the pigs reached the end of the aisle, Myrrh Cavanaugh drew her weapon and fired, unerringly putting a bullet in the head of each of the pigs that approached. The others immediately turned and ran. Cavanaugh gave chase.

Aimee turned and yelled. "Jimmy, what happened? Are you all right?"

"Yeah, Cavanaugh the cop showed up and shot the pigs. The rest are running back to the killing floor. How are you and Mary?"

Before she could reply, Mary fell limp into Aimee's arms, exhausted. "We're okay. I just have to redress her bandage." Aimee said, lowering her to the floor.

With her flashlight placed directly above her gun, Cavanaugh backed up the aisle till she reached Jimmy. "How many pigs are there?"

Jimmy looked past the dead pigs and down the aisle. "Hundreds."

"Where's the Impala?" Myrrh asked, surveying the area. She pressed the reset button on the emergency exit box. The alarm stopped.

"It exploded after crashing into the office lobby."

"So that's what that was. I was just outside when it happened and the force knocked me off my feet." She ran the flashlight beam up the sides of the metal shelving. "Is the driver dead?" she asked, then ran the beam down the length of the aisle.

"Yes, Father Santiago. Although we didn't see the explosion, we believe… he was inside the car when it happened."

Cavanaugh eyed him suspiciously, then jerked her thumb to the door. "Grab your friends and get out of here."

"We can't just yet," Jimmy said as he took out his cell. "Two of us are still inside the office. I'll call and find out where they are."

"Who?"

"Virgil and…"

"Virgil ? Virgil Vanderhill's here?" Cavanaugh asked.

"Yes, along with Brother Martaine," Jimmy said as he pressed Martaine's number. "They were at the bottom of the ramp at the back of the office building.

A few seconds later, Jimmy said, "Damn it! Voicemail." After the beep Jimmy shouted, 'When you get this, call me. We have to get out now!'"

Cavanaugh looked up the sides of the metal cabinets, turned to Jimmy and said, "Give me a boost."

As Jimmy knitted his fingers, he asked. "What are you doing?"

"Too dark to be wandering these aisles," she replied as she placed her foot in Jimmy's entwined hands, stepped up, grabbed a metal bar and climbed to the top."I can see a lot better from up here. I'll find Virgil and his friend. You three take off."

"No!" Jimmy protested.

"Do as I tell you!" Cavanaugh shouted. "The office building is on fire and once the flames reach the grease on the killing floor, this place will become a bonfire!"

With that, the young officer turned and vaulted over the tops of the shelves toward the catwalk.

*

Martaine and Virgil charged toward the slaughterhouse entrance with the trails of fire licking their heels.

"Once inside, we'll slam them closed," Martaine said as they ran, "Hopefully, that will block the flames and give us enough time to reach the exit."

Martaine blew through the slaughterhouse door first and immediately slid across the greasy foam-covered floor. Fortunately, he didn't fall but instead slammed into the catwalk railing making it vibrate like a tuning fork.

Virgil wasn't as lucky. As he burst through the doors he slipped, fell and slid directly toward the edge.

"Oh shiiiiiittttttttt!" he bellowed.

Martaine, rattled by the sudden impact couldn't stop Virgil from sliding over the side.

*

With Mary's damaged leg no longer able to support her weight, Jimmy placed her over his shoulder in a fireman's carry and with Aimee alongside, opened the door and stepped outside.

They found themselves on the side of the slaughterhouse, about 150 feet from Mary's truck. A cold breeze greeted them and Jimmy could feel Mary shivering. The light from the moon illuminated their surroundings as they carefully crossed the gravel toward the parking lot.

340

The increasing smoke from the office building was making it difficult to see. They had just turned the corner when they heard squealing and grunting coming from a darkened recess.

With eyes wide, Aimee grabbed Jimmy's arm.

Jimmy nodded but pressed forward. They had no choice; they'd never make it back to the slaughterhouse exit in time. Still, luck was on their side. Although a number of pigs had gathered inside that shadowy recess, they were fighting amongst themselves and didn't notice the trio.

Finally, when all three reached the truck, Aimee slid behind the wheel while Jimmy placed Mary on the back seat.

"All right," Jimmy whispered as he stood on the step to the passenger-side door. "Aimee, you drive Mary to the hospital."

"What?" Aimee said. "What about you?"

"Since Cavanaugh is in uniform, I'm betting that Buick is an unmarked patrol car. If so, there are rifles in the trunk. And once I get a hold of them, I'm going to start killing the pigs. If I don't, the people rounding them up will be possessed by the daemons and we'll be back where we started. It's got to end here."

"Jimmy, we don't know for sure if Father Santiago's prayer will protect you from being possessed. Plus you don't even know if that car door is open. What if we take off and it's locked?"

"Geez, I didn't even think of that," he said, climbing in. "Okay, drive over and I'll try the door."

Aimee started the engine, put it in gear, and pulled alongside the car.

Jimmy jumped out and looked inside. "Whoa, talk about luck!" he said excitedly. "Not only is the door open, the keys are in it."

"Sweet," Aimee said then studied the area. "Looks like you're in the clear. Pop the trunk and get the rifles. I'll blow the horn if any pigs show up."

Jimmy yanked open the door to the Buick, pulled the trunk lever, raced to the back and removed a shotgun and a semi-automatic. Realizing he didn't have a flashlight and with the very real possibility of having to go back in, he grabbed two road flares and stuffed them into his pocket. He slung the shotgun over his

341

back, snapped the clip into the semi, popped one into the chamber and returned to Aimee.

As she lowered the window, he said, "Turn the truck so the headlights shine on those pigs over in that recess," he said, pointing with the automatic. "I should be able to take them all out before they scatter."

She nodded and complied.

As the high-beams landed on the gathered pigs, Jimmy took aim and squeezed off a sustained volley. They were dead in seconds.

With Aimee and Mary trailing closely behind in the truck, Jimmy kicked the bodies to make sure there were no survivors.

There weren't.

Then he saw what caused them to huddle together.

In the mud were Abner's remains.

*

Following a thirty foot free fall to the Killing Floor, Virgil landed on the pile of pigs with a meaty thud. Fortunately, he landed on the side of the pile and tumbled several feet to the blood covered floor. He was bruised and the air had been knocked out of him, but sustained no injuries.

As he stood and staggered forward, one of the severely injured pigs lurched forward to bite him, but Virgil was acutely aware of his surroundings and jerked out of the way before the pig, buried under several others, could reach him.

He smelled smoke, looked up and saw Martaine.

"You okay up there?"

"As well as can be expected. You?"

"I seem to be in one piece but there are flames under the exit door behind me. Luckily, there's another exit on the far end. Should be one up there, see it?"

"I'll look. Wait, do you hear that?"

Virgil's eyes widened. "Pigs! I'll meet you at the truck."

*

Cavanaugh moved quickly over the metal shelving, jumped across the toppled metal shelf and saw the pigs squeezing under it. She continued until she reached the stairs that led to the catwalk.

She heard Virgil's voice.

She started running.

*

Jimmy jumped into the driver's seat of the patrol car, placed the rifles against the passenger seat and started the engine. Aimee pulled the truck in close, lowered the window and after he lowered his, she tossed him a flashlight. "You might need this."

Jimmy considered mentioning the flares but knew the flashlight was better. With a sad smile she reached over, took his hand and said, "Please be careful."

He squeezed it and said, "I will. Now get going."

She nodded, put the truck in gear and took off for the exit.

As Jimmy sat back and stared at the darkening crimson sky, he heard a voice. "You got eyes, boy, but you ain't seeing."

Jimmy turned and saw Ol' Ike sitting next to him. He was rubbing his sparse prairie grass beard and squinting through his spectacles.

"What ain't I seeing, old timer?"

"Remember what I told you about the rules of us talkin'?" the late prospector asked, tucking his thumbs into his suspenders.

Jimmy took a moment. "I think so. You said it was all right for us to speak because you chose to stay behind, not because you were afraid of the light."

"That's right, young fella. But they's other rules," he said holding up a cautionary finger. "One of them is I can warn you if'n you're in danger, but not when you *will be* in danger."

Jimmy scowled. "Try and make sense, old man."

The specter scowled in frustration. "I don't make the rules, and I'm only helpin' you to make up for all the years I mistreated you. So listen careful and I'll say it again. "You got eyes, but you ain't seeing!"

343

Jimmy ran the sentence over in his head but it made no more sense now than it had the first time. When he turned to ask Ike to elaborate, he was gone.

Jimmy exploded. "I hate this shit! I really hate it! Man! What I wouldn't give to be at home with a joint and a bottle of..."

He stopped, banged his fist on the door armrest and huffed in disgust. "Okay," he said through gritted teeth. "Just what *did* I see?"

He threw his memory into reverse. "We got rid of the pigs by greasing the catwalk, then ran to the emergency exit. Abner panicked and took off. Then Cavanaugh showed up and shot the pigs, then went to find Martaine and Virgil...

"Wait. If Cavanaugh made it to the emergency door without having to fight off the pigs, why was Abner chased and attacked when he left just a half minute or so before she showed up?"

Something doesn't add up.

Jimmy put the Buick in gear and drove to Abner's remains. He opened the window and used the flashlight to scan the surrounding area for pigs. Seeing none, he got out with the semi-automatic in hand, stepped over the pig carcasses and examined Abner's body.

Ike was right. He had been so startled to discover Abner's half eaten corpse that he hadn't noticed the gunshot wound directly in the center of his forehead and the blood spatter high on the wall behind.

*

After seeing Virgil charge through the exit door below, Martaine sprinted around the catwalk toward the door that led to the second floor hallway. As he opened it he said a silent prayer that he would not be met by a herd of ravenous pigs.

He wasn't.

It was something far worse.

*

As Virgil raced the past the first floor offices, he covered his nose and mouth with the bottom part of his jacket. Then, just as he reached the exit doors, the problem of what was wrong with the ectoplasmic bomb suddenly came to him.

Stunned, he stopped in his tracks, put his hand to his head and muttered, "Holy crap!"

The answer was so simple and obvious his jaw almost dropped. Yes, the math was correct, the chemistry was correct, even the theory was correct. Where he had made his mistake was with the explosive capacity of the ectoplasmic fluids. He had designed and built the device based on what had happened at the Blue Barn.

When the ectoplasmic gasses exploded there, the force was negligible, so he incorrectly assumed that when this device was detonated, the effect would be the same. But what he now realized was that the fire at the barn ignited only a very small portion of the fluid that had spilled from the shattered chamber.

The ectoplasmic bomb in Mary's purse was filled with a concentrate equal to that of the original chamber and without the previous chamber's constant recirculation of the gasses. This device, when detonated, would most certainly annihilate everything within a mile radius.

He shook his head in disbelief. *It's such an obvious mistake. Why didn't I realize that sooner?*

When he stepped through the exit door and checked the area for pigs, he heard a quick burst of automatic gunfire. Following that, he saw Jimmy approach several pig carcasses then fire two single shots into them. Virgil ran to join him.

"Hey," he said, breathing heavily as he pulled up alongside. "Where's Aimee, Mary and Abn... Holy shit! Where's the truck!?"

Jimmy saw another pig and shot it. "Aimee's driving Mary to the hospital. One of the pigs took a chunk out of her leg. Abner's dead.

"Abner's dead?" Abner asked, scouting the area. "What, the pigs get him? Not that I give a shit. Anyway, how we getting out of here?" he asked.

345

"I got the keys to that Buick. Where're Martaine and Cavanaugh?"

"Silvio should be out any second," he said as he reached into his pocket and pulled out his cell. "Is Cavanaugh the cop here? 'Cause I didn't see her."

Virgil dialed Mary's number and placed the cell to his ear. When Mary answered he said, "Mary, it's Virgil. Listen, be extremely careful with the device. I just realized my calculations were off. If that thing detonates, it will take out everything for a mile in all directions…"

"I don't have it," Mary replied. "I left it on the catwalk over the killing floor."

"Oh shit!" Virgil shouted and disconnected.

Jimmy shined the flashlight on him. "What's the matter?"

"Mary left the ectoplasmic bomb on the catwalk. Once the fire reaches it, the explosion will vaporize this entire area."

"What?" Jimmy eyed him. "I thought it would only…"

Virgil cut him off. "No, I miscalculated! If that thing detonates it will be equal to a truckload of C-4."

"Damn it!" Jimmy said as he slipped the shotgun from his shoulder. "See that hole in the reception area wall? I'm going in through there and I need you to bring the car over." He handled Virgil the shotgun and the road flares. "I don't have another flashlight so use the flares for light but only if you have to. The pigs…"

Without warning Virgil said, "No, I gotta do this!" and took off toward the hole.

*

When Cavanaugh reached the end of the shelving, she saw Mary's pocketbook laying on the catwalk near the doors. She climbed down the side of the shelves, jumped to the stairs and went up. When she reached Mary's pocketbook, she picked it up, opened it and saw the device. With a puzzled look she pulled it out, gave it a once-over, put it back, and slung the bag over her shoulder.

"Hang in there, Silvio," Virgil called out as he jumped through the hole and started toward the slaughterhouse entrance. He encountered two daemonic pigs who appeared confrontational but the moment he leveled the shotgun at them, they scattered.

"Smart move," he muttered as he raced into the hallway. The fire there had died down but the smoke was still thick. He kept low, placed his sleeve against his mouth and squinted to keep his eyes from stinging. He speed dialed Martaine but received a recording.

The number you have reached is not active at this time. Please check your number and dial again. The number you have reached...

What the hell is wrong with Silvio's phone?

He was pondering that question when he saw it.

The Impala was a burning, twisted hulk lying sideways against the wall. The tires had melted and the area reeked of burned plastic. Although almost completely charred, Virgil suspected if he got close enough, he would find the cremated remains of Father Santiago.

He momentarily stopped and bit his lip. "Thanks, padre," he said solemnly. "And if you got any pull up there, help me get Silvio out before that bomb goes off."

As he ran through the smoke toward the slaughterhouse he saw the hallway was littered with dead pigs. The explosion not only blew out the reception room wall, it decimated the cafeteria and turned the stairs to the second floor into a carpet of flame.

Well, at least, I don't have to worry about the pigs coming from there.

He kept low as he turned the corner and continued toward the slaughterhouse, jogging alongside the walls to avoid the dying fires.

I hope I get to that damn device in time.

*

347

D'Shaid had taken on a form Martaine couldn't quite comprehend. No longer was he a tar-colored liquid that slithered and snaked over floors and up walls.

No, this thing had mass, density and a darkness that his brain simply could not turn into a recognizable form. What he could fathom was that it was easily eight feet tall and reeked with an odor that gave Martaine an overwhelming urge to scrub his skin with a heavy brush.

Still, it possessed one very noticeable feature from its earlier form. Martaine discovered this when D'Shaid's snake-like arm whipped around him. Within seconds, Martaine was trapped within coils as tight as an anaconda.

It crushed his cell phone and snapped two ribs. The clergyman bellowed in pain.

*

When Virgil reached the slaughterhouse door, he kicked it open and cautiously strode in with the shotgun, careful not to slip on the catwalk entrance. He had no sooner entered when he was grabbed from behind, had his arm twisted against his back and felt the cold steel of a gun barrel against his temple.

"Are you the cop?" Virgil asked in a trembling voice. "I was told there was a cop in here."

A moment later the gun was lowered and his arm released.

As he turned, Cavanaugh said, "What's wrong with you people? Don't you have enough sense to get out of a burning building?" She motioned to the killing floor below where the flames had burned through the exit door and were literally roasting the pigs.

He saw the pocketbook and reached for it. "That's Mary's pocketbook. I need to take that."

She shoved him backwards. "No, you don't! Nobody touches this until the guys in tech check it out."

"You don't understand," he said reaching for it and again getting rebuffed. "I created that device. It's very dangerous."

348

"Yeah? How so?" she said as she took the shotgun from him and slung it over her other shoulder.

"No offense, but like I said, you wouldn't understand," Virgil said dryly.

Virgil suddenly saw stars when she bashed him on the side of his head with her gun hand. "Explain to me right now what it is and how it works or so help me..." she eyed him hard and raised her gun.

Frightened by the officer's increasing hostility, he quickly said, "All right all right! Calm down. You gotta understand, the longer you are in this area the more violent you're going to become." He rubbed his head. "The daemons are in the pigs and their presence makes people violent."

She eyed him. "What are you, a mental case?"

Virgil shook his head. "No, believe me, I'm damn serious. And that's why I need that device."

She opened the pocketbook, looked at it, then eyed him suspiciously. "So how does this thing work?"

"Let's go! We got to get out of here!"

She snarled and raised the gun. "Last chance. You start talking or..."

He stepped back. "Okay! Inside that canister are a number of highly volatile chemicals. And we are standing in an area that generates anger and violence. Not a good combination."

"I asked you how it worked!" she shouted.

"Okay! Just remember it's the daemons that are making you angry, not me," he said. He gently pulled the device from the pocketbook and gave a quick explanation.

After asking a few questions to make sure she understood, Cavanaugh stuffed the device back into Mary's purse.

"All right," she said. "Now take off. I'll find your friend and..."

"No!" he said firmly. "You can hit me all you like, but I'm not leaving until I find Silvio!"

Before she could reply, the halls echoed with the sound of someone howling in pain.

Virgil recognized the voice and knowing how physically powerful the clergyman was, anything able to make him call out had to be something exceptionally strong.

D'Shaid!

As the two raced across the catwalk toward the sound, Virgil reached into his pocket and pulled out a flare. Having spent time in D'Shaid's environment, he knew daemons were particularly sensitive to sulfur. He ripped off the top, lit it, flung open the exit door and saw a black leathery tentacle wrapped around Martaine.

Virgil lobbed the lit flare at the behemoth that was D'Shaid. The monster recoiled and released Martaine.

Virgil wasn't sure if D'Shaid's reaction was genuine or out of habit but it gave him just enough time to grab the clergyman and pull him toward the catwalk door.

As he did, D'Shaid recovered and shot two black tentacles at them but Cavanaugh had the shotgun at the ready and blasted away.

As the damaged tentacles dropped to the ground, the three slipped out the door. Virgil lit the remaining flare and propped it against the door jamb before slamming the door behind it.

"Hopefully that will buy us some time," Virgil said as they took off along the catwalk and out the slaughterhouse doors that led to the main hallway.

"What the hell was that thing?" Cavanaugh asked. Like Virgil, she had her arm wrapped around Martaine's waist, helping him run.

"King of the bad guys," Virgil remarked as he took Martaine's arm and placed it over his shoulder.

"Where... Where is my Black Box?" the clergyman gasped as he attempted to keep pace. He winced and held his side.

"Where you dropped it, just around the corner in the middle of the main hallway," Virgil replied.

"We must get it. It's our only hope."

Virgil looked at him in disbelief. "Are you nuts? We need to get back to the car, call in Navy SEALS and drive west till our hats float."

Martaine grimaced as a voice filled his head.

You and Santiago's meddling has ruined my plans. He has eluded my grasp but I will have my revenge by dragging you back to a world of never-ending torment.

Martaine paled and groaned in pain.

"How bad is it?" Virgil asked as he tried to adapt to Martaine's additional weight. "Did D'Shaid break something? You're holding your side like you're afraid something is going to fall out."

"He… He broke my ribs," Martaine replied. "But that's not the issue. Because he is here in his true form he intends to take me back to hell with him for ruining his plans."

"What?!" Cavanaugh said. "Can he actually do that?"

"I believe so," Martaine replied.

"Well, he won't if we manage to get the hell out of here," Virgil said.

"My friend, you've seen him. Your arrival only gained us some time. He will soon realize that sulfur doesn't have the same effect on him here as it does in hell. He will recover quickly and make good on his promise."

Behind them they heard something crash through a wall and then another.

"Sounds like our friend is all patched up and ready to play," Cavanaugh said as she pulled her service weapon and snapped in a fresh clip.

As they made the turn and Virgil spotted the metal Black Box in the center of the hallway and said. "I think I figured out a way to stop him."

*

Jimmy sat very still behind the wheel of Cavanaugh's car. He had heard the bellow of pain, the booming shotgun and the thunderous clatter of what he assumed was a collapsing wall.

He had parked the car near the hole to the left of the entrance. He saw Virgil disappear into it and hoped the man had enough sense to come out the same way.

351

But the noise from the gunfire and explosions drove the remaining pigs into a frenzy. They ran from the back, from the side and even from the diminishing fires at the office entrance. And seeing the Buick, they gathered around it.

Jimmy laid low and out of sight, fingering the automatic. He wasn't sure how many bullets were left, but he was pretty sure it wasn't enough.

So he made a new plan.

He decided when Virgil, Martaine and the cop approached the opening, he would turn on the siren, blow the horn and fire whatever bullets he had into the surrounding swine. He was betting that would make them scatter just long enough for all three to climb inside.

What he didn't know was that one of the three wouldn't make it.

*

Virgil discovered the handle of the Black Box was very hot, so he tore the sleeve from his shirt and ran it under the water of the hallway drinking fountain. After wrapping the damp cloth around the handle, he picked it up and said, "I'm going to lead us to a hole on the side of the building. When we get there, you take Silvio to your car," he said to Cavanaugh.

As the trio turned into the central corridor and headed toward the smoldering Impala, Martaine said, "What do you intend to do?"

Virgil didn't answer until they entered the reception office and neared the hole itself. "It's game time," Virgil said, panting. "Officer, take out the bomb."

As she did, Virgil lowered the black box to the floor and looked inside. He turned to Martaine, who was leaning against a support column with his hand pressed against his side, and asked. "Which one of these bottles contains Padre Pio's holy water?"

"The one… with the red label with the black… letter P on it," Martaine gasped, pointing to it.

Virgil removed the small vial from the Black Box and examined it, "Not much left, is there?"

352

"It is very powerful…" Martaine said, wincing as he pressed against his side. "Usually a mere drop or two with suffice."

"Well, we'll have to make do with what we got. Here's the plan," Virgil said as he unscrewed the top and poured the precious water on the floor in an oval pattern leading back to the reception room doorway.

"What are you doing?" Martaine called out. "It cannot… be replaced!"

"Hopefully, it won't need to be," he replied and stopped at the door jamb. He examined the bottle. "Okay, there's enough left to finish the job."

"What are you guys talking about?" Cavanaugh asked.

Virgil recapped the bottle. "Silvio told me this stuff is like Kryptonite to daemons. Makes them as weak as kittens. So when D'Shaid comes charging in here after Martaine, he'll be smack dab in the center of an impenetrable barrier consisting of Padre Pio's holy water. When he realizes it's a trap, I'll have poured out the rest to close the circle. And while he's trapped, you guys take off with Jimmy. He's in the Buick."

They heard a loud crash followed by the sound of something barreling toward them. They could literally feel it getting closer.

"But what about you?" Cavanaugh asked. She had her gun pointed at the floor. She was looking at the doorway, coiled and ready to respond as D'Shaid's destructive fury thundered toward them.

Virgil's expression became grim. From behind his dark eyebrows, he said, "Once you're all safely away I'm going to detonate the device. The explosion should level the building, kill all the pigs within a mile radius and most importantly, force D'Shaid back where he belongs."

"Absolutely not! I cannot…" Martaine began.

"You have no say in this!" Virgil shouted. "I'm responsible for everything that's happened. The machine I created brought about the deaths of everyone in this building, plus that of a young family, murdered because of what my machine let loose into this world. I opened the proverbial Pandora's Box and it's time I take responsibility. You're both innocent, why should you pay?"

353

With a cold stare Cavanaugh, with the device still in the crook of her arm and with gun in hand, raised her weapon and pointed it at Virgil. "I think the word innocent is a bit of a stretch. Now give me that bottle of holy water."

"But if I hand you the bottle, we'll be…" Virgil began.

"Just hand it over, Virgie," Cavanaugh said lowering the gun. "I'm not going to let you do this."

Virgil's face went white. "What did you call me?"

"Virgie, sweetie," she said as she reached over and took the bottle from the stunned scientist, "we're wasting time."

"Mom?!"

She winked. "Brother Martaine, take my son to the car and get out of here. I'll take care of D'Shaid."

Even with two broken ribs Martaine was formidable, and when his hand took Virgil's wrist it was as unyielding as a metal handcuff.

As Martaine pulled him toward the hole, Virgil called out. "But why, Mom? Why are you doing this?"

Lillian/Myrrh smiled and shrugged as she stepped behind the door. "Because I just realized that no matter how many bodies you get, sooner or later we all have to walk into that light, and so I figure if I do this one good thing, maybe I won't be judged a lost cause."

Reeling from the revelation, Virgil was dragged through the hole just as D'Shaid entered the room. Amid the sudden blaring of sirens, car horn bleats, flashers and gunshots from outside, he looked around and saw Martaine and Virgil climbing into the car.

As he started toward them he suddenly recoiled as if struck in the chest by a sledgehammer. Then as promised, Lillian/Myrrh slammed the door closed and poured what remained of St. Pio's Holy Water on the door jam.

"Release me, woman," D'Shaid demanded as he staggered toward her.

She shook her head. "I don't think so."

As he took another step toward her, his legs nearly gave out. "I SAID RELEASE ME!" he bellowed, but his voice was rapidly weakening.

354

She shoved him to the floor and watched with a smile as the car with its three occupants raced out of the parking lot.

Moments later she felt the temperature rise. She turned to D'Shaid and saw waves of heat emanating from his body.

Within a minute, even with the large gaping hole in the wall, the temperature was becoming unbearable. Then behind D'Shiad something formed in the shimmering air.

It was the netherworld.

On his knees, D'Shaid grinned and said, "Since you will not release me from this prison, woman, I have no choice but to bring you to mine!"

She felt the heat searing her lungs, felt the hair on her arms burn and the pain was making it difficult to concentrate. Still she watched as the car grew smaller as it raced back to 404.

Just a little longer; just a little bit longer.

She slowly reached into the pocketbook, placed her finger on the red button.

Well, she thought with a small grin. *It was fun while it lasted.*

She pushed the button.

Nothing happened.

"Are we far enough away yet?" Jimmy asked as the car raced over the bridge that connected the Little Piggy roadway to Route 404.

The speedometer read 103 miles an hour.

Sitting in the passenger seat and leaning over to read the odometer, Virgil replied, "Not yet. When it explodes, it will destroy everything within a mile radius. Another quarter mile or so and we should be…"

Suddenly Jimmy's head snapped back. He grabbed it in agony and screamed as if it were being twisted off. As Virgil grabbed the wheel, the engine shut down, the lights went off, the dashboard went dark and the car slowed.

"What's wrong?" Martaine asked as he leapt from the back seat.

355

"Get down!" Virgil shouted. "She detonated it. First, the magnetic pulse sweeps the area, then the explos…"

A thunderous roar filled the air. The windows burst from their frames as the Buick became airborne. The air bags filled as the vehicle was thrown nearly twenty yards before crashing and flipping into the bridge's guard rail.

The front axle shattered, sending a tire bouncing over the side and into the gorge. Smoke poured from the hood as chunks of bricks, splintered wood, twisted metal, and sections of pig carcasses rained down amid gale force winds. One side airbag was pierced by a shard of wood. A huge bowl-shaped dent appeared in the roof when a chunk of a brick wall careened off it. Another formed a huge dent in the rear panel, shattering the tail lights and popping the trunk. Then, just as the car began edging over the side, the wind finally relented and the vehicle fell back to the pavement.

Nearly a minute later, once the debris stopped falling, Virgil and Martaine staggered from the car. All three were bloody, beat up but very much alive.

Virgil helped Jimmy to his feet. "What in blazes happened to you?" he asked. "You were screaming like a lunatic."

"I don't know," Jimmy replied rubbing his forehead. "For a few seconds it felt like my brain was on fire."

In the distance they saw an inferno where the Little Piggy Hog Farm once stood. Thick black smoke billowed into the air like an oil fire.

"I think it worked," Martaine said. He was bent over, breathing heavily with his hands pressed against the Buick's rear door.

"Can't slip anything past you, huh?" Virgil replied sarcastically.

Martaine smirked. "What I meant was look at the sky, Mr. Freakin' Genius."

Virgil looked up and noticed the sky was dark blue and not a shimmering crimson.

"How's your side?" Virgil asked, coming over to him.

"Tolerable," Martaine replied. "It's still a long way back to the entrance and your car. We best get started."

They had only been walking a few minutes when they saw a truck approach. It was Aimee in Mary's Ford F-350.

When she reached them she slammed on the brakes, jumped out, ran to Jimmy and wrapped her arms around him.

"You're alive!" Oh thank God!" she said kissing the side of his face and squeezing him tightly. "When I saw the explosion I thought…"

"I'm okay, I'm okay," Jimmy replied with a smile as he returned the hug. As Aimee took a handkerchief from her silver mirrored pocketbook and dabbed the blood on Jimmy's forehead, he suddenly pulled back and asked, "Hold on, where's Mary?"

"She's on her way to the hospital. Just as I turned onto 404, I was pulled over by the police. Turns out Van Pelt, Warring and a few other officers were on their way to back up the cop at Little Piggy. I told them what happened and that Virgil had constructed a very powerful bomb to get rid of the push-ins.

"Van Pelt had one of the officers drive Mary to the hospital, and while I was giving him the rest of the information I saw the explosion and took off to see if you guys were all right. The cops should be here any minute, firemen, too. I… wait, where is the cop who shot the pigs?"

"The real Officer Cavanaugh…" Virgil began but Jimmy interrupted and said, Officer Cavanaugh sacrificed herself and detonated the ectoplasmic bomb. Without her sacrifice and that of Father Santiago, we wouldn't be talking to you now."

In the distance came the sound of approaching sirens.

In the Weeks that Followed

Mary underwent surgery to repair the damage caused by the pig bite. When she was released from the hospital she was brought in for questioning regarding Jess Maldonado's death. Jimmy and Virgil both confirmed Mary's statement that Jess had been suffering from psychotic episodes and was becoming increasingly violent. The autopsy collaborated Mary's version of what had happened. The investigation continued on for a while but eventually all charges were dropped.

All of Jess' worldly goods had been bequeathed to Mary which when lumped together came to about half a million dollars. However, because she was responsible for her best friend's death, Mary wanted no part of it. She signed over the ownership of Jess' house to Aimee and divided Jess' money equally among Jimmy, Virgil, Aimee and Brother Martaine. Sadly, without her best friend, Mary lost interest in everyday life. She never did another reading and officially retired as a psychic detective. Although Jimmy, Aimee (who now insisted on being called Sula) and even Virgil visited from time to time, within a year she passed away from natural causes.

As for Aimee, the MacFarland's demanded she be charged with murder. They had paid a princely sum to have the remains of the building cleared and Aimee's original body properly buried. However, the autopsy report showed that her death was the direct result of the building's collapse and nothing else. On the advice of her lawyer, she pleaded down to using a stolen debit card and because the amount taken was under $2,000 dollars, they were only able to charge her with a misdemeanor. When the judge learned of Sula's family's extreme poverty and the death of her stepfather and stepbrothers, he showed leniency and sentenced her to make restitution for the money taken and to pay court costs.

With her life now back in her own hands she returned to school as Sula May Hockenberger, made up for the time she lost, aced all her tests and with a letter of recommendation from the Wheatfield High Principal, applied to Vassar and was accepted.

Still it would take years before Aimee, with the help of Virgil, Jimmy and Brother Martaine, was able to convince the MacFarland's that they hadn't lost their little girl after all.

As for Virgil, he returned the $9,000 anonymously, signed the divorce papers and fully intended to leave Wheatfield never to return. However, before he could finalize his plans, he received a message from Brother Martaine. The two remained in touch and had developed a close friendship. According to Silvio, the populace of a village in Denmark was exhibiting the same symptoms they experienced at the Blue Barn and later at the Hog Farm. Would he be interested in accompanying him to look into it?

Virgil thought long and hard before replying. Did he really want to put himself in harm's way again? Did he really want to battle these murderous, supernatural creatures a second time?

No, he didn't.

But, when he took stock of his life, his career, his marriage and his obsession with his mother, he realized he hadn't really lived at all. As it stood now, should he die tomorrow, he would be looked back upon as just another soon to-be-forgotten nobody. And that, he decided, was not the fate a 'freakin' genius' deserved.

He replied to Martaine that he was on his way.

Jimmy believed he benefitted the most from their adventure. For the first time since he was twelve he wasn't visited by the dead begging favors. At first he thought it was temporary thing, but as the days grew into months without a single incident he realized the searing pain he experienced from the magnetic pulse had closed those portals, freeing him at last.

Following a special regimen of diet and exercise, his ulcers healed, his blood pressure fell to normal, the anxiety attacks ceased and his need to self-medicate lessened, then disappeared completely.

Impressed with Aimee's determination and drive to succeed, he returned to school and studied electrical engineering. Having spent the better part of his life dealing with the paranormal, the cold, hard science of electricity was a welcome change.

Jimmy and Aimee (now Sula) finished college and eventually married. Virgil was hired by the Vatican to assist Brother Martaine, which was a profession he kept till the end of his life.

And as for Father Santiago, Jess, Mary, Myrrh Cavanaugh and perhaps even Lillian Vanderhill, they were all doing just fine poolside at Jesus' house.

THE END

We hope you enjoyed The Dead Machine. If you would like to leave a review here's the Amazon review link
http://amzn.to/1TrFKTD

Turn to the next page to read a sample of Zackary Richards best-selling thriller The Messiah Complex.

The Messiah Complex
Chapter 1

Friday evening, February 4th

Hal Collins' breath came in short, panicky gasps, his eyes were wide and his hands shook as he held the steering wheel. He was trying to calm down, trying to make sense of what happened but each time his Ford Expedition slid or lost traction on the snow covered highway, his heart jumped in terror.

He wiped at the frost gathering on the inside of the windshield. Saw the ice caked wipers slapping back and forth at top speed. He checked the dashboard sensors and swallowed in relief when he saw there were no problems. Momentarily distracted by the smell, Hal looked down at the wisps of smoke rising from his still smoldering pant leg.

They must have slipped something into my food at the diner, he told himself. *That has to be it.* That's what he wanted to believe. It was the only reasonable explanation, but reasonable or not, the evidence said different.

I should have listened to those truckers. They tried to tell me, tried to warn...

He checked the rear view mirror. He could still see the fiery orange and red glow in the distance, hear the sirens.

Hold it. Is that... Is that...?

He held his breath.

No, it wasn't.

He exhaled deeply and absentmindedly pressed the button to raise the window, then remembered the window was gone. That... that *thing* had... That Thing!!!

A thin film of sweat covered his brow. He glanced at the pebbled glass and the tire iron on the passenger seat.

Just keep going. Just keep going!

He was nearly a mile from the accident when his headlights fell upon a group of children ahead. They were walking toward him on the shoulder of the highway. As he drew closer, he saw

361

they weren't children, but kids in their early to mid-teens, clad only in their underwear.

"What the…?" Hal said. "What the hell are they doing out here dressed like that? Shit! What are they doing out here at all?" He hit the brakes. The Expedition slid to a stop.

"Kids! Kids!" he shouted, jumping from the vehicle and slogging through the snow toward them.

"Wait!"

They didn't.

He placed himself in their path, motioning for them to stop.

They walked around him, staring vacantly, as if unaware of his presence, their predicament or their surroundings. The wind picked up and battered them with waves of fine crystal powder. Their hair flew wildly in the breeze.

"I have a truck," Hal called out as they plodded by. "I can squeeze you all in. Please come with me. You'll freeze out here!"

One small girl with black hair and dark brown eyes looked so cold Hal took off his coat and attempted to wrap it around her. She stopped only long enough for him to place it on her shoulders, but it fell to the ground as she walked away.

"Kids, listen to me!" he pleaded, picking up his coat. "I've got a truck and...."

They continued walking toward the area he had just escaped from.

"Kids!! Wait! Wait!" Hal said, lumbering after them through the thick snow. As they got farther and farther from the vehicle and out of the glow of the Expedition's taillights, they disappeared.

"Kids?"

Hal searched in all directions.

He was alone.

Standing in the center of the snow-covered Adirondack Northway, Hal donned his coat. As he did the distant sirens stopped and the fiery red glow faded.

I must have been drugged. Either that or I'm out of my mind.

Trudging back to the 4X4, he felt a vibration from the ground beneath the snow. He stopped, turned, but saw nothing. He picked up the pace.

Seconds later, he felt it again. Only this time, headlights snapped on.

He heard an engine rev. He began backing away. The headlights followed.

The semi! Oh dear God, it's the semi!

As it picked up speed and drew nearer, Hal could see the tractor-trailer's hood snapping up and down, and heard the gnashing metallic sounds that accompanied it. The headlights turned into eyes, cold and blood-stained. The wheels transformed into claws and thundered over the snow and tore into the asphalt. An air horn pierced the night then deteriorated into a sound that could only be described as a mechanical roar.

"Oh shit! Oh shit! Oh shit!" Hal yelped and frantically galloped toward the Expedition. The deep snow pulled off his right shoe and the ground shook under the weight of the approaching behemoth. "Screw it!" he said in panic as he charged toward the passenger-side door now only a few feet away. There was a roar. Hal lunged for the handle. He almost made it.

Almost.

Here's the link to the full version
http://amzn.to/1KWTCSc